# THE WORKROOM GIRLS

*'I wouldn't be a workroom girl for all the silk in the East!'*

Charlotte Grant is determined to marry for love. Running away from home to avoid an arranged marriage, her skill as a needlewoman earns her a place in the workroom of Court couturier Madame Last. Only then does Charlotte begin to realise that life for a workroom girl can be very, very hard indeed. The problems of her fellow seamstresses seem strange at first to middle-class Charlotte, but she soon becomes firm friends with the other girls and their closeness makes up for the long hours of gruelling work.

# THE WORKROOM GIRLS

# The Workroom Girls

*by*
Catherine Clifton Clark

**Magna Large Print Books**
Long Preston, North Yorkshire,
England.

British Library Cataloguing in Publication Data.

Clark, Catherine Clifton
    The workroom girls.

    A catalogue record for this book is
    available from the British Library

    ISBN 0-7505-1107-9

First published in Great Britain by Judy Piatkus (Publishers)
Ltd., 1996

Copyright © 1996 by Catherine Clifton Clark

Cover illustration © by arrangement with Piatkus

The moral right of the author has been asserted

Published in Large Print 1997 by arrangement with Judy
Piatkus (Publishers) Ltd.

Magna Large Print is an imprint of
Library Magna Books Ltd.
Printed and bound in Great Britain by
T.J. International Ltd., Cornwall, PL28 8RW.

There was no doubt the Grant household changed for the better when its master remarried. William Grant was a good-looking widower and his marriage took place at an auspicious time, with a general feeling of optimism in the air as the nation stopped mourning Queen Victoria and welcomed a new era under King Edward.

The man and woman in the street cast off their black armbands and the domestic staff at the house in Lancaster Gate looked forward to more cheerful times. The new Mrs Grant was a pleasant, easy-going young lady, not quite equal to her predecessor in looks but just as lighthearted and easily pleased.

'Funny thing how men always choose the same type,' remarked Mrs Vickery, the cook, as she drank her midmorning glass of stout. The maids were drinking tea. 'They don't know it,' she went on. 'Wouldn't believe it if you told them. Let's hope there are no ructions with this one.'

She didn't say this to denigrate the late Amanda Grant, who had driven her husband to distraction with her flighty ways. She always spoke of her with affection. Still, all things considered, the newly married pair stood every chance of happiness, and the only possible threat to it was Miss Charlotte.

Charlotte, the only child of William and Amanda, was almost eighteen and growing more like the mother she had lost every day. Mrs Vickery remembered the child's grief when Amanda died, and how she clung to Nanny, her nurse.

Her father didn't approve of Nanny or her methods. She was not one of those nurses who pushed prams in Kensington Gardens. She came of a family of thespians, spoke in a clear voice, enunciating her words distinctly, and although rotund in figure became a commanding presence on particular occasions. One of these occurred when William Grant told her he did not require her services any longer.

'You dismiss me at your peril, Mr Grant,' she declaimed.

'I shall risk it, Mrs Goode.'

'Your child will be the one to suffer.'

'Kindly go.'

She reached the door, turned, and treated him to the most withering of her assorted looks.

'Your ignorance of your child's needs is only equalled by your regrettable stupidity.

A reference from you would prove a drawback, I fear.'

He turned his back on her. She had been Amanda's childhood nurse and was easily persuaded to look after Charlotte. He suspected her influence on both of them and was determined to prevent his daughter growing up in the pattern of his late adored but impossible wife.

Nanny's departure increased Charlotte's sorrow. She was a neglected child. The governesses engaged to teach her knew next to nothing themselves. 'We'll learn together,' the last of them said, feverishly scrabbling through textbooks. Her father showed neither interest in her nor affection towards her. He threw himself into his work as an importer of dried fruit, grew richer, and spent his spare time at his club.

A series of housekeepers ran the establishment after Amanda died. They were always at war with Mrs Vickery, who was an old retainer of the Grant family and suspected each and every one of having designs on William. Each new housekeeper bathed the good-looking young widower in sweetness and light until Mrs Vickery warned him to beware. The change in these women when he gave them a month's notice always took him by surprise. Poison spilled out. Dear little Miss Charlotte became that dratted imp. The tails of his shirts were left rough dry. Mysterious holes appeared in his socks. His coats went unbrushed, and when he complained he was advised to hire a valet.

Charlotte's childhood and adolescence were spent in these unfavourable conditions, and but for Mrs Vickery she might have remained in a state of miserable ignorance. Her father didn't believe in education for girls—the less they knew the better, in his opinion. Mrs Vickery had opinions too, and hers were vastly different from his. She was a great one for education and did all she could to promote Charlotte's. She introduced her to the works of Dickens and Thackeray, and they spent hours discussing the characters who, Mrs Vickery declared, were all alive and kicking. 'You'll meet them as you go through life,' she told Charlotte. Privately she hoped Charlotte wouldn't notice the resemblance between her father and Mr Dombey.

Annie and Tilda, the two maids, enjoyed a different kind of literature. They devoured the weekly magazines. So did Charlotte. Both girls came from large families and before going into service lived in cramped conditions and saw their brothers bathing in a tub before the kitchen fire once a week. Charlotte found their descriptions of the male anatomy most peculiar and accused them of kidding, but when they told her why boys were different from girls she gradually came to believe them.

'No one else won't tell you, so we will,' said Tilda. 'Then it won't come as a shock when you get married.'

Charlotte had never even thought of marriage, but now, with her father bringing his second wife home, it was in the air and she was delighted, excited, exuberant at the prospect of having someone else to talk to. She told Mrs Vickery so, she told Nanny, for Nanny was a great friend of Mrs Vickery's and often came to tea with her. These were social occasions Mr Grant would not have permitted had he been aware of them, for they enabled Nanny to watch Charlotte's progress. She did this with some concern and a great deal of admiration, for the once sad little girl had inherited her mother's strong will, determination and optimism. Charlotte still felt the ache of her loss but she simply couldn't help being happy. She woke up happy, danced round the house, sang the music hall songs Tilda taught her and enjoyed each day as it came. She taught the governess much more than the governess taught her, and didn't confuse loving with liking.

'Of course I love Papa but I don't like him one little bit,' she told Nanny.

'Dear me, what next will I hear?' enquired Nanny.

'That I'm going to like my stepma very much though I don't suppose I'll love her. She must be a wonderful woman to take on Pa, don't you think?'

'Let us hope she's a wonderful woman in every capacity,' said Nanny, who was thankful to see Charlotte so eager to welcome the second Mrs Grant. Daughters often took exception to a father's second wife and felt themselves demoted. Not so Charlotte. She warmed to Ellen Grant on sight, and Ellen simply held out her arms to Charlotte.

Ellen was only ten years older than Charlotte, and as she didn't intend to usurp Amanda's place in her stepdaughter's heart an affectionate relationship developed between them. They soon found they had a good deal in common. They took enjoyment in simple things, and liked good food, pretty clothes, going to the shops and laughing at the conventions they had to observe.

Ellen had a flair for millinery and liked to trim hats. She had the means to buy whatever she fancied ready to wear but much preferred her own choice of trimmings with which to adorn plain straws, felts and velvets.

Charlotte's forte was dressmaking. Her great-aunt Mildred, a formidable lady who lived in Bournemouth, had taught her to sew from an early age. Miss Mildred Grant was William's aunt, and whenever a crisis arose in his household she came to London to sort it out. She followed an exceptionally strict code of conduct and Charlotte dreaded her visits, but at least her great-aunt had taught her to sew, to adapt patterns and to cut out, so that by the time she was in her teens she could make her own dresses and enjoyed doing it. Now she could go to the shops to choose materials with Ellen.

Ellen was amused by Charlotte's tales of Miss Grant and only half believed them.

'You'll see when she comes to stay,' Charlotte said. 'We have prayers before breakfast when she's here. Afterwards we do household tasks—she and I, that is. Then we read sermons for an hour. Next we ponder on them. After that a brisk walk. No window-gazing. No stopping to look at ducks or admire horses.'

'What does she look like?'

'Stately. Beautiful gowns that she makes herself. She's very strict about food, too. I have to stay with her for a fortnight every summer because she says I need a change of air. We have lots of spinach with one egg each. No puddings. I love puddings, don't you?'

'Very much,' said Ellen. 'Let's go out to tea. We can walk to Gunter's.'

So off they went, arm in arm, Charlotte chattering away, and Mrs Vickery, seeing them from the window, remarked that they could be taken for sisters.

The atmosphere in the house was so cheerful now that even the plants looked healthier. William began to give dinner parties and Charlotte was allowed to come down. Until now she had been served with her dinner at midday and tea in the early evening. Before the first of the dinner parties took place she talked about her changed situation with Nanny. 'I can't believe it. Pa's almost nice to me,' she told Mrs Goode, who was having a secret tea with Mrs Vickery at the time. 'I don't know if I'm pleased or sorry.'

'Enjoy it,' said Nanny. 'Make the most of it while it lasts.'

'Do you think it's only temporary, then?'

'Not exactly. It's a new phase. Your pa realises you've grown up. You'll be out when you're eighteen. Next thing you'll be married.'

'I don't know about that. Pa didn't have people home when he was a widower,'

14

'He's making up for it now,' said Mrs Vickery.

'And I'm observing husbands and wives together for the first time in my life.'

'What do you make of them?' asked Nanny.

'I think some wives have a lot to put up with,' Charlotte said. And then, with a smile, 'What was your husband like,' Mrs Vickery?'

'That would be telling,' Mrs Vickery said, upon which Nanny chuckled and Charlotte felt there was a secret understanding between them, as indeed there was. Mrs Vickery had never been married and only called herself Mrs in order to command the respect of her underlings.

Nanny, on the other hand, had enjoyed a short but happy marriage to an acrobat who was killed when he fell off a trapeze. 'He was wonderful, Charlotte. Handsome, generous, considerate. If you get a husband like Victor Goode you'll be fortunate indeed. Who knows? You may meet the very man at your pa's table.'

Charlotte enjoyed the food at the dinners but didn't like the company much. The guests were usually merchants, their wives and sometimes their sons. Charlotte wished they brought daughters, as she had no friends of her own age and there were all kinds of secrets she wanted to share with

15

other girls. Annie and Tilda were always ready for a nice long chat as they cleaned the silver or dusted the furniture, but they had a freedom of a kind she had never known. They could go out with young fellows on their free evenings. They were not constricted in the way she was. They had adventures. She didn't.

As the hostess, Ellen sparkled, but Charlotte found the conversation almost unintelligible. It was all about politics and the state of trade. The lady guests didn't contribute much but they looked as though they understood what it was all about and talked nonstop when they retired to the drawing room for coffee. Even here there was little to interest Charlotte—much of it was speculation about which of their acquaintances was in an interesting condition, or the way society was going now that King Edward had succeeded. The most fruity bits of scandal about him were retailed from ear to ear.

Although she didn't join in these gossipy sessions, Charlotte was glad to be away from the dinner table and the proximity of Albert Morton, a young man who was always placed next to her. He had little to say. His hands were large and looked clammy, and his face put her in mind of a frog's. She had never seen a real live frog so drew her impression from pictures and associated the creatures with bogs and general sliminess.

Apart from this, and she conceded it was only a minor annoyance, there was plenty to enjoy: shopping with Ellie, strolls in the park, the occasional excursion to Richmond to marvel at the view from the top of the hill. All this meant there was much more to tell Nanny when they met.

At Christmas Great-Aunt Mildred came to join in the festivities, which she did by casting a damper on them. She took exception to Charlotte calling her stepmother Ellie, something she had done from the first.

'Such disrespect is really not permissible,' she said, bolt upright in lace mittens.

'I can't call her Mama because she isn't,' Charlotte explained.

'Unpardonable. It must stop.'

'Shall I call her Mrs Grant then? Or Steplady?'

Aunt Mildred tapped her foot on the fender. 'I'm sorry to observe that Charlotte has grown very impertinent, William,' she said.

William, deep in *The Times*, hadn't been listening.

'Charlotte is absolutely right, Aunt,' Ellen intervened. 'I'm not her mother and it wouldn't please me at all if she called me so. I'm much too young to be her mother anyway.'

'But quite old enough to be mother to your own child, my dear Ellen. Almost too old, if you ask me,' replied Aunt Mildred.

'Which I don't.'

'It would grieve me to depart this life before my nephew has an heir.'

'How indelicate!' exclaimed Ellie.

William shook his paper violently, declared there was no peace with three women in the house, and stormed off to his club.

Aunt Mildred had been sewing. She pursed her lips, folded her work and put needles, scissors and thimble into her work basket. She stood.

'I leave tomorrow,' she announced and literally swept from the room, trailing discarded scraps of silk.

Charlotte and Ellen exchanged looks and smothered their laughter, but the next day, to please William, Ellen begged Aunt Mildred to stay a little longer. The older woman refused quite graciously and told them her presence was required in Bournemouth.

'But if I'm wanted here you have but to send a wire and I shall be on the next train,' she said, and added: 'Charlotte, a word with you before I go.'

Charlotte couldn't imagine what her great-aunt wanted to say to her in private, but she very soon found out. Aunt Mildred told her she was quite old enough to be married, and that no doubt her papa would soon introduce her to the man of his choice.

'Not of my choice?' queried Charlotte.

'I trust it will be your choice also,' said Aunt Mildred. 'But whether or not, you must remember the choice remains with your papa. Young women must be guided by their fathers in these matters. To choose for herself would be to put too much of a responsibility on a girl's shoulders.'

'I think that's terrible!' exclaimed Charlotte.

'You are not required to think,' returned her aunt. 'You are required to obey.'

Although she was inclined to laugh over this, Charlotte felt uneasy and wasn't helped by Nanny's response when she confided in her.

'I told you marriage was the next step,' she said.

'But to whom? Aren't I supposed to fall in love first?' asked Charlotte.

'It's to be hoped so, and if with the man your pa chooses, so much the better.'

'I shall choose for myself if and when I please,' Charlotte said, but she was oppressed by the fear of what might be in store for her.

Nineteen hundred and two promised to be a year unlike any other they had known, for the coronation would take place and all kinds of festivities, both public and private, were planned.

According to Ellen there were a hundred reasons for having new hats and dresses. William smiled indulgently and promised they'd go to Ascot at least. He had always been generous and was doing so well he could afford to be even more so. They were to have their own carriage and Ellen must choose the colour of the paint and upholstery. 'Your papa's an angel,' she said, and Charlotte's fear of she was not quite sure what diminished. She made herself a new dress, and when she pirouetted round the kitchen where Mrs Vickery and Nanny were enjoying one of their secret teas they both clapped and said it could have been taken for one of the great Madame Last's creations.

'You don't mean it,' said Charlotte.

'I do, my dear.' Nanny could speak with authority, for she was an old friend of the almost legendary court dressmaker and had succeeded in training her out of her cockney accent and into a manner of speech acceptable to her high-class clients.

Charlotte was so pleased with Nanny's compliment that she felt more confidence in herself. Her strange, indescribable dread receded still further and had almost vanished when her father called her into his study one day and told her that Albert Morton wanted to marry her and had been accepted as her future husband.

'*I've* never accepted him!' she exclaimed.

'That's of no consequence. I've accepted him for you. He is a young man of good character, his father is my business associate and the match is suitable in every way. Albert is in the drawing room waiting to speak to you.'

Charlotte's indignation was so strong she went red in the face and spoke to her father as she had never done before. 'He can propose till he blows up. I'm not having him. I hate him. He's horrible. Anyway, you can't make me marry him.'

'You will do as you are told. You will marry Albert Morton and there'll be no argument about it.'

'Oh, won't there just!' said Charlotte, so enraged she didn't care what she said. 'There'll be plenty of argument. I shall go and argue with Albert now.'

Mr Grant was so taken aback by this defiance that words deserted him. She left him spluttering, went into the drawing room where Albert was just about to fall on one knee, and said: 'What's all this nonsense about us getting married? Was it your idea?'

'No,' said the surprised Albert.

'Well, it's off. I'm not having it.'

'Your father insists and so does mine, so there isn't much we can do about it. I depend upon my pa and I suppose you do on yours. They both say they know best.'

'Let them.'

'Look, we'll be quite comfortable if we do as they say. Once we're spliced and have produced an infant we can go our own ways.'

'What an abominable idea!'

'It's the way of the world.'

'Not of mine,' she said, and the thought of getting into bed with Albert Morton and doing whatever was necessary to beget a child made her feel so sick she ran out of the room and retched all the way to the lavatory.

'We'll give her six months to come round to the idea,' William Grant told Ellen, who was deeply troubled about the match he had arranged. She knew how Charlotte felt and had promised to do all she could to thwart the plan. She had to allow there were material advantages, but without respect on both sides and at least a degree of affection she could see nothing but misery ahead.

'He has the most horrible ideas,' she said.

'It's a pity he didn't keep them to himself,' said William.

'How can you? I hope, oh I do hope you don't share them.'

'Of course not. How could I when I have you and you're all I ever wanted?'

'That's just it. We fell in love, didn't we? I'd like Charlotte to marry for love, just as we did.'

'We were both adults, my dearest. We could trust ourselves and each other. Who's to say Romeo would have stayed in love with Juliet? If they'd listened to their parents they wouldn't have ended up stiff while they were still in their teens.'

'William, please remember that Charlotte isn't in love with anyone at all, so romance doesn't come into it. That's not why she's opposing you. It's simply because she can't abide Albert, and no wonder. He does look like a frog.'

But no matter how fervently Ellen pleaded on Charlotte's behalf, and she returned to the subject so often that William told her not to nag, he remained adamant. Charlotte was to marry Albert if he had to drag her screaming to the altar, he declared.

There was not much happiness now in the house of William Grant. His friends came to dine as usual, and their wives visited Ellen on her At Home afternoons, but for Charlotte the prospect ahead was bleak. She didn't attempt to mask her dismay and talked about it to Mrs Vickery and Nanny and the maids.

'I wouldn't mind dying an old maid one little bit,' she said. 'I think it's splendid to be single. Miss Nightingale hasn't married, neither did Miss Martineau or Jane Austen, and look how they're admired.'

'But you're not them, Miss Charlotte,' remarked Annie.

'Who's to say I won't be when I'm their age? Oh dear, you don't understand me. None of you do.'

'Yes we do, dear,' said Mrs Vickery. 'Trouble is, young ladies like you have to obey their pas. Nanny will tell you the same.'

Nanny had to agree with Mrs Vickery on this, but she thought Mr Grant had made a very bad choice for Charlotte. 'You see, dear, in your class of society arranged marriages are the order of the day, and very often they succeed,' she said.

'This one wouldn't. I cringe when he passes me the salt.'

'Try another tack. Tell your pa how much you regret being unable to fall in with his wishes. Pile it on, my dear. Say you'll consider any other proposal but resist this one. Resist it for all you're worth.'

'I will,' said Charlotte. 'He won't browbeat me, the pig.'

'Tut, tut,' said Nanny. 'Have a crumpet, dear. It will do you good.'

Nanny pronounced crumpet in such a way as to rank it with the most delectable treat known to man. Charlotte ate two.

Ellen often took Charlotte out calling. Now that they had their own carriage they could include a drive, and this was pleasurable, but Charlotte really preferred walking.

One February afternoon, when they were almost home, Ellen remembered that she'd intended to call at a nearby shop for some ribbon she had ordered.

'Let me go and collect it. I'd like the walk,' Charlotte said.

Ellen was glad of the offer but warned Charlotte not to linger, as the weather was not to be trusted. The sky was unusually bright and it was almost too warm for the time of year.

'I think there's rain coming,' she said. 'Still, if you hurry you'll be back in time for tea.'

After collecting the ribbon Charlotte couldn't resist the lure of Oxford Street. It wasn't very far and there was no harm in going as far as Selfridges to admire the window displays. Such angelic millinery! Ellie would adore it. Lovely straw hats with exotic trimmings, bunches of flowers, artificial fruit that looked real enough to eat, especially the one with the cherries.

She didn't realise how long she had been out, or that heavy clouds were gathering, until a roll of thunder made everyone look up and then begin to hurry as enormous drops of rain fell. In no time the shower was a heavy, persistent deluge. She turned back but it seemed she was the only one heading for Bayswater, pushing against the crowd of pedestrians making for buses, hailing cabs or simply scurrying with all the speed they could muster.

The traffic in the road was scarcely moving: horse buses, donkey carts, a few motors, hansom cabs, a handful of riders, they were all pressed together in one of the jams she had heard about but never seen.

Somehow she must get home. It would be easier on the kerb side, so she made for that and half ran, half walked, frightened by the flashes of lightning and the noise. Not only thunder but ironclad wheels, horses neighing, motors sounding raucous horns. It was bewildering.

Her clothes were wet and getting wetter, and her shoes were not made to withstand heavy weather. She was being shoved this way and that and didn't see the uneven kerbstone that threw her over. She lurched forward, tried to stop, couldn't, and pitched flat in the gutter and the water that was rushing along it. Ellen's ribbons went flying, never to be recovered.

She was too shocked to move; then a voice said: 'Are you all right?' and before she could reply, she was on her feet again, picked up bodily and set down by a man who had dropped his open umbrella to help her. 'You've had a very nasty fall,' he said. 'Are you sure you're all right?'

'I think so,' she said shakily. His umbrella had gone under a carriage and was being transported to Oxford Circus.

'Have you far to go?' he asked.

'Only to Bayswater. I'll soon be there.'

'We'll get a cab. We're on the wrong side of the road. Take my arm and we'll cross.'

She was terrified of crossing. They had to duck under horses' heads and push in front of motors, but they reached the other side unscathed. A hansom was just putting down a fare and her companion pushed her in, asked her address and got in beside her.

The dusk had turned to dark. She couldn't see him clearly.

'You've ruined your dress,' he said.

'So I have. It's soaked.' She was aware

of the wet through to her legs, and her shoes felt as though they were falling off. 'Pa will skin me alive,' she said.

'Oh dear. Is it like that?'

'I hope we'll get home before him.'

'If I were your father I'd be thankful to see you safe.'

'But you're not,' she said.

He turned towards her, a broad smile on his face, or so it seemed, for she could only just make him out. He said something else. It sounded like 'I'm very glad I'm not', but she wasn't sure.

They were past Marble Arch and here was Lancaster Gate. The hansom rounded the corner and obedient to instructions drew up at her gate.

There was a glass canopy to the front door, which was open so the light streamed out. Her companion helped her down, told the driver to wait, and escorted her in. Her father, standing in the hall, had never looked so imposing: tall, slim, handsome, almost awe-inspiring.

'Where have you been, Charlotte?' he asked.

'On an errand for me, as I told you, William,' said Ellen, coming from the drawing room. The servants hovered in the background.

'Charlotte?' Mr Grant waited for her answer.

'I fell down and this gentleman kindly helped me and brought me home.'

'Are you hurt?'

'Not much. This gentleman has been so very kind. I'm so grateful to him.' By this time the shock of her fall was beginning to tell, and Ellen saw this was not the time for cross-questioning, so she gracefully thanked Charlotte's rescuer and took her away upstairs.

After she had disappeared from the scene Mr Grant's stern manner changed completely as he expressed his gratitude to the man, who now introduced himself as Richard Allen. They had all been extremely anxious about Charlotte out alone in such an unseasonable storm, he said, and he was thankful to see her safe home. Would Mr Allen perhaps take a glass of wine or some other refreshment?

Mr Allen excused himself. He had a pressing engagement, the cab was waiting and he must go, and so, with mutual expressions of goodwill, he departed.

Mr Grant, having discovered from their conversation that Charlotte had been in Oxford Street, went up to her room and gave her the wigging of her life. 'You are not to be trusted,' he said. Ellen did her best to soften his harsh tone and was later accused of undermining his authority. Charlotte closed her eyes and the scolding went over her head. She longed to ask what her rescuer was really like: Ellen had only been aware of his slouch hat and cloak. Annie and Tilda were both in the hall at the time but they hadn't noticed the gentleman, they were that worried about Miss Charlotte, they told her.

'I wish you'd had a good look at him,' she said next day. 'Still, never mind. Perhaps awful Albert won't want to marry me when he hears I was picked up in Oxford Street. It makes me a pick-up, doesn't it, Mrs Vickery?'

'Never, Miss Charlotte.'

'He was such a nice man, Mrs Vickery. And it's quite an experience to be lifted to one's feet by an unknown. I enjoyed it.'

'Well, you shouldn't have. I never heard of such goings-on. What did he say?'

'"I'm afraid you've had a very nasty fall." Such a nice voice, too.'

'Oh, I daresay. What else?'

'Nothing else much. End of adventure.'

It was not the end. Richard Allen was on his way home to Green Street when this young, pretty and clearly agitated girl fell over. She had an extraordinary effect on him, the lovely face, the enchanting voice, the lightness, the grace—he had never met another like her and wanted to see her again. Easy. It would be most discourteous not to call and enquire how she was after her fall.

The following day Charlotte and Ellen were having tea in the drawing room when Annie came in to say that Mr Allen was in the hall. She was asked to show him in.

No slouch hat and cloak this time. This was a young man in formal dress who laid his topper and stick by the side of his chair when Ellen invited him to sit. Charlotte was able to take a good look at him. Dark wavy hair, pale face with clear-cut features—how different from Albert Morton! The comparison went through her mind as she responded to his queries about her health and assured him she wasn't much bruised and was in fact as tough as a soldier's boot.

'Oh no. I'll never believe that,' he said with a smile, as though they were already friends.

Very soon they were all three laughing over what Ellen called 'Charlotte's escapade'. 'For just think, Mr Allen, you could have been the most dreadful villain. We're always hearing about the white slave trade, and just suppose you'd been a kidnapper! What would her father and I have done if she hadn't come home? Asked the police to watch the ports, I suppose.'

'Good heavens, Mrs Grant, what a

preposterous notion!' He smiled at Charlotte and she wished she could get a bit closer to see what colour his eyes were.

'You'll take tea, Mr Allen?'

There's nothing I'd enjoy more.'

Annie brought extra china, she handed dainty sandwiches and he took two. They talked of the weather and of yesterday's storm, not so much rain as hail, they agreed. And how dreadful if Charlotte had fallen in front of a horse.

'You had an appointment, I believe,' said Ellen. 'I hope you didn't miss it?'

'I had a few things to do before going on to Covent Garden,' he said. 'Have you been to the opera this season, Mrs Grant?'

'I never go. My husband doesn't care for music so I stifle my love of it,' said Ellen.

'I was brought up on opera,' he said. 'If you would care to hear *Traviata* tomorrow night I'd be only too pleased to give you tickets. Perhaps you could persuade Mr Grant?'

'That's very kind. I can't speak for my husband but I'm sure Charlotte would like to hear an opera, and so would I.'

'I'd love it,' Charlotte said.

'If your papa doesn't object,' said Ellen. 'Ah, here he is. We'll ask him.'

Mr Grant was just coming in as she

32

spoke, and after the customary greetings, which, to his family's relief, showed him at his most amiable, she told him of Mr Allen's offer and said she would really like to go.

'Well, my dear, I'll take you there and bring you back, and as you'll be wrapped up in the music you won't mind if I spend the evening at my club?'

Of course she wouldn't mind. They would all three enjoy themselves—he at his club and she and Charlotte at the opera.

'Charlotte?' queried Mr Grant.

'Of course.'

'Isn't she rather too young?'

Charlotte was only a few weeks off eighteen. 'Please don't bring age into it, Papa,' she pleaded. 'I shall die of disappointment if I don't go.'

'What does Mr Allen say?' asked Mr Grant.

'One can't be too young to enjoy music, so I hope you'll allow Miss Charlotte the pleasure,' said Mr Allen. 'I can promise an unforgettable performance.'

'Then I agree.'

Charlotte smothered a sigh of relief. Mr Allen was thanking her father, and Ellie looked so pleased and happy. It was good when Pa was in an agreeable mood. Now he was shaking hands with Mr Allen, who had picked up his hat and stick. He was as tall as Pa and had broader shoulders. Ever such a nice face, too.

'By the way, Mrs Grant, I expect you know that girls have to put their hair up for the opera? Otherwise they're not allowed in a box.'

'What's that?' demanded Mr Grant. 'Are you saying Charlotte has to put her hair up?'

'Just for this occasion. It's a rule at the Garden.'

'Is it, indeed?'

'Otherwise they have to go in the upper circle, and that's not nearly as good.'

Charlotte held her breath.

'If that's the rule we must abide by it, I suppose,' said Mr Grant.

All was well. Mr Allen took his leave and Mr Grant went so far as to escort him to the front door.

In the drawing room Ellie and Charlotte hugged each other. A crisis had been averted.

Mr Grant came back. Thunder. 'A nice thing when a man's told by a stranger that his daughter must put her hair up,' he roared. 'The fellow's a bounder.'

'Oh William, he's not!' exclaimed Ellie. 'If it's a rule it's a rule. You said so yourself.'

'Of course I did. But if I'd known about

it beforehand I wouldn't have allowed Charlotte to go.' He turned on her as he spoke. 'This is the first and last time you'll put your hair up before you're eighteen, and that's an order.'

'Yes, Papa,' said Charlotte.

Ellen thought Charlotte would look well with her hair dressed very simply; the hairdresser agreed, and when Charlotte saw herself in the glass she was surprised at the improvement it made.

She wore one of Ellie's evening dresses, hastily adapted to suit her. Blush-rose chiffon. She had never worn a dress with a train before and preened and paraded in front of the glass till Ellie told her to stop. Ellie herself was resplendent in green silk velvet and she carried a pink ostrich-feather fan.

Charlotte could hardly quell her excitement. Neither of them had ever been to the opera house and they were enthralled. Charlotte exclaimed at everything she saw: 'Look at the lady in white satin with the diamonds, Ellie! And the one in black tulle with gold gleaming through. Look!'

They had a stage box to themselves; programmes lay ready on the velvet-padded ledge with a bunch of violets on each. The scent was powerful.

'I can't believe we're here. It's a

fairy tale,' Charlotte whispered, and she wondered if Mr Allen was there.

The glitter, the air throbbing with the sound of voices, the rustle of silks, the swish of satins. Such an assemblage—the women all beautiful, the men handsome. Diamonds, rubies, emeralds. She tried to gather it all in, to register the sights and sounds so she would never lose them, but it was too much.

The members of the orchestra straggled into the pit; violins and cellos gleamed, flutes shone. They tuned up, haphazardly it seemed to her, but the effect was exciting. Then they were all assembled and the conductor mounted the rostrum and turned to acknowledge the applause.

Hush.

She leaned forward, hands pressed to her heart. He raised his baton.

Now!

She knew nothing of music, had never heard a full orchestra, but with the first notes of the overture she was captured, lifted out of herself, borne along unresisting on the tide of sound.

The curtain rose—the colours, the dresses, the glamour of that ballroom scene. And the singing! Oh, the singing. The characters had such lovely names: Violetta, Alfredo. Violetta's soprano had a rare quality, brilliant but mellow at the same time.

She was also unbelievably lovely, and the combination of physical beauty and grace with this exceptional voice made her unique.

The curtain fell on the first act, and when Charlotte recovered from her ecstasy she began to study the cast list. The names of the singers meant nothing to her, with the exception of one. Violetta was sung by Mary Allen.

'Ellie, look. Can this Mary Allen be related to Mr Allen, do you think?'

'Perhaps she's his wife.'

Oh no. Please don't let him be married. Yet why should she mind?

'Are you enjoying it?' His voice checked her flow of thought. Mr Allen, looking very fine in white tie and tails with a camellia in his buttonhole, had come into the box.

'It's superb,' said Ellie. 'Charlotte and I are carried away. I don't know how we can thank you enough.'

'Don't try.'

'I suspect you come here frequently?'

'Every night when Mary Allen's singing.'

'We've only just noticed that she sings Violetta. She's related to you?'

'She is.'

Don't let her be his wife, pleaded Charlotte silently.

'Mary Allen is my mother,' he said.

The disclosure was so unexpected Charlotte almost gasped. 'But she's so young!' she exclaimed. 'She's a girl.'

He had taken a seat between them and was closer than he had ever been. 'She's exactly eighteen years older than I am. There, what do you make of that?'

Charlotte didn't know. Was it eau de Cologne, like Pa used? Something much nicer. The way he smiled at her, and this scent, bewildered her and she didn't know what to say. She was so thankful his relationship with Mary Allen was established, she never thought he might be married to somebody else.

The audience had dispersed in the interval but now they were beginning to drift back. Mr Allen excused himself. 'If you'll wait for me afterwards I'll see you to your carriage. There's always a crush going out,' he said.

His hand was on the back of Charlotte's chair. She looked up at him, met his eyes. 'A transformation,' he said, and was gone.

What did he mean?

The curtain rose again and Charlotte thrilled to the intensity of the love between the doomed Violetta and her Alfredo. She lived their ecstasy, felt Violetta's agony when Alfredo misjudged her, and wept at her tragic death. Her eyes were streaming when the last curtain fell, but as the applause went on and on there was time to dab the tears away and marvel at Mary Allen as she curtseyed and accepted bouquet after bouquet until there were more than she could hold. She lost count of the curtain calls but at last the conductor raised his baton for the National Anthem.

'Your papa will be looking out for us. We'd better not keep him waiting,' Ellen said when it was over.

'But Mr Allen's coming to fetch us,' Charlotte reminded her.

'He may be delayed. I expect he takes his mother home, and she'll leave by the stage door.'

They put on their wraps. The auditorium was almost empty.

'Come along,' said Ellen.

Charlotte moved slowly to gain time. As they emerged into the corridor Mr Allen came hurrying towards them. He offered each an arm, said his mother's dressing room was packed with admirers and it would be some time before she could leave.

Ellen feared her husband would be angry if they kept him waiting. 'I'll go on if you don't mind,' she said.

'So you really enjoyed it?' Richard asked Charlotte, keeping her arm in his.

'It's another world. I want to hear it again, and other operas too.'

'I guessed you would.'

'How could you?'

'Intuition.'

'That's what women have.'

'Men have it too, plus something extra.'

They reached the exit and she could see her father outside and was glad he had his back to them.

'I want to thank you for this wonderful evening, but I don't know how to,' she said.

'You've thanked me by liking it and wanting to hear more.'

The way he looked, the sound of his voice—oh, the world would never be the same again. She held out her hand. He raised it to his lips, bent his head. He was kissing her hand! Was it real, or was she dreaming?

'Yesterday a charming little girl,' he said. 'Tonight an enchanting young lady.'

She was in a trance as she preceded him to the street, heard Ellen renewing their thanks as her father hustled them into the carriage. Then they were driving away.

In another carriage Mary Allen was almost smothered with bouquets. There was scarcely room for Richard to squeeze in. Her admirers pressed round, hungry for a last sight, and she waved and smiled and pulled out roses and camellias to give them. It was some time before the driver could urge the horses forward, but at last they were on their way home to Green Street.

'I caught a glimpse of that girl you rescued the other day,' Mary said. 'She's very pretty.'

'I wanted to bring her round to see you but her father was waiting. I gather he's one of those fathers to be reckoned with.'

'And that was the stepmother? She looked charming.'

'She is. But Charlotte! She's entrancing.'

'Dick, I believe you're smitten.'

'Rather more than that,' he said.

'Perhaps it's as well we'll be out of London for a bit, then.'

'Perhaps. But you know what they say?'

'Absence makes the heart grow fonder?'

'Just that,' he said.

For days and weeks Charlotte could think of nothing but the outcome of her escapade. She thought Mr Allen would call the day after the opera, was miserable when he didn't and comforted when he sent a postcard from Manchester addressed to Mr and Mrs William Grant. He said he was sorry not to have been able to call on them before going on tour with Mary Allen, and hoped to do so on his return.

'What a nice hand he has,' observed Ellen.

'Trying to muscle his way in,' snorted Mr Grant.

Charlotte's indignation rose. 'Papa, do you think that a pleasant way to speak of Mr Allen?' she asked. 'Why shouldn't he be received here and treated with the courtesy you show your other friends?'

'Because he isn't one of them, miss.'

She grew even more incensed. 'He's nicer than any of them,' she retorted. 'He's by far the nicest person I've ever met.'

Ellen had to intervene before William grew really angry, so the incident passed off. Mr Allen wasn't mentioned again but Charlotte thought of him constantly and hoped he would call soon, if only to give her the chance to test her opinion of him.

Several weeks dragged by. She felt unsettled, without a real purpose in life, and all the time the threat of marriage to Albert Morton hung over her. He made afternoon calls but never had anything to say. She went with her parents to spend a day at his parents' house at Marble Hill, and there was no denying their obvious wealth. The house, the furnishings, the large gardens and conservatories were far and away superior to anything they had at Lancaster Gate. There was a butler and a footman; at home they only had female servants.

Mrs Morton was very kind and Charlotte couldn't help liking her. She talked amiably, asking what interests Charlotte had, how she spent her time, and how happy she must be to have the company of Ellen. She admired Charlotte's dress, could hardly believe she had made it herself, and called upon Mr Morton to admire the fine handiwork.

'You'll be making your own trousseau,' she said. 'Perhaps you've already begun?'

Charlotte, surprised, horrified, shook her head.

'There! We've plenty of time. We thought about a year as you're so young.'

'A year for what?' Charlotte knew the answer before it came.

'A year till you marry, dear,' said Mrs Morton.

Charlotte managed a very small smile, and as Mr Morton summoned them all for a walk round the garden before the sun went in, nothing more was said.

They strolled along the walks, Mr Morton escorting Ellen, William with Mrs Morton and Charlotte with Albert.

'Like it?' he asked as they approached the house again.

'Top-hole,' she said, hating every beautiful bit of it.

At tea time a few days later Annie came in to say that Mr Allen was in the hall, and was bidden to show him in. The moment she saw him Charlotte experienced a whole range of new sensations. As formal words were exchanged, all she longed to say was: Don't go away again. I've missed you terribly.

Ellen wanted to hear all about the tour, which had been a great success and a new venture, as it was the first time Mary Allen had given lieder recitals in public. 'She begins to find opera a little tiring,' he said. 'Lieder is no less exacting, perhaps even more so, but she enjoys it so much, and so do I.'

'I suppose you have to work very hard,' remarked Ellen.

'My mother is never completely happy with her performance. There's always something more. I can't explain it,' he said, and went on to tell them that she was giving a recital at the Wigmore Hall very soon and if they would like to come he would get tickets.

'Yes please,' said Charlotte.

Was there something special in the way he looked at her? If they were alone would he say something meaningful? But what chance was there of knowing each other better within the strict confines of the social sphere?

The arrival of Albert Morton caused a diversion and gave Charlotte the opportunity to compare the two men. In looks Mr Allen scored heavily. Albert's complexion was greyish-greasy; Mr Allen's pale, almost ivory but healthy. His eyes were dark; Albert's colourless. She could have gone on, feature by feature, line by line but there was no need. The whole aspect of these two young men could not have differed more. Their looks, their behaviour: Richard Allen's unaffected charm, Albert's casual manner. 'Ma wondered if you'd like to come over and play croquet on Saturday,' he drawled.

'I don't know how to play.'

'Have to learn, won't you?'

'I'm not sure I want to.'

'Please yourself.'

He spoke with his mouth full of buttered scone, gulped half a cup of tea and took his leave.

Two of Ellen's special friends arrived as he was leaving, and Charlotte was thankful for the interruption. The exchange of farewells and introductions hid her embarrassment, and when she resumed her seat Mr Allen took his beside her.

Ellen's friends had called with a piece of gossip that obliged all three women to bend towards one another and talk in a series of disconnected phrases punctuated with screams of disbelief.

Charlotte sat looking down at her hands, swallowing hard, blinking, trying to compose herself.

'You're distressed, aren't you?'

She nodded. 'Is it so plain to see?'

'It is to me. Did that young man offend you?'

She looked full at him and met his steady, compassionate gaze. 'That young man is my intended husband,' she said, controlling her voice with difficulty. 'My father has chosen him for me.'

'Do you love him?'

'I hate him.'

'Then there's no question of marriage.'

'Try telling my father that.' Her voice was thin and shaky. 'You don't know. You just don't know.'

'I want to know, Charlotte.'

'Even my dear nanny says that girls like me have to obey their fathers.'

'Not in this.'

'I've no one to take my part. I haven't any friends.'

'Yes you have. Believe me, you have.'

This was the moment when he should have taken her hand, but of course he couldn't with the room full of observant women who missed nothing despite their incessant chatter.

'What's Mr Allen saying to make you

go pink, Charlotte?' one of them asked, and they nodded their heads and looked knowing. Ellen didn't join in.

'I expect they're talking about music. That's Charlotte's favourite topic just now,' she said.

'Very nice too. I simply love musical comedies, don't you? We should make up a party and go to a matinée. What's on at Daly's?'

Nobody knew, but under cover of the succeeding discussion Mr Allen was able to make an assignation. Charlotte often went for a walk in the park while Ellen took her afternoon rest. He would meet her there accidentally.

'Tomorrow,' he said.

'Suppose I can't get out?'

'I'll be there every afternoon until you can,' he said.

Mr Grant vetoed the recital at the Wigmore Hall. He liked Ellen to be with him in the evenings. Besides, who wanted to hear a woman caterwauling in German? he asked.

'I do,' said Charlotte, and was told not to be impertinent.

Her disappointment was mitigated by the prospect of seeing Mr Allen the very next day. She hardly knew how to wait for Ellen to put her feet up after lunch, and once out of the house with Annie as her chaperon she wanted to run all the way to the park.

Richard, for his part, had spent a long time in serious thought since leaving the Grants' house and as a result was thoroughly miserable. He was in love, no doubt about it, and stood as much chance of being accepted by Charlotte's father as a fly did of escaping from a spider's web. Compared with the abominable Albert Morton he wasn't even near the starting post.

Albert Morton was ill-mannered and ugly but his family's position and wealth put him in a superior class. He moved in a circle of bankers, merchants, stockbrokers, exporters and importers at such a high level they could cold-shoulder those in the arts.

As for me, Richard Allen thought, as he mooched up and down outside the park gates, what am I but my mother's accompanist? He forgot that he was a highly accomplished pianist, that he had mastered French, Italian and German in the course of his musical studies and that his unusual style as an accompanist had been noticed by eminent instrumentalists. He was frequently offered other engagements but didn't accept because the long hours of work and study with his mother left no time.

So what had he to offer a girl like Charlotte? He kicked the paving stones and scuffed the toe of his boot. He was so wretched he had half a mind to cut off home and try to forget he'd ever met Charlotte Grant.

Then he saw her. She was waving to him from across the road and looked so eager, so enchanting, so gloriously the one and only Charlotte that he flew over the tree tops, up in the sky and back down onto the pavement as she almost ran the last few steps. There she was, close to him, and they were miles away from the park, the traffic and the pedestrians, some of whom spared a glance for a young man and a girl who were so much in love.

He didn't even notice Annie, but she was there, waiting at a discreet distance. One outing was very like another to Annie but today, when Charlotte and Richard met, something happened that was so different from anything in her experience she felt quite odd inside.

She was fond of her Miss Charlotte, loathed Albert Morton and thought Mr Allen a very nice young gentleman indeed, but today she beheld such a transformation as she would never have credited. She told Mrs Vickery so. The way he looked down at her so tenderly and she up at him trusting and full of love was enough to make a person shed tears to see them, she said.

Richard drew Charlotte's arm through his and they went through the gates and along the path to a bench, where they became so absorbed in each other they didn't even notice Annie pass by, sit on the next bench and bury herself in the latest copy of *Peg's Paper*.

'I've been in such a state for fear I wouldn't be able to get out,' Charlotte said. 'You gave me so much hope yesterday.'

'Before you say another word, I just want to tell you one thing. You are not going to marry Albert Morton. If your father browbeats you into going through a ceremony it will be null and void without your wholehearted consent.'

'It will never have that.'

'What we have to consider now is your next move, or rather ours. You see my dear, dearest Charlotte, I love you with all my heart. I think of you, long to be with you, like you so very, very much.'

He had intended to keep all this to himself, but once he began he couldn't stop, and his feelings came pouring out in a cascade of protestations and declarations. He had never been in love like this in his life, hadn't known love could be so overpowering or so agonising when the object of it was out of reach.

She listened to words she had longed to hear. Her own feelings were as deep and strong as his and she had no hesitation in telling him so, and it was as though their two souls met and merged. They wanted to be together always.

'Look at me, Charlotte,' he said, letting go of her hands, 'I'm twenty-five and I've nothing to offer you. I'm never settled in one place for long. I've no independent means. So you see, my own dear darling, I can't possibly ask you to marry me.'

'Oh yes you can,' she said, in such a forceful voice that Annie, on the next bench, heard her and looking round saw they were locked in each other's arms, kissing. Yes, actually kissing out there in the park as common as you like.

'Lucky there wasn't no one but me about,' she told Mrs Vickery. 'If I hadn't coughed it's my belief he'd have eaten her.'

Ellen's afternoon rest was of prime importance to Charlotte now. Accompanied by Annie she was able to meet Richard every day, and the more they saw of each other the more certain of their feelings they became. But how were they to overturn the obstacles in their way?

Mary Allen was setting off on a tour of European capitals very soon, followed

51

by an appearance at the Metropolitan. Richard would go with her so there was very little time left for him to persuade Mr Grant to accept him as Charlotte's future husband.

She had no illusions. She didn't care a button for her father's blessing although she was overjoyed by Mary's approval. Richard had taken her back to Green Street one afternoon and his mother greeted her so kindly she thrilled to the warmth of Mary Allen's generous personality. Mary simply held out her arms in welcome. 'You dear, dear Charlotte! You're making Richard so happy and now I can see why,' she said, and they sat down together to talk.

Hardly knowing what she said, Charlotte told Mary even more about herself than she had told Richard. She spoke of her mother's time when the house was full of gaiety and love, punctuated by dreadful quarrels between her parents. She spoke of her father's plan to make her marry Albert Morton and the way the net was closing in on her, with the Mortons' frequent visits to their house and the reciprocal ones to the Mortons'.

'You are going to marry Richard, and if it can't be arranged before we leave, you must join us abroad and we'll have the wedding in Paris or Rome or wherever we happen to be.'

'Glorious!' said Charlotte, as she envisaged herself and Richard somewhere in Italy, at the head of a long table in the open, with crowds of fat, happy Italians swigging Chianti from straw-covered bottles.

Richard joined them and sat with his arm round Charlotte, and she marvelled at the ease, the uninhibited ways of the Allens, with Richard calling his mother Mary all the time. 'I can hardly call her Mama when we work together,' he said.

On subsequent days Mary told Charlotte of her hopes and fears for her son. 'I won't have him spending his entire life as my accompanist,' she said. 'He's a brilliant performer in his own right but he lacks confidence. Do try to instil some into him, my darling.'

'I will,' Charlotte said.

'I'm having a little evening party next week, and of course you'll come. Don't you think it would be a good idea for me to invite your parents? It would be a nice way for me to meet them and perhaps show your papa that we're not such outlandish people after all.'

Charlotte knew that her father was unlikely to be impressed by Mary's voice, but surely her superlative physical loveliness and her gracious manner would appeal, and he would have to admit he was glad of her acquaintance. She was overoptimistic. Mr Grant was not at all pleased to receive an invitation to Mary Allen's reception.

'Why does this woman imagine we want to visit her? Write the usual letter of refusal, will you, Ellen?'

'But I'd like to go,' Ellen protested. 'The Allens are going abroad very soon so they won't expect us to invite them back.'

'Very well. Go if you want to, my dear, but exclude me from your acceptance.'

Charlotte held her breath. She knew that Mary's invitation was extended to all of them and supposed her father hadn't noticed it. Nothing more was said but on the day of the reception Ellen changed her mind about going. 'It simply isn't worth rubbing your father up the wrong way,' she told Charlotte. 'He disapproves of Bohemians, as he chooses to call them, so I shall stay at home and play cribbage with him.'

'Does that mean I can't go either?'

'No. You must go and make my excuses. I shall order the carriage to take you.'

Charlotte thanked heaven and thanked Ellen. After dinner on the evening of the reception she changed into her prettiest dress and came down to find her father asking Ellen what the deuce the carriage was doing at the door.

'It's taking Charlotte to the Allens',' Ellen replied.

'The devil it is!'

'Now, William darling, don't get into a pet. There won't be any more parties or operas or anything else now the Allens are off abroad. And anyway, I'm staying at home with you.'

'Well, that makes all the difference. Charlotte, you are to be home by ten o'clock. The carriage will call for you. Is that understood?'

'Yes, Papa.'

'And mind you're ready. You're to be back here by ten sharp.'

'Yes, Papa. Thank you very much,' she said.

Mary Allen's front door was wide open when Charlotte's carriage, following a line of others, stopped outside, and there was Richard waiting to hand her out.

'Why are you alone?' he asked. She told him why and he said Mary would be disappointed and so was he.

Flowers were massed up each side of the staircase and Mary, looking radiant, was standing at the top, receiving her guests. Charlotte was overawed as she joined the procession: the women were in the latest creations, gowns of satin, chiffon, velvet and lace with trains looped up, such a dazzle of colour. Tiaras in their hair, ropes of pearls, and fans. Their escorts were resplendent in full evening rig—it was like Covent Garden in miniature. Richard took her hand. 'You'll soon get used to Mary's parties,' he said.

'I'm all of a shake.'

'So am I.'

'Why you?'

'You'll see,' he said.

They were at the top, and there was Mary in the most exquisite white dress Charlotte had ever seen, with diamonds everywhere. She kissed Charlotte twice and told her she looked lovely. 'But where's Mrs Grant?' she asked.

'Staying at home to smooth Pa's plumage. I'm to say she has a headache, but that's a fib and I don't believe in them.'

'Neither do I. But what a pity. Still, never mind. You're going to have a wonderful evening and I promise you a surprise. You'll have to tell her about it.'

Richard drew her away and they mingled with the crowd. He introduced her to more people than she could remember. They were all so extraordinarily kind, and so interested. They praised her dress, refused to believe she'd made it herself, wanted to know if her family had seats in the Abbey for the Coronation, and marvelled at how exciting the court would be now—all quite different from the dear old Queen's time. The King was having the chandeliers taken apart and cleaned so that the drawing rooms would be brilliant, and when was she to be presented?

'I'm not,' she said.

This drew forth exclamations of surprise and disappointment, and an elderly, over-painted woman in black told her that it could easily be arranged and she would see to it herself. She slipped a card into Charlotte's bag. 'Tell your mama my terms are most attractive. I could make you the débutante of the year,' she whispered.

'I don't know what she's talking about,' Charlotte told Richard.

'She's a pest. Influential, though, so one has to invite her. Let's go in to supper.'

There was a top table and two others at right angles in the supper room. Mary was at the centre of the top table, with Richard on her right and Charlotte next to him. Charlotte wished that Ellie was there to witness the splendour of the occasion and tell Pa. Better still if he could see it for himself. That would open his eyes.

The food was delectable, as was the wine. A good-looking middle-aged man on Mary's left made a graceful speech in her praise. He spoke of the pleasure she gave and how much she would be missed on the London scene. She returned thanks amid applause and invited the assembly to repair to the salon for a little music.

Charlotte saw this room for the first time and noticed the grand piano and some music stands near it. A number of chairs and sofas occupied most of the floor space. Richard took her to a sofa in a central position, and very soon the room was crowded. The scent of the flowers nearby and the babble of voices made her feel dizzy.

A footman came in and spoke to Mary, who had just taken a seat beside her. Mary shook her head and said something inaudible in reply. The man bowed and went away.

Four men carrying instruments came in: violin, viola, double bass and cello. The buzz of voices stopped. It must be a quartet, Charlotte thought, and turned to Richard to ask. He wasn't there. He was at the piano and she hadn't even noticed him leave her.

Not a quartet. A quintet.

The stillness.

Those opening notes. For the first time in her life she heard the music of Schubert. She sat forward, listening. How to describe a sound that was indescribable? Just listen. Just look. Richard. Can it be true he loves me? Me! Her eyes filled with tears at the wonder of it. No matter how many times she might hear this quintet in the years to come there could never be a time like this. She knew it, held on to it.

At the end everyone stood to applaud, and men and women gathered round the players. Charlotte stayed where she was, lacking the courage to go to the piano, and for a few moments she felt deserted, almost frightened, wishing she was with Richard on their park bench, far from this sophisticated assembly.

Then he was there, his arm round her, looking anxious. 'You needn't cry. It can't have been as bad as that,' he said, for the tears were running down her face and she hadn't even felt them.

'I'm lost. I knew you were special but—oh, I can't say. It just made me wonder why you have time for me.'

'You know why. You're getting maudlin. Anyway, when we're married you won't mind if I spend all day practising and all night studying?'

'Oh, when we're married!'

A clock struck. She began to count—nine, ten, eleven—it couldn't be. Twelve.

He heard it too.

'I should have been home hours ago!'

'This was a rather special occasion. We'll look for your glass slipper tomorrow, Cinderella.'

She couldn't laugh. This wasn't a joke.

Pa would be livid. Mary noticed how white she had gone and heard the fear in her voice, and came to reassure her.

'I'm sorry, my darling,' she said. 'Your carriage arrived just as the quintet was about to begin. You could hardly have left then, could you?'

'Pa will say I should have.'

'I can't believe even he could be such a philistine. Anyway, I'll take you home myself as soon as everyone's gone and plead with your father. I'm sure he'll melt.'

Charlotte began to think it was just possible with such an advocate, and was much more cheerful. After all, another half-hour wouldn't make much difference and it would be petty-minded to spoil Richard's début. She wanted to talk about that, to ask about the other members of the quintet, how often they met and how heavenly it must be to make music with them, and he enjoyed telling her.

Mary arranged for her own carriage to follow the Grants', but Charlotte's fears returned when her coachman, who had waited a long time, remarked that she wouldn't half cop it when she got home. It was not a carefree drive.

Mr Grant, watch in hand, was standing in the hall when they went in. He ignored Mary and fixed his eyes on Charlotte.

'What time do you call this?' he asked in the deadly voice he used to convey intense displeasure.

'Papa, there was the most wonderful concert—oh, I do so wish you had been there to hear it.'

'What time is it?' her father repeated.

'It must be one o'clock,' she said.

'And what time did I tell you to be home?'

'Won't you let me tell you why I'm late?'

'What time were you to be home?'

'Ten.'

'Ten what? Come along, come along. Ten what?'

'Sharp,' she whispered.

'Exactly.'

Mary interrupted. 'Mr Grant, I haven't the pleasure of your acquaintance yet but pray allow me to say that Charlotte isn't to blame for being late. The fault is entirely mine. I hope you'll accept my apologies.'

Mr Grant's cold stare went right through her.

'I have nothing to say to you but good morning, madam,' he said. 'Annie, close the door behind this lady.'

Charlotte was so appalled by her father's behaviour she tried to run after Mary, but the door was already shut and all she heard was the carriage moving away.

'How could you?' she cried, turning on her father.

'There's no need to distress yourself,' he said. 'You are overtired and overexcited. It's as well your Bohemian friends are leaving the country soon. They are not an influence for good.'

She was about to remonstrate, but he held up his hand with: 'That is enough.'

She was seized with such violent trembling it was as much as she could do to get up the stairs and into her room, where Annie was waiting to help her out of her dress. 'Well, if that doesn't take the biscuit,' Annie said.

'How could he, Annie? How could he?'

'There, Miss Charlotte, don't you fret yourself. I've no doubt we'll see Mr Allen tomorrow as usual.'

'After the way Papa behaved to his mother?'

'He won't let that stop him. He's fair gone on you, miss. I never see a young man look at his sweetheart the way Mr Allen looks at you. And what a beautiful lady his mother is. What a lovely face—and not a bit fat. I thought singers always ran to fat.' Annie rattled away non-stop but her well-meant remarks failed to comfort Charlotte and she was left dreading what was to come.

Ellen, having heard her husband's account of Charlotte's late return, said very little, but as soon as he left the house next day she asked Charlotte for her version and was horrified to hear he had been unpardonably rude to Mary Allen.

'Of course you shouldn't have stayed out so late, but it's hard to see what else you could have done in the circumstances,' she said. 'I really don't know what we can do to make amends.' William, much as she loved him, could be insufferable, and one of these days she would have to tell him so. She thought it high time he treated Charlotte as an adult and conversed with her in a reasonable way. As it was he snubbed her at every turn, and Ellen quite marvelled at the girl's resilience. She bobbed up every time.

Charlotte was not in a very bobbish mood that day. She was afraid Richard wouldn't come and felt very shaky inside as she went through the park gates with Annie, but there he was standing beside their bench and the first thing he did was to kiss her and draw her down beside him.

'Don't worry about last night,' he said. 'I'm coming back with you this afternoon to talk with your father. I shall tell him we want to get married and ask for his blessing.'

'You will?' Her spirits rose, only to plummet again. Richard didn't know her father as she did. Still, no matter how powerful he was she had to be stronger. Her whole being centred on Richard now and she knew she wouldn't be able to endure life without him. The warmth of his hands as he held hers on that chilly afternoon gave her such strength she was ready to combat a whole legion of fathers.

Mr Grant was not yet home when they got back. Ellen, too, was out, so Richard waited in the dining room and Charlotte, wound up so tightly she couldn't sit still, paced up and down in the drawing room. For them to be together in the same room without a third party present was simply not done, so they didn't risk it.

It was Annie's duty to tell Mr Grant that Mr Allen had called and requested an interview.

'Where is Miss Charlotte?' asked Mr Grant.

'In the drawing room, sir.'

Charlotte heard this and trembled. Then the dining room door opened and shut and she strained her ears to catch what was said.

Mr Grant wasn't aware of Richard's interest in Charlotte and the revelation came as an extremely disagreeable surprise.

'Am I to understand that you are making a serious proposal of marriage to my daughter?' he asked, after Richard told him that was exactly what he meant. The telling had been difficult, for as he spoke, pausing now and then in the expectation of some kind of response, Mr Grant had not uttered a word. He had allowed the uncomfortable silences to drag on until Richard spoke again. When he had dwelt on his love for Charlotte, his devotion to her and his determination to make her happy as his wife, he ended by saying that he was proud to know she loved him and all she wanted was her father's blessing on their union.

'That, sir, is impossible,' said Mr Grant. 'Are you not aware that my daughter is to marry Mr Albert Morton?'

'Charlotte's told me what you propose for her, but she dislikes Mr Morton and won't marry him.'

'You'll find my daughter will do as she's told. However, there's no need to discuss it with you. It is not your concern.'

'Indeed it is,' said Richard. 'Why should she be forced into a marriage that's thoroughly distasteful to her? Why won't you, as a loving father, consider me?'

'I'll mention a few reasons. Unlike Mr Morton, you have no position, no prospects, no permanent abode. You lead a vagrant sort of life. A few years ago you wouldn't have presumed to ring the front door bell. Theatrical persons went to the servants' entrance, Mr Allen.'

'You insult me. My profession as a musician is honourable.'

'As a musician, perhaps. As a man, no.'

Richard was so angry he couldn't prevent his voice shaking as he faced Charlotte's father.

'Mr Grant, you speak in an offensive way. You may think you own your daughter body and soul but you can't force her into a loveless marriage.'

'I can prevent her making a damned bad one.'

'Apart from you, who's to say I'm unsuitable? Tell me that.'

Mr Grant took a turn about the room. He had not offered Richard a seat and this added to his discomfiture. The sun had come out and was streaming through the window but he felt cold in its warmth. His hands were clammy, his throat constricted. He tried to swallow.

Mr Grant stopped in front of him. 'You force me to speak of a subject I would rather not,' he said. 'I understand your mother is unmarried, Mr Allen. And was unmarried when you were born.'

It was as though the room swung and there was a moment of blackness. A cloud had covered the sun, but that was not what caused the darkness. Richard gripped the table edge.

'I perceive you can't deny it.' Mr Grant's voice seemed to come from a long way off and became closer and louder as he continued. 'Mr Allen, as the honourable man you say you are, how could you suppose my daughter would want to marry you when she knows your origin? You, sir, are a bastard and your mother is a whore.'

Richard's naturally pale face was ashen. He clenched his fists in an attempt to master the frightening surge of anger that rose inside him.

'You have already insulted me. Now you insult my mother,' he said. 'If you were not Charlotte's father I would strike you across the face. Believe this. You've said nothing that will change my determination to marry Charlotte and you won't change her love for me either.'

With that Richard left the room and the house, but as soon as he reached the Bayswater Road he had to stop and hold on to the railings. His legs were shaking. He leant his head against the cold iron and wept.

The only thing that concerned Charlotte was her dread of never seeing Richard again. Her father told her everything but she didn't see why his birth affected his standing. Even if it did, why should she care? Mary Allen had her own special and highly honoured position in the world. If her father had seen the titled men and women at her reception he would have to admit it. And that wasn't counting the famous musicians who were there.

'You don't know what you're talking about,' her father told her. 'That man you appear to dote on is branded. He's a leper.'

'If he's a leper, so am I!' Charlotte was so disgusted with her father she almost screamed at him. The Allens were noble, they were devoted to music and their art, while the Grants depended on dried prunes.

Mr Grant was so taken aback by this show of spirit he could only think of one thing to say. 'Go to your room,' he shouted.

'Shan't,' said Charlotte, and she ran to the kitchen, where Mrs Vickery was ready to comfort her, although even she tempered her sympathy with cautionary words.

'Your pa's right in a way, my dear,' she said. 'People born out of wedlock get off to a very bad start, you know. I knew a man who would never marry because he was one of them.'

'Why not?' demanded Charlotte.

'It's the shame,' said Mrs Vickery.

'The ones who despised him should have been ashamed of themselves. That's what I think,' said Charlotte.

'You must mind your opinions don't get you into trouble, Miss Charlotte. Think so by all means but mind who you say it to. Still, I wish your pa would give you his blessing, and if I was in your shoes I'd stick to my guns and marry Mr Allen.'

'I will,' said Charlotte.

She was heartened by the cook's support but it wasn't enough, and who else could she turn to? She hardly slept that night for fear she might never see Richard again after the vile things her father had said to him. There was so little time left; they only had today and tomorrow, for the morning after that he would be on his way to Paris.

Ellen was miserable, too. She liked Richard and had encouraged him to call. Thinking about it, she supposed it was only natural that Charlotte would fall in love with him and he with her. There was a certain something about him, an air, a distinction she hadn't noticed in other men. To expect Charlotte to favour Albert

Morton was absurd, and she told William so. And for him to go making enquiries about the Allens and discovering the truth of Richard's birth was the last word.

'I'd never have thought it of you. It was abominable,' she said.

'Is a man not to protect his daughter's interests then?'

'Not in such a way. You might consider her own wishes more. Mary Allen is highly esteemed and received everywhere, even by the Queen, I'm told.'

'They are still rogues and vagabonds, and I'm not having Charlotte marry into that class.'

'Rubbish. They are highly cultured people and we are not,' she said, goaded by his blinkered outlook.

He told her the subject was closed, he was already late for an appointment and she was not to let Charlotte out of her sight.

Ellen was meeting friends for luncheon and if Charlotte chose to take an afternoon walk she would not be aware of it, so she did not reply to her husband's injunction.

Charlotte's heart thumped so hard it almost frightened her as she made her way to the park alone. He was already there. 'Thank goodness you've come!' he said. They kissed and laughed and felt each other's warmth as they linked arms and went their usual way.

He asked if her father had told her.

'Everything,' she said. 'He expected me to be shocked and was shocked himself because I wasn't. His mind is so narrow it's closed up.'

'He'll never give his consent, you know.'

'All the better. We can do without the consent of a man like my father. But we must be together soon.'

She had an entrancing vision of the future and it made her desperate to break out of her cage. It seemed to get smaller and tighter by the minute. Unseen bars were crushing her and if she didn't escape she would choke. She was terrified something would happen to keep them apart, perhaps for ever, and she told him so. 'No it won't,' he said. 'I'll give you my itinerary so that you'll know exactly where I am. It will be all right.'

He comforted her, assured her of his love over and over again and at length succeeded in quietening her fear. There was a great weight of responsibility on his shoulders and he almost regretted the tour he was undertaking. Yet it was bound to further his career. Apart from his regular work with Mary, he was engaged to accompany a leading violinist in three recitals, and there was the promise of more engagements. The quintet had been a marked success at Mary's reception and offers were sure to follow. This meant hard work both physical and mental, but with his ability, good health and stamina he was sure he would establish himself and have something worthwhile to offer Charlotte.

He told her all this and she wanted to know more: would there not be a great deal of travelling, who were the other members of the quintet, where exactly were they to perform and would it always be the Schubert? Her faith in him and his work was absolute and she wanted so much to understand it all. She longed to enter into his world of music. When she tried to describe her aspirations he looked at her with such compassion and love. Then he took her left hand and slipped a ring on to her third finger. It was gold with a turquoise set round with chip diamonds. 'I want to give you this now. It's not very precious, I'm afraid,' he said.

She knew nothing would ever be more precious and that she would treasure it all her life till the day she died. 'It's the colour of heaven,' she said. So they were betrothed, pledged to each other as surely as if they had taken a vow in church.

And yet.

She wanted one last meeting. He must come to the kitchen door after the opera.

She would steal down and let him in and they could spend a little while alone, within four walls, not on a bench in the park. It was worth the risk.

'Just think how wonderful it will be,' she said.

Heaven.

There wasn't a sound in the house when she tiptoed downstairs after midnight. Mrs Vickery and the maids had been in bed since ten o'clock; her parents retired later. There were no lights inside; the only illumination came from the gas lamp in the street which shed a gleam on the area steps. She opened the door gingerly and there was Richard.

Inside they clung to each other, she in her thin nightdress and shawl and he in white tie and tails. The meeting was spiced with the heady taste of the forbidden. She shivered, but not from the cold.

He sat in Mrs Vickery's easy chair and drew her down on his knee. They had never been so close and the slightly rough feel of his chin against her face induced the most delicious sensations. His face would be rougher by morning. How wonderful to wake up beside him, stretch her arms and legs as she always did and then turn for the first unshaven kiss of the day.

She didn't think of time, forgot it was

passing in the delight of this stolen tryst. He was more aware. A cinder dropped on to the hearth, the fire was almost out. He would soon have to go, and at that she cried, but he promised to come back as soon as he could. There were bound to be periods between concerts and he would seize the first of them to return and take her away. 'I want to marry you, sleep with you, live with you, love you all in the open, above board with everyone knowing,' he said.

'Oh, if it could only be like that!' The idea dazzled her. In her imagination she saw the exotic cities he was bound for and longed to go too. Paris, Vienna, Milan, Rome. She could almost smell the flowers on the Spanish Steps, weep in the room where Keats died, hear the tinkle of the fountains and enter into his world. Never mind the discomforts of travel, the dust, the stinks, the slightly less than clean lodgings. He told her about them and made her laugh. Fleas, bed bugs, they would be something new.

He gave her a small package, a gift from Mary to be opened after they'd gone. He promised to write often and she was to reply. Writing to each other would help to ease the pain of separation. He knew this would be much harder for her than for him, for Mr Grant was determined to crush her resistance. He warned her of his fear that her father would exert all his power to break her spirit.

'Don't be afraid. Nothing will shake my resolve,' she said, with such vigour he had to admit she inherited her determination from her father, just as the other traits he loved so much came from her mother.

'Think of me every day,' he said. 'No, don't just think. Concentrate. Do it when you're alone and undisturbed and I'll do the same. Let's make it a regular part of every day, shall we?'

She seized on the idea and chose the time. It was to be seven hours after midnight.

The fire was out. Not one glowing ember was left, just ashes. There were sounds from the street, wheels turning, heavy carts rumbling, and the window panes were no longer black.

He held her close, kissed her upturned face, loved her with all his heart and longed desperately to take her with him. How she would enjoy their travels, the foreign cities and above all the world of music that was his. 'My dear, dearest dear.' He lingered over the words, held her closer still, told her over and over again that nothing on earth could separate them.

They were so wrapped up in each other that neither heard Mr Grant come in, but he was there and saw enough. He struck a match, lit the gas and turned it full on. They were startled out of their embrace and faced him unnerved.

'What is the meaning of this?' His voice was quiet but his aspect frightening.

'It should be clear enough. I love Charlotte and she loves me. We are taking leave of each other but I shall come back and marry her.'

'You are trespassing,' said Mr Grant, ignoring Richard's reply.

Charlotte was trembling. She still held Richard's hand. 'Please, Papa, please,' she begged.

Her father grabbed Richard's stick which lay on the table and struck at their joined hands. 'Get out of my house,' he shouted, brandishing it. Richard was too quick for him. He wrested it away but knew that the longer he stayed the worse it would be for Charlotte.

'Very well, Mr Grant. I shall go,' he said, and looking past him to Charlotte he said: 'Keep faith and remember.'

'I will. I'll never give in. Not ever.' She heard the back door slam and there was a dreadful finality about the sound. Her father gripped her arm and gave her a savage shake. 'Get out of my sight, you brazen slut, before I give you the thrashing you deserve.' His red face and blazing eyes scared her. She ran out of the kitchen and up the stairs, clutching the rail, stumbling in the dark, and there was Ellen holding a candle aloft.

'Why, Charlotte! What on earth are you doing out of bed?'

Charlotte was too distressed to speak.

'What's going on? Is it burglars?' Ellen had her free arm round Charlotte. 'My poor dear, you're frozen. Aren't you well? You're shivering.'

'And well she may.' Mr Grant spoke as he reached the landing. 'She'll shiver a great deal more before I've done with her. She's disgraced herself, Ellen. I caught her in the kitchen with that oaf Allen. Practically naked. Look at her.'

Charlotte wore a chiffon nightdress. It was almost transparent and made her slim, lovely young body look even more alluring than if she'd been nude.

'She'll take cold,' Ellen protested. 'I'll get her some warm milk.'

'You'll do no such thing. She'll be lucky if she gets cold water.'

Charlotte, released from Ellen's protective arm, was already on the second flight, and Ellen, puzzled and worried, was pushed back into her room and forced to listen to her husband ranting on about the scene he had interrupted, until she fell asleep.

Safe in her own room, Charlotte let her sobs rip. She howled with grief and terror and misery. Richard had gone. Soon he would be out of the country, speeding further and further away.

There was no light to see by so she couldn't find anywhere to hide the gift from Mary. The bed was cold and it was impossible to get warm. Her hands and feet had never been so cold and she couldn't control the spasmodic fits of shivering. At last she pulled on two pairs of stockings, and rummaged in a drawer for winter combinations and climbed into them. With blankets and eiderdown piled on top, warmth gradually came back, but sleep didn't come with it. She lapsed into a comfortless drowse full of dread and foreboding.

Morning came. She struggled out of her torpor and into the reality of the day and the fear of what it would bring. Six o'clock. Tilda would be doing the fireplaces. But Tilda was at her door with a steaming cup of tea. She spoke in a whisper. 'Mrs Vickery reckons you'll get bread and water today, Miss Charlotte. We heard what went on, her and me and Annie. We was listening over the banisters. Here, drink this and hide the cup.'

Charlotte had never enjoyed a more

welcome cup. 'You're a real friend, Tilda,' she said.

'We all are. Mrs Vickery says she'd sooner meet a bull in a field than Master when his rag's out. Mustn't stay.' With that she withdrew quietly. Charlotte finished her tea and a warm glow spread through her. Then she opened Mary's gift and beheld a very pretty purse of *petit point* with a gold clip encrusted with diamonds, just like one she had admired in Asprey's and never expected to own. She opened it not thinking there would be anything inside and was surprised to find coins. Guineas. There were ten golden guineas! And a folded note in the bottom. It read: 'With fondest love, dear. From Mary Allen.'

It was so like her—the kind thought, the generosity. Charlotte had never had a penny piece to call her own; now she was rich. Her ring was under the pillow so she slipped it into the purse and hid the whole thing in a shoe and out of sight.

Seven o'clock. The hour they were to concentrate on each other. She knelt by her bed, buried her face in her hands and conjured up his image. She saw him plainly—waiting for her in the park, sitting at the piano, coming into the box at the opera—and her longing almost overwhelmed her. She knew he was dwelling on her at this particular time and that gave her strength. Her despondency vanished just as though he had willed it away. The more she thought of the time they had spent together the more confident she became, and when the clock struck eight she was ready to face her father's anger.

Should she go down to breakfast? She was dressed and ready. She peeped over the banisters and saw her father descending; Ellen followed. The dining room door closed behind them, and while she wondered what to do Annie came up the stairs.

'Oh, miss, you're not half in hot water,' she said. 'Master sent me to say you're to stay in your room and we're not even to give you a slice of bread.'

'I don't care,' said Charlotte.

The appetising smell of fried bacon wafted up from below and tickled her appetite. There would be kedgeree on the sideboard, poached eggs and a dish of that horrible stodgy porridge that was obligatory eating before the tastier dishes were allowed at her father's breakfast table.

'We're not half worried down in the kitchen. Mrs Vickery's afraid we'll catch it.'

'None of you had anything to do with it and I shall tell my father so if he tries to blame you.'

'That's ever so kind, miss. We're just praying everything will come right for you and your young gentleman.'

'Thank you, Annie. You'd better go down now. You'll be missed.'

Annie retreated and Charlotte sat by the window and thought about the changes in her life since Richard had come into it. If she had never met him she would have been content to stay at home and enjoy life with Ellen. Her coming had made an enormous difference. But there was the threat of Albert Morton. No, don't even think of him, think of Richard. He's coming back for me as soon as ever he can and we'll elope! The idea made her so happy, so thankful, so blessed her heart overflowed. There was colour in her cheeks and her eyes were sparkling. She longed to tell someone, Nanny, Mrs Vickery, the milkman, the butcher, the baker. Anyone but her father.

The door opened. Her father and Ellen came in.

'Charlotte, you have had time to consider your position,' he said. 'No doubt you realise you can't stay here. If the slightest hint of your disgusting conduct were to get about the whole family would be disgraced. No decent man would marry you.'

'Richard would,' she said quietly. 'If I'm

81

to be ostracised let me marry him and live abroad.'

'You will live at Bournemouth with your Aunt Mildred for the rest of the year,' he said. 'Our friends will be told that you require sea air and rest. At the beginning of next year you will marry Albert Morton, if he'll have you.'

'That I never shall,' she said.

'We shall see,' said her father and went out of the room, leaving Ellen behind.

As the door closed behind him Ellen looked very unhappy and shook her head. 'Your papa is simply furious with you,' she said. 'He sees your behaviour as a threat to our good name and tells me you're finished if Albert won't have you.'

'That's the best news I've had since Pa insulted Richard! Albert will be doing me a favour by jilting me. You see that, don't you?'

Ellen sat on the unmade bed, looking woebegone. 'Heaven knows I don't want you to be miserable, but you really asked for trouble seeing Richard alone at that hour of the night. Your papa has every reason to be angry.'

'I don't care a button for his anger. He can fly up and bust for all I care. I hope he does. I'd like to see his entrails spread on the wall!'

'Charlotte! This is going too far.'

'Pa may be angry with me but how do you think I feel, Ellie? How dare he speak to me like that? How dare he order my life?'

'He's your father, my dear, and you've been a bad girl.'

'Be truthful, Ellie. You don't want to see me sentenced to a life with Albert, do you?'

'You know I don't. I've pleaded with your father time and again.'

'Just think if you had to go to bed with him and he climbed on top and—'

'Stop!' shouted Ellen. 'You mustn't talk like that or think like it. I'm shocked to hear you.'

'How can you be? It must be heaven with the one you love and hell with anyone else. Admit you agree. You've often told me you fell in love with Pa, so you know what I mean.'

'We shouldn't be talking like this. Please don't make things worse than they are.'

'Why can't you be honest? We're friends, aren't we?'

'Yes, but I can't be disloyal to my husband.' Ellen was in a wretched position between father and daughter now. She was so fond of Charlotte and empathised with her in her difficulties. She wanted her to marry Richard but feared displeasing William if she took too strong a line.

Having fallen desperately in love with him when they met, she only discovered how tyrannical he could be after their marriage. This was a disappointment, but she was philosophical and took the sensible course of placating him in the home while keeping to herself her thoughts on topics he disliked. She was his wife when he was at home, herself when he was out, and as he was out a good deal she considered herself exceptionally fortunate to be able to go out and meet people. It would have pleased her immensely to know the Allens. She had taken to Richard on sight and from what Charlotte told her guessed she would like his mother very much too.

There wasn't a hope of knowing the Allens now. William had used swear words to describe them and told her to pack Charlotte's things in readiness for her long stay in Bournemouth. 'You're to be ready to leave in the morning,' she said. 'You'd better take a valise with you. The rest can be sent on. Papa is taking you to Aunt Mildred himself.'

'I won't go.'

'You'll have to. Don't think I favour the plan. I shall miss you dreadfully.' Ellen was on the verge of tears and Charlotte was beginning to see a whole new set of difficulties ahead. If she consented to stay with Aunt Mildred how was she to keep in touch with Richard? And where was the itinerary he'd promised?

At that moment it was under the crossing sweeper's broom, mixed up with twigs and dust and discarded scraps of food, for Richard realised he hadn't given it to her as soon as Mr Grant slammed the door on him. He waited till the kitchen gas went out and then pushed it under the door. Annie or Tilda were sure to find it and give it to Charlotte.

As it happened, Mrs Vickery was the first one to open the door that morning and see a piece of paper flutter away. She thought nothing of it. Rubbish was always blowing down the area steps and up again, especially when the wind was in the north, as it was that day.

Charlotte wasn't to know this. All she knew was that she couldn't write to Richard until she heard from him. Who would send his letter on if she succumbed and went to Bournemouth?

'Ellie, will you help me?' she asked.

'If I can, dear.' Ellen was at the wardrobe, trying to select the most suitable things for Charlotte to take.

'Richard will be writing. Will you post his letters on?'

Ellen hesitated and then said: 'I can't promise. Your father deals with the letters. He opens and reads them all, as you know, and he certainly won't allow you to have any letters from Richard.'

'What am I to do then?'

'I wish I could tell you.' Ellen picked up the chiffon nightdress and shook it out. It was the most exquisite piece of needlework, with rows of minuscule tucks and cut-out embroidery at the waist and hem.

'Your papa told me I'm to burn this,' she said.

Charlotte, staggered, considered this before she spoke. Hours of patient work had gone into the creation designed for her wedding night and knowing how far off in the future that night was she wore it for her last meeting with Richard.

Burn it. Never.

'If you burn it I'll never forgive you, Ellie. I shall hate you as bitterly as I hate my father.' She spoke with such vehemence and looked so wild that Ellen dropped the nightdress and stared in consternation. She didn't know this violent girl, and Charlotte didn't know herself. Something was welling up inside her, an emotion of such strength that she was afraid.

Unknown even to herself, she was rebelling against her life as the unloved child of a man so stuck in the mud of his own prejudices he would condemn her to a hateful marriage just to keep within the conventions of his kind. She would need patience, resolution and fortitude to hold her own, but her strength lay in her devotion to Richard. She only had to get through the time of waiting, and she would do it. Somehow. Somehow.

Ellen was sitting on the bed again, looking so wretched that Charlotte's heart softened. She remembered all there was to thank her for: Ellie had been a true friend and even now was not over-reproachful. Apart from the servants, she was the only friend she had ever had.

'Ellie dear, I'm sorry. I couldn't ever hate you. You're such a dear darling and I love you. Really I do. We've had lovely times together, haven't we?'

'We have, dear. I was so thankful you welcomed me when your father brought me home. Let us hope he will have a change of heart.'

They sat together talking of their happy times, but as they spoke Charlotte's mind was on her future, and the germ of an idea was born.

Presently Ellen realised that Charlotte had not had anything to eat since dinner the previous night, and decided to flout her husband's order to starve the girl. She rang for Mrs Vickery and told her to prepare a good breakfast for Miss Charlotte and serve it in the morning room. 'Don't trouble about bread and butter,' she said. 'Scrambled eggs on some of your special little potato cakes will do very well. And some good coffee.'

Mrs Vickery was only too delighted to comply. Mrs Grant had got round the order of 'not so much as a slice of bread' very neatly. Mentally she stuck her tongue out at the master of the house.

'You're an angel, Ellie,' Charlotte said when the tray was brought in.

'Well, dear, I try.'

Charlotte did justice to Mrs Vickery's excellent breakfast and for the rest of the day she did as Ellen advised.

The chiffon nightgown lay where Ellen had dropped it. Charlotte shook it and folded it carefully inside the flannelette one already in the valise.

That afternoon Ellen went to an art exhibition, so Charlotte spent an hour or two enjoying the comfortable companionship of Mrs Vickery and the maids. They told her she'd been very rash but seeing as how Mr Allen was going away, who could blame her? Such a lovely young gentleman, said Annie, with a sigh. And his mum, she added. 'Ooh, how I wish you'd a seen her, Mrs Vick. What a ma-in-law to have!'

All this heartened Charlotte considerably, and when Mrs Vickery said in a belligerent tone that sounded more like a threat than a promise: 'Love will find a way!' Charlotte hugged and kissed her and said she'd make sure it did.

While her parents were dining that evening, Charlotte was in her room eating the delectable meal Mrs Vickery had smuggled up to her. The ingredients had been intended for the master's table but she sent a message to the dining room to say the butcher was out of calves' liver so she had done her best with top-grade mince and hoped the rissoles would give satisfaction. Mr Grant ate four, supposed they were up to standard and trusted Ellen to see that Cook didn't get lax.

His dinner, good though it was, didn't bear comparison with Charlotte's, and she made the most of it for she didn't know where the next was to come from. Certainly not from Aunt Mildred's table, for she was most certainly not going to stay with her. The germ of an idea, planted when Ellie told her that her nightgown must be burned, had taken root and was flourishing.

It was Coronation year. There would be courts, balls, the races, celebrations of all kinds, and the demand for new outfits would be enormous. Dressmakers would be screaming for hands.

That was it! She was going to walk

out of the house with her belongings at daybreak, make her way to Hammersmith, where Nanny lived, and ask for an introduction to Madame Last, the court dressmaker.

Annie was surprised to find Charlotte in the kitchen eating bread and butter and drinking tea at the unlikely hour of six o'clock in the morning. She checked an exclamation as Charlotte put her finger on her lips and pointed to the valise.

'I'm off,' she whispered.

'Where to?'

'To see Nanny. I'm going to be a dressmaker.'

'Lawks!' said Annie, staring. 'How will you get started? You can't just set up without premises, you know.'

'I shall ask Nanny to introduce me to Madame Last.'

This statement, delivered in a firm and confident tone, knocked Annie back on her heels. Miss Charlotte, with no experience of life outside the confines of her comfortable home, was aspiring to work for Madame Last. Well, there's nothing like sauce to get you there, Annie thought. She felt bound to point out the dangers young and inexperienced girls were likely to encounter from wicked men and even wickeder women everywhere, but Charlotte only laughed and said heaven would protect an honest girl.

'I hope you're right,' said Annie.

'Annie, there's just one thing you can do for me, and it's the most important of all.'

'What's that, miss?'

Charlotte explained that she hadn't got Richard's address and expected a letter from him. As it was one of Annie's duties to pick up the post and take it to the master on a tray, would she extract this all-important letter and keep it safe? She'd know it by the foreign stamp.

'If I don't get it I'm lost,' she said.

'Right, Miss Charlotte. I'll make sure and snaffle it, but how am I to get it to you?'

'Re-address it to Nanny's.'

'Very good.'

Having settled this essential matter and received all kinds of warnings and good wishes from Annie, Charlotte stepped out into the waiting world.

It promised to be a beautiful day, and Charlotte was so elated she could have danced all the way to Hammersmith. As it was, she crossed the Bayswater Road, caught the first westbound bus she saw and encountered her first obstacle. The conductor eyed the sovereign she tendered suspiciously.

'Ain't you got nothing smaller?' he asked.

She had nine more exactly the same but didn't tell him so. It seemed he would need a busload of passengers several times over to give her change for her fare, and there were only two men and three women on board who all looked at her as though she had just arrived from the moon.

'Bit green, are they, where you come from?' he asked.

'They're the same colour as everyone else,' she replied.

'Sent you out with a guinea, did they? Did they know where you was agoing?'

Most of the girls who got on his bus were on their way to or from work. They wore serge skirts and nice plain blouses and their gloves, if they had them, were knitted. This girl's gloves were of such fine skin you could almost see through it, and he wondered how a person could do up such dinky little buttons.

Must be a rich girl, he concluded, and yet somehow poor. Not the kind of girl who went out so early and alone if all was well at home. Her sort was always accompanied. Besides that, why was she carrying a valise? He reckoned she'd upped and hopped it. Brutish father? Unfaithful husband? Going home to Mum?

'Tell you what, miss. You can owe me

the three ha'pence,' he said, for he saw her as a victim, a beautiful persecuted girl in need of a champion.

'Can I? But I don't know when I'll see you again.'

'Next time you're this way.'

'Thank you. Thank you very much. I shan't forget.'

Notting Hill. The streets were teeming with men and women going to work. She was used to a sedate stroll with Ellie, not to this bustle and hurry, not to newsboys shouting the morning papers. And there was so much to see she didn't know which side of the road to look out at. Shops were opening—butchers, bakers, grocers, haberdashers. Enormous slabs of ice were being carried in to the fishmongers. Men were pulling down canopies against the sun, shouting greetings to one another. Boys were pushing barrowloads of goods. Some rode bicycles with huge baskets on the handlebars piled so high they could scarcely see over the top, but they pedalled away as though Old Nick was after them.

This was life and she was part of it! So much to tell Richard, and what would he say? Soon she would have work to go to and a room of her own to live in, and always there would be Richard. Their reunion was on the horizon like a magnet pulling her towards it.

Shepherd's Bush. The end of the bus's route. She got off along with everyone else. But where was Hammersmith? 'If you want to know the way, ask a policeman.' Those were the words of a music-hall song Tilda often sang. Well, here was a policeman, so Charlotte asked him, but he didn't know of a bus that went to Hammersmith. The young lady had better take a cab or else walk there, though it was a fair step. He rocked backwards and forwards on his big boots and compared them with her dainty shoes. Very thin soles. She'd feel the pavement through them.

She said she would enjoy the walk, so he gave her minute directions and she set off, with only one small worry in mind. Somehow she must get change for a sovereign or she wouldn't be able to go on a bus or even take a cab. A sovereign must be worth a great deal, and she had ten of them. Annie's wage was fifteen pounds a year, she remembered. She had board, lodging and all found, as they said, so in a way it was pocket money. It made Charlotte think. Things she had always taken for granted would have to be earned. Food, lodging, coal, clothes. What about washing? Think of that later. All those girls scurrying off to work managed it, so she would as well.

Now the road thronged with children. A

bell rang. School. Swarms of boys and girls were running to their separate entrances as she passed the building. Chattering, shouting, crying, falling over, pushing past her as though she were a pillar or a post. The girls wore pinafores and hard straw hats with elastic under their chins. They had stout buttoned boots.

Fascinated, she stood and watched until the last one was inside and all was quiet. As she went on, a burst of song brought her to a standstill again. The children were singing their morning hymn and the sound of the young voices touched her heart. These children had a certain security, at least for the present, but what was before them? They were not to know, and that made their singing all the more poignant.

The valise was getting heavy. She had changed it from one hand to the other several times. On she went, but not so fast. If there were a bench she would sit down for a little. The street seemed to go on and on, an endless terrace of little houses, most with their front doors open and women going in and out, chatting to one another, staring at her as she passed. There was something vaguely inimical about them; it was like being in a strange country and not knowing the language.

She came to a turning at last and to a street the policeman had told her to look out for. Nearly there. She had been repeating his directions in her head, and here at last was a much quieter, more pleasant street with lace-trimmed curtains at the windows and little front gardens.

Round the corner and there, tucked away, was a pretty little double-fronted house standing alone. Number 35. She put down her valise and knocked at the door.

Nanny, unaware that she was to have a visitor that morning, was in the scullery doing the washing. She had looked up at the sky and hoped it wouldn't rain, at least not until the sheets were dry. She had fixed the lines that crisscrossed the paved yard, which was bordered all round by narrow flowerbeds.

She often discussed having it grassed over with her son, Will. 'Grass would be nice for Lily to play on,' she said.

'Lily can bounce her ball better on paving,' was his reply, so they never reached a decision.

Lily, Will's young daughter, was the heart of his life. Lovely to look at but simple. Tenpence in the shilling, people said, and tapped their heads. He would never admit it but Nanny knew it was true. At twelve years old Lily was still in the infants' class. Nanny's heart contracted with grief for both of them as she got Will's shirts out and went back for the towels.

She had just pegged the last in place when there was a knock at the door. Probably a neighbour wanting to borrow a box of matches or a cup of sugar. They all came to her when they ran short and usually forgot to repay their borrowings.

There was the knocker again. Must get the kettle on. Dying for a cup of tea. The knock came for the third time as she put the kettle on the hob, snatched her apron off and opened the door to a fashionable young lady who was certainly not one of the neighhours.

A pretty hat, a pretty face, and something so familiar about it.

Amanda!

Of course it wasn't. It was Charlotte.

'Nanny! I was afraid you were out, or had moved, or gone to Margate for the day.'

Charlotte was safe with Nanny's arms round her, and what a relief it was.

Nanny didn't have to be told there was something badly wrong for Charlotte to be calling on her so early—and with a valise. Was it because her father was going to marry her off to that horrid Mr Morton when she was madly in love with Mr Allen? Mrs Vickery had told her that Mr Allen was a most eligible young man: he had style and accomplishments, and most of all he truly loved Charlotte. Pity he was born the wrong side of the blanket, but so were plenty of top-drawer people.

While these thoughts were in her mind she was saying comforting things: Sit in Will's chair, dear. You must be tired after your journey. Drink your tea and have a biscuit, then we can have a nice long chat. Is all well at home?

She very much feared that all was far from well. Fire, flood, financial ruin, smallpox? Had Mrs Grant eloped or Mr Grant run off with one of the maids? Stranger things had been known to happen.

'I've left home,' said Charlotte.

Nanny was so lost in a maze of imagined catastrophes she didn't hear this, and Charlotte had to repeat it.

'I've left home.'

'What!'

'I've run away.'

There was Charlotte, pretty as a picture, putting her empty cup on the table and saying she'd run away. There was a pause. Then Nanny said: 'You don't mean it.'

'I do. Oh, if you only knew, if you'd only been there. Pa was going to send me to live with Aunt Mildred for ages and then make me marry that toad Albert Morton.'

'So you haven't managed to talk your pa out of that idea then?'

'He's adamant. He's a hard, cruel, puffed-up pig. Richard and I did something a bit stupid but it was only because Pa was so horrid and we were desperate. And now Richard's gone abroad and I haven't even got his address and I do love him so much, Nanny. And he loves me. He'll be worried stiff about me now.'

The idea of Richard speeding away in a French train made her clutch one hand in the other and look so pitiful that Nanny drew up a chair beside her, took both her hands and said: 'There, there, don't fret so, dear. But whatever was this stupid thing that made your pa so cross?'

Nanny wanted to sympathise with this young couple in love, but when she heard of Richard's visit in the early hours she shook her head. It was foolish in the extreme. Asking for trouble, she said. Only natural they should want to see each other, but any father would be angry and shocked by such behaviour. 'Really, Charlotte, what could you have been thinking of?' she asked.

'Can't you imagine how I felt knowing Pa had insulted Richard and his mother? Called him a bastard and her a whore! If you'd been me wouldn't you have wanted one last meeting? I know you would.'

Nanny almost felt the cold cloud that

had enveloped Charlotte after Richard's dismissal. Who could blame her for that secret assignation when they knew the depth of her love for him and his for her? Charlotte had never looked more like Amanda than she did at that moment and Nanny had a powerful reminder of her favourite charge who had died so young, leaving her little girl to a father with no paternal feelings at all. Of course she understood. She'd have done the same herself in a similar situation.

'You need help, and you can count on me every inch of the way,' she said. 'Now, what's your plan?'

'I shall take a room somewhere and get work so I can keep myself,' Charlotte said, thankful and grateful to find Nanny was on her side.

'I ought to warn you, it's one thing to run away from a home like yours—quite another to face life without all the comforts you've been used to, Charlotte. What kind of work did you have in mind? Governess, perhaps?'

'Dressmaking. I'd like to get a place with Madame Last.'

'I see.'

Charlotte found the silence between this and Nanny's next observation rather uncomfortable. Then Nanny said: 'You'll find the life of a workroom girl very

100

different from what you've been accustomed to.'

'I expect I shall. I know it won't be easy but I shall be earning my right to marry Richard. You will help me find work, won't you?'

Nanny was in a quandary. It was easy to promise, not so easy to perform.

'You must let me think, dearie,' she said.

She was a woman who always looked cheerful but often felt anxious. Her son's wretched marriage was over but she was concerned for his future with a child who would always be dependent on him. His wife, a nasty woman called Ruby, had gone off with a publican when Lily proved to be lacking in wits. She said she wasn't going to spend the best years of her life looking after a half-potty kid, even though she'd brought her into the world.

When this happened Nanny considered she had no choice but to give up her work as a children's nurse and join forces with Will. He found the delightful little house in Hammersmith where she now lived, keeping house for him and looking after Lily.

'Charlotte,' she said, when she had considered the best course to take, 'I'm going to see Madame Last.'

'Oh, bless you, darling Nanny!' cried

Charlotte, who had been sitting on pins.

'Yes, but I want you to stay here and keep Lily company till I get back. Will you do that?'

'Of course I will.'

'I shall call on your pa first,' said Nanny.

'Oh dear, I wish you wouldn't.'

'It's my duty. He's probably got the police out looking for you by now. He'll be thinking goodness knows what.'

'Serve him right. Serve him jolly well right!'

Echoes of Amanda, Nanny thought. 'That's not the way,' she said.

Charlotte felt some of the sparkle had gone out of the day. She ached for Richard; the sound of his voice, her arm through his. It would soon be time for their assignation in the park, with Annie walking demurely on ahead—oh, how could she bear it without him! All this dreadful common sense. If I knew where he was I'd go after him. As soon as I know where he's staying I jolly well will. I'll get a passport and use Mary's money for the fare. I wish I'd learned to speak French properly. Wish I'd brought my grammar book with me.

Nanny left on her mission as soon as Lily came home from school. She was rather large for her twelve years, with a smooth, almost beautiful face. Nanny introduced her to Charlotte and told her to behave nicely, to go out to feel the washing every now and then, and to fold the sheets the way she'd been taught. Yes, she could play the piano to her new friend and they could go for a walk during the afternoon. She might like to take Charlotte to see the ducks on the pond.

It was the first time Charlotte had met anyone with less than the full complement of wits, and her heart warmed to Lily, who took to her at once. She wanted to try on Charlotte's hat and touch the locket she wore.

'Is there a picture in it?' she asked.

Charlotte opened it to display a miniature of Amanda.

'That's you!' exclaimed Lily.

'No, it's my mother,' Charlotte said.

'I haven't got a mum,' said Lily. 'She scarpered.'

'She did what?'

'Scarpered. Ran away. Don't you know nothing?'

'Not much, I'm afraid,' Charlotte said, wondering how Lily came by such a strange expression. It must be school. It was certainly not Nanny. So although Lily was slow, Charlotte learned from her, especially when they went for a walk and saw crowds of children playing in the street and doing things she'd never seen before, like swinging from lampposts on ropes.

'I'd like to do that,' Lily said.

Some of the children stared at her and made grimaces. 'She's dotty,' one of them said, and others took it up like a chorus, jeering. 'Ain't you all there, then? Where'd you leave the other two penn'orth?'

Charlotte hurried Lily away, hoping she didn't understand the meaning of these jibes but fearing that in some dull kind of way she did.

Nanny, meantime, had arrived at Lancaster Gate, seen and talked with Mrs Vickery and the maids and been shown in to the dining room, where Mr Grant joined her after a few moments.

'I understand you have news of my daughter, Mrs Goode,' he said, without preamble.

'Charlotte is with me. She is perfectly safe and well and I have come to relieve your anxiety.'

'Indeed. I'm grateful to you, but extremely angry with her, Mrs Goode. She is a stupid, disobedient girl and deserves a good whipping.'

'She deserves some love and understanding,' said Nanny, bridling.

'What's that? What's that?'

'I think you heard, Mr Grant.'

'You condone her conduct? Have you any idea of the brazen way she's behaved? Or of the worry she's caused Mrs Grant and me? It's intolerable. It's past belief. She's ruined in the eyes of society.'

'Have you asked yourself why she did it?'

'Because it's in her nature to be rebellious, just as her mother was. I try to save her from an illegitimate scamp of a musician and this is the thanks I get. Justify that if you can.'

'The scamp of a musician, as you call him, gave her the one thing she needs, Mr Grant. He gave her love.'

'And how long will that last, pray? No steady income, just the odd engagement now and then.'

'I believe Mr Allen is well thought of in his profession, with every prospect of advancement. Charlotte loves him. Can't you bring yourself to approve an understanding between them?'

'You must allow me to know what's best for Charlotte, Mrs Goode. From all you've said it's quite clear you're much too pliant and easy-going with her. I'm afraid you are not a good influence on her any more than you were on her mother.'

This reference to Amanda raised Nanny's blood pressure. 'I see you are as pig-headed

105

and intolerant as ever you were,' she said, rising as she spoke.

'Wait a moment. My carriage is at the door. Bring Charlotte home and she won't even be scolded unless she persists in her disobedience.'

'Will you allow her to correspond with Mr Allen?'

'Most certainly not.'

'Then she won't come.'

'In that event I've finished with her, and you may tell her so.'

'Think again, Mr Grant.'

For answer he tugged the bell rope and went out of the room, leaving Nanny defeated and confused. Annie showed her out, and having heard most of what had been said returned to the kitchen to tell the others the master was in a towering rage and they'd better give him white fish for dinner or he'd explode.

Nanny was so upset by Mr Grant's intolerance that she went into a teashop to get over it before proceeding to Madame Last's establishment in Mayfair. If she failed to secure a post for Charlotte there... But why consider defeat before it happened? Look on the bright side.

She had a Bath bun and butter, and a pot of tea, and felt much better. Better still when Madame Last—Bessy to her—made her welcome as an old and valued friend.

Nanny had known Bessy Weller when she was a fat and formidable child whose first words had been that she hated potatoes and didn't mean to hump sackfuls of them like her parents. The Wellers were prosperous greengrocers but Bessy intended to be a person of consequence, so when she grew up and met weak-kneed Henry Last she promptly married him, learned all she could of his family's lucrative dressmaking business and very soon took it over.

In the course of her rise to fame she decided to shed her cockney accent. 'Teach me to speak proper,' she told Nanny, who was a friend of her parents.

'Properly,' Nanny corrected, and teach her she did. Now corsetted, coiffed, and with a strong preference for fruit preserved in brandy rather than fresh, she was known for the excellence of her gowns and blouses. A garment with her name embroidered in an inconspicuous place was a prize. In spite of her outstanding success, however, she never forgot old friends and always had time for them.

'I'm glad to see you, Nanny, 'pon my word I am,' she said when Nanny was shown in. 'How are you?'

'Worried,' Nanny said.

'Not on account of Lily, I hope?'

'No. I've another girl to worry about.

She's the daughter of my favourite charge.'

'And you want my help?'

'I do.'

'Tell us what it's all about and then we'll have a nip of brandy.'

Madame Last's stays creaked as she sat down before the fire and invited Nanny to do the same. Her private sitting room, just off the elegant salon where she saw clients, was furnished for comfort, of which, as she often said, she could never have enough. There were two enormous armchairs upholstered in crimson velvet, with footstools to match. A small table was laid ready for lunch with heavy silver cutlery and cut-glass wine glasses.

'I'm having a bit of smoked haddock today. Like to join me?' she asked. 'I'm on my own else. Henry's out and my Algie doesn't often show up.'

'I hope they're both well,' Nanny said.

'Henry gets the screws. Young Algie's fit as a flea and pretty well as active. Can't get him to take an interest in the business. Still, it's your troubles we're talking about today. How about the haddock first?'

'No, thank you kindly, Bessy. I mustn't be away too long. Now, about Charlotte. She's with me now and wants work. She's run away from home—'

'On account of falling in love with a man they don't like, I've no doubt.'

'You've hit the nail right on the head.'

'Say no more. The less I know about this young person the better. You're aware of my soft heart, Nanny?' she said, laying her hand on it and screwing up her face. 'I can't abide having it touched, and in my business sentiment is O-U-T. Begin to feel for your workers and you'll face ruin. So never mind about your young friend's trials and tribs. Just tell me one thing. Can she sew?'

'She can.' Nanny produced the nightgown as evidence and Madame Last examined it and made a sound very like a whistle.

'My word! Call this a nightgown?' she said. 'More like a top-class whoring gown, I'd say.'

'My Charlotte is an innocent, I'd have you know, and her young man's a gentleman. There's been no hanky-panky there.'

'I believe you, Nanny. Thousands wouldn't. It just happens that one of my best young women hopped it with a policeman day before yesterday so I'm short of a hand. What with the season almost on us, and then the Coronation, I'm pretty well pushed. Send this Charlotte of yours to see me at ten thirty tomorrow morning.'

'Thank you, Bessy.'

'She won't get favours. She'll be treated just like the others, fair and square. It's hard work but a sight better than a factory. What's her other name?'

'Grant. Charlotte Grant. Oh, and there's just one more thing. What about the digs round this way? She'll need a room.'

'The girl who hopped it was sharing with one of the others at a house owned by a very respectable woman, name of Blunt. I'll give you the address.'

Madame Last hoisted herself out of her chair, smoothed down her dress and went to her desk. Although she moved in a stately way and wore a handsome gown in the latest fashion, Nanny noticed the roll of fat bulging over the top of her corsets.

'You're putting it on, Bessy,' she said. 'Those stays are pulled in much too tight.'

'Don't I know it! I'll have to get fitted for another pair. Still, I don't wear too bad, do I?'

'Remarkably well, all things considered.'

Madame Last handed Nanny Mrs Blunt's address and poured out two glasses of brandy. 'My doctor tells me there's nothing better for the circulation,' she said as she raised one to her lips.

Nanny was tired out by the time she got home that afternoon. She was thankful

Bessy Last was willing to give Charlotte a trial, but not at all enamoured with Mrs Blunt, the landlady. A gorgon if ever I saw one, she concluded as she was shown the room Charlotte was to share. The house was cheerless, and so was the room, with its threadbare brown oilcloth, ugly washstand, and clothes horse with one thin towel placed near the window to dry. There was a tiny open fireplace with newspaper, a few sticks and a small bucket of coal in the hearth.

'Where do they cook?' Nanny asked.

'They don't. They can boil a kettle on the Primus stove for their tea. Food's to be had from the cookshop. Cooking I do not allow.' This was a surprise as a smell of boiled cabbage pervaded the house.

'What about washing?'

'There's the basement scullery for underwear. Bed linen is done by the house. Fair enough?'

In view of the low rent Nanny had to admit it was, but she wondered how long Charlotte would be able to endure it after the good fare and comfort she was used to, and was almost ready to wager that a fortnight would be her limit.

Charlotte was not at all disheartened when she heard of the disadvantages and begged Nanny not to pile it on so. 'I'm doing it for Richard so I don't care how hard it is,' she said. 'You're a darling to take all this trouble for me—where would I have been without you?'

'Back home, I should think,' Nanny said.

'I'd rather have gone to the workhouse,' said Charlotte.

Evening closed in, the fire was full of pictures. Lily was frowning over a book. She moved her lips as she tried to puzzle words. Her father came in, and at the sound of his footsteps in the hall she jumped up and ran out to meet him.

Charlotte had never seen an affectionate greeting between father and child and she never forgot the way Will spoke to Lily, asking her what she had been doing all day, keeping his arm round her, encouraging, praising, loving her. It made her cry inwardly. This little house was home to a devoted family, and no matter how welcome they made her—and they did—she was alone.

Charlotte felt a cold shiver run through her when she saw her room at Mrs Blunt's the following morning. Nanny had insisted on accompanying her there so she could leave her valise before going on to Madame Last. She also wanted her to learn the geography of the district, the shortest way to work and the locality of the cheapest shops. 'Though

I've no doubt your roommate will show you the ropes,' she said.

'I hope she's friendlier than Mrs Blunt,' remarked Charlotte.

'Mrs Blunt's got her soft spot like everyone else. You'll just have to find it,' Nanny told her.

There was just time for a cup of coffee, and having walked a fair way exploring they were both glad to sit down. The shop they went into was in a fashionable part of Mayfair. People at other tables were well dressed, looked affluent and as though they hadn't a care worth mentioning.

Charlotte almost envied them, and then chided herself for her ingratitude. She had Richard, his ring was on her finger, and she had escaped from the suffocating atmosphere of home.

'You won't be able to come here very often,' Nanny said, breaking into her thoughts.

'No, but this time I must change one of my guineas,' said Charlotte, refusing to allow Nanny to pay and making her accept half a crown to buy something pretty for Lily.

'I shall want to know how you get on, so you must come to see us at the first opportunity,' Nanny said when they reached Madame Last's establishment.

Now they were there, Charlotte felt

very fluttery inside. 'As soon as I turn the corner ring the bell,' said Nanny after a final hug and kiss. 'Don't be frightened now.'

'I'm not,' said Charlotte. She watched Nanny out of sight and was just about to press the bell when the door was opened by a young footman who stared at her, winked, and said: 'The young person for Madame, I believe.'

She was taken aback by this familiarity. 'I have an appointment with Madame Last. Kindly inform her I'm here,' she said.

'And what might your name be, if I may make so bold as to ask?'

'Miss Grant.'

'Follow me and don't be tempted to pinch me calf as we go up,' he said.

Charlotte was far too concerned about her interview to pay any attention to this remark. Everything depended upon making a good impression on Madame Last, so she scarcely noticed anything in the private sitting room when she was shown in, and was only aware of a large woman in an armchair who told the footman to set a chair for the young person.

It was a hard, straightbacked chair. Charlotte sat on the edge and murmured, 'Good morning' before she could stop herself; for perhaps this was not the right thing to do, especially as Madame

Last was staring at her so hard she felt uncomfortable.

'Mrs Goode tells me you can sew,' said Madame in her most highly cultured tone. 'I want another hand and she recommended you. Is that right?'

'Yes, Madame, and I'm very grateful to her,' Charlotte said.

'It's quite plain you've never worked before, and I shan't enquire why you want to do so now. Young girls from good homes have been known to get ideas about independence and set out to prove some notion or other before this. I don't enquire. Has anyone told you what the life of a workroom girl is like?'

'No, but I think working on fine materials and making elegant clothes must be a very satisfying occupation.'

'You do, do you? Well, that's one way of looking at it. I never heard it put like that before. Some call it drudgery.'

'It may be monotonous but that's the best of it! You can think all kinds of thoughts while you're sewing hems. You can be off anywhere in your imagination— China, India, France.'

'Indeed. Before your fancy runs away with you, let me tell you that the life of a workroom girl is tough. Long hours, exacting work, getting in on time no matter what the weather. I wouldn't be a workroom girl for all the silk in the East. But you'll find that out for yourself if you're really asking me to give you a trial.'

'I am,' said Charlotte.

Madame Last gave her a long, hard look out of her dark, calculating eyes. 'Miss Prescot shall decide. She's my forewoman and you'll take your orders from her if she thinks you're up to it.' She pulled a bell rope and Charlotte heard its tinkle from somewhere far away.

She kept her eyes down while they waited, noticing the design of the Turkey carpet and the toes of her glacé kid shoes. They were comfortably familiar but not at home on this strange carpet, accustomed as they were to the ones at home. They knew the wide staircase there, the polished linoleum of the upper floors, the flowered doormats. Here they were alien and far too fragile. She should have worn stouter ones. She hoped they were in for a fine dry spring.

These thoughts were banished by Miss Prescot, who burst in looking as though the hounds of Hell were after her. She was a thin, almost skinny woman of about thirty and seemed to have pins stuck all over her plain dark dress. Her eyes, behind black-rimmed spectacles, were blinking hard and she was obviously in a state of extreme agitation.

116

'Look, Madame! Just look at this!' she exclaimed, shaking out a delicate piece of fabric. 'We found this as we were packing up Mrs Seymour's order just now. That young hussy Jones had hidden it. Never let on she hadn't finished it—only half the insertion, see? I don't know what Mrs Seymour will say. You know her and her threats.'

'Give it here, stop panicking and sit down,' said Madame. She shook out the object Miss Prescot gave her and Charlotte saw that it was an unfinished blouse with only one sleeve sewn in.

'We mustn't upset Mrs Seymour,' Madame said.

Miss Prescot sniffed.

'Haven't you got a hankie?' asked Madame. 'Honestly, Miss Prescot, you give me the wind sometimes.'

'Sorry, Madame,' said Miss Prescot.

'It's your circulation. I'm always telling you. As to this blouse, I'll finish it myself if the worst comes to the worst. On second thoughts, this young person here might be able to dig you out of your hole.'

Miss Prescot appeared to notice Charlotte for the first time and blinked in her direction.

'This young person, name of Grant, wants me to give her a trial, and it seems you want another hand now Jones has taken herself off.'

'I do. There's only Clarice and Victoria on blouses today.'

Madame Last turned her attention to Charlotte. 'Are you up to finishing this garment?' she asked. 'It needs three rows of lace insertion each side, then the pleats. Set the other sleeve in, do the collar—boned, Miss Prescot? Right. Boned. Neaten all seams and finish off.'

'I can do that. I'd love to,' said Charlotte.

'I don't want it messed up, mind. It's a very expensive blouse.'

'I'm quite capable. Nanny—I mean Mrs Goode—would tell you so if she were here.'

Madame Last didn't doubt it, having seen the nightgown. Her warnings were given for form's sake.

'There you are then. You can start straightaway.'

Miss Prescot looked as though the sun had just come out and she was basking in it. 'Follow me,' she said, addressing Charlotte, who had scarcely had time to thank Madame Last before she was hustled up a flight of back stairs and into a small room where two girls were sitting at a table sewing.

'Clarice,' said Miss Prescot to one of them, 'Madame has engaged this young person, name of Grant, to carry on with the work Jones left. Kindly show her the amenities of the establishment and explain the rules. Refer to me if there are any difficulties.'

'Yes, Miss Prescot,' said Clarice.

The door closed behind the forewoman and Charlotte found herself in totally unfamiliar surroundings with two strangers and the blouse she was to finish in her hand.

'Well, name of Grant,' said Clarice, 'come in and take a seat. You needn't be scared. Vic and me won't bite you, will us, Vic?'

'Course we won't,' said Vic. 'What are we to call you? What's your Christian name, I mean?'

'Charlotte,' she told them, and she felt safe and comfortable in their presence.

Pandemonium broke out at Lancaster Gate on the morning Charlotte ran away.

The servants were summoned to the dining room and questioned exhaustively by Mr Grant at his most fearsome. Mrs Vickery kept wiping her eyes, Tilda giggled with nerves and Annie shook so much her answers came out in jerks. They all denied any knowledge of Miss Charlotte's intentions and it was not until later, when Nanny came, that their fears subsided.

Ellen was thankful to know she was safe but wretched about her own part in the affair. She blamed herself for not standing up to William more vigorously, and once Charlotte was home again she meant to oppose him with all the strength of her convictions.

She didn't expect to be put to the test that very day, but his reaction to Nanny's news brought out her sharpest feelings.

'I wipe my hands of Charlotte,' he told her after his interview with Nanny. 'Heaven knows what we're to tell the Mortons now.'

'Is that all you can think of, William? The effect this will have on the Mortons?'

'They're not likely to let Albert marry her after this, are they? Isn't that important?'

'Very important to her. It's the last thing she wants, as I've so often told you.'

'You, my dear, are a very poor judge of these matters. It's a great embarrassment to me. It can hardly be covered up either. What the devil do you suppose we can say?'

'Why say anything? You were going to tell them she'd gone to Bournemouth because she was run down and needed sea air. Why add to that?'

'It may work for a time, I suppose,' he groused.

She had scored a minor point. He had

120

accepted her suggestion.

Below stairs the relief Nanny brought was beyond measure. 'She's got courage, that girl. I knew she had,' said Mrs Vickery, squaring her shoulders as though daring anyone to contradict her. She gave Nanny her own well-worn copy of *David Copperfield* for Charlotte to read when she felt depressed. 'She wept buckets over it first time and there's nothing like a good cry to raise the spirits,' she said.

They all felt quite cheerful as the day went by. Annie would send Mr Allen's letter on as soon as it came, and once Miss Charlotte knew where he was things would take an upward turn and no mistake.

Unfortunately they took a downward one. A carpenter arrived and fitted a box with lock and key on the front door so that all the letters would fall into it.

'The master's done it on purpose to catch the one from Mr Allen,' said Mrs Vickery.

'Beast,' said Tilda.

'Now what?' asked Annie.

'You'll just have to watch out when you're serving. See if there's one with a foreign stamp. See if you can look over his shoulder and twig the address.'

'Easier said than done.'

It was William's custom to open all the letters, no matter to whom they were addressed. Now he collected them from the box himself and laid them beside his plate at the breakfast table.

'Anything for me?' asked Ellen.

'In good time. The bacon's getting cold,' he said.

Annie watched him cutting through the rashers, breaking a roll, eventually plastering butter and marmalade on another with maddening deliberation, and all the time those letters lay unopened.

At long last he crumpled up his table napkin and dropped it on the floor, a habit that annoyed Annie. Nobody else did it. 'Does he suppose we might be tempted to iron it without washing it first?' she enquired of Tilda, who had an answer that was not flattering to Mr Grant.

When the expected letter arrived, as it did, Annie caught a mere glimpse. Mr Grant put it in his pocket and dealt with the rest of the post. Ellen followed him into his study.

'William, is that a letter from Mr Allen?' she asked.

'It may be, my dear. We'll see.'

He slit the envelope, drew out a closely written page and glanced at the signature. 'Signed by a person called Richard,' he said.

'It's to Charlotte, isn't it? You don't mean to read it, do you?'

'I do.'

'That's despicable.'

'I beg your pardon?'

'I said it's despicable, and it is.'

Ellen had strung herself up to object and it took courage.

'You are overwrought,' he said.

'I am concerned for Charlotte.'

'Then stop condoning her behaviour.'

'Why don't you show a little fatherly love? As far as I can see you never have yet. You treat her as though she's a chattel to be kept under control, like a dog on a short leash.'

'It's the only way to treat a stupid, wayward girl. I soon saw she'd inherited her mother's worst characteristics, and it's been my object to obliterate them.'

'How glad I am you've failed. You'll be sorry, William. Just see if you're not.'

'You had better take a powder,' he said.

Ellen didn't exactly slam the door behind her but she certainly shut it very hard. She felt exhilarated, but not in a pleasant way. The only quarrels they ever had were over Charlotte, and that was disturbing.

She thought back to when she had met William at the Mayor's ball in Sidmouth. Since her father was the Mayor's chaplain, the ball was an occasion in the life of the Hunt family. At the advanced age of twenty-six Ellen was still unmarried. She didn't mind in the least, for as no one believed she was more than twenty, there was time enough yet. She didn't want to follow in her sister's footsteps and spend her life bearing children and cutting down left-off clothes to fit them.

'If I don't meet the man of my dreams I shall remain a contented spinster aunt,' she said.

The women at this particular ball outnumbered the men so there was always a rush when the Ladies' Excuse-Me dance was announced. Ellen had noticed a tall, good-looking man she'd never seen before, so she made a beeline for him and got there just ahead of about six other eager young ladies. The next moment he was whirling her round in a Viennese waltz. He asked if she lived in Sidmouth, and told her he was there for a change of air and thought it a delightful place. They sat the next dance out and went on talking about themselves, so by the end of the evening she knew something about him.

Next day they met by chance on the Esplanade. She was with her mother. They stood chatting until Mrs Hunt said she must go as some parishioners were coming to tea, and would Mr Grant care to join them? They would have it in the garden, which he would see at its best. He didn't need asking twice. Tea on the lawn with scones and cream and strawberry jam. Never mind the wasps. They were all part of the scene.

'What a very pleasing young man,' remarked Mrs Hunt after the guests had departed. 'Quite a catch for some lucky girl.'

He called the next day in a hired carriage and invited Mrs Hunt and Ellen out for a drive. His shares went higher still. It was the first of several drives and daily calls. Ellen soon learned that Amanda, his young wife, had died some years earlier, leaving him devastated. She saw that he was still in need of consolation, for his grief at Amanda's untimely end was mixed with anger and irritation which he had never yet been able to talk about to anyone. In Ellen he found the ideal confidante. He told her how Amanda had been uninhibited to the point of recklessness. 'She would insist on going to some country place to hear the nightingales and refused to wear a coat or even a shawl. It was cold. We stood ankle deep in wet grass and froze. She was shivering. The wretched bird didn't even croak and by the time we got home—well, you can imagine.'

Ellen found he was holding her hand.

'You wouldn't be so silly, would you?' he asked.

'It's romantic—to want to hear nightin-gales,' she said. 'I think I'd take a coat. But there—you can never tell.'

'I think I can.'

What exactly did he mean by that? she asked herself.

'I begin to think Mr Grant's interested in you,' said Mrs Hunt.

Ellen hoped he was, but he left Sidmouth without even saying he wanted to see her again. She felt pangs of disappointment, told herself not to be ridiculous and tried to fall back into her well-worn rut as though he was no more than a casual acquaintance.

It was not long, however, before he wrote to Mrs Hunt thanking her for her hospitality and enclosing a note to Ellen, in which he said that his pleasure in his stay at Sidmouth was almost entirely due to her and that he hoped to come back very soon. He arrived the following weekend and on several succeeding ones, and having made sure his feelings were reciprocated he proposed himself to her father. It was an exceedingly good match and the Hunts were delighted with it. William and Ellen were both sure they would be ideally happy together, and so they were until Charlotte unwittingly disturbed their peace.

Thinking of all this, Ellen began to wonder if she had erred in defending

Charlotte so strongly. From the first, William's attitude towards his daughter had puzzled her. She came from a loving, close-knit family, and thought she would have died if her own father had been as insensitive and strict with her as William was with Charlotte.

And yet poor William. Poor Charlotte. Poor me.

While she was worrying over all this in the drawing room, William was reading his daughter's letter in his study.

My dear, dearest Charlotte,

Here I am in Calais and at last able to write. What a fool I was not to give you my itinerary but I'm pretty sure you got it as I pushed it under your kitchen door after that revolting scene with your father. What a way to leave you! You'll realise the distress I felt and continue to feel for all you suffered that night, and I hope and pray he won't treat you harshly for loving me, as I know you do. It won't be easy for you but I'm sure your stepmother will be kind and understanding.

I know you will resist his plan to make you marry that objectionable oaf who can't even drink his tea in a civilised manner! I shall seize the first chance to come back and rescue you. A ladder at your window? Gretna Green? Why not! We'll probably think of something a little less theatrical but married we will be before the year's out, depend upon it. I think of you night and day, my dear, darling, one-and-only Charlotte. Remember seven hours after midnight as I do and concentrate hard. Write when you can. Tell me everything. Just a few crosses and an assurance you are well will do if more is impossible. Mary sends her love to her dear future daughter-in-law.

I love you with all my heart,
Richard.

William crushed the letter up and tossed it into the waste basket. 'Objectionable oaf' indeed! On second thoughts he retrieved the letter. Annie was quite capable of smoothing it out and noting the address. Seething with indignation, he took his hat and stick from the hall stand, opened the drawing room door a crack and said: 'I'm going.'

Ellen raised a languid hand but didn't rise.

No goodbye kiss, no tender words? She usually saw him to the gate. What were things coming to? Well, it wasn't his fault. His disobedient daughter was to blame.

Ellen had felt vaguely queasy when

she got up this morning and hardly touched her breakfast. The manner of William's departure surprised and upset her. He always came right in and they went through the hall together. Oh, dear.

She thought of Sidmouth, home and Mother, and of herself walking on the Esplanade without this odd nauseous feeling and the uncomfortable prickling of her nipples.

Charlotte had so much to learn on her first day at Madame Last's she couldn't spare a moment to think of home and the disruption she had caused there.

She had no sooner begun work than Wilfred, the footman, came to ask if the new young person would be having dinner, as Cook wanted to know on account of how many spuds, and if she was where was the three-three farthings?

Victoria explained. Madame provided a midday meal for her girls, for which they had to pay. 'It's worth it,' she said. 'Otherwise you have to go out. It costs more and there's your shoe leather to think of.'

Charlotte gladly produced sixpence and held out her hand for the change. Wilfred winked at her, counted twopence farthing into her palm, closed her fingers over it and told her not to spend it all at once unless she fancied treating him to a little something after work.

'She'll treat you to a box round the ear'ole if she has any lip from you, Wilfred,' said Victoria.

'Oh, indeed. You're the one to watch your step, miss,' retorted Wilfred. 'There's eyes everywhere, so watch out.'

'Take yourself off or I'll tell Miss Prescot,' said Victoria.

'Tell-tale-tit.'

Clarice took his arm and pushed him out, but not before he shouted: 'Tongue shall be split.'

Charlotte bent her head over her work. Miss Prescot came to inspect progress from time to time, and once a very smart young man bounced in with a lively, 'Good morning, pretty ones, and how's my chuck today?'

He was Algie Last, Madame's only child, and his chuck was Victoria. He whispered in her ear and drew her into the window alcove, from where kissing, giggling, and other sounds of endearment were clearly audible.

Clarice glanced at Charlotte and shook her head to indicate disapproval. 'If Madame catches you she'll give you the order of the boot, Victoria.' There was no response from the alcove.

'Suppose she comes in?' said Clarice, louder.

'Suppose she does?' Algie emerged holding a coat button. 'Came to ask you to sew it on, didn't I?' he said. 'Come on, Clarice. Where's the needle and thread?'

'Don't ask *me*. You pulled it off on purpose. It's the same one as yesterday. Shame on you, Algie Last.'

Algie, who was very nice-looking, beamed at Charlotte and said he was quite sure the new young lady would sew it on, upon which a slightly dishevelled Victoria came out of the alcove. 'Oh no she won't, and it's not fair to ask her,' she said. 'I'll do it meself, dinner time.'

He seemed pleased with this suggestion. 'You are a fool, Vic,' Clarice said when he'd gone. 'Suppose Miss Prescot came in? What would you do if you got the sack? I bet young Algie wouldn't help you.'

'That's my affair, ain't it?' countered Victoria. 'We're not all so lucky as you with your Mr Blades, hanging his hat up and everything.'

'I know I'm lucky,' Clarice said, and she smiled at her secret thoughts. It wasn't often that a girl from her station in life was sought in marriage by a man like Herbert Blades. Very soon now she would leave Madame Last's for ever and become

131

Mrs Herbert Blades, with a house in Wimbledon, a live-in maid and a woman for the rough. All the girls in the workroom were agog, for what had happened to Clarice might very well happen to them. Even Madame herself was impressed and indicated her intention of attending the church for the wedding ceremony.

Charlotte became vaguely aware of this on her first day and learned the whole romantic story bit by bit.

Clarice was a good-looking girl, tall, slim and well made. She had a slender neck, a well-set head and graceful movements. She was twenty and had earned her living since she was twelve, first in a tailor's sweatshop, then hemming sheets for a lady who employed her aunt as a charwoman, then getting a place with a dressmaker, and eventually finding a job with Madame Last.

'And let me tell you, this place is a picnic compared with other jobs I've had,' she told Charlotte, for Madame Last's philosophy was that hungry workers were incapable of good work, so the midday meal was substantial. Madame also believed in the value of fresh air, not for herself, but for the young, so they were permitted to sit out on the flat roof for ten minutes before resuming their various tasks.

It was during these breaks that Charlotte

132

got to know about the lives of her colleagues, although she, Victoria and Clarice could chat all day in the seclusion of their little sanctum.

Clarice liked to recall the manner in which she had met her Mr Blades. She was gazing into the window of a sweet shop one evening after work, wishing she could afford to take something home for her Aunt Cassie, when Herbert Blades came out, caught her eye and raised his hat. She was astonished and he apologised.

'I beg your pardon. I mistook you for somebody else,' he said.

'Oh, that's all right.'

'You are so very like Lady Jane Adam. A quite remarkable resemblance.'

'Really?'

'Quite remarkable. They say she will be the most sought-after débutante of the season. She'll be married by the end of it, you may be sure.'

'Indeed? I'm afraid I don't know the lady and have no idea what she looks like.'

'Stunning. Absolutely stunning.'

Clarice was flattered but rather embarrassed. Men often tried to pick her up but they weren't like this one. He was obviously from a high-class family, his clothes and the way he spoke made that clear. He had probably been educated at a public school and was far above her socially.

'Excuse me, but I have to buy some sweets so I'll wish you good evening,' she said, for she thought she had better go into the shop just to get away from him. It was a surprise to find he had followed her in. She ignored him and asked for an ounce of fruit drops.

When she emerged from the shop he was beside her. 'Have you far to go?' he asked.

'I'm going home.'

'It seems we go in the same direction.'

She stopped short. He was an extremely personable man, with an air of prosperity about him. He had a moustache, waxed and turned up at the ends, and his grey topper was perched at a rather rakish angle. She guessed that his next move would be to ask her out to dinner. He had designs on her.

'We may be going the same way but I prefer to walk by myself, so once again I'll wish you good evening,' she said.

'Oh, come now. Surely we may share the same pavement?'

'At a distance,' she said. 'Pray don't force your company on me.'

'I'm sorry. No offence was intended,' he said, raising his hat and turning the other way.

Clarice walked on as fast as she could, but she rather regretted discouraging him, and if home had been a pleasant house and not two rooms in the bowels of a run-down warehouse she wouldn't have objected to his accompanying her there.

Still, it was a bit of an adventure, something to laugh about with the girls at work.

As she didn't look back she was not to know that Herbert Blades followed her home at a safe distance and noted where she lived. He had seen her several times before in the vicinity of Madame Last's and been captivated by her looks. Now he had heard her voice and liked that too.

He was doing very well in what he referred to as his business. 'I'm in business,' he would say when asked what his occupation was, and if pressed further would mention jewellery.

He had a great wish to marry and settle down but had never met a girl he really wanted until he saw Clarice and fell in love on sight. So by careful manoeuvring, by contriving to meet her accidentally as she went to work or came back, he at last managed to persuade her it was not a bad thing to have an escort. One Saturday he asked her to tea at Gunter's and followed it with a walk. The time came when she accepted his invitation to dine out. By now she liked him very much indeed, and he had made his intentions clear. After this dinner he asked her to marry him.

'I can't,' she said, although she wanted to so much.

'Why not?'

'I couldn't leave Aunt Cassie.'

'How's that?'

Because she was thoroughly straightforward she told him exactly how she was placed and how much she owed to the aunt who had taken her in when she was left an orphan and been a mother to her ever since. Together she and her aunt managed to keep a roof over their heads. The more she said, and the worse her situation seemed, the more he loved her, so when she finished he simply told her to stop worrying because Aunt Cassie would live with them when they were married and be taken care of for the rest of her life.

Clarice was in heaven. Never, in her most extravagant dreams, had such wonders floated into her mind. To be married to this generous, good-looking man and live in a pretty little house in Wimbledon! To be Mrs Herbert Blades! The world that had been so hard all her life became soft and luxurious. It was full of flowers and chocolates and she loved everyone in it, so when Miss Prescot brought Charlotte Grant into the workroom she was more than happy to help her.

'We're so lucky to have this little room to ourselves,' she said. 'The main room isn't nearly as nice, with Miss Prescot waiting to pounce all the time. Which dressmaker were you with before?'

'This is my first place,' Charlotte said.

'Gracious! Do you hear that, Vicky? However did you manage to get taken on here?'

'I think it's because somebody left.'

'Amy Jones. That's right. Have they landed you with the work she didn't finish? How do they expect you to do it when you've no experience?'

'I've done a lot of sewing in my time, ever since I was quite little, so I think I can manage,' Charlotte said.

'Well, Vicky and me will help you out if you get stuck, won't us, Vic?' said Clarice.

'Shouldn't wonder,' said Victoria, and added: 'You must be the young lady who's to share the room with me at Mrs Blunt's.'

Charlotte assented, and Victoria went on to tell her that Mrs Blunt was an old cow if ever there was one. Then she said: 'Bless her,' as though those two words absolved her of any hard feelings towards Mrs Blunt.

'It's Mr Blunt you've got to beware of,' she said.

'Why is that?'

'You'll see,' Victoria said, and she pursed her lips and shook her head.

Charlotte didn't like to enquire further. She took up the work and began to measure the pleats that ran from shoulder to waist. She liked the feel of the material, and the working conditions were good. The large table was covered with a white cloth that almost touched the floor, and there was ample light. Soon she was engrossed in her work, and while she was doing it she thought of Richard and tried to imagine which stage of his journey he had reached. How she wished she was with him!

The workroom girls poured out of Madame Last's establishment at eight o'clock in the evening and made their separate ways home. Charlotte caught a glimpse of a tall man standing under a lamppost, and Victoria told her it was Herbert Blades waiting for Clarice as he did every evening. Then he took her somewhere to dine.

'Lucky for her. Algie brought some ham and rolls in when I sewed his button on,' said Victoria. 'We can get something extra at the cookshop. What do you fancy? Saveloys?'

'I've never tasted them.'

'Coo! You've got a treat in store.'

There were plenty of shops on their way back to Mrs Blunt's, and Victoria knew which ones to patronise. She bought a pot of jam, a loaf and a screw of tea at one, and then went next door for the saveloys, which were steaming hot.

'There, we won't do so bad,' she said. 'We'll go halves, shall we?'

'Of course we will,' said Charlotte. She was very tired but still had enough energy to enjoy the shopping. Mrs Blunt gave her lodgers door keys, so Charlotte opened the door with hers to try it out and was greeted by the unappetising smell of Irish stew, which, as Victoria observed, was enough to put a dog off its feed.

Mrs Blunt poked her head out of the door that led down to the basement, and having ascertained there were no followers withdrew it faster than a jack-in-the-box.

The two girls creaked up the uncarpeted stairs to their room and Victoria immediately set about lighting the fire while telling Charlotte how to get the Primus going and to make a cup of tea as it wasn't half nippy.

Charlotte was quick to learn, and before long they were sitting down to their supper and enjoying it. Algie had supplied Victoria with a generous portion of ham off the bone, the saveloys were bursting with richness and Charlotte pronounced them simply scrumptious. It was all so free and easy and so different from the strictures of home.

'I'll lay you're tired,' Victoria remarked. 'Your first day and everything. You look washed out.'

Charlotte admitted it and longed to be tucked up in bed, but although her legs ached and she could hardly keep her eyes open she insisted on helping to clear up and wash the crockery at a sink on the landing.

There was only one thin blanket under the quilt. 'Doesn't Mrs Blunt give us two? she asked.

'Not likely. You'll have to put newspapers under the quilt. There's a pile in the corner there. You'll be real warm that way. Here, I'll help you.'

Victoria was an expert at this economical bedmaking and collected every clean newspaper she could find for the purpose. 'Best thing's for you to hop into bed straight away, seeing as how you're flaked,' she said. 'I'm going out for a bit.'

It appeared that Victoria took the air most nights, much to the displeasure of Mrs Blunt.

'Where are you off to?' she asked, as Victoria tiptoed through the hall.

'Got to post a letter,' said Victoria.

'You posted one last night.'

'And I'll do the same tomorrow, like as not.'

'Door's bolted at eleven thirty, mind.'

Victoria ignored this. She had found a way of squeezing in at the scullery window, with the help of Algie Last, who always saw her home after their nightly assignation.

Being short of funds, they mostly went for a stroll, stopped at a coffee stall for refreshment and then looked out for a dark doorway where they could make love unobserved. They were going to get married as soon as Algie plucked up enough courage to tell his mother.

'We don't want to wait too long,' Victoria always said.

'Have to catch her in the right mood. She's at her best when the season's over.' Algie knew what he was talking about and Victoria believed him.

'It's risky,' she whispered.

'Not when you do it standing up,' he said.

'Honest?'

'Injun.'

Victoria had to shake Charlotte out of her sleep the following morning, and there was only time for a lick and a promise in cold water, a hunk of bread and jam and a cup of tea before they scuttled off to work, joining the stream of others who all seemed as hurried as they were themselves.

They didn't talk much on the way. Victoria was thinking of Algie and wishing they could do it in bed, lying down, and Charlotte's mind was on Richard. It was such a short time since their last, disastrous meeting, but it seemed years, and no wonder considering all that had happened. What would he say when he knew what she was doing? And how was he? *Where* was he? She longed for Saturday, which was half-day, so she could go to Nanny's and find his letter waiting for her. To think she was free! Out of the house of bondage. That was how she thought of home now, except for darling Ellie and Mrs Vickery and the maids.

She was tired by the time Saturday came, and felt she had lived through several lives, but as soon as the morning's work was done she felt brand new. She was off to Hammersmith.

'You've perked up,' said Victoria. 'Got somewhere nice to go?'

'An old friend of my mum's,' Charlotte said. Words like mama were out now, and she referred to Nanny as Mrs Goode. 'If I'm not back tonight it's because I'm staying there. What about you?'

'Depends if Algie can get out.'

Charlotte was sorry for Victoria, as she had been brought up in an orphanage and had no idea what it was like to have a

142

proper home, no matter how poor. She looked longingly at furniture in shops and talked about the things she'd like to have and the way she would arrange her sitting room if she had one.

'I expect we'll just have two rooms, Algie and me,' she told Charlotte. 'Clarice can't see any future for us two—she can't see Madame allowing him to marry me, but you can, can't you?'

'You might have to do without her approval but you mustn't let that stop you,' Charlotte said.

'Sounds as though you speak from experience.'

'I'll tell you one of these days,' said Charlotte as she hurried off to catch her bus.

It had been the most exhausting week of her life. Sunday had seen the disastrous end to her assignation with Richard; Monday, disgrace; Tuesday, escape, Wednesday, a working girl. And here was Saturday, and what would Richard say when she told him all this in the letter she intended to write? Could he possibly sense it in those precious daily minutes when she concentrated on him and he on her?

She didn't find concentrating easy with Victoria dodging about their room, raking out the ashes, making the tea and heading off Mr Blunt, who always tried to get his

143

foot in the door when he brought up their bucket of coal.

It was Charlotte's job to cut the bread and butter and wash up afterwards, and she found the best time to think was when she was dabbling out the crockery at the sink on the landing, although even here Mr Blunt managed to brush past her much too close, and when she looked up it was to see him leering at her from the top of the stairs.

None of this mattered now that she was on her way to Hammersmith by a much more direct route than her first journey there. Just a short walk along a squalid street, then a better one, round the corner and there was Nanny's double-fronted cottage with its little front garden full of daffodils.

The door opened almost as she put her hand on the knocker. How lovely it was to see Nanny and be kissed and hugged and made welcome, although there was something in the atmosphere that was not quite right. Was it anxiety, foreboding? Lily was holding her hand and looking puzzled. And why was Annie in the sitting room, looking strangely unfamiliar out of uniform and in her own neat coat and skirt?

'Annie?'

'I'm that sorry, Miss Charlotte,' Annie

began, and was unable to go on.

'What's wrong? Where's my letter?'

'I don't know, miss. In the fire, like as not.'

'Don't let us jump to that conclusion,' Nanny put in. 'The fact is, your papa got hold of it and there's nothing anybody can do. Annie will tell you.'

And Annie did, at great length and with many observations of her own and Mrs Vickery and Tilda thrown in, but so far none of them had discovered a way of getting the letter that meant everything to Charlotte.

She heard all Annie said but she couldn't speak. She was too stunned. Looking from one woman to the other she saw pity in their faces. They were as powerless to help her as she was to help herself. It was like seeing Richard vanish into nothingness.

'None of us foresaw this,' said Nanny.

Charlotte still couldn't speak. The full impact of her father's action would take time to sink in but it was clear he meant to prevent her from having any contact with Richard.

After a long time she said: 'There will be other letters.'

'But how am I to get them?' It was Annie who wept, almost as though she was the cause of Charlotte's dilemma.

In a desperate, groping kind of way

145

Charlotte tried to find a straw to clutch at. There must be a way to locate Richard, but the distance between them had never been so great as at that moment in Nanny's sitting room.

Worst of all, she couldn't even remember what he looked like. The face she loved so much had gone, wiped from her memory.

How could he disappear, go beyond her reach, when he was only in France? She was as much lost to him now as he was to her, and for the first time since she left home she was afraid. She had believed herself safe but now she saw there was no such thing as security. She had stepped out into the world, thinking that her term as a working girl would be brief and that any hardships would earn her the right to future happiness with Richard. Her reunion with him was the heaven just within her reach until her father snatched it away by stealing her letter.

Annie broke in on the confused thoughts that were jostling in her brain. 'I don't see as how you'll ever find out where Mr Allen is the way things are, miss,' she said. 'Your pa has the key of that letter box so it won't matter how many letters come.'

They sat puzzling over what seemed an insoluble problem, although Nanny kept reminding them there was no such thing, while Lily, unable to make out why they were all so gloomy, stole away and into the street to seek forbidden adventures.

Charlotte considered going home and demanding the letter; she thought of appealing to Ellie for help or asking the servants to admit her after her parents were in bed so that she could raid her father's desk; but that would put them in jeopardy and she would never do that.

'Besides, we're not allowed in his study, not unless the missus is there,' said Annie when the idea was mooted. 'Seems you're in a cleft stick. I don't see as you'll gain anything by working yourself to the bone at Madame Last's. You might just as well come home and be miserable in comfort.'

This was exactly the spur Charlotte needed.

'How can you say that, Annie?' she cried. 'I'm proud to be working and I'll find a way to contact Richard, so don't you ever doubt it,'

Nanny had been suffering all manner of agonies. Foremost among them was the fear that Charlotte might succumb now she faced such formidable odds. More than once she had voiced this fear to Annie in an undertone while Charlotte absorbed the implication of the stolen letter.

'Well said! I knew we'd see what you're made of!' she declared, for Amanda was in every line of Charlotte's resolute expression.

'It's only a setback,' said Charlotte, although the disappointment was so sharp it felt like a physical pain. Even so, her inflexible resolve to succeed remained strong and steady and already a plan was beginning to take shape in her mind.

Richard had promised frequent letters and they might come by any of the four deliveries. The last was quite late in the evening, so after work she could waylay the postman at Lancaster Gate and ask him to give her any that were addressed to her personally. She hugged the idea to herself and decided to tell Nanny when she had procured one and not before.

Annie had come laden with clothes and another pair of shoes so Charlotte wouldn't have to buy anything, and Nanny had received a postcard from Madame Last that morning. It depicted her establishment on the front, and written on the back in a large, bold hand were the words: THAT GIRL IS A TREASURE. THANK YOU FOR SENDING HER. B.L.

'See that and gloat, my dear,' Nanny said, presenting it with a flourish.

'Me?' queried Charlotte.

'Who else? You're the only girl I sent her.'

It was not merely a crumb but a whole

slice of comfort. It cheered Charlotte, filled Nanny with pride and gave Annie something special to tell the others at home. 'And it's time I was going,' she said.

'Not till you've had tea,' said Nanny, going to put the kettle on and coming back at once to ask, with a note of anxiety in her voice, 'where's Lily?'

Lily was nowhere to be found. She was not upstairs or down, or in the garden or by the front gate or in the adjoining road. They looked everywhere. Nanny hurried along the road, asking at various doors, but no one had seen Lily. The noise from the next street was rough and raucous; dozens of children were there, skipping, playing hopscotch, dancing to the strains of a barrel organ, but Lily wasn't among them.

The appearance of Charlotte in her becoming clothes and fashionable hat made them stop and stare, but none of them answered when she asked if they'd seen a young girl with fair hair who would probably be looking lost.

So on to the next street, which was rougher still and even more crowded. There was a barrel organ here too, grinding out 'The Soldiers of the Queen', and Charlotte was seized by a young coalman, clasped round the waist and danced up and down as though she was a puppet. He was laughing at her but she was not laughing back. His hands and face were black with coal dust and he stank of beer. She managed to struggle out of his clutches and that made him angry. 'Stuck-up bitch! Get back to yer meadow!' he shouted.

Annie caught up with her and they went back the way they had come, and there was Lily by a lamppost with a crowd of boys and girls, who were daring her to take a swing the same as they did.

There was a rope tied to the arm of the post and a girl was swinging on it, high off the ground. Others pushed at her so she rose higher still. Round and round she went and Lily kept shouting: 'Me next. Let me. Let me.'

As they reached the crowd Nanny came running from the other end of the street and pushed her way through to Lily. Charlotte thought she would grab hold of her but she simply took her by the hand and said gently: 'Come along, Lily dear. Dad will be home soon and it's time for tea.'

'I want to swing,' said Lily with a pout.

'Dad will make you a swing in the garden if you ask him,' Nanny said. 'What a silly face you're pulling. Mind the wind doesn't change or you'll get stuck like it.'

Charlotte was surprised that Nanny hadn't spoken sternly to her granddaughter, but Annie told her that wasn't the way. It was no use scolding a child with Lily's mentality and Nanny had her work cut out taking care of her.

'It's a bit rough on Nanny. She's no chicken,' Annie said.

Nanny and her son took it for granted that Charlotte would stay with them until Sunday night, and once again she was drawn into the heart of the family and felt the warmth of their affection for one another extending to her.

Will had a workshop in the garden and spent his spare time making miniature cabinets, stands for looking glasses, picture frames and boxes, all expertly crafted and ornamented with carvings. It was fascinating to see him at work, and Lily spent hours watching him.

Charlotte was touched by his affection for his daughter and his unlimited patience. It was pathetic to see her trying to spell a word, and when she succeeded his triumph was even greater than hers.

On Sundays they all went to church in the morning, and after that the day was their own, so in good weather they took an excursion, a trip on the river, a visit to Kew Gardens or to one of the parks to hear a military band.

On Charlotte's first Sunday with them they went to Richmond, had midday dinner at Lockhart's and then walked up the hill to the park to sit round the bandstand and listen to the brass band playing classical overtures and popular tunes.

Charlotte was entranced. She had never seen men, women and children in their Sunday best enjoying themselves in this uninhibited way. Going home was less pleasurable. There were long queues for buses, tired children grizzled, exhausted mothers' shoulders drooped and men's boots, already tight, grew tighter still.

How glad the Goode family was to get home to Hammersmith and gallons of tea, but what a wonderful day they'd had and how happy Charlotte would have been but for the nagging worry of the missing letter. To think her father had read words that were meant for her! Loving words. She could just see him holding the letter at a distance, drawing himself up with such disdain he looked like a man about to give vent to an almighty sneeze.

When it was time to go, Nanny accompanied her to the bus stop and refused the contribution she insisted on making towards the day's expenses.

'It's little enough,' said Nanny in her

grandest manner. 'The Goodes wouldn't think of it.'

'Charlotte would.'

'Pouf!'

'Charlotte won't come again if Mrs Goode won't take it.'

'Oh, very well then.' This after a long pause. 'But it will go in Lily's money box.'

'What a ripping idea!'

They both chuckled, the bus came and Charlotte got on, with all the bundles Annie had brought. How glad she was to have them. A week in the same pair of shoes had been rather trying.

Once she had waved Nanny goodbye she settled down to work out how to get Richard's address, but a feeling that was very close to fright kept recurring, and it was all she could do to keep it down.

Her spirits sank lower still as she approached Mrs Blunt's, and when she went in and was assailed by the stink of boiled scrag and cabbage she sank to her lowest point yet.

Her room was depressingly squalid after the comfort of Nanny's house. No Victoria yet. She would be out with Algie. And I should be out with Richard, Charlotte thought, and was so overcome by the hopelessness of her situation she threw herself down on the bed and howled out loud without restraint.

A prolonged knocking at the door made her stop. She half opened it and came face to face with Mrs Blunt demanding to know what all the fuss was about.

'What fuss?'

'Sounded like a dog howling.'

'It probably was.'

'Have you got a dog in there?'

'Of course I haven't. It's the dog next door.'

'They haven't got one.'

'Next door but one then. How should I know?'

'If I find you're keeping a dog in there your name will be Walker.'

'And if you ever find a dog in here you can have half the money I get for selling it. Good night, Mrs Blunt. And Mr Blunt too.'

She added this because Mr Blunt was close behind his wife and treated her to a really lascivious wink before she got the door shut.

The exchange made her laugh, and as Victoria came in before her mirth died down she told her all about it.

'Good for you,' said Victoria, but after taking a keen look at Charlotte she wanted to know what was wrong, and as she felt so desperately low Charlotte told her everything.

Victoria already knew Charlotte was engaged—the ring on her finger told her so—and although neither she nor Clarice meant to pry they had asked a few questions that were perfectly natural between girls working together, so they knew Richard was a musician and had gone abroad and that Charlotte was waiting to hear from him.

This part of the story was beautifully romantic but the rest of it, the autocratic father and his treatment of Richard, the horrid Albert Morton with his clammy hands, was enough to make the most timid girl run away, and Charlotte was far from timid. They talked late into the night, drank cup after cup of weak tea, and when Victoria knew everything she said: 'Don't you worry any more. I'll come to Lancaster Gate with you tomorrow night and we'll beard the postman together.'

'Won't you be going out with Algie?'

'He can come with us if he's a mind to. Anyway, him and me can do our bit of spooning after you've got what you want.'

The dearest of friends could not have made a more generous offer, and Charlotte was so comforted she was asleep almost before she rustled into bed under the newspapers.

Algie Last fancied himself as he strolled down the Bayswater Road with a girl on each arm the following night. They stopped at a pull-up for cabmen, for ham rolls and coffee. Compliments on his discerning taste flew, and nobody could deny he was favoured with two of the prettiest girls in town. What smart titfers they sported, and what stunning clothes!

There was no question of this. Madame Last prided herself on her girls' good taste, so although their shoes might leak and their petticoats be in tatters, their outward appearance always did credit to her establishment.

At nine thirty they made their way slowly towards Charlotte's old home and were rewarded by the sight of the postman delivering letters nearby. Urged on by the other two, Charlotte approached him and asked if he had a letter for Miss Charlotte Grant. If so, she was Miss Grant and would be obliged if he would give her the letter, which had come from France.

'How do I know you're Miss Grant?' he asked.

'If you've got a letter and it comes from France that proves it, doesn't it?'

'Not as I see it.'

'Then how did I know where it had come from and which number it was going to?'

156

By the light of the lantern fixed to his belt she could see the French stamp and the writing which she knew to be Richard's on the top of the bundle the man carried.

'That's it!' she cried. 'That's the one I'm expecting. I'll take it.'

'Oh no you won't,' said the postman. 'It's my duty to deliver the mail through the doors, not to hand it out to people in the street.'

'But it's mine!'

'If that's your name and address you can go inside the house and pick it up when I push it through the door.'

'I can't. You don't understand.'

'It's none of my business. It'd be more than my job's worth, so don't ask me.'

'Please. Please! It means everything to me. I'll go mad if I don't get it. It's from my fiancé.'

'Whose name is?'

'Richard Allen. Why?'

The postman turned the letter over. Richard's name and address were on the back.

'Correct. Tell you what. You can take a gander at what's written on the back if you like.'

Charlotte pulled out paper and pencil, and managed to scribble down the name and address of a hotel in Paris before the postman turned the envelope over again.

'I didn't ought to have shown you, so keep it under your hat *if* you please,' he said, and was on his way round the corner to deliver it into her father's hands.

The thought of this put her in such a frenzy she had to sit on the coping of a front wall to get over it. The sight of the letter had made her so strung-up she couldn't stop shaking. To think she had seen, almost touched it. Yet she wasn't allowed to have it. It was wicked.

Victoria and Algie had seen and heard everything from close by and they came to offer what consolation they could.

'Anyway, you can write to him now you know where he is,' said Victoria. 'You're a lot better off than you were this time last night.'

'But just think of Pa reading my letter! I expect he's slitting it open this minute. It's too horrible. He's blighting our lives and enjoying it.'

'Now look. It's no use carrying on like this. Me and Algie will walk you home and you can sit yourself down and tell Richard all about it. How's that?'

'Sounds a good idea to me,' said Algie.

She had to comply but the walk back seemed much longer than coming, and Mrs Blunt's neighbourhood was less attractive than ever, with howling children outside every pub door waiting for their parents. A little girl not even seven was borne down by the weight of the baby she was holding. Tears made rivulets in the dirt of her peaky white face. Algie gave her a penny and she said: 'God bless you, mister.'

Victoria was right. Pouring her heart out to Richard on paper did Charlotte so much good that forebodings vanished and her mood swung up. What was there to complain about? Before long he would know all that had happened since he left her. Perhaps—perhaps he'd come rushing back.

By the time she went to bed she was her usual optimistic self, and once the letter was safely posted she would be able to lean back and treasure unexpected joys as they came.

Herbert Blades was prospering so well his generosity overflowed. Towards the end of a hard week's work Clarice, her face shining with pride, told the girls he wanted to take them all to dinner at the Criterion on Saturday, then on to a show at the Alhambra and after that supper at Rules.

'We'll be on top form on Saturday,' she said. 'We'll sparkle.'

As far as she and Victoria were concerned, that was certain; they each had a beau, for Algie was invited and was to bring a friend to make up the numbers. But that friend was not Richard and how Charlotte wished it were. Still, he would have her letter by then, and with luck she might even have his answer. She threw herself heart and soul into her work, for the rush was on and exquisite dresses were being created.

Madame Last was striving to fulfil orders for the first court of the new reign, which would undoubtedly be one of the most exciting events for many a long year. Courts would be vastly different from those in the dear old Queen's time, she told the staff. Splendid though she was in her way, she'd been a proper stickler. White gloves all round—now they could have them dyed in shades to match their ensembles. Not the debs, of course. White for them, colours for their mas. Madame visited her workrooms every day to see how the orders were progressing.

'We've got to hold our own with these dressmakers coming over from Paris,' she told Miss Prescot, who was on her knees with a mouthful of pins. She was arranging the folds of a white Chantilly lace dress embroidered with raised velvet leaves and poppies. The silver tissue lining gleamed through.

'French dressmakers here?' gasped Miss

Prescot, losing most of the pins in her astonishment.

'Taking rooms at the Savoy, if you please. And other places. Anywhere they can get their French feet in.'

'Shouldn't be allowed. Should be stopped at the ports!'

'We're not likely to have another Coronation for some time, let us hope. Come to think of it, them having no king and queen of their own they're going to make the most of ours.'

'That's their impudence for you.'

'I don't *think* they'll put us in the shade, Miss Prescot. Not from what I see in *my* workrooms. Who did that embroidery?'

'Victoria.'

'Tell her I'm pleased with it. And mind you don't swallow those pins.'

Madame Last was delighted with her whole collection and felt she was to be congratulated. When times were good, as they most certainly were now, she gave her staff an outing at the end of the season, and she was beginning to wonder what form it should take this year. They'd had dinners and theatres. It could be a picnic but that meant extensive organising, and after they'd eaten and drunk too much what was there to do but lie on the grass?

As she passed the small workroom she almost collided with Algie coming out.

'And what might you be doing here?' she asked, looking him up and down. 'I thought you was to go riding after breakfast.'

'So I did. Matter of fact I was looking for one of the stock books. You're always on at me to take an interest in the business so I've been checking up.'

'I'm glad to hear it. But you're not likely to find stock books in there. We keep them in the office along the passage, as I'd have expected you to know. If you've been distracting my girls with your chat I'd advise you to leave off. They've all got more than enough to do.'

'Right, Ma.'

'And don't call me Ma. Not up here. I'll tell you one thing you can put your mind to. The end-of-season outing. I'd welcome some fresh ideas.'

'How about a river trip?'

'Not Margate! Not the Golden Eagle!'

Madame Last had endured more trips downriver than she cared to remember. Everyone on deck eating hard-boiled eggs. You couldn't move for the shells.

The coast was the last thing Algie had in mind. 'Upriver. Maidenhead,' he said. 'Lunch at a riverside restaurant, then a nice trip up to Marlow for tea and back by twilight for supper. Lots of fairy lights, lanterns, music.'

162

Algie relied on his friend, Eustace Bright's, graphic descriptions of these scenes. Eustace liked punting and spent his weekends on the river. Algie longed to get away from home to be with Victoria so he led his parents to believe that he went punting with Eustace. He enlarged on the delights of the Thames to his mother.

'Sounds interesting,' she said. 'I'll leave you to see about it, and I don't want nothing skimped, so you can lay it on thick.'

'I will,' he said, and the minute she was safely in her own domain he nipped back for another kiss from Victoria.

There was no letter for Charlotte by the time Saturday came, and she was bitterly disappointed.

'Give him a breather,' Victoria told her. 'If he's anything as pushed as us he mightn't get a chance till Sunday.'

'Perhaps,' said Charlotte, but she couldn't honestly believe Richard would put off replying, no matter how busy he might be.

'Are you sure there wasn't a letter for me?' she asked Mrs Blunt, not for the first time.

'Course I'm sure.'

Mrs Blunt, in a sackcloth apron, was hearthstoning the front step. She was not in the best of tempers; doing the step was her husband's job, but, as usual, he was sleeping it off. Still, she'd rather have him asleep than up to some of his other pranks. There was nothing sacred once he was in his cups, and to think what a handsome young man he'd been! He'd have blushed, blushed he would, to think he'd ever go so far as to piddle over the mangle. Her worry was keeping it from the lodgers.

The girl was still standing there. Mrs Blunt supposed the letter she expected was from her young man.

'If it's in the post you may be sure it'll get here,' she said. 'You'll be late for work.'

Here came the other one, Victoria, clattering down the stairs. Bit of a mystery about her. Went out most nights and was never yet caught coming back. Little alley cat. Smart though. Might catch some fellow's eye with those saucy looks. She watched the two girls walking down the street talking secrets. All about *him*, no doubt, whoever he was. What he said, how he looked, no good pretending a him wasn't the centre of every girl's world.

She gave a sigh for the him who'd left her to scrub the step. The sigh was for what he once had been; an angry shake of the head was for what he'd become. Passing the bedroom door she rattled the handle. 'Get up, you lazy slob,' she shouted.

The postman pushed something through the door. A bill. Nothing for Miss Grant.

Letters for Miss Charlotte Grant continued to arrive at Lancaster Gate and William took them straight to his study to be read when convenient.

Richard Allen always put his address on the back, and the addresses changed. The latest was from Vienna. Didn't that just go to show how right William had been to send him packing? A wandering minstrel. Charlotte would soon have tired of trailing round with him. Still, might as well see what he had to say this time.

He skipped the usual opening endearments and went for the main part:

...I hoped beyond hope I'd find a letter waiting for me here but there was nothing. How can I tell if my letters are reaching you? I begin to fear you are not receiving them and are in a void, just as I am. Without any news at all I can't help imagining things which I hope are wide of the mark. Are you well or ill? Neither of us thought life would be easy until we found a way to overcome our difficulties, but I'm afraid you are being made to suffer. My God, I hope and pray that isn't so. My own news is good, much better than I ever expected. You remember the young violinist at Mary's party? Tall and straight. He spoke to us, remember? Well, he is to give a recital in Vienna and has asked me to be his partner! So here I am. We are to play the Kreutzer Sonata and oh, my dear, darling Charlotte, you can have no idea how wonderful it is. If only you could hear it. One day when we are together you will and you'll wonder where such sounds come from. How I long to see you, kiss you, talk with you. Is there no hope your father will relent?

No there isn't, thought William. He put the letter in the pigeonhole reserved for these missives and went to join Ellen in the drawing room.

'All right, darling?' he asked.

'Nausea. It's the same every morning.'

'What does the doctor say?'

'That old ass knows nothing.'

'It's a trial that has to be endured, I suppose.'

'I'd like some husbands to try it.'

He patted her shoulder and thought of his own trials. He was finding it very hard to sit opposite her at breakfast and see her toying with a piece of dry toast while he demolished a pair of kippers.

Mrs Vickery had told her that green apples helped morning sickness so she usually crunched into one, and the noise put his teeth on edge.

'Was there another letter for Charlotte?' she asked.

'Yes. And you needn't look at me like that. I'm acting in her interest, not against it.'

'What odd notions you have, William.'

He put his arm round her. 'The whole thing's most unfortunate but it would be worse if she married the fellow. He's not our class so it wouldn't work. Misalliances never do. And don't forget his parentage.'

'He's not to blame for that.'

'If he were a gentleman he wouldn't presume to ask a girl of good family to marry him. Or any girl at all.'

'That may be the common opinion but it isn't mine.'

'Well, don't parade it among our friends. I'm pretty sure Charlotte will get tired of her independence before long and come crawling back. You'll see.'

She didn't answer and her attitude worried him. They'd been so blissfully happy at first and agreed on so many things, but then, of course, nothing like this had occurred. He was shocked to find what lax views she held. It was surprising in a clergyman's daughter. Still, he loved her so much and wanted to please her, especially now with a baby on the way.

'Ellie darling, don't let's quarrel. I can't bear it when we're not in accord,' he said.

'We would be if you changed your tune.'

He stared at her. How like Amanda. That was just the kind of thing she would have said. What would he do if Ellen was another Amanda? Could that outrageous behaviour be catching? Women were supposed to defer to men, daughters to their fathers, wives to their husbands, but a lot of them were getting out of hand and it was disturbing.

Ellen looked so sad and the bit of knitting she had done was a disgrace. All uneven. He almost remarked on it but remembered her mood might be due to her condition and it behoved him to be considerate and patient. Amanda—trust her—had never been off song for a second. She had practically waltzed through her pregnancy and boasted that it only took half an hour to bring her redfaced, bellowing baby into the world. She put it all down to olive oil, of which she took a whole tablespoonful every morning. He was the one to feel bilious when she poured the greenish-yellow mixture out and planted an oily kiss on his lips after she'd tossed it down.

No, he must not, whatever he did, begin to compare Ellen with his late wife. His best course was to humour her, keep her amused, take her about, perhaps to a few shows. There were plenty to choose from.

Although her deep longing for Richard dominated Charlotte's feelings, she was excited at the prospect of the entertainment Mr Blades offered. Victoria told her he had included her and Algie in several outings before and took them to places she would never have dared enter except by the back door.

'I know you wish Richard was coming but Eustace Bright's been invited to make up the party, and he's ever such a nice young man. Proper gentleman, same as Mr Blades. Mr Blades is right out of the top drawer. Could be a lord the way he goes on. Manners! My word.'

Charlotte soon found that Victoria wasn't exaggerating. Mr Blades sent a cab to pick them up and, with Clarice, was waiting to greet them at the Criterion. He was charmed to meet Miss Grant and honoured that she had accepted his invitation. His dear Clarice had told him she had difficulties, and if ever he could be of assistance in his small way she had only to mention it.

She was impressed. He was very good-looking: waxed moustache turned up at the ends, beautiful hazel eyes beneath strongly marked brows, and dark hair with a soft natural wave.

'We're all here, I think, so we'll go in. Oh, first some flowers.' He beckoned a waitress with a tray of posies for the girls to choose from. She obviously knew him, for she wished him good evening and he hoped she was well and asked after her mother. She fixed a white carnation in his buttonhole. Algie chose a green one, as did his friend, Eustace Bright, who had been introduced to Charlotte.

'Naughty,' said Mr Blades, shaking his head at their choice.

'Go on with you!'

Clarice had a pink rose, Victoria violets. Charlotte noticed camellias and her heart looped. The sight of them brought back her evening at the opera, and it was almost as though Richard was beside her, as he had been then, with a camellia in his buttonhole. She couldn't suppress a little gasp as she put out her hand to take one.

'Are you all right?' It was Eustace who noticed her slight hesitation.

'Perfectly all right, thank you.'

He offered his arm. The head waiter was ushering them in, his politeness and deference so marked he was clearly out to please a very important patron, and the moment they were all seated waiters came hovering round. Champagne corks popped with scarcely a sound, oysters arrived in a mountain of crushed ice on a silver tray, and Charlotte prayed she wouldn't have to eat one. The others were swallowing them whole.

'Go on,' said Victoria. 'Open your mouth. The oyster knows which way to go.'

Mr Blades was smiling at her. She couldn't be so ill-mannered as to refuse so she took one and was agreeably surprised. It was rather fun. So was the champagne that went with the oysters so well. She had several more.

As she had never been in a restaurant in her life, everything was strange and exciting. The brightness, the busyness, the dexterity of the waiters whisking dishes away and conjuring up others as if by magic. Since becoming a workroom girl she had eaten only the plainest food and was almost bewildered by the variety offered here. Huge joints of beef or mutton under enormous covers were tempting enough, but first there was soup, fish, game, and afterwards delicious puddings, ices and fruit, and the accompanying wine.

The others, even Victoria, had been

171

there before and knew what to expect. There was plenty of laughter and good-humoured chaffing. Eustace Bright was a very sprightly young man and the champagne made his slightest remark seem witty to him and amusing to her. She couldn't help liking him.

There was only one hitch and it was not remarkable enough to make any impact at the time. Mr Blades had given Clarice a brooch in a velvet case that evening. She showed it to the others but he objected. 'I don't want anyone to see it until I've had it reset for you, dearest,' he said.

'But it's lovely as it is.'

'I'd rather you didn't show it yet. Put it away.'

She was reluctant.

'To please me,' he said.

She did as he asked but looked downcast till he consoled her by saying that only she could display the jewels to their full advantage when they were set to his design.

After dinner they strolled along to the Alhambra and were shown to their seats in the centre of the dress circle. The house was packed, a very different audience from the one at the opera, more high-spirited, only a few in evening dress but innumerable hats to admire.

Charlotte thought of Ellie and wished she could see them. She was wearing a most becoming creation of ostrich feathers herself. It was one Annie had smuggled out and she was especially fond of it, as Ellie had insisted on buying it for her. It enhanced the prettiness of her face and Eustace asked if he could borrow it to wear in the park on Sunday. 'I'd be taken for a lifeguard in his busby,' he said.

'You're more likely to be run in,' said Mr Blades.

People nearby noticed the lively young people who were having such an entertaining evening before the curtain went up. None of them knew they had attracted attention but it was no wonder, for they were all remarkably good-looking—the men handsome, the girls attractive: Clarice with her classical features and delicate colouring; Victoria with something of the gypsy in her aspect. She had taken a pair of cherries at dessert and hung them over one ear, because, as she said, 'I'm a poor girl what ain't got no jewellery.'

'Stick to fruit,' said Algie. 'I'm struggling to buy you a ring.'

'Honest? What kind?'

'Plain gold. I can't run to twenty-two carat so you'll have to make do with eighteen.'

'A wedding ring?'

'What else?'

'Ooh,' she said. 'Ooh, Algie.'

173

Just before the lights went down Mr and Mrs William Grant were shown into a stage box. William had chosen to take Ellen to the Alhambra as it was the best variety show in town, according to friends who had seen it. They had dined at the Savoy first and she had been able to enjoy the food and the surroundings. She had persuaded herself that William couldn't keep up his rigid attitude to Charlotte much longer. He must surely declare an armistice and welcome her back home, for her prolonged absence was already provoking curiosity, and Mrs Morton had asked for Aunt Mildred's address. The Mortons were going to Bournemouth in the summer so would have the opportunity to call and see how dear Charlotte was doing.

How will he get out of that one? Ellen wondered as the orchestra struck up a rousing overture and the curtain rose on the first of the many turns. She slipped her hand into William's and he responded with a gentle pressure. It was not the thing to hold hands in public but he couldn't resist her.

In the circle Mr Blades was holding hands with Clarice, Algie with Victoria, and Eustace Bright wished he had the nerve to do the same with Charlotte.

Something told him he had better not try, although she was easy enough to get on with and not at all stuck-up. She struck him as unusually green. The way she'd goggled at the oysters told him she was as good as brand new. Not a bit like a girl who earned her own living and shared digs with Victoria.

She was lapping up the turns now as though she'd just left the schoolroom, nearly diving out of the circle when the trapeze artists performed, laughing her head off at the comedians, marvelling at a male impersonator, and then, when a rather unusual act appeared, growing tense, gripping the rail in front, and then leaning back.

It was only a singer, a soprano, he thought. But Charlotte was crying, or rather trying not to. Eustace could almost feel her forcing back tears and it worried him. It was quite a nice tune.

He was not to know what this aria from *Traviata* was doing to Charlotte. The whole evening, from the moment she had chosen the camellia at the restaurant to this particular music, seemed designed to bring Richard before her and yet sent him further away than ever. How she ached in her heart, how she longed for him, and how empty her life was without him.

The operatic interlude stirred recollections in Ellen's memory too and brought back that evening at Covent Garden with Charlotte. Where was Richard Allen now, she wondered, and where was Charlotte? Oh, if only those two were together, married and happy, as she was sure they would be.

The first part of the show ended and the house lights went up, giving Ellen her first chance to look round the theatre. There was a great deal of movement, with people leaving their seats for the bar or simply standing to stretch their legs. She noticed a girl wearing an ostrich feather hat in the dress circle. There was something familiar about it and she wondered where she could have seen it before. Then the girl turned her head. Charlotte! Oh!

Ellen's first impulse was to draw William's attention to his daughter but she immediately thought better of it and managed not to exclaim aloud. They were having such an enjoyable evening together and this would ruin it. He was smoking a cigar and looking so placid. From what she could see, Charlotte was among friends, and very nice ones by their appearance.

The second half of the show was even better than the first. There was tumultuous applause at the end and then the solemn moment when the conductor raised his baton for the King. How still the house was. Nobody moved till it was over. Then came the hustle to get out.

The strength of her memory of *Traviata* had left Charlotte disturbed in her mind but she was determined not to be a wet blanket and spoil the evening for the others. They made their way downstairs but she got separated from them in the foyer, although she managed to keep them in sight and could see them waiting for her just inside the entrance.

A tall man with his arm protectively round his companion was blocking her way. 'Excuse me,' she said.

He turned, looked, stared. She stared back. There was a momentary pause after the shock of recognition, but the resentment of a lifetime was packed into it. Now that she had seen parental love demonstrated at Nanny's, she missed what she had never had. She owed nothing to this man who was her father. She had no love for him or duty towards him and was thankful she had run away.

Ellen was not surprised by this meeting but she felt William positively bristling. His daughter, an exquisite young girl, here at the Alhambra enjoying herself.

'What are you doing here?' he demanded.

'Trying to get out,' she said.

'Are you with those people over there?'

'They are my friends.'

By now they were almost alone in the foyer. She could simply have walked out but Ellen clutched her hand and said how lovely it was to see her and wasn't it strange they should hear that aria tonight?

'We were together last time and so happy, weren't we, Charlotte dear? Don't you think we can mend matters? I miss you so much.'

Before Charlotte could respond her father said: 'You had better come home with us, Charlotte,' but without any warmth in his voice.

'Will it be different? Will you tell me where Richard is?' Perhaps, after all, there was a glimmer of hope.

'Certainly not,' he said.

'Then I shan't come.'

'In that case there is no more to be said.' It was beneath his dignity to argue with this stupid, insubordinate child, looking so damned like Amanda he could have choked. He gave her a cold, dismissive look.

'Come along, Ellen,' he said to his tearful, protesting wife. She had no choice, but she cried all the way home in the cab.

Although she had stood her ground Charlotte was shaken by this encounter and didn't find it easy to explain to the others at supper. They were all concerned for her and thought her situation impossible. Mr Blades said he had a very good mind to consult his lawyer, as Mr Grant could be in trouble for withholding the letters. 'They are your property. You may have a case, Miss Grant. You might be able to sue him for them.'

Charlotte saw herself in court, surrounded by barristers in wigs and gowns, and shuddered. Papa in the dock. Ellen weeping in the gallery.

'I'll never do that,' she said.

'It's a pity your papa is so adamant. But what a fine-looking man, Miss Grant. A merchant, I think you said?'

Charlotte didn't remember saying exactly that but was ready to accept she had. She was sorry they had met, but the others didn't agree.

'I think it's lucky you did,' said Clarice. 'It shows he doesn't care a button how you feel.'

'Fancy trying to shove you off on a toad like Albert,' said Victoria.

'It all boils down to money,' Algie said. 'An alliance with another prosperous merchant would be right up his street.'

'That makes me a pawn!' cried Charlotte.

'So you were till you hopped it,' Victoria declared.

The others all agreed.

Mr Blades ordered another bottle of champagne and they raised their glasses to Charlotte and her bid for freedom.

This was all very fine, but Charlotte woke with a headache the next morning and no sense of elation. Victoria too was nothing like as cheerful as usual. She had a weight on her mind but Algie kept telling her not to worry. She'd only missed once, and like as not it didn't mean what she was afraid it meant. Anyway, there was no sense in talking to his mother, with the first court nearly on top of them and all the orders to complete. Ma would go off the deep end and cut his mingy allowance. Wait till August, he said.

'It'll show by then,' said Victoria, close to tears.

'Don't you trust me, Vicky?'

'I would if you'd take more interest in the business, like your ma's always telling you. As it is, you leave everything to your dad, and how are we ever to get a place to live if you don't earn a wage?'

This made Algie think, and he was

serious when he said: 'Righto, then. I'll buckle down to it.'

He meant it by learning how to keep the books and deal with the wholesalers and the buying side. Madame Last marvelled at the change in him. Little did she know he had bought Victoria a wedding ring, and although she couldn't wear it her confidence came back.

'I can be proud now,' she said when she showed it to Clarice and Charlotte as they were taking the air at dinner time. 'End of August we can announce our engagement in style, just like the nobs,' she told them. 'Mr Algernon Last to Miss Victoria Clink. It'd look good in *The Times*, wouldn't it?'

'I never knew your name was Clink,' said Clarice.

'Well, it's not. I don't know what it is. I was called Clink because I was left in Clink Street. By my mum, I suppose. Poor thing. I bet she was a girl just like me. Some bloke let her down. I was three days old, they said. Oh, dearie me! My poor mum! I wish I could find her, tell her I'm all right. Indeed I do.'

She burst out crying and the other two did their best to console her. Charlotte had grown fond of Victoria and felt protective towards her. It was remarkable how she kept cheerful, especially now she had, in her own words, got herself in the pudd'n' club.

'I'll kill that Algie if he lets her down,' Clarice told Charlotte.

'How could he? I'm sure he won't.'

'Poor little Vic's a bit of a guttersnipe, isn't she?'

'She can raise herself up.'

'That'd spoil her,' Clarice said.

The ever-vigilant Mrs Blunt was suspicious of Victoria. 'What's happened to your rags these days?' she demanded one evening. 'I reckon they've twice been missing from the line.'

'And what business is it of yours to go reckoning, I'd like to know.' countered Victoria.

'I only let rooms to respectable young women. That's what my business is.'

'Then you can stuff it. I've found a good laundry. Same one the Queen has. Satisfied?'

'No, I'm not,' said Mrs Blunt.

'Hard luck,' said Victoria, going upstairs to a supper Charlotte was getting ready as a treat. She was in low spirits herself, as Richard's expected letter still hadn't arrived and she was certain there was something amiss. She had no means of telling if he was still in Paris or if her own outpourings had reached him. Her news would surprise him so much she was certain he would get in touch with her as soon as he received it. She couldn't understand it, and although Clarice and Victoria tried to think up reasons they were puzzled too.

Nanny found explaining it almost impossible, but she did the best she could and tried to persuade Charlotte that the news was following him round and hadn't caught up yet.

'I'm getting desperate,' Charlotte told her when she spent her usual Sunday with the Goodes.

'Despair is destructive,' Nanny said. 'You've got to build, Charlotte.'

'How?'

'Use what you've got around you. That poor child Victoria needs help in her situation. Make sure you give it to her.'

'That won't help me discover where Richard is.'

'I never thought I'd hear you sound so selfish,' said Nanny, in a tone of surprise and disappointment. 'Of course it won't, but it'll help your backbone. Do your best for others and you'll be surprised at the strength it gives you. Here endeth the first lesson.'

As a result of this, Charlotte bought a frying pan and half a pound of pork sausages on her way home, and had just got them going on the Primus when Victoria, fresh from her contretemps with Mrs Blunt, rushed in.

'Here! You can't fry things!' she shouted.

'Why not?'

'She'll be after us.'

The sausages had already begun to splutter and their savoury smell pervaded the air.

'Let her,' said Charlotte, turning them over.

Footsteps were heard on the stairs as she spoke. The girls looked at each other, flung the window open, got the Primus and pan out on the sill, closed the window and were innocently buttering some rolls when Mrs Blunt banged on the door.

'What's cooking in here?' she demanded when Charlotte opened it.

'Nothing,' said Victoria.

'Then what's the smell? It's all over the house.'

'Makes a nice change from cabbage then,' Victoria said. 'It ain't in here, Mrs Blunt, and on that I'll take my oath.'

Mrs Blunt sniffed, nose in the air.

'Coo, a bloodhound couldn't do better,' said Victoria.

'You know the rules of the house, and if I find you cooking in this room your name will be Walker, my fine young lady. I am *not* satisfied.'

She peered all round the room, sniffed again, and withdrew.

'Next time I'll start it on the sill,' said Charlotte as they sat down to one of the nicest meals they'd had since they shared a room.

Her life seemed to consist of major disappointments and small triumphs now. She was doing well at work, there was another splendid evening out with Mr Blades, and her weekends with Nanny were comforting, but always, dragging her down, was the complete lack of news from Richard.

Annie came to Hammersmith when she could. Letters still arrived from abroad, she told Charlotte, but she never got so much as a peep at them. The master was ever so good to the missus. They were like a honeymoon couple, and Miss Charlotte might be pleased to know she would have a little brother or sister later in the year. Mrs Vickery was of the opinion that underneath it all the missus was rather sad and it was a sin and a shame.

'Anyway,' Mrs Vickery had said, 'Mr Allen's sure to come to the kitchen door when he's back home, so tell Miss Charlotte to keep a stout heart.'

Annie delivered this message and Charlotte asked her to be sure to thank Mrs Vickery. She also got her to smuggle a note to Ellen. 'Darling Ellie, I'm so happy to learn your news. I think of you a lot,' she wrote.

Then the unbelievable happened. She got home from work on a Saturday afternoon to find Mrs Blunt coming up from the basement with a package in her hand.

'This here came for you,' she said.

It was a small parcel carefully wrapped in brown paper and sealed with red wax. Just a plain seal. Her name was printed in black ink.

'Who brought it?' she asked.

'A young fellow. Mr Blunt took it in. Aren't you going to open it?'

'Of course I am,' said Charlotte, and she ran upstairs leaving Mrs Blunt to vent her unsatisfied curiosity on her husband by hiding his boots so he couldn't go to the pub.

Charlotte's heart beat fast. In a strange way she knew what the parcel contained before she opened it, and there it was—a bundle of letters tied with blue ribbon. Richard's letters. She tore them from the packet. They were postmarked Paris, Vienna, Milan, Rome. It seemed sensible to read the last one first, but her hands shook as she opened it. To think his pen had written it, his hands held it. She began to read:

Oh, for a single word from you, my dear, dearest Charlotte! We are so far apart and it's hard to go on without knowing what's happening and why you don't write. I'm convinced it's because you are prevented against your will, but sometimes the most horrid doubts come into my mind. Has she been ground down by a will stronger than her own? Has she tired of me and of this wretched situation? Is she intimidated, browbeaten, subjugated? My dear, if you knew how I love you, more now than ever, you would appreciate how miserable I am, especially when I'm at my lowest ebb in the small hours. Then the seventh hour comes and I concentrate on you, see us together in the park, at Mary's concert, all the happy times, and once again I know you are as unwavering as I am. So, my dearest, I send you all my love.

Charlotte read it again and again, and sometimes she could hardly see for the tears blurring her eyes. Relief, joy, thankfulness. Doubts and fears melted away. She spent a long time with the letters, taking them in order and following him from place to place in her mind.

He had many plans for the future and spoke of the success of the Kreutzer Sonata in Vienna and the probability of repeating it in other locations. 'But don't deceive yourself, my darling,' he wrote. 'I shall never be one of the great pianists, I'm no Paderewski! I like being an accompanist, to both singers and instrumentalists, and have some more engagements to keep. Mary is so pleased—we work together, of course. She gave several Lieder recitals in Vienna and brought the house down each time. I'm pretty sure I can earn enough to keep the wolf from our door when we're married, and, after all, we don't crave riches, do we?'

All the envelopes had been opened, so her father must have taken all this in, and she wondered if he was reconsidering Richard, though it had not seemed so when they met at the Alhambra. What was she to think? He must have relented enough to send her the package but there was no message with it, nothing to show where it came from.

Anyway, what did that matter now she had them? Now all was sunshine and light. Her pen almost scratched holes in the paper as she expressed all her emotions as fast as she could get them down.

'My dear, you've heard from Richard! Your eyes are shining!' cried Nanny when Charlotte arrived rather later than usual.

'At last!' She was out of breath, having run all the way from the bus stop. 'Just wait till I tell you.'

'Take your time,' said Nanny.

She listened to everything attentively and asked several questions, but was not nearly as pleased as Charlotte expected her to be.

'What can have brought about this change of heart in your father, do you suppose?' she asked.

'It must be Ellie's doing,' Charlotte said. 'I know she misses me at home, and she's always liked Richard. I expect she got to work on Pa after we met at the Alhambra.'

'I wonder.'

Her doubtful tone made Charlotte protest. 'It must have been Pa who sent them,' she said.

'Somehow I can't see him doing any such thing.'

'You're throwing a damper on it.'

'Not a damper. Just a word of caution. It's unwise to jump to conclusions, even such an obvious one as this.'

'Oh, don't say that.'

'I do say it, Charlotte.'

'Nanny darling, do try to imagine how I feel. I can forgive Pa and even be a dutiful daughter now. Isn't that as it should be?'

'It is, my dear,' said Nanny, but she saw

Amanda in Charlotte's impulsive readiness to believe without proof that her father had relented.

'Anyway, I'm going to thank Pa straight away and I'll come back and tell you all about it. Do say you think it's wonderful. Say you're glad.'

'I'm glad to know you've heard from Richard at last. Of course I am.'

But Nanny shook her head as she watched Charlotte hurry away. In her opinion Mr Grant was not a man to have a change of heart.

It was early evening when Charlotte walked up to the so-familiar front door of her old home and told Annie she had called to see her father.

Annie looked worried but there was no chance for them to exchange a word, for Mr Grant appeared and invited Charlotte into his study. His tone was far from gracious.

Ellie was already there and, like Annie, she looked anxious. 'Come and sit by me, Charlotte dear,' she said in a slightly tremulous voice.

'Sit *there*,' ordered Mr Grant, pointing to a chair on the other side of the room. This was not at all what she had expected, but she sat, smoothed her skirt and said: 'Papa, I'm here to thank you for sending me Richard's letters. I'm so—well, I'm just overflowing with thanks and gratitude. You've made me so happy.'

Mr Grant held up his hand. 'Stop!' he said. 'How did you come by those letters?'

'You sent them to me, Papa.'

'Answer my question. How did you come by them?'

'A young man delivered them in a packet this morning. They were beautifully done up and sealed.'

'Were they, indeed? Have you kept the wrapping paper?'

Charlotte, already discomfited, began to have a sense of foreboding. 'I didn't think you'd want it back,' she said.

'It's wanted for a particular reason.'

'I don't understand. What's wrong with it?'

'Those letters were stolen from my desk. That's what's wrong.'

'Stolen?'

'Stolen. And I mean to find out who took them.'

'I thought it was you who sent them.' She was bewildered and apprehensive now. Her joy was fading, and the hope that her father had forgiven her gave way to the miserable fact that he had not. She drooped, sank into herself, her voice

191

no more than a whisper: 'Does it mean someone broke into the house?'

'Isn't that obvious? Someone entered the house for no other reason than to steal those letters. Nothing else was taken. You don't need to be Sherlock Holmes to deduce that the thief was a person of your acquaintance.'

'Nobody I know would do that. I don't know any thieves.'

Ellen had listened to all this, seen Charlotte's joyful expectations dashed away, and felt such pity for her she was driven to speak. 'William, it's quite clear Charlotte knows nothing at all about this theft,' she said. 'Can't you understand what the receipt of that package meant to her? She thought you'd changed your mind.'

'I did. Oh, I did,' cried Charlotte.

'Then she deceived herself,' he said, ignoring his daughter. 'We will not enter into an argument, Ellen.'

He turned to Charlotte. 'I wish to know the names of the people you associate with,' he said. 'You had better tell me, for if you don't the police will ask you.'

'Does it matter? The letters are mine by right. They are addressed to me.'

'That's beside the point. My house was entered and the police have been informed. Now. Who were the people you were with at the Alhambra?'

'The two girls who work with me at Madame Last's. Madame is a court dressmaker.'

'Yes, yes.' He tapped the desk top irritably. 'Who were the men?'

'Only young Mr Last, Madame's son, and his friend, Mr Bright. He's a medical student. And Mr Blades. He's engaged to Clarice and she'll be leaving to be married soon.'

'And what does this Mr Blades do?'

'Really, Papa, I've never asked him. It wouldn't be civil to ask a gentleman what he does. Clarice once said he's in business.'

'Did she indeed? That covers a wide field. Who else do you associate with?'

'No one really. Just the other girls in the workroom—that's all.'

'Very well. That will do to go on with.'

'Papa,' Charlotte faltered, and groped for her handkerchief, 'I'm so sorry it's like this. I hoped. I dared to hope you had changed your mind about Richard. You've read his letters so you know he's doing well. I hoped you might give us your blessing.'

'You will have my blessing, Charlotte, when you marry a man of my choosing. Richard Allen is not that man.'

He gave the bell rope such a tug it

almost broke, and Annie came in so fast it was obvious she had been listening at the door. She was told to get on her outdoor things and accompany Miss Charlotte to her abode.

Charlotte was too bewildered and frightened to speak. She longed to be back with Nanny so that she could talk things over, but above all she wanted Richard. She was adrift in an angry sea of doubts and suspicions.

Ellen saw her to the door. 'Oh, Ellie, I did so hope,' she said.

'So did I,' said Ellen.

Her father had turned his back and was sitting at his desk.

Annie couldn't throw any light on this extraordinary theft. She only knew the master had kicked up a terrible hullabaloo when he missed the letters, had them all up for questioning, and Tilda was so frightened she wet her drawers. Not that she knew anything about the robbery. Mrs Vickery was most indignant. She told the master so. 'You've had an effect on that poor girl's bladder,' she told him.

'If you speak to me like that you can look for another place, Mrs Vickery,' he said.

'And glad to. I'd have no trouble finding one,' she retorted.

'And she wouldn't,' Annie told Charlotte. 'Still, it's very strange someone should get into the house and take nothing but those letters. Whoever it was knew exactly what he wanted. There's lots of good stuff, as you know, and none of it touched. Couldn't be anything to do with Mr Allen, could it?'

'Of course it couldn't.'

'Well, I call it weird. It fair gives me the creeps. I don't like to think of someone sneaking in and out of the house. Why, he could cut our throats if he'd a mind to. They've never caught Jack the Ripper yet.'

'Oh, don't be so fanciful,' Charlotte said.

The wrapping paper was nowhere to be found. It appeared that Mrs Blunt, in an excess of zeal and curiosity, had used all the odd bits of paper to light her fire, so Annie had to go back without it.

Charlotte was so disappointed with the outcome of her visit home she couldn't help crying. Deep down, so deep she was hardly aware of it herself, was the wish to be at peace with her father.

Her weekend with the Goodes wasn't as pleasurable as usual because they couldn't help trying to find explanations for what had happened. On Sunday afternoon Mrs Vickery came on one of her rare visits to have tea with the family.

It was a very grand affair in the dining room, which was only used on state occasions, and in which the furniture, from the overmantel to the arms and legs of the chairs, had been richly carved by Will.

'It should be in a museum,' Mrs Vickery said, to which Nanny responded that it most likely would be at some unknown date in the future.

The conversation turned to the theft at Lancaster Gate, which had left the domestic staff unsettled. Poor Tilda couldn't remember if any of the windows were open that evening, although she was certain she had closed them all by bedtime. Mr Grant himself always checked the whole house for security last thing, but even he hadn't noticed if the letters were in the pigeonhole in his desk. Annie overheard him discussing this with his wife the next morning, for he only discovered the loss when another letter arrived from Mr Allen.

'Thunder wasn't in it, my dears,' said Mrs Vickery, addressing the whole table and selecting a fish paste sandwich from the plate offered to her. 'Of course it's disturbing when something like this happens. We were all suspects. Us! If he can't trust us downstairs, he can't trust anyone.'

'Could it have been Mrs Grant?' suggested Will.

'I'm sure she wanted me to have them but she'd have used persuasion, not deceit,' said Charlotte.

'I have my doubts about Mr Blades,' Nanny said.

'Oh no! Why suspect him?' cried Charlotte.

'Who else knows of your plight, my dear? He seems to be generous and kindhearted. He could have paid some petty thief to do it.'

Will intervened. Lily was getting restless and this always worried him. 'I reckon we ought to stop guessing and just be glad Charlotte's heard from her sweetheart and knows where he is,' he said. 'We don't know the answer, do we, Lily?'

'When's the piano lady coming?' asked Lily, away in her own little world.

'Next week, love,' said Will.

He told Mrs Vickery Lily had a piano lesson every week, and she suggested Lily might play a tune for her.

'After tea,' said Nanny firmly.

They did justice to everything on the table, various sandwiches, sliced bread and butter, jam, watercress, celery, a large Victoria sandwich and rock cakes, all washed down by copious cups of tea.

As soon as it was cleared away they sat

back to listen while Lily picked out 'The Bluebells of Scotland' with one finger and a lot of help from Charlotte.

Next day all the workroom girls puzzled their heads over the mystery of Charlotte's letters. Some said it was the doing of an international spy, Miss Prescot favoured a disaffected postman, Clarice just wondered, and Victoria had a fit of the giggles.

'A nine-day wonder,' said Madame Last when Miss Prescot mentioned it to her. 'I've said before and I'll say again, it don't become me—or you, for that matter—to interest myself in the ups and downs of those girls. And I wish you'd learn to pin your hair up proper. There's enough pins sticking out for a knife-throwing act.'

'Sorry,' said Miss Prescot, wishing her hair was thick enough to support the numerous pins she kept pushing in to hold it up.

A few days later Charlotte had another shock. Her own letter came back, returned by the Italian postal authorities.

'Funny,' said Mrs Blunt, as she handed it to her. 'I never seen anything like this before.'

Charlotte hadn't either, but it was clear that Richard had never received it and consequently knew nothing of events since their parting. Her heart plummeted. It was as though the postal services on both sides of the Channel were conspiring to prevent her from communicating with him, and the effect was frightening. She had no resources, he was further from her than ever and she longed for him desperately. She was powerless against this invisible force, yet there must be an explanation and a way to get through.

Who could she turn to for advice? Mr Blades came to mind. He was a man of the world. Would Clarice mind if she appealed to him?

'Of course not,' said Clarice. 'Come home with me after work. Herbert's bringing some supper in, so you must join us and we'll get this sorted out for you.'

It was the first time Charlotte had been to Clarice's rooms and met her Aunt Cassie, a jolly old woman who made light of her rheumatic pains, prided herself on still being able to do a bit of charring, and offered up prayers of thanks every night for the good fortune that had thrown Mr Blades into the path of her beloved Clarice.

'What a world it is where such things can happen,' she remarked to Charlotte. 'Him so handsome and so generous. Thinks nothing of bringing in a couple of pounds of best rump, and frying it, too. What's on the menu tonight, Clarice?'

'Steak,' said Clarice.

Apparently the squalor of the basement flat had been banished as soon as Mr Blades saw it. Nice oilcloth on the floors, one or two rugs, a dresser for the crockery, three armchairs and plenty of coal in the cellar.

'We don't feel ashamed to ask people in now,' said Aunt Cassie.

Clarice put on an apron and began peeling potatoes; Mr Blades arrived, put his arms round her and gave her a hug, then he kissed Aunt Cassie and called her his second sweetheart. He still called Charlotte Miss Grant.

'Clarice tells me you've got a puzzle,' he said.

She explained her quandary over the returned letter and he took it to the table to look at it under the lamp.

'Ah, I see. It's come back because you've addressed it to Richard Allen Esquire,' he said. 'The Esquire's the trouble.'

'Isn't it right?'

'Only in the British Isles, Miss Grant. Foreigners are likely to take it for a surname.'

'Oh!' She felt a great rush of relief. 'How stupid of me,' she said.

'You weren't to know. Hotel clerks ought to understand but they don't. The best thing is to put the name with no title. Then there won't be a mistake.'

Charlotte was thankful for the explanation, mad with herself for displaying such ignorance and worried because Richard was still in the dark.

'Never mind. You can start afresh now,' Aunt Cassie said.

'I shall. I'll write as soon as I get home, and post it tomorrow.'

'There now. Nothing more to worry about,' said Clarice.

Mr Blades took off his coat, rolled up his shirtsleeves and donned the chef's apron and cap that hung behind the door.

'Always dress for the part,' he said, and set about frying the steak and onions, while Clarice mashed the potatoes.

Soon they were sitting down to supper and talking about the remarkable increase in trade due to the Coronation.

London was being transformed, there were lavish decorations, affluent visitors were pouring in and so were foreign royals. There would be illuminations, fireworks and goodness knows what all, as Aunt Cassie said. 'I did hear as how the King was giving big dinners to the poor. In tents, on the commons,' she added. 'Still, I don't suppose they'll have anything as good as this steak.'

'They say the weather's been specially

ordered,' said Mr Blades.

'About time too. I never knew such a miserable spring. Wet and cold all the time,' Clarice said.

'Never mind. This will be a year to remember if ever there was one,' said Mr Blades.

'We'll have to go and see the debs lining up in the Mall next week, Charlotte. Madame likes us to spot her creations.' Clarice said.

'Why don't you make up a party like when you go out to dinner?' suggested Aunt Cassie. 'Then you can come back here and tell me all about it.'

'Splendid idea. Over a good bottle of port.' Mr Blades leaned back in his chair, the picture of ease and contentment.

'And some Stilton. Nothing I'd enjoy more,' Aunt Cassie said.

'You're a good old girl,' said Mr Blades, and Charlotte could see he was genuinely fond of her. There was no doubt of his love for Clarice. The warm, comfortable atmosphere was all-embracing.

It was not in Charlotte's nature to be envious but she couldn't help comparing the unhampered courtship of this couple with her own, and thinking how lucky they were.

At the end of the evening Mr Blades escorted her home and their conversation turned to the mysterious theft of the letters.

'Papa is determined to find out who took them,' said Charlotte. 'He's informed the police. Isn't that dreadful?'

'A bit strong, perhaps, but natural enough. Nobody likes to be invaded.'

'I believe they'll be calling on everyone I know.'

'I don't think your friends have anything to tremble about. All this is routine.'

'But somebody got in and I can't imagine who.'

'If I were in your shoes I'd forget the whole thing,' he said. 'Don't give it another thought.'

'I'll try not to,' she said.

He saw her into the hall at Mrs Blunt's and went off whistling a jaunty tune. It was a pity Mr Grant had told the police about the theft, he thought, but as he had never been near Lancaster Gate himself there wouldn't be much he could do to help them.

A day or two later Clarice arrived late for work and said it was because a police officer had called and asked her a lot of questions. 'Personal ones too,' she said. 'He wanted to know if I was engaged and asked who the lucky man was. He even asked to see my ring. He admired it. I should say so, too. It's the best Herbert could buy, and I told him so.'

Clarice seldom wore her ring because Aunt Cassie said someone would knock her down for it. It was a gold hoop set with large diamonds that flashed so boldly it would attract attention anywhere.

'I don't know what the police thought I could tell them about a burglary at your pa's house,' she complained.

Charlotte didn't know either, and felt very uncomfortable about it.

Victoria had a visit from the police too, much to the displeasure of Mrs Blunt, who told her she'd get the house a bad name.

'Who's to know the copper didn't come to see your old man?' retorted Victoria. 'He's not particular where he commits his nuisances, is he? He don't only wet the mangle, Mrs Blunt. We'll see his name in the papers one of these days.'

'Don't you sauce me, young woman. You're no better than you ought to be.'

'And how much better is better, I'd like to know?'

'Fewer inches round the waist, or I'm much mistaken.'

'You bet your life you are,' said Victoria.

Again Charlotte felt distinctly uncomfortable. She had precipitated these enquiries by assuming that her father had sent her Richard's letters. How stupid she had been not to heed Nanny's advice.

Algie Last and his friend Eustace Bright were also asked if they could throw any light on the affair, and an officer even called on Mrs Goode, who told him he was wasting his time in pursuing something that didn't matter tuppence one way or the other.

'Miss Grant is the rightful owner of those letters and now she's got them. So why bother how?'

'The bother is that someone entered Mr Grant's house. That's what interests us, madam,' said the officer.

'Why don't you go and catch the Ripper? That would be much more sense than making enquiries like this,' said Nanny.

This comment did not please the officer, but he wished her a polite good day and went off to interview Mr Herbert Blades, the last person on his list.

As soon as Mr Blades heard about all this activity he took certain precautions. He told Clarice he might have to go up north at short notice, as an important deal was pending.

'By the way, dear, your ring needs cleaning. You'd better let me have it,' he told her.

She parted with it reluctantly, as it hadn't lost any of its sparkle as far as she could see. 'When will my brooch be ready?' she asked. 'They've had it ages.'

'Any day now.' He took a sealed envelope from his pocket and asked her to take care of it for him.

'It's a certificate. I don't want to have to take it with me if I go away on business.'

'I hope you won't be away long,' she said.

'No longer than I can help.'

She was accustomed to his short trips and thought nothing of it. They arranged to meet on the evening of the first court of the season, as already agreed.

Their venue was the Mall; Charlotte and Victoria went with her straight from work, and Algie and Eustace were already there. There was no sign of Mr Blades.

'It's not like him to be late. He's always here first,' Clarice said.

Five minutes went by and he didn't appear. He would have let her know if he'd had to go away, and he was never so inconsiderate as to keep her standing about in the street.

After half an hour she told the others they had better go nearer Buckingham Palace without her; she intended to stay where she was until he came, and when he did he'd get a right flea in the ear.

It was disappointing for the others, but once they were mingling with the crowd that always gathered on such occasions, they were caught up in the spirit of the evening.

It was a new scene for everyone, as the old Queen had held her courts in the afternoons, when most of her subjects were at work. This was new, exciting, unprecedented. There were plenty of young blades in the crowd, amusing themselves by cheering on the prettier debs and giving plain ones the thumbs down. They pressed their faces against carriage windows, made horrible grimaces and did everything possible to make the debs lose their composure. Matrons sat stony-faced; some of the debs tried not to giggle, some looked indignant, while others were so nervous they shook in their seats.

Charlotte and Victoria were busy searching for dresses that came from the house of Madame Last, and identified several.

It was not a warm evening and Charlotte felt her position as a poorly paid working girl when she peered into the carriages. Those debs, in their white dresses, with jewels sparkling in their hair, were about to step into an enchanted world of romance. Balls would be held for them, grand dinners given, and by the end of the season the majority would enter yet another world—that of matrimony.

The pavements were cold under her feet

and she was hungry.

'Seen enough?' It was Victoria who spoke. She was tired and hungry too.

'I wonder what became of Clarice?' asked Charlotte.

'I expect she met Mr Blades and they went off to supper somewhere.'

'We were to go back to Aunt Cassie.'

For some inexplicable reason, premonition perhaps, none of them wanted to prolong the evening. They had cocoa and hot dogs at a coffee stall, then Eustace saw Charlotte home while Victoria and Algie went off for their usual stroll.

Next day an anxious Clarice had still not heard from Mr Blades and feared he must be ill and unable to send a message.

Her fear was partly justified. Herbert Blades couldn't send a message but it was not because he was ill. He had been visited by the police on the day of the first court. He wasn't surprised to see them, knowing as he did about the break-in at Mr Grant's house. He had no trouble in convincing them that he had nothing to do with it, and they believed him. The annoying thing was their interest in his sapphire cuff links and his past history.

He had to admit that he had been a gentleman's gentleman to a very distinguished gentleman indeed, and had spent many a Friday to Monday in various country houses in that capacity.

It could be a coincidence, the police said, but jewellery of enormous value had disappeared from those houses, not while he was there on duty, but afterwards.

He could explain it all but they insisted he did so at the station. A cab was waiting.

Clarice knew nothing of this at the time, but when a week went by without a word she decided to go to his rooms to enquire.

She had never been there before and was afraid his landlady might misconstrue her reason for calling, so Charlotte offered to accompany her and they set off for Sackville Street after work. 'Just the kind of house I'd expect him to live in,' remarked Clarice as she rang the bell. 'It's his style.'

A liveried servant answered, and when Clarice said she had come to enquire after Mr Blades, they were invited to step inside.

After a very few minutes a stout, pleasant-looking woman bustled in, summed the girls up at a glance, decided they were respectable and invited them to sit.

'I understand you wish to see Mr Blades,' she said. 'Are you by any chance related?'

'Mr Blades is my fiancé,' Clarice said.

The landlady was impressed by Clarice's good looks and quiet manner and felt very sorry for her. 'Oh, dear me,' she said, not knowing how to break the news.

'May I see him—if he's in?'

'He isn't in, my dear, nor likely to be. You say you're engaged to be married to him?'

'Yes, at the end of the summer.'

'Then what I have to tell you is bad news, I'm afraid. Mr Blades was taken away a week ago.'

'Taken? What do you mean? He was to have met me that evening and he didn't turn up. I haven't heard a word since. Who took him?'

'Why, my dear, it was the police. Of course it may all be a mistake, and I hope it is, for a nicer lodger I never did have. I understand he's to be charged with burglary.'

'No!' Clarice looked dreadful. Her colour changed.

'It's true, I'm sorry to say.'

Light dawned on Charlotte. 'It must be the letters!' she exclaimed.

'Nothing to do with letters,' said the landlady. 'He's accused of stealing jewellery. There, I had to tell you. You'd have heard about it sooner or later.'

Clarice only heard a terrible rushing

sound as she slipped off her chair in a faint.

This was the one time when a state of unconsciousness was a mercy, by the landlady's reckoning. For Charlotte the revelation and its effect on Clarice shocked her into acting like an automaton. She had to get her friend home, and the only way was to take a cab, which the maid called. The landlady supplied burnt feathers, sal volatile and encouraging words.

They almost had to carry her between them, for the way she moaned and kept lapsing back into a faint alarmed them.

It was midnight before they reached home, and then Charlotte had to break the news to Aunt Cassie and witness her distress. She saw the old woman's world come crashing down and had to steel herself or she would have been no use. She helped Aunt Cassie get Clarice to bed, wondered if she should call a doctor, knew they couldn't afford it, and then remembered the guineas in the purse Mary had given her in that other world, that different life of long ago.

Aunt Cassie knew where a doctor lived and Charlotte walked there through filthy streets, running past men and women whose atrocious faces peered out at her from dark doorways. They were like figures in a cartoon, exaggerated in their degradation, but she kept on and at length reached the doctor's house and woke him by repeated bangings on the door.

She had to shout her message to an upper window and plead with him to come, for he didn't want to. He was a young man not long out of medical school, finding it hard to make his way. Without the allowance his father gave him he would not have survived as a doctor, for his patients were mostly too poor to pay him more than a few pence of his modest fee.

Charlotte told him of Clarice's collapse and part of the reason for it. She was not sure how much she should say and left it to the discretion of Aunt Cassie, who told him a great deal more.

He could only advise rest and restoratives, which he prescribed. No one could put back the clock for these three people, the old woman, the young one who clutched his hand and begged him to tell her it wasn't true, and the girl who seemed to be in charge of them. It was she who paid his fee, and he wondered why she was there, for she seemed of a different kind.

Although there were not many hours till dawn, Charlotte had never known such a long night, and her feeling of responsibility for Clarice came from the knowledge that it was her father who had set the police on her friends. They had investigated each one of them and taken the strongest interest in Mr Blades. He was older than the others, apparently rich and unusually generous.

She looked round the room he had made so comfortable for Aunt Cassie, who sat huddled in her chair while Clarice sobbed into the pillows of the large double bed they shared.

It was the hour to concentrate on Richard and she did so on her knees, willing him to sense her trouble, to come back and help her. It was like praying into the godless dark. And then it was time to go to work. There was no possibility of Clarice coming.

She made tea, persuaded Aunt Cassie to drink it, and stoked up the fire. Then, promising she would be back in the evening, she called at a chemist and paid for the medicine which was to be sent.

She was late at Madame Last's, and that meant losing money.

'Where's Clarice?' demanded Miss Prescot.

'She isn't well.'

'How inconvenient!'

Victoria was dying to know what had happened and if Mr Blades had come back.

'I wasn't half worried when you didn't

come home all night,' she said.

Charlotte told her the reason and it was received with disbelief at first, then with pity. Victoria couldn't bear to think of Clarice without her Mr Blades.

'And to think it all started with your pa,' she said. 'You mustn't half feel awful.'

'I do,' said Charlotte, worried sick by what she saw as her part in the downfall of Mr Blades.

They had to work even harder than usual because the dress Clarice was sewing had to be finished, so there was no time to talk. When they left that evening, Charlotte bought food from the cookshop and told Victoria she was taking it to Aunt Cassie.

'I've got something to tell you first,' said Victoria.

They went to a cheap teashop they passed every day, and sat at a marble-topped table.

'I suppose you wonder who really took those letters of yours,' she said as she stirred her dark-brown tea. 'Well, hold your hat on. It was me.'

'You? You couldn't have!'

'Couldn't I just? I'm very good at getting into places. Ask Mrs Blunt.'

'How? I don't see how you could.'

'I'll tell you. Algie and me thought we'd take a look at your house—only out of nosiness. We saw a lady and gent come

214

out and get in a carriage. It was your pa and ma. All in evening dress. Ever so posh and handsome.'

'You might have told me,' said Charlotte. 'I'm telling you now.'

Victoria and Algie had both had the same idea. The coast was clear, so why not do Charlotte a good turn and snaffle her letters? They could hear the servants laughing and talking in the basement. One of them was singing a music-hall song. The lights were on in the hall, and doors were open, so they could see into the rooms from outside. They soon spotted the study. The window appeared to be shut but Victoria could just get her fingers under the frame and raise it a little. She squeezed in. There was only the light from the hall to see by, but that was enough.

She let down the lid of the desk and saw a row of pigeon holes inside. In one of them was a bundle of letters. She took them out to the hall to make sure they were what she wanted.

'So that's how it happened,' she told Charlotte. 'Algie wrapped them up and paid Wilfred sixpence to deliver them.'

'I don't know how you dared,' said Charlotte, gasping at the thought of Victoria actually invading her father's sanctum.

'I like a bit of a risk. Wouldn't be in

the pudd'n' club if I didn't, would I?'

'But why do this for *me*, Victoria?'

'You're not going to tell me you're sorry you've got the letters, I hope,' Victoria said with a characteristic sniff.

'Of course I'm not. I was getting so low, not hearing anything and wondering if I ever would. But to think you—oh, I don't know how I can ever thank you properly.'

'You was getting run down. Me and Clarice both saw that. It's been very hard for you. We're used to roughing it but you're not.'

'No, but I have Richard to think of all the time—the only hard bit is being out of touch with him. I shall tell him all about your goodness to me as soon as ever I can.'

'Stuff it! Ask me to your wedding if you want to give me a treat.'

'I will. Would you be my bridesmaid?'

'I don't think I'll be the right shape,' Victoria said.

They looked at each other, burst out laughing and couldn't stop. The sound of their merriment caused two dreary-looking women to comment that it was lucky some people had something to laugh about.

Later on Charlotte found Clarice and her aunt in the same state of bewilderment as when she'd left them that morning.

They'd had nothing to eat all day and had spent the time going over and over the fate that had overwhelmed them.

So many things fell into place. The diamond ring, the brooch, the extravagant outings, the presents.

'Like Robin Hood,' Aunt Cassie said, but all Clarice could say was that she couldn't bear it and would probably go mad.

'I always noticed how quiet he moved,' observed Aunt Cassie. 'Went upstairs on tiptoe. You never heard him coming or going.'

'You never said.'

'What difference would it have made if I had?'

'None, of course.'

Charlotte spread out the food she had brought, washed the cups which still had this morning's dregs in them, made fresh tea and persuaded them to come to the table and at least try to eat a little.

'You're very good to us,' Aunt Cassie said.

'It's nothing.'

'It's a lot, my dear.'

'We must get Clarice well. She was missed at work today.'

'You hear that, Clarice?' Aunt Cassie was trying to rouse her niece.

'You'll come to work tomorrow, won't

217

you?' Charlotte urged.

'No. Not ever again.'

'But what about your wages?'

'I'd sooner starve. I can't go back to Last's and face all the pity. And the shame. Some of those girls envied me green, with my rich fiancé and the good times he gave me. They'll be as pleased as Punch about this.'

She was different from the Clarice they knew, her white face disfigured by tears. She was hardly able to grasp the truth of the calamity that had struck, with Herbert Blades snatched away, leaving nothing of himself. And yet there were the comfortable chairs, the great bed in which she and Aunt Cassie slept so well—all these were gifts from him. She thought of his kind eyes looking into hers as he told her how much he loved her and spoke of the home and children they would have. They both wanted a family. And she wept again because she had set her heart on these things.

'I wonder what was in that envelope he gave you?' Aunt Cassie's question jerked her out of her reverie. She fetched the envelope and opened it.

'It's a pawn ticket!' exclaimed Aunt Cassie. 'What's he got in hock, I wonder?'

'You'll find out if you go and ask,' said Clarice stonily.

'That I will,' Aunt Cassie said.

Charlotte left them very late that night with a promise to return the following evening. She walked back to Mrs Blunt's, half running most of the way as she was so frightened of the drunks lurching about and the men trying to bar her way as they made suggestions she was beginning to understand only too well.

'I hope you're not turning into a night bird.' Mrs Blunt, grim in the hall, gave her a searching look and decided it was more likely she had been on an errand of mercy.

Next day the workrooms were buzzing with the news. It was in the papers. Herbert Blades had been up in court charged with stealing jewellery. He would be tried at the Old Bailey.

'That'll put a certain young lady's nose out of joint,' remarked Miss Prescot.

'I hope you're not pleased about it,' said Madame Last. 'You look a sight happier than usual.'

'So I should. The war's nearly over.'

'I suppose your young man will be coming home from South Africa then?'

Who's a cat now? thought Miss Prescot, but she said nothing and gathered up a batch of the illustrated monthlies Madame took in order to know what was going on in society.

The girls enjoyed looking at them in their dinner break. So did Miss Prescot, and in a fairly recent one she noticed photographs of some pieces of jewellery stolen from the country house of a certain Mrs Graham, who also had a house in Curzon Street. She wondered if these had been appropriated by Mr Blades and felt quite excited. She took it in to show Victoria and Charlotte. Neither of them said a word, but they recognised the brooch Mr Blades had given Clarice and refused to let her wear until it was reset to the design he favoured.

'I don't know how I managed not to gasp,' said Victoria as soon as Miss Prescot left them.

'Neither do I. We saw it that night he took us all out.' This led to a flood of recollections about Mr Blades: his attire, his various tiepins, his gifts to Clarice and the generous outings they had all enjoyed.

'There was certainly something about him,' Victoria said. 'He won't look so good in broad arrows.'

Charlotte shuddered at the thought. She didn't know how to wait for the day to be over. Once more she bought food and hurried to Aunt Cassie's.

It didn't come as a great surprise to learn that the pawnbroker's ticket related to the brooch Mr Blades had given Clarice. Aunt Cassie had seen it in his shop that very morning and Charlotte told them there was no doubt it belonged to Mrs Graham, from whom so much had been stolen.

'She can have the ticket for all the good it is to us,' Clarice said. 'Herbert must have been pushed for cash. I can't think why he didn't sell it.'

'He meant it for you, dearie. He pawned it so he could get it back,' Aunt Cassie said.

Clarice sunk her head in her hands. What was she to think? And what was he thinking, shut up in a prison cell? Were his thoughts of her?

'We'll be well shot of that ticket,' Aunt Cassie said. 'You'd better take it to her, Clarice. Soon as you feel fit enough to go out.'

'I couldn't,' Clarice quailed at the very idea. 'Would you take it, Charlotte? As a special favour. Would you?'

Charlotte had to consent, although she wasn't happy about it. Clarice was in enough trouble and in no state to call on an aristocratic lady and present her with a pawn ticket for a stolen brooch.

After work the next day Charlotte went home, put on her best blouse with the Brussels lace panels, her black velvet bolero and the ostrich feather hat.

'My, you do look a gun,' said Victoria.

It was true. Charlotte looked enchanting, and no one would know she had holes in her shoes. Luckily it wasn't raining.

At Mrs Graham's house she was shown into a large drawing room when she told the butler she had called about some missing jewellery and gave him her name.

She sat in the corner of one of the sofas and was much too worried to notice her surroundings. It was difficult enough trying to remember the words she had so carefully rehearsed.

Mrs Graham did not keep her waiting. She was a middle aged lady who still retained much of the beauty that had distinguished her in her youth.

Charlotte rose and whatever she had intended to say went straight out of her head. She stood there trying to summon words that wouldn't come.

'Miss Grant? I believe you have some news for me.' Mrs Graham's voice was as pleasant as her appearance.

'Do sit down,' she went on, and when Charlotte was seated: 'Is this visit connected with the jewellery that was advertised in the *Illustrated London News?*'

'Yes. It's the brooch,' Charlotte replied. 'It was given to a friend of mine some time ago.'

'Given? By whom?'

'The man she was to have married, but now...' She faltered, dried up and could only say how sorry she was. She was just beginning to realise how deeply she was involved with Clarice, with Aunt Cassie and even with Mr Blades, and it was not like anything she had ever imagined.

To support herself independently until she and Richard could be reunited had been her one and only object when she left home. Now she was mixed up with large-scale burglary and was so apprehensive she almost wished herself back at Lancaster Gate.

Mrs Graham was speaking in a calm, soothing manner. She did not show the surprise she felt at the sight of this unusually lovely, elegant young lady giving her such a strange piece of information. For a moment she wondered if the girl was making it up, seeking notice like people who confessed to crimes they had never committed just for the notoriety. But there was the envelope with the pawn ticket.

She began to question her about this, and before long most of the story came out. It intrigued her. It was easy to see that Charlotte was not cut out to be a workroom girl. The way she spoke, the clothes she wore, even the way she sat showed she was a girl of gentle birth from a good home.

'I want to know a great deal more about this poor friend of yours,' Mrs Graham said. 'Is she dependent on her wages?'

'Entirely. Her aunt earns a few pence scrubbing, but that's all.'

'I see. And may I ask why you are taking so much interest in her?'

'We work together at Madame Last's and she was so kind to me when I started. If it had not been for me, or rather if my father had not set the police on to my friends because his house was entered and something of no importance to him taken away, this would never have happened.'

Mrs Graham didn't ask for an explanation, although she wanted one. It must wait for another time.

'And that makes you feel responsible for Clarice?'

'I *am* responsible.' Charlotte was positive about it.

'But don't you think your friend is better off without this man—this thief?'

'Oh, I can't think of Mr Blades as a thief! I suppose he must be but he was so kind. And very helpful to me. He loved Clarice dearly, I'm sure he did. And does.'

A young man came in, saw that his mother was engaged and was about to go out again when she stopped him.

'Edward. This young lady has brought me some astonishing news. I think we may recover my brooch.'

'Golly! How topping,' he said, his eyes on Charlotte.

'Miss Grant has been with me for a long time now and I'm sure she's tired, so I'll tell you all about it later. Perhaps you'd see about a cab to take her home.'

'Please, not a cab. I always walk,' Charlotte intervened quickly.

'It's much too late to walk through the streets,' said Mrs Graham, realising that Charlotte was afraid she would have to pay the fare. 'Edward, dear, I think you can arrange things.'

'Right, Ma,' he said, and left them. Charlotte rose but Mrs Graham laid a hand on her arm, rang the bell and gave the butler an order.

'You must have some refreshment before you go,' she said. 'I suspect you came without your supper.'

Charlotte had only had a slice of stale cake since her midday dinner. She was exhausted and when a tray was brought in and set before her she realised how hungry she was. A wing of roast chicken with a most delectable salad. Some fruit jelly. A glass of sherry. Just what Mrs

Vickery would have served to anyone out of sorts.

'Oh dear.' Charlotte pressed her handkerchief to her lips. 'Oh dear!' She had difficulty in keeping back the tears at the thought of Mrs Vickery and the maids all comfortable at home.

Mrs Graham guessed there was still a lot she didn't know, and felt a strong interest in this attractive girl who seemed to be caught up in a serious scrape. She said soothing things, encouraged her to eat and, by asking judicious questions, gradually elicited most of what she wanted to know. It unrolled before her eyes: she saw the household at Lancaster Gate, the overbearing father, the arranged marriage, and the young musician whose ring Charlotte wore.

If Charlotte had only known, she could have told Mrs Graham that Richard was in Rome, a city he loved but could take no pleasure in because he was so miserable about her.

He mooched up the Spanish Steps every day and through the gardens of the Pincian Hill, simply for the exercise, not for the beauty of what was to be seen.

He would have appreciated it if she had been with him, and when his tour began he kept a journal to show her, although even then he feared she might not have his itinerary and that if her father confiscated his letters she wouldn't know where he was.

He chewed over the problem with Mary practically every day, and she too feared Charlotte wasn't receiving his letters. It was an impossible state of affairs.

'Write to the cook. Vickery. Wasn't that her name?' she suggested.

'Mr Grant wouldn't give it to her when he saw it came from me.'

'I don't suppose he would. I wish you could go back but there's no time between engagements. Not until June.' She was consulting their diary. 'You could snatch a week in June.'

'I mean to.'

They were at breakfast in their hotel suite. A servant brought the newspapers and the morning's post.

'One for you from London,' Mary said, handing it to him. It was from the music publishers for whom he had already transcribed a series of songs and operatic arias for the piano. Now they wanted more. He handed it across the table.

'It's a very generous offer. Will you accept?' she asked.

'Perhaps. I don't know. I hoped it was from her, though I bet her writing doesn't look like that.'

Mary noticed how tired he looked, how on edge. He spent hour after hour practising and his technique was superlative, but there was so much more to his playing. She had never known any other accompanist to be in such accord with the soloist as Richard, or to interpret the composer's music as he did. Other singers heard and wanted him. There were several extremely able accompanists around but none had Richard's touch, and Mary could see him as pre-eminent in the field before he was much older.

That Mr Grant! To be spurned by such a philistine. He'll lick Richard's boots in the end, she thought, and she walked up and down the room trying to control her indignation.

'What's the matter?' Richard asked.

'Charlotte's father is the matter,' she said.

'Don't I know it!' He seized his hat and went out. Up and down those damned Spanish Steps again, trying, trying to decide what to do.

But Charlotte knew nothing of what was going on in Rome. She told Mrs Graham a good deal about her problem, she even told her how she thought of Richard at a fixed time every day and trusted he still thought of her.

'I'm sure he does,' said Mrs Graham.

'It's a pact and a very good one. You mustn't let doubt creep in.'

'I won't,' said Charlotte, sitting up very straight. '*That* I won't,' she said with great determination, just as Edward returned to say the carriage was ready to take Miss Grant home.

'Now I want you to bring your friend to see me as soon as she feels equal to it,' said Mrs Graham, reverting to the subject of Clarice. 'You will do that, won't you?'

Charlotte promised. Mr Graham escorted her to the carriage, handed her in and surprised her by getting in too.

'There isn't any need to accompany me,' she said.

'I want to.'

Although she would have preferred to go home alone Edward Graham was such pleasant company she found herself enjoying the journey, especially when he enthused about the motor car he had scraped up enough money to buy.

'Practically new,' he said. 'Only made last year but the fellow who sold it to me wanted the latest thing so I got it second hand. It goes like anything.'

'What colour?' she asked.

'Yellow. It's a Sunbeam.'

'How apt. I've never been in a motor. It must be thrilling to have an engine instead of a horse.'

'Instead of several horses,' he said. 'A bit nippy, this weather, though. There never was such a beastly cold spring. When it warms up a bit you'll have to let me take you for a tootle.'

'I'd love that.'

'Then I'll call one afternoon.'

'It will have to be a Saturday. I work all the week, you see.'

'You *work?*' He didn't believe her.

'At a court dressmaker's. I'm a needlewoman.'

'Go on!'

'Truly.'

'But you—well, you don't seem the sort. I don't know any girls who go out to work—except servants, of course.'

'I'm in the same boat as servants. If I didn't earn I'd starve.'

He was still unconvinced. 'There are a few debs who go slumming, I've heard. Trying to find out how the other half lives, I suppose.'

'I could tell them. I don't do it from charitable motives. Simply to keep myself.'

''Pon my word, do you really?'

They had left the fashionable streets of Mayfair and reached the less salubrious area in which Mrs Blunt's house was situated. Silence had fallen between them and Charlotte thought her revelation had made Mr Graham recoil. Perhaps he

230

did not wish to pursue an acquaintance with a working-class girl, and that was understandable. Young men of his station in life simply did not mix with the lower orders and would not feel comfortable with them.

The carriage drew up at her door. Mrs Blunt's house was clean but drab, with one small gaslight in the hall and skimpy curtains. There was an immeasurable gulf between her house and the Grahams' in Curzon Street.

The coachman alighted and had knocked at the front door before Charlotte could stop him. Mr Graham handed her out.

'Thank you. Good night,' she said.

Mrs Blunt was at the door, peering at them.

'I say,' he was shaking her hand, 'I think you're an absolute corker! Going out to work! You're one in a thousand.' There was no mistaking his admiration.

'Not in a thousand. I'm one of quite a few million working girls,' she said, and sailed in before he could say another word.

Mrs Blunt gave her a searching look. 'Coming up in the world, aren't we?' she said.

'I am not aware that I ever went down,' said Charlotte, proud to be what she was.

Clarice thought about Herbert Blades until she was dizzy. She tried to imagine what must have been going through his mind. Did he really believe his crimes would go undetected for as long as he lived? Had he ever thought of what life would be like for her if he were to be caught? Sometimes she almost choked with anger at the way she had allowed herself to be duped. And yet. One of the worst things was the effect of his unmasking on Aunt Cassie. The poor old thing had to take on more charring: Charlotte had been keeping them in food, always bringing in things she knew they liked—fish and chips, meat pies, cheese, butter, screws of tea—but it was high time they paid their own way.

One day Clarice looked in the glass and what she saw made her decide to act. She must straighten her back, grit her teeth and find work. There was plenty of it about, with the Coronation so close, but she couldn't go back to Madame Last. The first thing was to see this Mrs Graham and get that over. She decided to brave it and go alone. And she wouldn't go crawling either. Herbert had treated her to good shoes, fine kid gloves and a fashionable skirt. She always had blouses. The workroom girls made them when things were slack, hiding them on their laps under the tablecloth if Miss Prescot was about.

By the time she was ready, with her hair arranged in a bunch of curls at the back and her hat just so, she looked, as Herbert would have said, fit to kill.

The walk to Curzon Street did her good, but when she reached the house she almost wished Charlotte was with her. It took so much courage to approach the imposing front door and lift the knocker.

She stood as tall as she could, gave the butler her name and said that Mrs Graham had invited her to call. He asked her to step in, as though he knew she was expected.

Mrs Graham came almost immediately. In appearance she was just as Charlotte had described her: softly waved grey hair, a lovely face with a touch of rouge on the cheeks. But the striking thing was her gracious manner, her way of putting Clarice at her ease.

'I'm very glad you've come to see me,' she said, shepherding Clarice into the drawing room.

'Charlotte—Miss Grant, I mean—told me you would like me to come,' Clarice said.

'I thought it so good of you to let me have the ticket when you could easily have destroyed it. My brooch means a great deal to me for sentimental reasons.'

'I'm sorry Mr Blades ever gave it to me,' said Clarice. 'Not that he let me keep it for long.'

'So I understand from Miss Grant. But don't let's talk of it now. I know you've had a dreadful shock and are under great strain now. That's what concerns me.'

'It's all come to nothing! I wanted—oh, I did so want! And it's my poor aunt, too. I've let it get me down. You see, so much was promised.' Clarice made a tremendous effort to control her agitation. 'Still, we managed before Mr Blades came along and we'll manage again,' she said, but she was trembling as the reality of her situation smote her yet again. She was penniless, weak, ill, and if she couldn't work, couldn't earn, what was there for Aunt Cassie but the workhouse? The thought of that froze her blood.

She could not have told anyone how she felt or described her fears, but the little she said, the hesitations, the flashes of courage, the black despair were all there for Mrs Graham to see. If anybody ever wanted help it was this poor, proud, disenchanted girl.

'Are you seeking work?' she asked.

'I'm about to,' said Clarice. 'This is the first day I've been out since Mr Blades—since I found out about him and

234

it got in the papers. I can't go back to Madame Last. I just can't. I shall look for work where no one knows anything about me.'

'Would you like to come here as my sewing woman? There's a surprising amount of needlework to be done in a family like mine. The woman I've employed for many years has just retired, so her post is vacant.'

'Are you offering it to *me?*'

'If we can come to terms, and if you prove suitable.'

Clarice was too surprised to speak. A little colour came into her face and her eyes brightened as Mrs Graham outlined what her duties would be. She was to have a little room with a sewing machine; a midday meal and high tea would be provided; she would come for five days a week from nine in the morning until six in the evening and have Saturdays and Sundays free. Her pay would be half as much again as she earned at Madame Last's.

'This is wonderful! How can I ever thank you?' she cried.

Mrs Graham smiled and told her not to try. She had never seen anyone change so quickly, for Clarice was full of hope now. Her confidence was returning. She had an object in life.

'Aunt Cassie won't have to go charring any more. Oh, she will be so glad.'

Mrs Graham did not need more thanks than that.

Charlotte had good cause to be pleased with Clarice's visit to Mrs Graham. It proved they had been right to give her the pawn ticket. But just as she pined to hear from Richard, so did Clarice long to see Mr Blades. She missed him at every turn, and when she was told how lucky she was to have escaped marrying a hardened criminal she didn't answer. There was sadness in her face and a much deeper sadness in her heart, grateful though she was for her post at Mrs Graham's.

But Herbert! The ache was physical. Aunt Cassie understood. 'Remember the good things, dearie,' she said.

Clarice straightened her back, held her head high. 'I shall always love Mr Blades,' she said. 'Don't let no one ever doubt that.'

Charlotte missed Clarice at work, and so did Victoria. Neither of them liked Miss Sharp, who was engaged to take her place. She had a thin face, prominent teeth, a spiteful nature and no sense of humour.

The atmosphere in their workroom changed. Miss Sharp said Algie fancied himself as a lady's man and any girl who trusted him would be out of her wits. Consequently Victoria couldn't mention him in her presence and he didn't come in so often.

Miss Sharp very soon gathered that Charlotte's fiancé was abroad. The idea of having a young man who left the country and never told you when he would be back cast serious doubt on his sincerity, she said. She threw out plenty more nasty hints as the days went by.

'Of course we can all have an absent sweetheart,' she said one morning, 'but when we don't get a letter or a message or anything for months on end it makes people wonder.'

'Wonder what?' demanded Charlotte.

'Wonder if there's any such person as him that's supposed to be abroad.'

'Are you implying that my fiancé doesn't exist?'

'Put the cap on if it fits.'

Charlotte wanted to shake her till her teeth fell out but Victoria intervened. 'Miss Prescot forgot to put her milk down today. Cats get nasty without it. Especially them that can't get a tom,' she said.

Charlotte got on with her sewing. Victoria could be trusted to cap Miss Sharp's malicious thrusts but it didn't compensate for the friendliness that had warmed her heart ever since she began working at Madame Last's, and she viewed the prospect before her with some despondency and the weekends at Nanny's as so many oases on her way through the desert to Richard.

She usually spent the first part of Saturday afternoons attending to her wardrobe, mending stockings, cutting out cardboard insoles for shoes that had worn into holes and washing blouses and underwear in the basement scullery.

The latter was not an easy operation if Mr Blunt happened to be about. He would come and offer to turn the mangle for her, and when she told him she wouldn't dream of letting anything of hers near it he said he could wring the things out by hand and why wouldn't she let him?

'No thank you,' she said.

'Go on.'

'Certainly not.'

'I see 'em on the line, don't I?' He nudged his shoulder against hers. 'Tickly frills and things.'

'Go away, you horrible old man.'

'Come on. Give us a kiss.'

'Don't be ridiculous. Go and ask your wife for a kiss if you want one.'

'Kiss her what's got a chin like an old scrubbing brush?'

There was no need for Charlotte to respond, for Mrs Blunt was on her way.

'Valentine!' she bawled. 'Come out of that scullery before I fetch you one.'

Charlotte shook with laughter over Mr Blunt's inappropriate name. He should have been Bert, Bill or Sid—anything but Valentine. What was more, Mrs Blunt had a quart beer bottle in her hand and looked ready to use it as a truncheon. She was short and spare, her husband twice her size, but he cowered before her.

'I heard you,' she said. 'I heard what you said about Miss Grant's drawers.'

'Never mentioned her drawers.'

'Thought it though. I know all about your sinful thoughts.'

'Must have some yourself or you wouldn't know,' he muttered.

'You don't leave this house today, Valentine,' said Mrs Blunt. 'You won't find your boots no matter how you search.'

'What have you done with them? Where are they?'

'Uncle's minding them till Monday. Where else was I to get the two bob for our vittles?'

The couple were retreating from the scullery and up the basement stairs, quarrelling all the way. What had she done with the lodgers' rent? he demanded. Paid the landlord, hadn't she, and why didn't he go out and earn? How could he with no boots?

It sounded like a comic turn and Charlotte could laugh at it but she also saw the grim side of their lives. There was no colour, no singing, no joy, and it made her shudder for fear Richard never came back and she had to go on scraping to survive until she was too old to work any longer.

Some of the senior hands at Madame Last's, neatly dressed and spotlessly clean though they were, spent day after monotonous day without hope. It wasn't life, it was mere existence, but although they felt sad and endured hardship they could laugh and joke among themselves. She feared she wouldn't be like that if she ever shared their fate.

She was leading this life by her own choice, but could she have done it if she had not had a dazzling star on her horizon? It was not a comfortable thought.

By mid-afternoon she was ready to go to Nanny's. The miserable weather was improving and getting warmer, so it was good to be out. She noticed a young man on the pavement outside—a very nattily dressed young man pretending to read a newspaper.

It was Edward Graham.

She hesitated. He raised his hat. 'Good afternoon. I just happened to be passing,' he said.

'And I just happened to be coming out. What a strange coincidence.'

'Is that what you call it?' He had a rather impish grin and very lively eyes. 'My motor's round the corner,' he said.

'Well, fancy that!'

'I wondered if you'd like to come for a spin?'

'That's just what I'm doing. Spinning off to Hammersmith.'

'Let me drive you there,' he offered.

As a well-brought-up young lady she should have refused—in a motor with a man, unchaperoned: whatever next? But she was a working girl now, so she could jump at it, and she did.

'I don't know what my fiancé would say if he could see me,' she said.

'Is he likely to?'

'No, worse luck. He's abroad.'

Mr Graham helped her into the car, which wasn't much more than a box on four wheels. Its chief recommendation was novelty as it couldn't boast of comfort or of speed, but it was fun and his pleasure and pride in it amused and rather touched her. He obviously expected her to be impressed, so she pretended to be.

They drove down Park Lane to Knightsbridge and on to Kensington, and Charlotte kept on thinking how much faster she could have got there by bus, or better still, the underground.

Edward Graham seemed to be lost in thought for a long time. She supposed he was concentrating on his driving but presently he said: 'So you're to be married?'

'Yes, before the end of the year,' she said.

'Then why on earth are you slaving in a dressmaker's? Are you an orphan?'

'Good gracious, no. I'm a refugee.'

'Oh, come on. You're pulling my leg.' He sounded quite hurt so she couldn't resist telling him why she had run away. Perhaps she shouldn't have told a young man she hardly knew so much about herself, but that was the best of it. He was a stranger, and a stranger was a listening post. She even told him about Nanny and what a help and blessing she had been. 'I don't know what I'd have done if she hadn't been there for me to run to when I left home.'

'I wish I'd known you then,' he said. 'Still, I'm here now and if you ever need any help you will ask me, won't you?'

'That's really generous.'

'I mean it.'

He thought Charlotte by far the most attractive girl he had ever met. She was lovely to look at, and courageous as well.

She had taken an enormous risk when she walked out of her comfortable home and threw in her lot with people who might well have resented her. He liked the sprightly way she countered his remarks, warmed to her innocent flirtatiousness and hoped he wouldn't fall too desperately in love. It was clear no one stood a chance against this Richard Allen she kept talking about. It was Richard this or Richard that all the time.

They had almost reached their destination and were in a crowded narrow street. He had to drive with great care as people were all over the road, hurrying in the same direction. Something was wrong, it was in the air. An accident, the unhealthy curiosity that drives people to look at a person mangled under cartwheels, was drawing them along. Towards a lamppost.

Charlotte had a sickening premonition.

'Stop. Please stop!' she cried, and she scrambled out and started to run with all the others.

The rope had broken. The children who had been swinging round the lamppost were standing still, and sprawled in the road lay a child in a pretty dress.

'Lily!'

Charlotte was on her knees in the gutter. 'Lily.' There was no movement.

The crowd parted for a woman, who

knelt by the child, felt her pulse, her heart. She was Lizzie Wilson, the local midwife, and everyone knew her. Charlotte clutched her arm. 'Can't you do anything?'

'I wish I could.'

Charlotte had Lily's hand in hers and it was warm. She couldn't be dead. Mustn't be.

Women in the crowd were saying it was Lily Goode, her that was slow-witted. Her that wasn't allowed to play in the street.

A doctor was there now, making an examination. Lily had cracked her head on the sharp edge of the kerbstone. She'd swung ever so high—the children were beginning to talk, telling the doctor—right over the road she went.

That was when Will Goode, on his way home from work, stopped to see what was happening. Charlotte would never forget the look on his face when he saw it was his daughter lying on the ground. Her fair hair, blue ribbon, blood.

The doctor and midwife were trying to tell him what had happened; the children who had seen the whole thing spoke in chorus. She swung right out, she did, and the rope broke. The rope broke. The rope broke.

He didn't speak. Didn't hear. He gathered Lily up, and Charlotte knew he would carry her home, and she ran,

ran, faster, gasping, breath gone.

Nanny was at the door. She had just realised Lily was not in the house and was looking anxiously up the road as Charlotte stumbled up to her, saying something about an accident and trying to lead her inside before they came. But it was too late. Will was there, and behind him the men and women who had gathered at the lamppost.

Will laid Lily on the horsehair sofa in the best room. He tried to smooth back her hair, chafe the hands that were growing cold.

In the hall the doctor and Lizzie Wilson were conferring with a constable.

'...inquest...'

'...mortuary...'

The voices were low but Will heard.

'You're not taking my Lily to a mortuary,' he shouted. 'She'd be frightened.'

'She won't know,' said Lizzie gently.

'Get out of here. Get out! Get out, the lot of you!'

They left together.

Nanny hadn't spoken. Her face was ashen and she didn't answer when Charlotte coaxed her to sit down. It was frightening not to be able to get through to her, not to know what to do. There were things to be done but she had no idea how to go about any of it. There was no one to ask. Dusk was beginning to fall. At least she could close the front door.

As she did so she saw Edward Graham by the gate. She had forgotten all about him.

'Isn't there any way I can help?' he asked.

'Could you take a message?'

'Of course.'

She wanted Mrs Vickery to be told. As Nanny's oldest and dearest friend she was the one to give comfort.

'Would you go to her?' Charlotte asked. 'I know she'll come when you tell her what's happened. You'd better go to the side door. Do you mind?'

He was anxious to do anything for this stricken family who meant so much to Charlotte. 'But what about you?' he asked. 'Will you be going back to town tonight? May I call for you?'

'Thank you, but I shall stay here until Sunday evening,' she said.

The quiet in the house was overpowering. In the ordinary way Nanny and Will would be talking, Lily would be trying to use the abacus or laboriously copying pothooks and hangers on her slate, murmuring under her breath as she did so. There would be the chink of china, the kettle singing, the scrape of chairs as they were pushed back from the table.

There was noise enough outside. People from the surrounding streets were drawn to the house by a miserable kind of excitement.

Mrs Vickery lost no time in coming, for Mr and Mrs Grant were out to dinner, as they usually were on Saturdays, and she was free.

The news Mr Graham brought her came as a complete shock, and she knew it would shatter Will. His devotion to Lily touched her heart whenever she saw them together, but part of the sadness was caused by his imperishable belief that the girl would improve. He really thought Lily would gain the wits she lacked as time went by. She looked lovely, she tried hard, she could read three-letter words—with time she would be as bright as other children. She was only a bit slow, he said.

Nanny knew he was deluded and often told Mrs Vickery so. What's to become of her when I die or if he dies? was her constant question. At least that worry had gone, thought Mrs Vickery, as she pushed her way through the mob outside the house. At the front door she turned round and addressed them.

'This isn't a peepshow. It's a house of mourning. Go home, all of you.'

'Ain't they bringing her out?'

'No they are not. Go away and give this family peace and quiet.'

'Ain't nobody going to *say* anything?'

'*I'm* saying something. I'm asking you to show respect for the dead and pity for the living by going away.'

Muttering among themselves, they began to disperse.

Charlotte had heard the whole exchange for she had the door open a crack, and now she flung it wide and hugged Mrs Vickery. 'I'm so thankful you've come. Nanny hasn't said a word and I don't know what to do.'

'Leave it to me, my dear.' Mrs Vickery took off her bonnet and shawl, went into the kitchen and sat beside Nanny, whose face was buried in her hands.

'I've come to lend a bit of help, Nanny,' she said gently, patting her friend's arm as she spoke.

Nanny looked up. 'It was my fault,' she said.

'What do you mean?'

'I nodded off after we'd had our dinner.'

'No wonder. You were tired. We all drop off now we're getting on in years.'

'*I* don't. I have to keep awake to see she doesn't slip out. I should have bolted the door. She can't reach the top bolt. How am I to bear the guilt of it?'

'There isn't any guilt. You fall asleep and Lily takes advantage. She wants to play with the others. There's no guilt on anybody.'

'Her father won't believe that. He'll never forgive me.'

'Don't say that, Nanny. It isn't true.'

'Oh, I don't know. I just don't know how I could have forgotten to do it.' Nanny bowed her head in her hands again and Mrs Vickery went on trying to console her.

Charlotte heard a soft rap at the front door and found Lizzie Wilson outside. 'Mr Goode's in no state to see to things so I took the liberty of calling on the undertaker for him,' she said. 'Are you a relation?'

'No. Just a friend. I'm staying here.'

Mrs Wilson went into the kitchen and Charlotte heard Nanny say: 'I knew you'd come, Lizzie. You brought her into the world and now you're going to see her out of it.'

There was more murmuring, then Mrs Vickery joined Charlotte in the hall. 'We can make ourselves useful,' she said. 'We'll put fresh sheets on Lily's bed.'

They made the bed between them, and doing so gave Charlotte an almost eerie feeling. She had shared this bed with Lily every Saturday night for a long time now, and the thought of the girl lying there alone, stiff and cold, sent shivers through her. Her tears began to stream, and Mrs Vickery was crying too. They sat on the bed with their arms round each other and wept.

'It does you good to cry,' said Mrs Vickery at last.

'Sometimes I feel so sad. I miss you all so much and I'm so worried at not hearing from Richard.' She had been elated when she talked to Edward Graham in the motor, but now, overcome by sorrow, tiny doubts began to surface. 'Do you think he's forgotten me, Mrs Vickery?'

'You know he hasn't, Miss Charlotte. He's as true to you as you are to him,' said Mrs Vickery stoutly.

'Oh, I do hope so.'

They went on talking, grieving for Nanny and Will in their sorrow, going from one thing to another, the funeral, weddings, music, Richard, it was all mixed up, the joy and the sorrow.

'Lily always wanted to try on my hat,' Charlotte said.

'Ah, she knew there was something not quite right, although she couldn't say so,' Mrs Vickery said.

They talked until the time came for Mrs Vickery to go, as it was late and dark.

'Nanny darling, would you rather I went too?' Charlotte asked.

'No. Stay and be a comfort to me,' Nanny said.

So Charlotte accompanied Mrs Vickery to the bus, saw her safely on board and then walked back through streets that were now quiet and deserted. She hated passing the lamppost but there was no other way, and she thought of Will having to pass it every day.

It was impossible not to be weighed down by the hush indoors. Will kept vigil beside Lily all night and all the next day, while Charlotte stayed with Nanny and made endless cups of tea for the friends who called to condole.

By the time Charlotte left, as dusk was gathering on Sunday, Nanny was beginning to recover from the worst effects of the shock and to talk more philosophically. Charlotte refused to let her come to the bus stop, as it meant passing the fatal lamppost. She felt intensely sad as she left and didn't look forward to the journey home, but when she reached the gate she found Edward Graham waiting.

'I didn't like to think of you going home alone after such a sad visit,' he said. 'We can get a cab at the Broadway.'

It was a cold, miserable evening. 'Take my arm,' he said.

Mrs Blunt was out in the hall the moment

she heard Charlotte's key in the door that Sunday evening.

'There's some flowers come for you,' she said.

Mingling with the unmistakable smell of cabbage was the scent of roses, and there, stuck in the umbrella stand, was an enormous bunch with large heads of wide-open flowers.

'There's a letter with them,' said Mrs Blunt. In fact there were two. One in a sealed envelope; the other written hastily in pencil folded and tucked into itself.

'Who brought them?' Charlotte was in a tizz.

'Young fellow with a little pointed beard,' said Mrs Blunt, thus dispelling the hope that it was Richard.

Mrs Blunt had watched him get out of a cab and come up to her door carrying the roses and a violin case. She sized him up as one of those street musicians who put their hats down on the pavement and are told to move on by the police.

'We don't take fiddlers here,' she told him.

'Madam, I do not wish to be taken. I wish to see Miss Grant,' he said in heavily accented English.

'Ho. Wait outside *if* you please,' she said, closing the door on him and calling up the stairs for Miss Grant, who didn't answer as she wasn't there.

Mrs Blunt told the fiddler so. No, she had no idea where Miss Grant had gone, she went off Sat'day and came back Sunday night.

'Alas!' he said and hit his forehead with his hand. He thrust the roses into Mrs Blunt's arms.

'I had a right job to understand him, he spoke so thick,' Mrs Blunt told Charlotte. 'He said the roses and the letter was from a Mr Allen.'

Charlotte picked up the roses and sat on the bottom stair. To think, oh to think that she had missed Richard's messenger.

'What else did he say?'

'He said Mr Allen wanted news of you partickler and was you quite well, so I said to the best of my knowledge the young lady's in the pink. Anyhow, he couldn't stop as he was on his way to Manchester to play with a trout.'

The Trout. Oh, the Trout! There was music in Charlotte's ears.

'Funny place to go fishing,' remarked Mrs Blunt.

'Yes, isn't it.' On an impulse Charlotte pulled a rose out of the bunch, gave it to Mrs Blunt and ran up to her room. She was out of breath when she got there, fumbled for the matches, lit the gas and tore open the envelope.

My dear, darling, precious Charlotte,

At last! These months without a word have been unbearable and I was half-demented with worry about you and imagined all kinds of things had happened. Then your long, wonderful letter came and sent me straight to heaven. How crazy we've both been! I for not giving you my itinerary—what happened to it?—you for—no, you are not crazy. You are a marvel and I'm still gasping at the way you walked out, got work and threw in your lot with those poor girls you tell me about. I imagined all kinds of things—nothing like that. I can't wait to get back to you. We'll have our own home and our own fireplace to sit by. The very day your letter came Hans set out for England and there was just time for me to scrawl this and ask him to deliver it so I'd be certain sure you'd get it. Much, much more to follow. Meantime I was, am and will be yours with more love than ever, Richard.

It was too much to take in all at once and she read it over and over and laughed and cried and hugged it to her heart. How she longed to tell someone, but the one to tell was Nanny and that took her thoughts back to the sad little house at Hammersmith.

The other note, which she had forgotten, lay on the table. Hans Braun had written it in the hall and simply said how sorry he was to have missed her. He had left Richard well and in high spirits and he hoped to play the fiddle at their wedding before very long.

This message, slight though it was, brought the future straight into the room. Richard would be back. And when he came she would only have to consider *him*. Nothing and no one could come between them.

At last she heard Victoria coming in and couldn't wait to tell her. 'Oh, what a weekend it's been!' she cried.

'What's up then? Coo! I believe he's wrote!'

'He has. I'm so happy! And so miserable.' She didn't know she was going to cry but that was what happened, for all her emotions seemed to crowd in together: joy, sorrow, fear, bewilderment and sheer physical exhaustion.

'Here, hold on,' said Victoria. 'Let's get the fire alight. I'm froze. Then you can tell me all about it.'

Charlotte couldn't have found a more sympathetic confidante than Victoria, and that evening the companionship they enjoyed deepened into a strong friendship.

Victoria had always been a perkily cheerful character. Even as a three-day-old abandoned baby it was said she soon managed a chuckle, and all through her childhood in the orphanage she kept a stoical outlook and felt sorry for those who allowed their parentless state to turn them into submissive nonentities.

The authorities let them know they were children of shame, for hardly any had been born in wedlock, and consequently they were taught to be humble and subservient to those of an entirely different race who lived in houses, were becomingly dressed and even drove about in horse-drawn carriages.

To rush out with shovel and bucket to scoop up the manure left by these quadrupeds was one of the tasks assigned to sturdier orphans, of whom Victoria was one.

She was the only child who enjoyed it. Never mind the stink if it got you into the street, she said, and to her the street was life.

It wasn't long before she was exchanging banter with passing tradesmen. The coalman who came by daily always had a word with her. He told her she was just like his own little girl and would grow up to be a right pretty lass. He said if she had any sense she'd take a bucket of manure into the next street and sell it to the old women with gardens for a ha'penny.

She took advantage of this advice and managed to sneak away unobserved. The street, which lay behind the orphanage, turned out to be a blind alley and had virtually no traffic. It was called Lordship's Trust.

There were six small houses on either side, occupied by very old women who wore little lace caps and shawls. Each house had a front garden alive with cottage flowers, pinks, mignonette, wallflowers, stock, nasturtiums—not all out at the same time, of course, but each one a revelation to Victoria, for there were never any flowers at the orphanage. She stood and stared. She saw bees going in and out of the flowers in their busy way; she saw a bumble bee and decided he must be the foreman as he was so much bigger and better dressed than the others. She saw a spider in the middle of a web slung between two hollyhocks. She saw a sparrow.

An old woman sitting beside her front door in the sun called out and asked what she wanted.

'A ha'penny for this,' said Victoria, holding up the bucket.

'Come here.'

She opened the gate, went up the flagged path and stood in front of the old woman, goggling. She had never seen anyone so old, clad all in black with a little lace apron, long jet earrings, a gold chain round her neck and an enormous book open on her lap.

'Are you from the orphanage?' she asked.

Victoria nodded.

The old woman felt in her pocket and produced a penny. 'Tip it over there,' she said. 'In the corner.'

Victoria did as she was told and was given the penny and a bull's-eye.

'Bring another bucket tomorrow,' the old woman said. 'Run along now or you'll be missed.'

She got to the gate just as the others were filing in, and the supervisor was so busy shouting orders she didn't even notice that nothing came out of the bucket Victoria tipped up.

She looked back on that day as the one that changed her life. The flowers, the bees, the whole penny and the old ladies of Lordship's Trust who had all been governesses or housekeepers to families of the nobility. Long before any of them had been born, a rich and altruistic peer built the houses for the benefit of his servants when they retired. When Victoria first saw the houses they were over a hundred years old and had all the beauty of antiquity and none of its frailties.

The residents matched their surroundings. They had the mysterious grace conferred by age and experience. Servants they had been, obsequious they never were.

Miss Parker, who gave Victoria the penny and the bull's-eye, was interested in the tough, pretty little girl and realised she would never get very far in the world without more help than the orphanage was likely to provide. She began asking what openings there were. Factory work mostly, with starvation wages and no prospects.

Miss Parker mentioned Victoria to one of the nuns in a nearby convent and was told that help was wanted in sewing plain cassocks. The nuns depended on selling cassocks, vestments and altar cloths to churches and religious orders all over the country.

A great deal of the work was done by voluntary helpers. There was no pay, but it was a unique opportunity to learn. If Miss Parker's protégée, showed any aptitude the sister-in-charge was willing to give her a trial.

Victoria jumped at the chance. It meant being away from the orphanage all day, and when Miss Parker took her to the convent she was almost bewildered by the extraordinary peace that pervaded the place. The nuns spoke quietly, they seemed to glide along the cloisters without a sound. There were no hobnailed boots, no shouted commands, no harsh voices and no horrible smells. Beeswax and incense. It was a world apart.

The sister-in-charge soon saw that the new recruit was capable of more than plain hems and set her to sew on the lace and do simple embroidery. Victoria learned fast and hoped she would eventually be allowed to work on the vestments, for she loved the glowing colours, the richness of the silk and the intricacy of the designs. Cardinal scarlet, emerald green, gold, white with the metallic gleam of silver and gold thread.

All this whetted her appetite for things of beauty, and yet, loving it as she did, she was always aware that this was not her world. She wanted the excitement of the streets, the banter of tradesmen, the whistles of the errand boys, the vitality of life outside the reclusive peace of the convent.

Some of the lady helpers wore stylish clothes in fine materials, and Victoria compared them mentally with her own drab uniform. These ladies were impressed by her application to her work, and one of them suggested she might earn her living in one of the better dressmaking establishments.

She didn't know anything about dressmakers. Everyone in the orphanage, even the overseers, wore uniform, and they told her that when she was sent out to earn her living she would still be in uniform. She would be a skivvy. That or cover buttons at sixpence a day and nothing found, they told her.

Nonsense, said the ladies. Between them they contrived to fit Victoria out in good plain clothes and sent her off to see Madame Last, who engaged her on the spot when shown samples of her work.

'So I wasn't half lucky,' Victoria said when she recounted her progress through life to Charlotte on the evening they exchanged confidences. 'I don't even know who those ladies were, and dear old Miss Parker's gone to heaven. I was thirteen when I came here, and now I'm nearly twenty.'

'And engaged to Madame Last's son,' said Charlotte.

'Ah, who'd have thought it? I haven't done so bad since me bucket and shovel days.'

'You've done wonders.'

'I didn't know who he was the first time he spoke,' said Victoria dreamily, looking into the fire.

261

She had seen Algie Last several times in the street before he bobbed out of an area entrance and raised his hat one day when she was on her way to work.

'You're the prettiest girl I've seen for many a long day,' he said, raised his hat again and scooted.

'He did it for a bet,' the other girls said when she told them.

'Think what you like,' she retorted.

Next day she met him near Madame Last's front door as she went into the staff entrance. He wished her good day and remarked on the beautiful weather.

'It's raining,' she said.

'Seeing you makes it a beautiful day.'

'Go on with you!'

She was used to the backchat of the streets and enjoyed exchanges with the young clerks and artisans in passing, but there was something different about this young man. He managed to cross her path every morning and he always spoke. Once he gave her a bunch of violets. She found herself thinking about him, wondering. One morning she asked him if he worked round that way.

'I live here,' he said, and he took a key from his pocket and put it in the lock of Madame Last's front door.

'You don't!' she exclaimed.

'I do. My name's Algie Last.'

'Tell us another.'

'There isn't one to tell. Honestly.'

'Oh,' she said, and turned away. 'That's all then.'

'Wait. Do wait.'

But she ran to the staff entrance and hurried in, feeling stupid and upset. He'd been having her on. He knew what his mother would say if she discovered he was making up to one of her workroom girls.

If she saw him again she'd tell him straight. There must be no more of it. Having decided upon this she realised how sorry she was. And disappointed. Yes, that was it. Disappointed because she liked him so much and would miss him.

Despite telling herself not to be a fool, and trying to be extra cheerful all day, her efforts made her feel lower still.

It was drizzly and miserable that evening. Her shoes let in water and her coat was getting wetter by the minute. It wouldn't be dry by morning if she couldn't get a bit of fire going. She bought a bundle of firewood at the oilshop. Outside she dropped a penny she couldn't afford to lose, picked it up, slipped it inside her glove and heard someone say: 'You'd better come under my umbrella.'

And there he was, Algie Last, tucking her arm through his, holding her hand, telling her she needn't think it was going to end for he simply must see her every day and if she refused he would be the most miserable wretch on earth.

It was no wonder she succumbed. For the first time in her life she had found someone who honestly cared, and who loved her so much he wanted to marry her. The very idea of that filled her with a happiness she hadn't known existed.

Algie was supposed to be learning the business side of his mother's establishment, not only keeping the books but dealing with manufacturers' representatives and obtaining the best possible terms. As all the advantages of a well-to-do young man were so tempting, he didn't find work to his taste at all and annoyed his parents by skimping it and running up bills.

'We are not a gold mine, Algernon,' his mother told him at regular intervals. 'When you set your mind to your work in earnest we'll pay you a proper salary. Not before.'

He didn't take any of this seriously until Victoria informed him he would be a dad long before Christmas, and even then he shirked telling his mother before the season was over.

'I can't let my skirts out any more. There ain't enough left in the seams,' she eventually told him. 'It's daft to be frightened of your ma. Why should she be any better pleased when the season's over? Let's get married on the q.t. and invite her to the christening.'

'What a brilliant idea. I can't wait to see her at the font,' he said.

They didn't take aimless walks any more. They started looking for unfurnished rooms.

'Now that's really sensible,' said Charlotte, and she took a great interest in the places they saw and the rents asked, because it wouldn't be long before she and Richard were home-hunting too.

Nanny and Will went to Broadstairs soon after Lily's funeral and decided to stay for a fortnight. Nanny told Charlotte there was no sense in stopping at home to mope when a change of scene might work wonders. Lily had been the centre of their lives for a long time but now they must turn their energies in other directions.

When they came back, Will thought about buying a bicycle and joining a cycling club so as to get out of the house on Sundays. Nanny had no trouble filling her time. There were two weddings and a christening to look forward to, and as Charlotte and Victoria worked such long hours she would be happy to do the plain sewing for them.

'And soon I suppose I'll be knitting.

You must think about the layette,' she told Victoria when Charlotte took her to see the flat they had chosen. It was just what they wanted, situated on the fourth floor of a tall house in Clapham. There were two rooms and a tiny kitchen all on the one floor, and as they were at the top no one would be passing their doors. The furniture would be sparse at first, but now that Algie was earning more they could get things gradually. Their first purchase was a double bedstead, iron-framed, with brass knobs. Charlotte bought Victoria a tin of metal polish and some rags, for a joke. Nanny promised a bolster and two pillows; Eustace Bright pitched a yarn to his mother about a poor old couple he knew who hadn't a blanket to their name and was given two quite thick ones. Clarice decided she wouldn't need all the things she had been hoarding in her bottom drawer for years and gave Victoria a set of towels.

It was the beginning of June, and the Coronation was only three weeks away. The weather continued to be cold and damp but the brilliant illuminations brought the crowds out at night and they swarmed about in their thousands. They came up from the country and in from the suburbs, pushing and shoving on the pavements to see the flags and banners waving in the drizzly air.

They came from abroad, too, and the natives elbowed stout Germans and shrill French out of their way as though they had no right there, because it was *their* King who was being crowned.

By now thousands of soldiers were camping in the parks and an unusual number of girls took to strolling past the railings to catch the eyes of the men inside. Naturally they didn't admit it—if asked, they were on their way to the Palace in the hope of glimpsing a foreign royal, for there were plenty of them about.

Charlotte and Victoria were positively cool about all this excitement. Victoria's wedding was far more important to them than any king being crowned, and having to keep it secret added just that touch of risk Victoria liked. It would never do for Madame Last to find out, but as the ceremony was to take place at a dingy little church in Mrs Blunt's locality there wasn't much chance of it.

One thing worried Victoria. There was no one to give her away. Eustace Bright was to be Algie's best man, so he was out, and she didn't know any other men. It was a quandary until Nanny came up with a brilliant idea. What about Will?

Nanny was always ready to help any girl who had made her own way in life, especially if she was alone, as Victoria was.

'A very nice, jolly girl,' she told Will. 'The kind who stands up for herself.'

So it was arranged that Will should give her away, and there would be a small gathering at the Clapham flat afterwards to celebrate.

Victoria went to see Clarice one evening after work to tell her about the arrangements and persuade her to come.

'It won't be much of a do, but it'll be nice because we're all friends, and I don't see myself getting married without you being there, Clarice. After all, you and me, we've been pals a long time, haven't we?'

Clarice agreed, but she was thoroughly miserable over her own blighted prospects, and thought of Herbert Blades every day. She often found herself looking for him in the crowd when she was out of doors and had to remind herself that he was in prison with hair shorn, hands ruined by hard labour, feet in stinking boots and body in a uniform marked with broad arrows.

Of course it was wrong to steal jewellery, or anything else for that matter, but look at the comfort he'd given Aunt Cassie, look at the lovely warm vests he had bought her, and the cosy slippers. And who hadn't done a bit of stealing in their time? Hopped off the bus without paying their fare, used Madame Last's Silko to sew their own garments, got up to all kinds of subterfuges to save a few ha'pence? Who?

Now she was blessed with well-paid employment, a warm room to work in, good meals in the upper servants' dining room. Pleasant company, too. The butler, housekeeper, footmen and head parlourmaid all struck her as very superior, far above the folk she was used to in their manners and conversation.

She had plenty of work, with Mrs Graham's dresses and underwear to make, as well as various garments for the grandchildren and a good deal of mending.

Mrs Graham herself was a most considerate employer, she was never in a rush for things and sometimes sat down for a talk. This beautiful, dignified young woman had been cruelly treated by a man who was now serving a long prison sentence. Mrs Graham had once hinted that Miss West might possibly find happiness with someone who was worthy of her. Clarice met her eyes and shook her head.

'Oh no,' she said. 'I am engaged to marry Mr Herbert Blades.'

The reply made Mrs Graham feel uncomfortable. Loyalty. There was no other word for it.

Clarice appreciated Mrs Graham's kindness, but there was one fly in this otherwise delicately scented ointment, and that was Mrs Graham's second cousin, Arthur Heston.

Mr Heston had his own rooms in the house and to all intents and purposes was its master. He was thirty years old, rich, good-looking, sought-after, but much too interested in Clarice.

He came to her workroom every day, leant against the doorpost and talked, asking her all kinds of questions, trying to find out her likes and dislikes, paying her compliments, and looking at her. No matter how industriously she plied her needle and kept her eyes on her work, she felt his intent gaze fixed on her.

It was disturbing, because he was very like Herbert Blades in appearance. He had the same type of looks and figure, and what upset her even more were his clothes. She could have sworn he patronised the same tailor as Mr Blades, wore the same kind of hand-made shoes, similar neckties and carried an almost identical silver-headed cane.

'What are you making now, Miss West?' he asked one day, touching the rich chestnut-coloured satin she was working on.

'A tea gown for Mrs Graham.'

'That's your colour. It would suit you perfectly. I'd like to see you in just such a dress.'

'Well, you won't.'

'Not even if I gave it to you? As a present?'

'Certainly not.'

'Why?'

'Because there's no reason for you to give me a present.'

'Am I not to be pleased, then?'

'Mr Heston, I'm very busy, as you can see. I know you're not serious, but even if I wanted a dress like this, where would I wear it?'

'In a drawing room.'

Clarice laughed. This kind of light chatter was all very well but there was an undertone that made her nervous. She should have put a stop to it there and then and regretted her response as soon as she made it.

'Whose?' was what she asked.

'Mine,' was what he answered.

She went quite cold. The atmosphere had changed.

'Think about it, Miss West,' he said, and went away.

She was upset and worried, not sure what he meant or if she was imagining that a suggestion lay under this monosyllabic exchange. She remembered other hints he had made, such as asking if she didn't think it would be nice to live in a luxurious flat.

'Anyone can think if they've a mind to,' she'd said.

'But what do *you* think, Miss West?'

'Why are you interested in what I think?'

'Everything about you interests me,' he said.

'It's none of my business, Mr Heston, but if you really want to know, I think you should get yourself a hobby,' she said.

'Ah, but I have one,' and he gave her a look that brought her out in gooseflesh, for it clearly implied that she was his hobby and he was pursuing it.

'He wants you for his fancy lady,' said Victoria when Clarice told her all this.

'Oh, don't!' cried Clarice.

Victoria saw nothing against Clarice being a rich man's fancy now that Mr Blades was banged up inside. More than one of Madame Last's tiptop ladies was exactly that, and no one thought the worse of them. In fact, the whole establishment practically fell on their knees when one particular lady came for a fitting, because she was the extra-special friend of the King himself. Oh, how Madame Last kowtowed to her and practically licked her dainty little boots.

'You could do worse, Clarice,' she said,

breaking the silence that had fallen between them.

Clarice gave her a long, cool look. 'Not with my feelings, Victoria,' she said. 'Pray never say any such thing again. Or even think it.'

Shamed, Victoria switched the conversation to the subject of Charlotte and her affairs.

'She don't half seem to cop it, what with her pa being such a swine and then that dotty kid getting killed. Still, things are settling down a bit since she heard from her young man. She's like a puppy chasing its tail these days.'

Clarice was glad to hear it. 'I don't know where Aunt Cassie and I would have been without Charlotte,' she said. 'She took charge of us. Kept us in food, ran errands. Even stopped the coal cart and paid for a quarter of a ton to be delivered and wouldn't take a penny.'

If they had but known it, Charlotte was very nearly at the end of her pennies, for she couldn't resist buying a table Victoria had fallen in love with in the second-hand department of a large furniture store. It was a round table with the revolving top covered in dark-green leather. It had four drawers and stood on a moulded pedestal with three feet. A rent collector's table, they were told. Tenant and landlord sat opposite each other. The tenant put his rent in a drawer and the landlord swivelled it round and took it out.

The idea appealed to Victoria. She looked forward to the day when she and Algie would have a house and take in a lodger or two.

'How much?' she asked.

When told it cost three guineas she simply said, 'You can keep it,' and walked out. But she was disappointed, and Charlotte, elated now that she had heard from Richard, wanted to give it to her as a thanksgiving token. She went back later and managed to persuade the salesman to let her have it for two and a half.

Now she had exactly one guinea of Mary's money left, over and above what she earned, but what did that matter now that wonderful letters from Richard plomped on the doormat nearly every day?

She came up from the basement to the ground floor of this magnificent furniture shop and walked straight into the path of a fashionably dressed middle-aged woman, who stared at her in disbelief and said: 'Can it be Charlotte?'

It was Mrs Morton, Albert's mother.

Charlotte tried to retreat but Mrs Morton was too quick for her. 'Charlotte!' she called, and then again, 'Charlotte!'

Charlotte stopped and didn't know what to do. She simply stood.

Mrs Morton was shaking hands, and the look on her face showed concern as well as surprise. 'Are you alone, dear?' she asked.

Charlotte said she was, and Mrs Morton enquired after her health, remarked that she'd grown thin and asked when she'd come back. All this was a puzzle to Charlotte. She had never given a thought to the questions likely to be asked when her absence was noticed by an old friend who clearly knew nothing of the circumstances. Yet as she had nothing to hide, there wasn't any sense in being evasive.

'I haven't been out of London,' she said.

At this, Mrs Morton looked still more concerned and took Charlotte's arm.

'But, my dear, you have,' she said, in the comforting tone reserved for invalids who don't know how ill they are. 'You've been in Bournemouth staying with your Aunt Mildred for a long time now.'

So that was what friends had been told!

'To recover your health,' Mrs Morton went on. 'We were very sorry to learn you weren't well. There now. I was going to buy some curtain material, but it can wait.

I'll take you back to Lancaster Gate.'

Charlotte had always liked Mrs Morton and didn't want to upset her, so she thanked her for her solicitude and said she didn't live at Lancaster Gate any more.

'Not live there? But you've been at Bournemouth, surely?'

'No. Papa intended me to go there. I was to stay with Aunt Mildred for a long time but I couldn't have borne it, so I—oh, Mrs Morton, however am I to tell you?'

It was impossible to continue in this wide aisle, with customers coming and going all the time.

'There's a restaurant on the first floor where we can talk more easily,' Mrs Morton said.

She wanted to escape but Mrs Morton was leading her to the restaurant, where people were having tea and drowning the three-piece orchestra with loud conversation. They were shown to a table in a secluded corner.

Charlotte had never thought she might meet any of her parents' friends. Now she would have to explain herself, and Mrs Morton was entitled to know what had happened more than anybody, barring Albert himself.

Tea was served, Mrs Morton poured and Charlotte watched, hypnotised, as the amber liquid streamed from the spout. Her father must have deceived the Mortons into thinking that her marriage to their son would take place when she recovered from her supposed indisposition.

'It seems things are not as we supposed, Charlotte,' said Mrs Morton, passing her a cup. 'Do help yourself to milk. That's right. Now, tell me why you didn't go to your Aunt Mildred, dear.'

'It was because I ran away from home.'

'What?' Mrs Morton put down her cup without even taking a sip. 'What did you say?' she repeated.

'Papa was sending me to Aunt Mildred as a punishment for falling in love with somebody who wasn't Albert.'

There was a shocked silence from the other side of the table.

'So I ran away.'

Mrs Morton heard but could say nothing.

Charlotte waited a second before rushing on with: 'I've been earning my living ever since and living in lodgings with another girl. We're needlewomen at a court dressmaker's.'

There was still no response, so Charlotte spoke again: 'I was in love, you see. I couldn't marry anyone but the man I was in love with, could I?'

Mrs Morton was remembering a dream of her girlhood. It was a belief that a perfect partner existed for her, and that one day they would meet and know each other instantly.

She had spoken of this to other girls as a certainty when she was very young. Most of them agreed with her; some were more down-to-earth. As she grew up she clung to this belief but those who had shared it with her gave up. They married for other reasons, the main one being that they didn't want to stay on the shelf.

At twenty-five she was the only spinster in the large group of girls who had been friends, but she had little in common with them any more. So, just to be in the swim, and because she had never glimpsed her ideal, she married Freddy Morton. She was never in love with him, nor he with her, but they got along together pretty well. The match pleased both families, so it was all very comfortable.

Now, looking at Charlotte across the table, she felt a surge of emotion, a strange kind of longing for what she had missed and would now never have. She had not had cause to do as Charlotte had done, but if she had, would she have dared? Would she have run away, shut herself off from everyone she knew, got work and shared her life with companions of such a different order? She would not.

But Charlotte had.

On an impulse Mrs Morton leaned across the table and took Charlotte's left hand.

'Then why are you not married?' she asked.

Charlotte told her.

Amy Morton could not have felt worse if Charlotte had knocked her hat off. She automatically lifted her hands to adjust it, found there was no need so let them flutter down to her lap again. It must be her head, not her hat, that needed adjusting. How was she to order her conflicting thoughts, and was it possible to do so? Some must be smothered, but which?

As she listened to Charlotte, several quite wicked ideas occurred to her, and although she came out with conventional advice such as: 'We don't always like the men our fathers choose for us. We get to like them after we're married,' an inner voice shouted: 'Oh no we don't.'

She tried to ignore it, and said, so loudly that the three ladies at the next table turned to look: 'We all fall in love with handsome, charming young men and find out what terrible husbands they make when it's too late.'

She only raised her voice because the rebel inside was telling her that since she had never tried one, who was she to say they made bad husbands?

'Fathers know best,' she said.

'Mine doesn't,' said Charlotte.

This was enough for the three ladies next door to start a debate which, from a cool beginning, became quite heated.

Mrs Morton's trouble was that she agreed with Charlotte and for a while even envied her. How wonderful to fall in love, to stand up to a tyrannical father and walk out to face the world at daybreak, young and beautiful and bold.

But it was no use giving way to these impossible fancies. She must be practical and positive and act upon what she had just been told.

'It seems you have jilted Albert,' she said.

'I never consented to marry him, Mrs Morton. Everyone knew that. Albert, my father, my stepmother, Nanny, the servants. I told everyone.'

'Everyone except the Mortons.'

'I'm sorry about that. Truly I am.'

An overlong silence between them followed, though the discussion at the next table went on. Mrs Morton, confronted by problems she would need time to sort out, set them aside temporarily by uttering these words: 'Let us say no more,' asking for the bill and drawing on her gloves.

She gave the impression that there was

a great deal more to be said, and Charlotte began to feel miserable. She wouldn't have upset Mrs Morton willingly and hadn't thought of informing Albert that she had not gone to Bournemouth. It was not her place to do so anyway.

Mrs Morton had no heart for curtain material when she parted from Charlotte with a rather strained goodbye. The evenings were still dark and the weather deplorable; there was nothing to stay out for, so she took a cab back to Marble Hill and arrived to find that her husband had already left. It was ironic he should be dining with William Grant, at Simpson's, where they were to entertain a merchant from Turkey.

It wasn't an occasion Freddy had been looking forward to, as he couldn't endure foreigners who spoke broken English and always said he felt worn out after a session with them. That was why he had raked in William Grant. He wanted someone to share the listening.

Amy knew he wouldn't have been in the mood to hear about her encounter with Charlotte, and now she was back in her own surroundings she was beginning to feel her matronly self again.

It was all very well to have fanciful notions; her own had been very dear to her until she saw she was being left behind because of them. That was when the chance of a conventional marriage came her way. She took it and had conformed ever since. Consequently she must stop thinking of Charlotte as courageous and see her as rashly impulsive. Also, it would be as well to remember that Charlotte was Amanda's daughter and was said to be like her.

She had never met Amanda but knew enough about her pranks from hearsay. Amanda had been a trial to her husband. She smoked cigars, read risqué French novels and refused to retire to the drawing room with the other ladies after dinner, saying that she much preferred talking to men and adored port wine.

So, with such a mother, was it any wonder Charlotte was unconventional too. Would she have made a suitable wife for Albert?

How she wished there was someone she could talk all this over with on that long, chilly evening broken only by a dinner of two very small cutlets and three Brussels sprouts. Cook had taken her at her word when she said she didn't want much.

Albert was out playing billiards somewhere. There wasn't even a dog or a cat for company and she was too worried and upset to read. Freddy had told her not to wait up, so she went to bed early with two hot-water bottles and was woken at one a.m. when he fell in beside her.

'I want to talk to you, Freddy,' she said.

He greeted her request with a snore loud enough to disturb the servants in the attics.

Things were not much better in the morning. He had a thumping head brought on by overindulgence the night before. The merchant from Turkey spoke flawless English and his knowledge of what the capital had to offer astounded his hosts. He knew hot spots Freddy and William Grant didn't think existed on their side of the Channel, and took them on a tour to broaden their outlook. William stayed cool, drank moderately and closed his eyes. Freddy drank too much and kept his open.

By lunch time he was recovering but the time wasn't right for Amy's bombshell. She wasn't sure when to drop it.

'You're very edgy, old girl,' he remarked as he set about carving the Sunday roast, sharpening the knife on the steel and testing the blade with his thumb. 'Anything wrong?'

'I can't decide about the curtains,' she said, judging this a good way to lead into yesterday's shopping expedition and its outcome.

'What's wrong with these?'

'Nothing. Except we've had them a long time.'

'In that case, let's keep them a bit longer. Beef's tough.'

'I'll speak to the butcher.' This was a problem she knew how to deal with, but she still had the more difficult one to settle.

'So you had a good evening with Mr Grant?' she said.

'Capital. He did all the talking. He's an excellent fellow.'

Now for it. 'Did you ask after Charlotte?'

'No. We had our Turkish friend with us.'

'Only I met her in Maples yesterday.'

'Did you? Looking better, was she?'

'Freddy, Charlotte never went to Bournemouth as we've been led to believe. She ran away from home and works as a seamstress. She lives in a lodging house with another girl. What do you think of that?'

He had a large piece of Yorkshire pudding speared on his fork, his mouth open ready to receive it. Instead of putting it in he planted both elbows on the table, holding knife and fork up straight, and stared at her.

'What?' he said.

She repeated the story, adding much

more detail and finishing with the news that Charlotte was in love with a man who played the piano and meant to marry him.

'She can't. She's engaged to Albert.'

'Not formally, Freddy.'

'It's an understood thing.'

'So we thought.'

'Does Albert know?'

'I haven't told him,' she said.

She knew that Freddy would blow up, and he did. He said that his Sunday dinner, his favourite meal of the week, was ruined. Damn the pudding. He didn't want any. The Grants had deceived them and they were not putting up with it.

'Get your bonnet on. We're going to see them,' he said.

'I'm not at all sure it's wise to call today,' said Amy. 'And I wish you wouldn't call it a bonnet. It's a hat.'

She had chosen the wrong time. She was aggrieved. She had been nursing this news ever since yesterday afternoon. If only he had come home at a reasonable hour last night, they could have discussed it then. As it was, she had lain awake all night while he slept—noisily—she added.

'Don't nag,' he said.

Ellen and William were in the drawing room when the Mortons were shown in.

Afternoon tea was being served, so Freddy couldn't broach the reason for their visit while Annie was clattering about with trays and plates and an enormous silver teapot.

While this went on, William innocently referred to the success of the previous evening, and Ellen admired Amy's hat.

At length Annie withdrew and Ellen began to pour tea.

'No tea, thank you,' said Freddy. 'We didn't come to tea.'

His tone surprised Ellen. She put the teapot down. William raised his eyebrows and treated Freddy to a conspiratorial look. 'Perhaps you had too much champagne last night,' he said. 'It can leave a sour aftertaste.'

'It's not the champagne that's turned sour. It's your behaviour, Grant.'

William, not expecting this, stiffened. 'I don't think I forgot my manners,' he said.

'No, but you forgot to tell us your daughter had run away. You let us go on thinking that the understanding with Albert still stood. Amy met Charlotte by accident on Saturday and got the whole story out of her. What do you say to that?'

William's composure suffered a shock but he recovered in a flash. He put the tips of his fingers together and leaned back in his chair, elbows on the arms.

'And what leads you to suppose a temporary aberration on my daughter's part changes that understanding?' he enquired with studied deliberation. 'Better this should happen now than after she marries Albert, I should think.'

He was master of the situation. Here he was at tea with his wife in his own drawing room. To be disturbed in this way was unwarrantable. Much as he desired and needed the goodwill of Freddy Morton this was not the way to discuss affairs of the heart, if indeed the heart came into it at all.

He was angry with Charlotte, infuriated by her disobedience and her rejection of his plan for her life. She was her own worst enemy, but let anyone, even so important a person as Freddy Morton, say one word against her and the hair on the back of his neck bristled.

Ellen was so pleased with the way he was handling the matter, she couldn't resist throwing in her weight with his. 'This may be news to you, Mr Morton, but girls have their adventures, you know. Few of them have the nerve to run away. Their romances are all in their heads. I can assure you I had mine, and I've no doubt Mrs Morton had hers.'

'Allow me to speak for myself, if you

please,' exclaimed Mrs Morton, red in the neck and trusting that she wouldn't be asked to account for her secret dreams.

'Charlotte's little escapade will be swept under the carpet, no matter whom she marries,' said Ellen. 'Now, won't you change your minds and have some tea?'

'No, we will not have tea. You've properly led us up the garden path, and I don't like it,' said Freddy.

Ellen was trying to decide which animal he reminded her of. Mrs Morton came into the feline category, plump, pussy-like, peevish. He could have been a rabbit with that twitching nose, but she had never yet seen an angry rabbit so that wouldn't do.

'There's no need to see us out.' Freddy was on his feet. 'We know our way. Come, Amy.'

Amy rose and so did William. He opened the door for them and Annie got her ear away from the keyhole in time to show them out of the house.

Alone, Ellen and William gazed at each other. Then they began to laugh. 'What impudence,' he said.

'It was simply wonderful the way you dealt with that. You were so anxious they wouldn't find out. Now you don't seem to care. Why?'

'Freddy made an ass of himself last night. He left all the talking to me and I got on so well with our Turkish customer I'm pretty sure a very good thing will come of it. It won't be due to Freddy, and he knows it.'

'How clever you are!'

'Yes, I think I am rather clever,' he said.

At Marble Hill Albert took the news with little surprise and no disappointment.

'You should have heard the way Charlotte carried on when I popped the question,' he said. 'A proper little minx, I can tell you.'

'She won't do for you, my boy, so there's an end of it,' his father said. 'Pity. I can't afford to lose Grant on a business footing. He has a way with foreigners.' He took a cigar from a casket on the sideboard and made a great to-do about lighting it. 'Pour yourself a whisky, Albert, and one for me,' he said, sinking back in his great armchair.

Amy took out her knitting, then put it away. The sound of needles clicking irritated Freddy, and now that he had calmed down it would be silly to disturb him.

She thought of Ellen Grant and her provocative remark about romantic dreams. She thought of Charlotte. She looked at Albert. He was holding his glass between his hands, sitting forward by the fire, ruminating. It occurred to her that he was not a young girl's dream. She gave herself an angry shake. Where in the world did these outrageous ideas come from? He was her son. Their son. He was a good catch, let there be no doubt about that.

He spoke. 'One thing. She's got plenty of spunk for a girl. I'll say that for her,' he said.

There have to be a few fine days in even the worst of summers, and the Saturday Victoria married Algie was one of them. Just before she emerged from Mrs Blunt's house for the last time, the clouds rolled away, and as she stood on the step with her arm through Will Goode's, the sun came out. There she was, resplendent in all her finery, which included Charlotte's ostrich feather hat.

Clarice had made her sprigged lawn dress, which allowed for her expanding shape; a pair of blue satin garters from Nanny kept her stockings up. The rest of her kit, as she called her underwear, was old, so everything was as it should be. Something old, something new, something borrowed, something blue.

Will gave her a little bouquet of pink carnations and gypsophila to carry when he arrived in the cab that was now waiting to take them to the church. Charlotte and Nanny were to follow in another cab, so to Victoria's delight and surprise it was all being done properly.

Charlotte, Nanny, Clarice and Will had conspired to make it the happiest day of her life, and that was not to mention Algie. She was yet to see the wedding breakfast he had organised at the Clapham flat and didn't know that Charlotte had bought her the round table she had admired so much. Now it was installed in her sitting room. Eustace Bright had bought armfuls of flowers to bedeck the room. He had borrowed jugs, jam jars, vases, anything that held water, to put them in. He had borrowed chairs, too, and the other flat-dwellers were pleased to lend them when they heard that a newly married pair would be coming home that day.

It had been a worrying week for Charlotte. She almost expected an angry visitation from her father now the Mortons knew she had run away, but as she heard nothing she was left wondering exactly what was going on at Lancaster Gate. Nanny couldn't offer any answers as she hadn't heard from Mrs Vickery or Annie, so all she could do was to tell Charlotte that worrying never did any good and it was much more important to live for the present, plan for the future and forget the miserable bits of the past.

'And the sooner you marry Richard and settle down, the sooner I shall be able to make a list of the platitudes I've poured into your ears ever since you ran away,' she said.

'Are there so many?'

'We'll count them up one day.'

Nanny was laughing but Charlotte felt ashamed. She ran to Nanny whenever she was troubled, and although she prided herself on being independent she was nothing of the kind. Without Nanny, without Victoria and Clarice, where would she have been? Back at home or at Bournemouth with a heart full of hostility, no hope of a reunion with Richard and nothing but an obnoxious marriage or a lovelorn spinsterhood ahead.

The wedding cake, iced to perfection by Will, was all ready to be boxed and taken to Clapham. Nanny had made it herself, although she was no cakehand, as she readily admitted.

'But it looks perfect,' Charlotte said.

'That's Will's handiwork, not mine.'

'It's good enough for a confectioner's window.'

'Why not for a society bride?' Nanny pretended to be huffed. 'Confectioner's window indeed. When did you ever see a masterpiece like that in a cake shop?'

'Never.'

'And let it be known this is only one of Will's accomplishments,' Nanny proclaimed, standing back to admire the cake.

There were three tiers, all expertly iced and decorated. Will had acquired his skill by icing cakes to delight Lily. Nanny was justly proud of him and liked to fancy he would grow rich. His workboxes, their lids inlaid with a variety of veneers, were in steady demand now. The one he had just finished was for Victoria, and he promised Charlotte he would make one for her when she married. Her fear was that he would have plenty of time to make it.

She was not happy at the prospect of living at Mrs Blunt's without Victoria, and there was no one else she wanted to share with so she would have to pay the full rent. Better by far to seek a single room. She began looking at advertisements in the newsagent's windows and writing to the likely ones. Several replies came, and Victoria was curious about the increased correspondence.

'What's going on?' she asked.

'Nothing.'

'Tell us another. What you up to, Charlotte?'

'If you must know, I want to move to a single room after you go.'

Victoria was frying steak and tomatoes on the windowsill at the time. She had her back to Charlotte and didn't answer straightaway. She dished up.

'We'd better give Mrs Blunt notice today,' she said as they took their places.

'We? I can't leave here until I've found somewhere else.'

'You've found it. Clapham with me.'

Charlotte didn't take Victoria's meaning. No newly married couple wanted a third party living with them, and anyway, there wasn't any room at the flat.

'Come on. Wake up.' Victoria was quite sharp. 'Algie can only live at the flat weekends till August,' she said. 'You go to Nanny's Saturday afternoon to Sunday night, don't you? We'll put a camp bed in the sitting room for the other nights.'

She began tucking into her steak. Charlotte didn't even pick up her knife and fork. She was fascinated by Victoria's matter-of-fact approach to a problem that quite honestly didn't concern her. The solution was unexpected, wonderful, impossible.

'I couldn't. I can't intrude on you like that,' she said at last.

'Intrude? I like that. You'll be paying us rent, my girl, and me and Algie can do with it. There's all sorts of things we'll be wanting.'

'If you put it that way...'

'That's the way I put it. I'm keeping on at Last's till Algie sorts it out with his ma, so you and me will come and go together. It'll work out fine. You'll see.'

Charlotte, full of gratitude, began trying to thank Victoria, who shut her up without ceremony.

'Cut the cackle and get on with that steak while it's still alive. Now. Not another word.'

Charlotte didn't utter one, but she thought a lot.

As Victoria paused on the step and looked up at the clearing sky on her glorious wedding day, she was not prepared for the large handful of rice hurled at her from behind by Mrs Blunt.

''Ere! What's that for?' she shouted, wheeling round on her late landlady.

'Good luck, of course. We don't keep confetti in stock,' returned Mrs Blunt.

'That's for after the wedding. Not before.'

'There's other things gone before what should have come after,' retorted Mrs Blunt.

Will cut in before Victoria could come back with the reply that sprang to her lips. 'The cab's waiting,' he said. And so it was, and the driver had the door open, so she stepped in and wasn't sorry she'd let the ugly old geezer have the last word. There wasn't much in life for Mrs Blunt, but she, Victoria Clink, soon to be Mrs Algernon Last, had everything her heart desired.

Wedding guests are expected to shed a few tears, and with the exception of the bride, her groom and his best man, most of those present were glad of the excuse. Their sorrows were no secret, but by the time the party reached Clapham and Algie attempted to carry Victoria over the threshold, they were all laughing.

Victoria, seeing the round table for the first time, and the wedding cake displayed in the middle of it, just gasped that it was all a dream, she didn't believe it, and it was too good to be true, whereupon Charlotte told her to give it a twist, which she did. Then came the raptures. She was bewildered to find herself in her own home, with things she had never hoped to possess, with friends treating her as though she was a real somebody, and Algie so devoted and in love. And best of all, he was her husband now.

'Is it true? Is this fat little party really me?' she whispered in Charlotte's ear.

'There's no doubt about it, Mrs Last,' Charlotte said, hoping it would not be too long before she could be called Mrs

Allen. But why think of that distant day when she was with these special people who had come to mean so much to her? And to see them all as though they hadn't a care, Nanny and Will, Clarice—who would guess at her disappointment when she could laugh and talk with Eustace Bright as she was doing now? Nothing could mar the pure happiness here, and Charlotte revelled in it. And what a day it was, with the sun coming through the window.

'Lucky you didn't choose last Saturday, Victoria,' she said.

'Coo!' Victoria shuddered at the recollection of that freezing wet day, wet week, if it came to that. 'Told you I was lucky, didn't I? I'll have a drop more port, whoever's pouring it.'

Will was in charge of the bottles. 'Lemonade in it?' he asked.

'You joking?'

There was plenty to eat and drink: Algie had really gone to town and provided all the delicacies he had been saving up to buy. What with the food, the wine, the flowers and the superb cake, which was yet to be cut, it was a wedding day none of them would ever forget, and Eustace had even taken photographs to serve as lasting mementoes.

It was dusk and time to light up

when Charlotte noticed that Nanny had disappeared and found her in the kitchen washing up.

'We couldn't leave it for them to clear away,' she said. 'Victoria's tired out, and so are you, my dear. It's been a long day and a pity you had to go to work this morning.'

'We couldn't afford to lose the money,' Charlotte said, taking a cloth to dry the dishes.

Nanny had brought greaseproof paper with her and was wrapping up the leftover food. 'We'll go when this is done,' she said. 'And tomorrow you must have a good rest. We won't go gallivanting.'

Charlotte agreed. They rejoined the party. Nanny announced that it was high time for them all to leave, and although Victoria and Algie said it wasn't, the others all declared it was. The day ended with hugs and kisses all round. Eustace saw Clarice home, and the other three set out on the long trek to Hammersmith. They kept nodding off on the tram, and were too tired to talk when at last they got home. Hot cocoa. Bed. Sleep.

As they weren't going anywhere on Sunday there was no need to get up early. Nanny didn't hear the knocker next morning, neither did Will, but Charlotte did.

She lay in bed, wondering if it was a real knock or if she had dreamt it. It came again, a gentle tapping, a mere agitation of the knocker, as though whoever was outside didn't want to cause a disturbance. Perhaps she had better see who was there, just open the door a crack and peep out.

No one. But there had been. The caller was quietly closing the gate, walking away down the road. Her heart started to thump like mad.

Richard!

'Come back!' she shouted with all the power of her lungs.

He stopped. Turned. Then rushed rather than ran, and she was in his arms and he was hugging her fit to crack her ribs, kissing her breathless, holding her away to gaze, gathering her to his heart and just saying, 'Charlotte, Charlotte,' over and over.

There were questions in her mind but she was too full of joy to ask them, too thankful to have him safe home after the fears of those first long months of separation.

They were still in the same place when Nanny came down, took in the scene and went quietly to the scullery to put the kettle on. So he was home. She felt little tingles of excitement mixed with some apprehension, for Charlotte had staked everything on his return to marry her. What if she lost, even now? Nanny touched wood. There had been times when it was hard to conceal her anxiety, for if Charlotte hadn't established contact with him, who could tell if he would have kept faith, far away as he was in the glittering world of Mary Allen?

From all Mrs Vickery and Annie had said, Richard Allen was a most attractive young man, and although Mr Grant had spurned him, there was so much in his favour he was bound to be a prize in the marriage market. But he's here, so why worry? Will must make another wedding cake—the wedding would be at the parish church—how her mind ran on!

All these jumbled thoughts were milling in her brain when Charlotte, exultant, lovely Charlotte, ran in, dragging Richard with her and saying: 'He's here, Nanny. He's home! Isn't it wonderful?'

Nanny stretched out her arms in welcome. 'At last we meet,' she said, clasping Richard's hands in hers. 'How glad I am to see you. Safe and sound, I trust?'

He was not quite the Adonis Charlotte never tired of describing. Unshaven, dishevelled, in need of soap and water and with his shoes unlaced.

'He's been travelling from Milan for days,' Charlotte said. 'He had to sit up all night on a hard wooden seat.'

'Forgive me. I was so mad to get here I couldn't wait to stop at the barber's. I'm afraid I'm an embarrassment to Charlotte, turning up like a tramp.'

'You are here and that's what matters,' Nanny said warmly. 'Now, you must both have a cup of tea while I get breakfast. Sit yourselves in the kitchen. I want Richard to be as much at home here as you are, Charlotte.'

There was something regal about Nanny, even when she was doing the most mundane things, like setting their tea on the table, whisking back the curtains to let in the sun and enquiring if Richard would like two eggs and would it be toast or bread and butter? If her coffee wasn't as good as they made it on the Continent, she said, at least it had the virtue of being English.

'If it's as good as your tea it will be delicious,' he said.

Charlotte glowed. To find Richard and Nanny getting on so well together added to her happiness. Soon he would be eating an egg! She was actually to see him crack the shell, or would he slice off the top as Papa did?

Before this important point could be settled, Will came down, disturbed by the sound of a male voice when he had expected to have a peaceful lie-in. The

301

sight of Charlotte holding hands with a rough-looking fellow who turned out to be the eagerly awaited Richard Allen came as rather more than a surprise, but he managed to control his features. He didn't open his eyes wide or allow his jaw to drop but greeted Richard with a firm handshake and expressed his pleasure at seeing Charlotte's fiancé under his roof.

Nanny was very much in charge. As Richard's luggage was at Victoria Station, she was quite sure Will would lend him a razor. Having shaved, he was to have several hours' sleep in Will's bed, which she would prepare for him as soon as breakfast was over. While he slept she and Charlotte would press his suit, as it was more crumpled than she cared to see.

He allowed himself to be manipulated.

Charlotte had never thought where she and Richard might meet again. The time and place were not important, it was being together that mattered, and this little house was exactly right. Nanny was loving, generous, sensible and undemanding, and as Charlotte watched her expertly pressing Richard's trousers she knew no place could have been better. She couldn't help putting her arms round Nanny's neck and calling her a darling.

'Careful. This iron's hot,' said Nanny,

putting it on the stand and redamping the pressing cloth. 'What do you mean, I'm a darling?'

'Doing so much. Taking Richard in hand.'

'He certainly needed taking in hand.'

'You *do* like him, don't you?'

'I'll tell you when I know him.'

'But first impressions?'

'Don't go by them. A scruffier young gentleman I never did see. Pass the other iron and put this one on the stove.'

'Shouldn't I be pressing his trousers?'

'Time enough when you're married, my dear.'

Ah, then. Then.

But when? Except for the preliminaries —calling the banns and that kind of thing—Charlotte thought they could get married tomorrow, and while Richard made up for lost sleep in Will's bed she sat with Nanny in the garden and talked about the wedding.

Nanny, with her usual cautious approach, tried to warn her of the difficulties likely to beset any young couple beginning a life together, but these were all brushed aside, and when Richard at last appeared, shaved, polished and looking undeniably handsome, Charlotte knew exactly where her heart was because it started to turn over.

He came and sat between them on the bench and leaned his head back to feel the sun on his face. 'It's so good to be here,' he said. 'So very, very good.'

He saw the honeysuckle that covered the garden wall, and the wisteria climbing over the workshop, the great bunches of flowers scenting the air. It was all as Charlotte had told him in her letters. And Nanny too, how beautifully she spoke, how graciously she moved, what a wonderful, wonderful woman she was. He made an attempt to thank her but she patted his arm and said: 'You two want to talk about your plans. I'm going to clear up indoors.'

He had so much to tell Charlotte he scarcely knew where to begin, but her first question set him off.

'Why ever did you travel third?' she asked.

'It's cheaper. I only go in style when I'm with Mary.'

This was news to her. 'But you're always with Mary,' she said.

'Not always. I went to Vienna with Hans. Remember?'

'Aren't you Mary's accompanist any more?'

'Of course, when she wants me, but she doesn't think it right to keep me under permanent contract to her, and neither do I.'

'But you always were, weren't you? It was a good arrangement?'

'It was splendid. But she saw the limitations.'

Charlotte, surprised, waited for him to amplify this, but he said: 'Let's make up for lost time and talk about ourselves. I've been living for this.'

'So have I. Oh, you don't know...'

'Don't I just! You've been so strong—working yourself to the bone, taking care of poor Clarice—I don't suppose I know the half of it. You left bits out, didn't you? What's it really been like?'

He wanted to know all about Madame Last's establishment, and she told him of the long hours they worked there, and how her back ached. It was awful when she pricked her fingers for fear of getting blood on things. She told him they walked to and fro to save ha'pence but their shoes wore out. She took off one shoe to show him the holes in the sole. Mrs Blunt's house was always cold, and the room she'd shared with Victoria could only be called squalid. But they'd had such fun there, such laughs, as they outwitted the old geezer by cooking their meals on the windowsill.

He wanted her to go on and on, so she did, but she didn't say much about her encounters with Valentine Blunt for fear Richard might want to knock him down.

He heard it all and marvelled at her fortitude. What had he done to be blessed with the love of a girl like Charlotte? he asked her, and that made her laugh and throw her arms round him.

'You're marrying a workroom girl,' she said.

'I don't know how you bore it,' he said.

'It was only until you came home. If you hadn't been on the horizon I really don't know what would have happened. But you were and now you're here and it's heaven.'

He said the best thing of all was to be in love with someone you really liked and he called it a guarantee of happiness, which pleased her immensely.

'And just think. We're both free. No irate fathers laying down the law. We can be married almost at once, can't we?'

She was too happy to notice his slight hesitation and went on to tell him she thought it her duty to go to Last's as usual in the morning. 'I think I owe it to her for taking me on, don't you?'

He agreed. He had various commissions to execute for Mary that would take up most of the following day, but the evening was hers and she must choose how to spend it. On Tuesday he was to meet the publisher who was bringing out the classical songs he had adapted as pieces for the piano, and in the afternoon he was rehearsing with Hans Braun.

'That brings us to Wednesday,' she said. 'Nearly half the week gone. Shouldn't we put up the banns?'

'Wait a moment. Hans has a series of recitals covering the next three months. Don't you think it splendid?'

It was very nice for Hans, she thought, and asked, more from politeness than genuine interest, where the concerts were to take place.

'London next week. Then Paris, Vienna, Milan. It's an unbelievable opportunity.'

She knew Hans was already an acclaimed violinist and didn't see why Richard was so excited about it.

'It isn't exactly an opportunity for him, is it?' she said. 'He doesn't need one.'

'But I do, my dear darling, and he's engaged me to accompany him on this tour. I'm the one with the opportunity. Just think what it means to me!'

'To you? Not to us?'

She withdrew her hands from his and sat with them in her lap. She swallowed hard. 'I thought you had come back to be with me. I thought we were to be married as soon as we could. You talked about our own fireside. I was to be with you all the time.'

'And so you will. But not straight away. Look, it's only three months.'

'Three months is as long as forever.'

'No. Be sensible.'

'Sensible indeed! I'm very sensible.'

'Then you know I love you with all my heart, and you also know that money comes into it.'

'You never mentioned money before,' she said.

'Don't let us quarrel over it,' He got up and paced backwards and forwards on the narrow path. Then he sat beside her again. 'You've been so brave and I've been trying to make the best of what talent I have. I want to be someone worth having and I know I can be.' He paused because she didn't answer and then went on: 'In the past only the soloist was noticed. An accompanist was practically invisible. Mary always said the piano part ought to be appreciated. Can you understand that?'

'Yes,' she said flatly.

'I'm only getting some notice now because of the way she taught me. She listens to every note, every shade of meaning. Schubert and Schumann composed marvellous accompaniments.'

Again she was silent.

'Don't you see?' he asked.

'Not really.'

'Hans had an accompanist who didn't

suit him, so he asked me. How could I refuse?'

'You could have told him about us.'

'He knows.'

'You said something about Paris and other places, didn't you? Why can't I come with you?'

'Not this time.'

'Oh!' she cried, face red, eyes streaming. 'You didn't come back to get married at all! You just came back to work with Hans and see your publisher and anyone but me. You're cruel and I can't bear it.'

She ran inside and up to her room, where she flung herself on the bed and wept tears of bitter misery that scalded her eyes and ruined her face. After all the hard work and privations she had suffered since she left home, this was the result.

She had never given way to self-pity before, but it was impossible not to wallow in it now and ask herself how she could go on. She felt her mind shattering. She was frightened. Alone. Abandoned. He was going away again. Without her.

Nanny, glancing out of her bedroom window a little later, saw Richard sitting alone on the bench and fancied he looked despondent. She went down, thinking that Charlotte must be inside making coffee. There was no sign of her. She went out to Richard, whose pale face was paler than

309

usual. He looked up and she knew from his aspect that something was badly wrong.

'I've upset Charlotte terribly and I don't know what to do,' he said. 'Perhaps I'd better go.'

'You'll do no such thing,' said Nanny. 'At least not until I know what this is all about. Where is she?'

'Indoors. She accused me of coming back for the sake of my career and not to see her at all. She didn't give me a chance.'

Nanny couldn't help thinking of Amanda and the impetuous way she used to jump to conclusions. Richard looked so miserable. He still had grime under his fingernails, no doubt because his toilet things were with his luggage at the station. That was rather touching. She felt she was going to like him.

'You probably know what Charlotte's life has been like since she left home,' she said. 'She has lived for this day and had many grievous setbacks and disappointments while she waited.'

'I know it,' he said. 'I didn't expect to come until September anyway, and then I got this chance. I thought we could set the date of our wedding. I'm going to marry her, Nanny, and I mean to make damn sure she's happy with me. I love her to death. I adore her. I admire her.' He was all but wringing his hands. His hair, so neatly combed when he came into the garden, was almost on end.

'Did you tell her so?'

He shook his head. 'I told her I was going on a three-month tour with Hans Braun, and she took it all the wrong way.'

'Gracious heaven, can you wonder?' cried Nanny, throwing up her hands. Of all the idiotic, crass ways to go on, this took the biscuit. She told him so, and he told her how important it was for him to enhance his reputation as an accompanist and be recognised for his musicianship. She listened and gathered more than he put into words. She appreciated his integrity. By seizing an opportunity that might never come again, he could attain that advancement.

'And not only that,' he said. 'Mr Grant insulted me. He called me what I am. A bastard. He said I had no right to get married at all. Very well. But this particular bastard means to prove himself.' He spoke with passion, all the more impressive because he did not raise his voice. 'Do you see, Nanny?' he asked.

'Yes, I do, and so will Charlotte when she understands.'

'What shall I do?' he asked her.

'If you have half an ounce of sense, my

dear boy, you will go up to her room, take her in your arms and cuddle her. Then, when she stops crying, tell her what you've just told me.'

'Will she listen?'

'Not if you lead off with your career. Ask her to look out for a house to live in, one with no near neighbours so you can practise your piano. Ask what kind of a wedding she wants. You'll think of things.'

He was already thinking. He would be able to rent a house. He had heard that Barnes was a pleasant locality. After his tour with Hans, and the winter season ahead, he would get all the work he could manage at home. That, and the fees from his publisher—the possibilities were endless.

'Nanny, you are the world's wonder!'

'Limit it to Hammersmith,' she said, making Hammersmith sound even more exotic than Xanadu. 'Oh, and before you go upstairs you might put a match to the oven. You'll find the box on the stove.'

It was a long time before Charlotte came running out to the garden. 'Nanny, Nanny, you'll never guess! Richard is to play at the Wigmore Hall with Hans Braun this very Wednesday, and you and I will be there to hear him!'

'Well, I never did. What next will I hear?' said Nanny.

'Just that we think of settling at Barnes. It's only over the bridge so I'm to look out for a house. Oh, Nanny, I'm so terribly happy.'

'So you should be,' said Nanny. 'I'll tell you a secret. Your future husband has won my heart.'

'That makes me happier still.'

'Good. And now to practicalities. The beef will be ready at six. Take Richard for a stroll by the river, and by the time you are back it will be time to sit down.'

There had never been a livelier meal than the dinner at Nanny's that evening. By contrast, the one at Lancaster Gate was a far more solemn affair, as Aunt Mildred had arrived for the Coronation.

The atmosphere was strained, as William had not seen fit to tell her that Charlotte had run away for fear she might upbraid him. She did more. She as good as said that the whole thing was his fault, and although she was sure it was a father's duty to choose the right husband for his daughter, it was madness to expect a girl to marry a man she found repulsive.

'I told Charlotte the last time I saw her that she must obey you in the question of choice, but I gave you more credit than to choose a creature like Albert Morton,' she said.

'I agree with you, Aunt,' cried Ellie. 'Oh, how I wish you could have met Mr Allen.'

'And who, may I ask, is Mr Allen?'

'The man Charlotte wanted to marry. Good-looking, charming, accomplished—'

'Don't mention that unmentionable at this table,' roared William. 'His mother is a single woman and as bold as brass.'

Annie was handing the vegetables as slowly as she could and lapping up the conversation to repeat to Mrs Vickery.

'A disadvantage, to be sure, but not insurmountable when treated with discretion,' said Aunt Mildred. 'I understand certain aristocratic members of society have fathers who are not their mothers' husbands.'

'And do you condone that kind of thing, Aunt?' enquired William with heavy sarcasm.

'I am not called upon to condone or condemn, so I do neither,' replied Aunt Mildred. 'Tell me more about this Mr Allen, if you please.'

William sulked, so it was left to Ellen to tell Aunt Mildred of Charlotte's romantic attachment to Mr Allen and the proposal that had resulted in his dismissal. This had led to the final assignation in the kitchen after midnight, and William's plan to send Charlotte to stay with her aunt at Bournemouth for as long as it took to bring her to heel.

William sat in sullen silence while Ellen recounted this. Aunt Mildred was all attention, but when it came to the plan to send Charlotte to Bournemouth she sat up straight and said he had never consulted her on the matter. What had he meant by it? she wanted to know. Had he intended to dump Charlotte on her doorstep without notice? Had he the impertinence to expect her to accept his refractory child for the purpose of breaking her spirit? Did he not know that she could put up with Charlotte for a fortnight in the summer but no more? Had he no idea of her mode of life—her work with various committees, her obligation to friends, her involvement with the Bournemouth Amateur Operatic Society as their honorary secretary?

At this stage William, not for the first time in his life, accidentally tipped the gravy boat in his aunt's direction, causing her to rise with alacrity for fear of getting a lapful of the contents.

By the time the cloth was changed and the table relaid for pudding, nobody had much appetite for it, and although the subject was dropped Aunt Mildred came back to it later.

She was horrified to learn from Ellen that Charlotte was working as a needlewoman and mixing with low-class people who no doubt pumped her full of revolutionary ideas. William had shown Mr Allen the door. Well and good. If he had asked her advice she would have told him to introduce Charlotte to eligible young men and do everything possible to divert her mind from Mr Allen.

'You say he's abroad,' she said. 'Out of sight, out of mind.'

'I don't think so,' Ellen said.

She was surprised to find that Aunt Mildred disapproved of William's actions and could almost be called broad-minded, but after several conversations she understood how it was. Aunt Mildred believed in a strict upbringing for children and young people. Above all they must learn the difference between right and wrong. If, in adulthood, they chose to grow lax, to take a light view of marriage vows, at least they couldn't be hypocritical about it. 'They know they are wrong but that's for their consciences, not for other people's,' she said.

For the present, all Aunt Mildred's attention was on the Coronation and the state of the King's health. She noted with concern that he hadn't been to Ascot the previous week but that he would be driving from Paddington to Buckingham Palace in semi-state on Monday. She was determined to see the procession.

'If it's a fine day you must come with me, Ellen,' she announced. 'I shall go whatever the weather.'

Ellen's pregnancy was progressing well. The green apples she crunched every morning banished nausea and she felt uncommonly healthy. She would enjoy watching the procession.

After such a long spell of cold, wretched weather the day of the procession was fine and warm and the crowds turned out, thankful for a touch of summer at last.

Aunt Mildred decided the Mall would be the best vantage point. They went there in their own carriage, alighted above the Duke of York's steps and went down to the road, where there was still ample room for onlookers. The decorations, flags, bunting and arches had survived the recent lashing rain and looked triumphant in the sunshine.

'We shan't have to wait long for Their Majesties. They are due to be at the Palace in time for luncheon,' Aunt Mildred said. There was already the buzz of anticipation which heralded the approach of royalty.

Very soon a detachment of cavalry appeared followed by the first of the carriages. They heard distant cheers that grew louder as the royal coach came into view and drove slowly up the Mall.

'Curtsey, Ellen,' Aunt Mildred commanded, dropping a low curtsey herself as the coach passed them. The Queen acknowledged the cheers with graceful waves. The King didn't raise a hand. Grey beard, greyer face, he sat slumped in his seat, an old, tired, ill man in pain, whose appearance shocked everyone who saw him.

People turned to one another, spoke to strangers, concerned by what they had seen.

'They say it's only lumbago,' came a voice from the crowd.

'Go on. Where'd you hear that?'

'It's in the paper.'

Aunt Mildred shook her head. 'I fear for His Majesty. How is he to go through all the ceremony of a Coronation in his condition?'

'He'll have to, Aunt. It's all arranged,' said Ellen.

'If it is lumbago, perhaps a good rub with liniment will do.'

A lady standing beside them remarked that the terrible weather at Aldershot where he had been to review the troops must have affected his health badly. 'I expect he's taken a chill,' she said.

'Let us hope that's all,' said Aunt Mildred.

'I believe the Queen took the review in his place. He was far too ill.'

They went on talking in the same vein, just as other onlookers were doing, gathering in little groups to discuss the King's health.

Aunt Mildred had another reason to linger. The lady she was speaking with seemed vaguely familiar. Her voice and general demeanour were not those of a complete stranger. The fact that she was accompanied by a young man of equally pleasant appearance added a further complication to the riddle. Curiosity overcame natural courtesy. Aunt Mildred was driven to enquire. She said she couldn't help feeling they had met before. 'I have been thinking the same. How very odd,' said the other.

Odd indeed. In the next two breaths they discovered they had met at Bournemouth long ago. A family by the name of Lennox had lived in the same district as Miss Mildred Grant. Mr and Mrs Lennox were her contemporaries: they attended the same church, took the same daily walks on the promenade and went to the same concerts, usually accompanied by their daughter, Rose. Consequently they became acquainted, passed the time of day and had the occasional chat, mostly about some local event.

This continued until Rose married Henry Graham. He was rich, well born and moved in the higher echelons of society. Rose visited her parents from time to time and in summer was to be seen on the promenade with her husband and a nursemaid pushing a baby boy in a perambulator. Then Mr and Mrs Lennox moved away and out of Miss Grant's orbit.

Now both ladies, the elderly and the middle-aged, were embarking on a flood of reminiscences. Introductions were made, Edward Graham was introduced to Miss Grant and her niece-in-law, and at his suggestion they drove to Berkeley Square in their separate carriages to eat ices at Gunter's.

A good many other people had taken advantage of the change in the weather to do the same, and some fashionable carriages were already drawn up under the plane trees opposite the shop.

Once there, Aunt Mildred and Ellen joined the Grahams in their more commodious equipage, and a waiter ran across to take their order and was back with a loaded tray held aloft almost before they could blink.

William had never thought to give Ellen this treat, and she was amazed at the way the waiters dashed in and out of the shop and never collided with one another, just as though they were performing a circus act. It was a very lively scene and she enjoyed it enormously. A pity about the stink. Sometimes she longed for a breath of Sidmouth air but it wasn't as bad here as in the Mall, and the sweepers were active with their shovels.

Mrs Graham and Miss Grant, seated side by side, were deep in conversation, and Edward took advantage of this to ask Ellen if by any chance a young lady named Charlotte was in any way connected with her.

'She's my stepdaughter and dearest friend,' exclaimed Ellen. 'How strange you should speak of her. Do tell me how you became acquainted. You see, she hasn't lived at home for some time now.'

'I know.'

Ellen felt her position keenly at that moment. The family situation was extremely uncomfortable and it seemed quite wrong for her to have to ask a young man she had only just met, and that by chance, for news of her stepdaughter. But, being Ellen, she quickly dismissed any scruples and sought as much information as he could give her.

He, for his part, sensed the genuineness of her affection for Charlotte and found it easy to talk to her. He told her how they had met, how much he admired her, how he engineered meetings by being there when she left work every evening, and on Saturdays ran her down to Hammersmith in his motor car.

Ellen soon perceived that there was a great deal more than admiration in Edward Graham's feelings for Charlotte, and thought it only kind to let him know he didn't stand a chance.

'I expect you know Charlotte considers herself engaged,' she said.

'So she tells me. But the knot isn't tied, and until it is I shall continue to hope,' he told her.

She was touched. Here was the ideal suitor right beside her, the kind of man Aunt Mildred had told William he should have sought for his daughter, one she herself would have wholeheartedly approved if he had come on the scene earlier. As it was, could there be any going back? Was Charlotte likely to be persuaded to favour Edward Graham as opposed to Richard Allen? Oh dear, oh dear, how lucky I was to have had only one suitor, Ellen thought. William, my dear, difficult, misguided William, you need someone to love you and it's lucky you have me.

Edward, having confided his affection for Charlotte to Ellen, leaned across to speak to his mother, only to find that she had just discovered the connection too and was telling Aunt Mildred how much she admired her great-niece.

'Such courage in so young a girl,' Mrs Graham said. 'But for her I would never have recovered a brooch that means so much to me. It was a gift from my husband when Edward was born.'

'Indeed?' said Aunt Mildred. 'And how did all this come about?'

Mrs Graham liked telling people about the theft of her jewellery and the strange way in which this one precious piece was recovered, so the conversation went on until they noticed the time. Other carriages were moving away; Aunt Mildred and Ellen alighted from the Grahams' and were handed back to their own. Farewells, but not goodbyes.

'What a lovely afternoon we've had,' said Ellen as they drove out of the square.

'Pleasant for us, not so good for His Majesty, I fear,' Aunt Mildred said. Ellen had forgotten all about the King. She had heard he ate too much and thought he had only himself to blame if he had a bilious attack.

'Mrs Graham is just as I would have expected her to be had I ever spared her a thought,' Aunt Mildred remarked as they drove home. 'She was such a lovely girl, and the years have treated her kindly in spite of being widowed so young. Perhaps on that account.' She seemed to be musing over the advantages of youthful widowhood for some time.

Ellen was thinking about Edward Graham, and decided she wouldn't tell William about the young man's feelings for Charlotte. After all, he had told her in confidence, so she would keep that confidence to herself.

'What a pity we didn't know the Grahams before that silly girl became enamoured of an organ-grinder,' Aunt Mildred remarked as they neared their destination.

'I don't think anyone could call Richard Allen an organ-grinder, Aunt.'

'If I have an opportunity I shall form my own opinion, Ellen. For the present I am concerned for His Majesty's health.'

'Yes, Aunt,' said Ellen.

Aunt Mildred was only one of many thousands concerned for the King. His illness, and there was little doubt he was ill, could seriously damage business everywhere, besides causing all kinds of constitutional problems.

Henry Last, happening to be near the processional route, went out of his way to take a look and was horrified by his glimpse of the sovereign's ghastly pallor. He hurried home to tell his wife.

'I never saw a man look nearer death's door,' he said. 'He'd only have to lift his hand and he'd be knocking on it.'

'I hope you're exaggerating, Henry,' said Madame Last.

'If they put a crown on his head he'd sink under the weight. They'll never get him to the Abbey. Mark my words.'

'If you're right there's plenty will be ruined. Think of the crowds that's coming by rail. The trains won't run. They'll go broke.'

'So will the pubs.'

'Well, let's hope it's only the result of overindulgence in a bit more than food and drink. There's nothing a good dose of salts won't cure, as well you know.'

'He's only got tomorrow to recover. And don't forget he didn't go to Ascot.'

'Everyone else did and we met all our orders for it, Henry. What's more, we've just dispatched the last of the gowns for the Coronation. I think our clients will be a good advertisement for us.'

Although the weather was so much warmer, Madame Last still kept a fire burning in her sitting room, and when Algie came in that late afternoon he puffed and blew and said he didn't know how she and Dad could stand it.

'Old bones,' she said.

'You ain't old, Ma. You're in your prime,' said Algie.

'How many times have I told you not to say ain't? You never used to. I hope you're not keeping low company.'

Algie laughed. He'd caught it from Victoria but naturally he didn't tell his mother so. Victoria was the most wonderful thing that had ever happened to him, the secret he was saving up until August, his wife. His very own wife!

'You don't seem to catch the sun out punting,' his father remarked.

'Well, there ain't—sorry—hasn't been much sun lately, and anyway I wear a straw hat,' Algie said.

'With all the rain we've had, I'd expect to see the brim round your neck,' said his mother, whereupon Algie thought he had better go before he committed himself further.

Left by themselves, his parents sat in silence for a full minute. Then Madame Last spoke. 'Funny thing. I've never seen Algie's straw hat in this house,' she said. 'I wonder where he keeps it?'

'Ah,' said Henry, closing his eyes.

'I suppose he *does* go on the river?'

'You'd better ask him.'

'No. I shan't interfere. He'll only be young once, so he may as well have his fling,' said Madame Last.

Henry kept his eyes shut. He had seen Algie walking with one of the girls from the workroom. They were arm in arm and so wrapped up in each other they didn't notice anyone. Madame didn't know. She'd probably sack the girl if she found out. Well, he wasn't going to tell her. Things would settle themselves without any intervention from him.

Richard stayed at Nanny's until midnight on that wonderful Sunday of his return, and was back early the next morning with a cab to take Charlotte to Last's.

Consequently she was not in the right frame of mind for work that day. There was so much to tell Victoria, in whispered snatches.

'What's up with you two?' demanded Miss Sharp suspiciously.

Victoria winked at Charlotte and they both collapsed with laughter.

'I suppose it don't mean anything to you, the King being took ill,' said Miss Sharp.

'Not much,' said Victoria. 'Not to me anyway. Matter of fact I got married Sat'day. I'm Mrs James Smith now.' She had told Charlotte long ago that she intended to be known as missus so that she could wear her wedding ring and be accorded the respect due to a married lady in an interesting condition.

'Congratulations, I'm sure,' said Miss Sharp nastily. 'Perhaps you'll show us a likeness of Mr Smith sometime.'

'There's no need to sniff. I was at the wedding and it was lovely,' Charlotte said. She was not inclined to tell Miss Sharp that Richard was home. She would have found something unkind to say about the brevity of his visit. She was resigned to it now, and had so many things to think about and arrange she would have to get her ideas into order. Mary was coming to the wedding, Nanny would help her find a house, and there were only Saturday afternoons and Sundays to sort everything out.

For the first time since she began at Last's she had to unpick a seam, and Miss Prescot said she wasn't surprised at the lack of concentration, for only heaven knew what was to become of them all the way things were going.

'We'll be taking orders for mourning before very long,' she said. 'I hope you girls have got black hats. That and armbands is all that's expected of the poor when royalty dies.'

'Which royalty's going to die?' demanded Victoria. 'If you're talking about the

King, I'll bet my boots he's only got a bellyache.'

'Mr Last has seen him this very day,' said Miss Prescot.

'Mr Last's as pickled as Madame's plums,' said Victoria. 'He saw his own reflection in a window.'

'Keep your disloyal remarks to yourself and get on with your work,' said Miss Prescot as she left the room.

'Lucky I didn't bring me bow. I'd have played a tune on her fiddle face,' said Victoria.

Somehow they got through the day. Richard would be waiting for Charlotte and she wanted Victoria to meet him. In her excitement she forgot that Edward Graham was likely to be outside too.

As she emerged they both stepped forward, two tall, good-looking men raising their hats simultaneously.

'Richard!' Charlotte lifted her face for a kiss. Then, holding his hand, she said: 'This is Victoria—' and paused. 'Oh, and here's Edward. Mr Graham, I mean.'

She was so excited she was doing it all wrong. She should have presented Richard to Victoria, not the other way round, but Victoria was behaving beautifully. 'I have long wished to meet you, Mr Allen,' she said, taking him in. Not quite her style, but certainly a bit of all right, and just fine for Charlotte.

'And I'm delighted.' He raised her hand to his lips and sent her into a fit of giggles.

'The pleasure's mine,' she managed to say.

Charlotte turned to Edward and introduced him to her fiancé who had arrived in England only yesterday. 'Or more truthfully on Saturday night. I believe he waited till morning on Nanny's doorstep.'

'I did,' said Richard.

The two men bowed stiffly to each other and an edgy silence fell on the group until Richard said he had booked a table at the Savoy and they had better hail a cab.

'There's something special I want to tell you, Charlotte,' Edward said, for he was full of his meeting with Ellen in the Mall.

'It must wait for another time,' she replied, her arm in Richard's.

Edward turned away disappointed. Now he was stranded with Victoria.

'May I drive you home?' he asked.

'Thank you but I can't risk being jolted,' she said. 'Besides, I'm meeting a friend.'

'Then I'll wish you good night.'

'Thanks all the same.'

She went off to meet Algie and go back to Clapham, where he would stay until midnight. They had agreed he should return to Mayfair every night until, as he put it, he spilt the beans when the season was over.

'What was that Graham fellow doing outside Last's?' Richard wanted to know.

They were in a hansom on their way to the Strand.

'I told you about him,' Charlotte said. 'He's been a great help one way and another.'

'He was waiting for you, wasn't he?'

'He often does.'

'Does he indeed?'

'Don't sound so suspicious. There's nothing in it.'

'There had better not be.'

'I believe you're jealous.'

'Of course I am.'

'You make me feel ever so important. I wonder if you'll challenge him to a duel? They usually have them at dawn on Wimbledon Common. Or they did. It's not allowed any more.'

'I can wring his neck anywhere.'

'You really are a chump! Wringing poor Edward's neck. Really! Put your arm round me and tell me how you got on with the publisher.'

Richard was pacified, but worried too, because he realised that men were bound to be attracted to Charlotte. Edward Graham

331

was a personable young man with natural advantages that made him a formidable rival. But perhaps, as she assured him, Graham was no more than a good friend, and he'd be a fool if he expected her to limit her male acquaintances to her fiancé.

All the same, it reinforced his determination to be recognised as an accompanist of the highest order, and he was sure she understood how important it was.

He told her the first set of arias he had adapted as pieces for the piano would be in print by late summer, and that he had a commission for another six.

'How will you do it? How can you fit it in with your tour?' she asked, concerned for him with his already packed programme.

'Midnight oil,' he said, and he hugged and kissed her until she begged him to stop as they were nearly there and her hat was all crooked.

'I like it that way. You look adorable.'

The cab drew up at the entrance. She managed to adjust her hat and they sailed into the hotel hand in hand. She looked radiant and he so much in love that people noticed them and asked one another who this glamorous young couple could be.

Charlotte always ran out of superlatives when she spoke of the evening, when she and Richard were so entranced with each other they didn't even hear the paper boys shouting or feel the sense of impending disaster that affected everyone else.

Next morning at Last's, even Victoria looked solemn. The papers were all wrong kidding the nation the King only had lumbago, she told Charlotte. The poor old basket had got something 'orrible inside and they were going to cut it out soon as he'd had his lunch.

'He won't be having any lunch,' said Miss Sharp.

'Coo. He must be bad,' Victoria said.

Universal gloom.

Madame's heart went out to the shop-keepers and caterers all stocked up with eatables that would be left on their hands.

They could give it to the poor, muttered Victoria. But that wouldn't benefit trade, as Miss Prescot tried to point out, and she conferred with Madame on the advisability of giving a big order for black crêpe.

'If the worst comes to the worst there'll be a rush for mourning costumes,' she said.

'We had enough of that when the old Queen went,' said Madame Last. An armband manufacturer she knew was working overtime and she didn't intend to follow his example. 'No, Miss Prescot. Look on the bright side, we've already got one. Those French dressmakers are all going home, I hear.'

'Frogs,' said Miss Prescot. 'Leaving the sinking ship.'

Madame cast her eyes up to heaven. The stupid woman didn't know the difference between frogs and rats.

Wilfred was out much longer than usual on various errands, and came back to say the Coronation was off, if anyone still had any doubts about it. He'd managed a sneak round the Abbey where the dress rehearsal was being held. Good as the real thing, he said, until someone whispered in the Archbishop's ear and the whole lot of them fell down on their knees and started praying like mad.

All this provided food for talk in the workrooms, for Madame didn't begrudge her girls slacking off once in a while.

Charlotte's own concerns didn't allow her to dwell on the trials of the nation for long. She had the rest of June and the whole of July and August before her new life dawned in September. Victoria understood this very well, as August was to mark her own changed status. 'Won't it be a lark when we're prop'ly settled, Charlotte? Me in Clapham and you at the top of some tree in the concert world.'

'Yes, won't it!' echoed Charlotte.

Richard was outside Last's when they

left work, but there was no sign of Edward Graham, so there were no altercations. They dined at the Savoy again but there were very few guests in evidence, although a great many servants all jabbered and gesticulated in French and German over the piled-up luggage outside. Richard asked a commissionaire what was going on and was told the foreign visitors were leaving and that it was the same all over London.

Charlotte immediately feared for the Wigmore Hall recital. 'It's all right. All the seats are sold,' Richard told her.

Although she wanted to hear the recital, especially the Kreutzer Sonata, she almost dreaded it, for it would be their last evening together and they wouldn't be spending it alone. They, with Nanny, were to be the guests of Hans Braun for supper afterwards, and early on Thursday the two men would leave for Paris. It was hard to bear the thought of parting again, so how could she endure the reality when it came?

'It won't be like it was before,' Richard assured her. 'There won't be any confiscated letters and I shall be back before you know where you are.'

This should have comforted her, but a niggling sense of danger persisted. It was like a grain of sand in her shoe.

Wednesday was not a comfortable day. The King had come through his operation much better than anyone expected. The outlook was good but an air of despondency hung over the capital. Workmen took the decorations down. Flags, banners, garlands were all dismantled, and the columns and flagstaffs looked skeletal without them.

Long queues of people bound for home formed at the main railway stations. It was no use staying in town now that the Coronation was off.

Hotels, boarding houses and spare rooms emptied out. There had never been so much bed linen to wash all at once, so at least the laundries flourished.

Charlotte felt almost dazed as she arrived at the Wigmore Hall with Nanny that Wednesday night. She was overtired after the late nights and almost feverish excitement of having Richard home. Every emotion was stressed because they were to be parted so soon.

Nanny knew Charlotte was strung to breaking point and feared there would be a dramatic reaction. Bessy Last was a good employer and Charlotte had made a tremendous effort to adapt to the life of a working girl, but it was time she stopped, for the strain of the past few months was telling on her.

Days later, when she looked back to the evening of the recital, Nanny saw it as a disappointment in many ways. The music was superb but the hall was half empty. Although all the seats were sold they were not taken up, so the applause was thin and scattered where it should have been thunderous.

Charlotte thought it a disaster. Her eyes kept filling with tears but she managed not to shed them. Hans Braun, unperturbed, said it was due to the Coronation being cancelled. 'People are not in the mood for music just now,' he said.

Richard was stoical. It was a pity but who wanted to pay for another night in town just because they had bought a concert ticket? It was easily understandable.

Hans took them to supper at a small, exclusive restaurant they had never heard of because its élite clientele preferred to keep it a secret, as did the management.

The food was delicious, and Charlotte brightened under the influence of the wine. It behoved her to encourage Richard rather than deplore a recital which deserved the highest praise but would probably go unnoticed.

There was a lounge furnished with sofas and armchairs where they could enjoy their coffee and liqueurs after supper. Hans knew that Richard wanted to talk to Charlotte, so by mutual accord he and Nanny sat together and had plenty to say. He spoke a great deal of Richard's prospects and rated them as good. He had the highest opinion of his favourite accompanist.

On the other side of the room Charlotte was reminding Richard not to forget to give her his itinerary this time. He handed her a notebook in which he had carefully written all the dates, locations, hotels, halls, train times—everything. 'Don't lose it,' he said. 'That's my immediate future mapped out, but I want to talk about yours over the next three months. I don't like you working at Last's. It's not right. A twelve-hour day, scrappy meals. You are exhausting yourself'

'Not for much longer,' she said.

'One more day is too much. I wish you would leave tomorrow.'

'How can I? They pay us enough to live on. Just.'

'Have you still got the purse Mary gave you?'

'Of course I have. It's one of my most treasured possessions.'

'The money's all gone though, hasn't it?'

She nodded, puzzled by these questions. Then it struck her that she couldn't have managed without it. All the expenses with

Clarice. The table for Victoria. Cab fares. All kinds of things.

'Where is it?'

'Here.' She took it from her reticule.

'I'm going to fill it up again,' he said. 'There will be enough for you to leave work and take life easy until I come home.'

'Oh no,' she said. 'I can't take money.'

'Why not?'

'It wouldn't be right.'

'You'd take it if we were married.'

'But we're not.'

'Charlotte!'

'Please don't ask me. If you do I shall think you don't understand me. I've used the money Mary gave me, but that was different. Keeping myself, being independent is a thing I simply have to do. I've got so far with one object in view, and I think you know what that is.'

He knew very well.

'Let me finish it,' she said.

He bowed his head. 'How can I look you in the face after all you've endured because you loved me?' he said at last.

'Don't put it in the past tense. I've never stopped loving you.' She put her hand over his, and of the two his was by far the more beautiful. Her fingers were marked with needle pricks, his were smooth, long, well shaped. She thought of him working ceaselessly, practising for long hours, listening, learning, studying, thinking. His life had been no less arduous than hers. This interlude, magical, sad, joyous, shadowed, must not end in misunderstanding.

'Don't let's spoil the rest of our time together,' she said. 'It's been hard for both of us being parted and worried about each other, but I'm sure we'll weather the next bit.' And then, because he didn't respond at once, 'Aren't you?' she asked.

He wanted words to express his feelings but couldn't find them. Soon he must leave her and his heart was hurting already. He took both her hands, and his voice sounded husky as he said: 'Yes, Charlotte. I am.'

She woke the next morning knowing that he was already far away and thought of their last embrace, the strength of his arms round her, the feel of his lips and the fervour of his words. This would sustain her, along with his letters, written after midnight when he was so tired that sometimes his pen dragged across the paper.

It was his first experience of a concert tour without Mary. There were often long distances between engagements, sometimes pianos were less than perfect and there was trouble with tuners. Life was hectic; there were few chances to relax.

Her own life settled into a predictable routine. The seasonal rush was over, so work slackened off at Last's. Madame knew that the girls kept their own sewing on their laps under the cloth and got on with it behind her back. She could afford to turn a blind eye, for the firm had never done so well, and now the King was on the mend it was a blessing she hadn't followed Miss Prescot's advice and laid in quantities of black cloth.

Miss Prescot had recently drawn her attention to Victoria, now married to a Mr James Smith and rapidly putting on weight.

'It's not the extra pounds so much as the way she walks,' Miss Prescot observed. 'She's kind of leaning back, as if she has to balance something.'

'How she walks is no concern of mine or yours, Miss Prescot,' said Madame Last. 'I've told you before and I'll repeat it now. It doesn't do to get interested in how employees live. So long as they are punctual and industrious and maintain a good appearance, I ask no more.'

In spite of what she said, Madame Last felt a certain amount of sympathy when a worker's trials came to her ears. She couldn't help feeling sorry for Clarice

West, let down so badly by a burglar. Then there was Miss Grant. She continued to be a valuable acquisition. The girl had apparently run away from home on account of a forbidden love affair. As she was still here, Madame supposed it must have fizzled out. She was much thinner than when she came, and sometimes looked as though she had been crying.

Charlotte did cry into her pillow. She missed Richard so much, almost more now that he had been and gone. She didn't expect to see Edward Graham again as he had met Richard, but a few nights later there he was when she left work.

'I've been dying to talk to you,' he said. 'Something miraculous happened. I suppose you haven't heard?'

'Heard what?'

'Look, we can't talk in the street. Let me take you to dinner.'

'I must go home, Eddie. Victoria's gone on to buy some chops and she'll be waiting for me.'

'Just this once.'

'No, I can't. It isn't proper and Richard wouldn't like it.'

'Blow Richard.'

'What?'

'You may well ask what. So shall I. What's wrong with sitting down at table with me? I know a very cosy little restaurant. I'm sure Mrs Grant wouldn't object to us going there.'

'How on earth do you know what my stepmother would say?'

'Because I've met her. There. I knew that would shake you. We got on famously and had a long chat about you.'

'Did you indeed! Look, Eddie, I really can't stay now. Please don't try to keep me.'

He saw she was determined, swallowed his disappointment and gave way gracefully.

She went on her way, puzzled over the meeting he had described. Ellen would be sure to tell her some time just how it had happened, so she didn't dwell on it for long.

A few days later a letter in an unknown hand arrived. The daily letter from Richard was there as well and was much more important, so she put the other in her pocket and didn't open it until after midday dinner, when she and Victoria were sunning themselves on the flat roof. It was from Mrs Graham and she read it with disbelief.

'What do you make of this, Victoria?' she asked, passing it over.

'Plain as a pikestaff. She's inviting you to tea Sat'day,' said Victoria.

'But why?'

'Are you dim or something? She says

she met your stepma recently. By a happy chance, she says. That's why. Ain't it nice?'

Charlotte supposed it was but didn't want to accept. She was going to explore Barnes with Nanny on Saturday. Will Goode had promised to make enquiries at an agent and to tour the area on his bicycle so they wouldn't waste time looking at places that were no use. Now this invitation had come along and changed everything.

After work on Saturday she went straight to Hammersmith. Nanny hadn't expected her so early and echoed her surprise when she read Mrs Graham's letter.

'It's very nice of her to ask you, and who knows but it will help heal the rift with your family,' she said.

'There isn't one with Ellie,' Charlotte said.

'No, but it forges a link. The Grahams are a good family and it's as well for you to associate with people like that. Remember how thoughtful young Mr Graham was when we lost poor Lily.'

Charlotte hadn't forgotten. Neither did she forget the number of times he had waited for her after work with no other object than to see her home, or so she liked to think. He would stay outside shops while she went in for various groceries and then carry the parcels.

'He's fair gone on you,' Victoria remarked more than once.

'He knows I'm engaged.'

'He wouldn't half be a good catch,' said Victoria.

'I don't doubt it.'

'He's on the spot, Charlotte.'

'What are you suggesting?'

'Just that he's here and Richard ain't.'

'Kindly keep such observations to yourself, Victoria.'

'All right. Hold your hair on. But it's obvious, ain't it?'

'No it ain't,' said Charlotte crossly.

The Grants' carriage was among those drawn up outside the house in Curzon Street when Charlotte arrived, so she knew Ellie was there and hoped her father wasn't. It was a fine afternoon and she saw the house in the daylight for the first time. When she'd called to give Mrs Graham the pawn ticket it was dark and she had been too concerned with her mission to notice its size and magnificence.

She felt quite strange as she approached, and afterwards couldn't clearly remember entering the drawing room. It was all in a haze, though she recalled Mrs Graham's welcome and her own efforts to print on her mind the names and faces of the ladies

345

she was introduced to. Of the men, she knew only Edward Graham; Mr Heston, a distinguished-looking gentleman, was a stranger although she had heard he took an interest in Clarice, to her friend's discomfort. No Papa, thank goodness.

And then there was Ellie. 'I've kept her until last,' said Mrs Graham. 'There, my dear, is this not wonderful?'

'Yes, it really is wonderful,' Charlotte said, and gazed at Ellie.

Ellie, no less moved, patted the empty seat beside her, and Mrs Graham told Charlotte to sit down and hear all about the chance meeting that had given them both so much pleasure.

'You look so well,' Charlotte said, and Ellie replied that she was very well indeed. She didn't remark on Charlotte's looks but noticed that she was much thinner and that her young prettiness was giving way to beauty. It betrayed hardship and privation with inner strength, and made Ellie sad. How she wished William would take his daughter back on her own terms. But Charlotte was asking how she had met Mrs Graham, and Ellie gave her an account of the day she went to the Mall with Aunt Mildred to see the King's procession.

'Mrs Graham lived at Bournemouth as a girl, and your Aunt Mildred was acquainted with her family. Mrs Graham has called on me since and I've heard all about her brooch and your involvement with that dreadful burglar.'

Charlotte wasn't expecting this and sprang to the defence of Mr Blades. 'Ellie, Mr Blades is not dreadful,' she said.

'That's scarcely a matter of opinion, dear. One could hardly describe him as admirable, could one?'

'He was very kind and helpful to me and I shall always be grateful to him,' Charlotte said.

'Were you with him at the Alhambra that night?'

'Yes. He gave us a lovely evening.'

'I suppose he organised the theft of those letters from your papa?'

'He had nothing to do with it. Oh dear, when I think of it! The police would never have called on him if Pa hadn't made me give him everybody's name. And poor Clarice! Look what it did to her. You can't imagine how guilty I've felt about that.'

Charlotte was beginning to show distress, and Ellen saw it wouldn't do to pursue the subject. 'We'll talk of all this another time,' she said. 'Let's not get excited about it now. There's young Mr Graham dying to speak to you.'

She turned to the lady on her other side and Edward took the opportunity to engage Charlotte's attention.

'I've been desolate without you,' he said.

'Now don't be silly, Edward. I'm still to be found in the same place. I suppose you were going to tell me how you met my stepmother last time I saw you.'

'You didn't give me a chance.'

'I was too wrapped up in Richard, and can you wonder?'

'I can, to be truthful.'

'Oh?'

'How can he let you go on slaving at that dressmaker's? He may be very clever and very talented, but if you ask me, he hasn't got any sense.'

'I don't ask you, Eddie dear.'

'That hurts.'

'What does?'

'Endearments you don't mean.'

She was rather sorry she had said it, but after exchanging so much frothy banter with him, surely he knew how to take it. She liked him and enjoyed being met and taken home after work, but, as she kept reminding him, she was engaged to Richard Allen.

'Where is Mr Allen now?' he asked.

'On tour with Hans Braun.'

'Then he's not in London?'

'No. They're abroad until September.

'Good,' he said, and moved away to be

replaced by Mr Heston.

'I believe Mrs Graham's brooch was restored to her through you, Miss Grant,' he said. 'I can't tell you how glad she was to have it back. We're all grateful to you, you know.'

Charlotte said she was pleased to have helped but it was only what anybody would have done.

'Was it not intended as a gift for Miss West when it was in the wrong hands?' he went on.

Charlotte agreed and wished he wouldn't stare so. He was taking her in, inch by inch.

'Being deprived of it was a great disappointment to Miss West, I suppose.'

'She lost a lot more than a brooch, Mr Heston. Her whole future vanished overnight.'

'You know her very well?'

'Indeed I do.'

'I understand you worked with her at a dressmaker's, Miss Grant.'

'I still work at the same place. I shall be leaving in September.'

'For better things, presumably. I'm quite sure you were not cut out to be a working girl.'

'I certainly was not, but I've squeezed into the mould.'

'And retained a remarkably lovely shape,

if you'll allow me to say so.'

'Well, Mr Heston, I can hardly forbid you now you've said it, can I?'

Mrs Graham joined them. 'I hope you're not teasing Miss Grant, Arthur.'

'As if I would.' He saw that his cousin wanted to speak to Charlotte and moved away.

'How is the world treating you, my dear?' Mrs Graham asked. 'I hear your fiancé returned from abroad recently.'

'He did, but only for three days. He's on a Continental tour with Hans Braun now.'

'Ah. Hans Braun is very much to the fore nowadays. They say he's quite a Paganini.'

'I never heard Paganini,' Charlotte said, at which Mrs Graham laughed and said neither had she. 'None of us have. He's a legend. But I suppose touring with Hans Braun must be very strenuous? A good deal of travelling, no doubt.'

'And getting acclimatised to different halls, too. But Richard will be in London for quite long periods, so we'll be able to take a house and settle down in the autumn.'

'Very nice, dear. But I expect Mr Allen's work will often take him from home, will it not?'

'I think it's bound to, but I shall go with

him whenever possible.'

Mrs Graham shook her head slowly. 'I gather a steadier situation wouldn't suit him. Teaching perhaps at an academy of music, with regular hours and a regular income.'

'I don't think that would appeal to him,' Charlotte said. 'He has so much energy and such talent. I'd never try to stop him doing what he feels he must.'

'Don't you think it would be nicer for you to have a husband in a steady occupation rather than one who's here, there and everywhere?'

'But that wouldn't be Richard,' Charlotte said.

'So long as you recognise the drawbacks,' said Mrs Graham with a smile.

Charlotte managed to return the smile but sensed danger. Yet how could there be any in this room full of men and women who had no reason to harm her? She told herself it was something in the atmosphere of wealth, class, leisure, standing. Just as she, a workroom girl, was superior to the match-sellers, flowergirls and crossing-sweepers, so were these people superior to her.

Occasionally she was struck by her lack of security, of depending on her wages for her every need, and it frightened her. Absence from work meant loss of pay, and when a workroom girl fell ill the others clubbed a few pence together to buy her food.

She thought of Richard with greater longing than ever. How safe she felt when he was by her side, and how vulnerable without him. She twisted the ring on her finger, almost forgetting where she was, but the guests were leaving and Ellie was saying it was time for them to go.

They took leave of Mrs Graham with many compliments and warm assurances of future meetings.

'That was a pleasant occasion, don't you think?' Ellie said as they drove away.

'I didn't like it. It gave me the shivers,' Charlotte said.

'Goodness me, why was that?'

'I felt out of it. I don't fit in with people like the Grahams and their friends any more.'

'They're no different from us. They may be richer, but that doesn't matter. I believe the late Mr Graham was a gentleman farmer with the largest flocks of sheep in England. Of course they're an old family, landed gentry—but not ennobled. You shouldn't feel out of place with them.'

'It isn't that. I don't think you know what I mean and I can't explain.'

'Perhaps it's because you're mixing with

working-class people now,' Ellie suggested, and Charlotte didn't remind her that it had almost always been so. She had spent more time in the company of the servants than with anyone else after her mother died.

'I do wish you were at home, Charlotte. I miss you every day. And you're not in any danger from Albert Morton now. Your papa has quite given up the idea of an alliance there.'

'Does he think any more kindly of Richard?'

'No. He's as adamant as ever where Richard is concerned, I'm sorry to say.'

'Oh.' This was no surprise but it was a continuing disappointment.

'By the way, dear, young Mr Graham is really taken with you. He told me so himself. But perhaps I shouldn't tell you.'

'It doesn't matter. Edward knows I'm engaged. I really like him. He's rather like a brother. We flirt a bit but it doesn't mean anything.'

'It does to him, Charlotte. You've made a conquest.'

'You won't tell Pa, will you? Promise.'

'I've already decided it's one thing I should keep to myself,' Ellen said.

They jogged along in thoughtful silence which Ellen broke by asking when Richard would be coming home.

'He's been and gone again,' Charlotte

said, and she felt so low, weak, lonely
and poor that it was a comfort to respond
to her stepmother's sympathy and tell her
what had happened and how hard she was
finding it to keep up her strength. Not that
her resolve was any less. It was simply that
she missed Richard terribly and he was
such a long way off.

Ellen was deeply concerned about her.
They had arrived at Lancaster Gate but
stayed in the carriage talking, and it was
wrong to feel they couldn't go into the
house to continue their conversation. At
last, with a heavy heart, Ellen got out and
instructed the driver to take Miss Charlotte
to Hammersmith.

When William heard Ellen in the hall
he was out to greet her, asking her what
she would like. Tea, or perhaps a glass of
sherry would do her more good.

'Whisky with plenty of splash.' She sank
down on the sofa in the drawing room and
put her legs up.

'Tired?' he asked, handing her a glass
of pale liquid and replenishing his own.
'Have you been doing too much?' He was
all solicitude.

'Not tired. Rather upset.'

'Oh? How was it at the Grahams'?'

She took a sip before telling him.
'William darling, Charlotte was there this
afternoon. We had a long, long talk.'

'Is she as pigheaded as ever?'

'She's as faithful to Mr Allen.'

'Then I'm not interested.'

'I am. It worries me to know she's leading such a hard life. It's telling on her.'

'She chose it,' he said, in that cold voice that made her long for Sidmouth.

'How can you be so...' She hesitated, trying to find the word she wanted, rejecting 'brutal' and plumping for 'heartless.'

'Because I don't want to see her tied up to that wandering minstrel.'

'That's not fair, William.' She wanted him to know all that Charlotte had told her about Richard's progress, his work transcribing songs, his tour with the highly acclaimed Hans Braun. Instead she told him something that was far more likely to impress him. 'The Grahams think very highly of Charlotte,' she said. 'She's held her own all this time and I think you should be proud of her.'

He shuffled his feet on the carpet. Charlotte had inherited Amanda's stubbornness, her looks, her impulsiveness, even her voice, and had she been faced with the same dilemma he guessed she would have done exactly what Charlotte was doing.

'I'm sure I don't know what Mrs

Graham must think of you for allowing your daughter to go out to work and live in a common lodging house,' Ellen went on.

'Would you like me to drag her back by the scruff of her neck?'

'I'd like you to ask her to come home,' said Ellen.

He tossed down his whisky and poured more. He was having a struggle with himself. It hurt to give in but in the end he had to, because he loved her.

'All right. If it would make you happy I will,' he said.

On Monday he took a cab to Mrs Blunt's street, noting that it was a fair step from Mayfair and Madame Last's establishment, which he had already made it his business to inspect.

It was a fine evening but the late sunlight magnified the shabby appearance of the houses. The street itself had the crushed, depressed look of a place that had never seen better days and certainly did not expect any in the future.

He dismissed the cab at the end of the road and walked to Mrs Blunt's, observing her skimpy brown curtains and the peeling paint on the window frames.

Her door was shut but most of the other houses had theirs open, emitting the stink of boiled bones, cabbage and other appetite-killers. Several small children squatted on the kerbs. Most had sores round their mouths, bare bottoms and horrid square faces, and they stared.

Mrs Blunt kept him waiting for several minutes before answering the door. She had been taking a good look from the window, and knew he was unlikely to have any business with her and had probably come to the wrong address.

'Well?' she challenged.

She spoke so sharply he took a step back. 'I wish to see Miss Grant,' he said.

'Ho, do you? Well, you've come to the wrong shop. Miss Grant don't live here.'

'I understood she did. Do I take it she has moved away?'

'I don't know how else you'd take it,' she said, and went to close the door.

'One moment.' He raised his hand in a commanding gesture. 'Be so kind as to give me her present address.'

'That I won't,' said Mrs Blunt. 'Addresses is confidential.'

'Miss Grant is my daughter and I wish to see her.'

'Then you ought to know where she is, not come poking and peering round here. How can I be sure you're her father? You could be up to no good.'

'Madam...' He almost choked with indignation.

'There's many a top-hatted swell pretends to be the father of unprotected girls like Miss Grant. You don't look old enough to be her father. Where's your mutton-chop whiskers? Ho, no. You don't get me divulging.'

This last was because he had put his hand in his pocket, thinking that half a crown might soften her. Unluckily for William, Mrs Blunt had taken an active dislike to him.

'A likely father,' she said. 'What father would let his daughter share digs with a fast little cat like Victoria Clink? Your girl's learnt some sly tricks since she's known that one. No cooking in the rooms. That's the rule of the house. Miss Grant got round it by cooking on the windowsill. I found it covered in fat when they left. Valentine!'

She had no need to shout, for Mr Blunt was there, looking over her shoulder. Dirty toes stuck through the holes in his socks.

'Tell this gentleman how you had to go out for more scouring powder for the sill after those girls left.'

'It was Miss Grant started it,' said Mr Blunt.

'We never smelled frying till she came here. Couldn't catch her at it. Didn't twig. I reckon she was craftier than the other one.'

Mr and Mrs Blunt, for once in accord, were railing at William in unison. They came out on the step and rivalled a tom cats' chorus.

Mr Grant had acquired a stately walk over the years but found himself retreating from the Blunts at an unseemly speed. He was thankful to round the corner and sink down on the only bench in a scrubby patch of grass that called itself a park and was not much bigger than his own back garden.

He took off his hat and mopped his brow, shocked and disgusted by the unspeakable Blunts. Their belligerent attitude, their determination to withhold his daughter's address and their unwarrantable assumption that he was not her father but some kind of roué made him feel caught up in a waking nightmare.

He had never let himself imagine where or how Charlotte existed, but now he had seen for himself. The street, the house, the Blunts themselves formed an entity she should never have known and would not have done if she had been the dutiful daughter he had every right to expect her to be.

Apparently she walked to work every day, three miles at least, and back again at night. Well, the exercise was good for her. Why should he blame himself? He mustn't. He had asked her to come home that night at the Alhambra, Ellen wanted her there and she was fond of Ellen. No. The whole trouble was that damned Bohemian organ-grinder she'd fallen in love with.

It wouldn't last. Get her home.

He got himself home, hot, weary, defeated. Ellen's eager look of expectancy turned to dismay when he shook his head.

'Don't ask for explanations. I've been through a shocking ordeal.' It was hours before he could bring himself to tell her what had happened, and even then he omitted all Mrs Blunt's disparaging remarks, dwelling only on her refusal to disclose Charlotte's address.

'I suppose she was right,' Ellen said. 'Don't worry, William. *I'll* find Charlotte for you.'

You'd better. You're the one who wants her, he thought, and just managed not to say so.

Charlotte was in a hurry to get home, as all her stockings needed darning; those she had on were dropping into holes, not that it mattered, as the legs didn't show under her skirt though the heels did.

She ran down the stairs and into the street, and there was her father's carriage outside. She wouldn't have believed it was his if Ellen had not been looking out of the window. She was waving and beckoning.

'How lovely to see you!' exclaimed Charlotte. 'Are you thinking of patronising Madame Last?'

'No, dear. She's a bit too expensive for me. Jump in and I'll tell you why I'm here.'

Charlotte was glad to comply. Being seen in a carriage might not endear her to the other girls.

'Where are you taking me?' she asked as they drove off.

'Home,' said Ellen.

'To Clapham?'

'So that's where you live! Your papa went to Mrs Blunt's and was told you'd left. I think they were horrid to him. They wouldn't tell him where you'd gone. He came home quite shaken and wouldn't give me any details.'

The idea of her father being confronted by Mrs Blunt was so preposterous it made Charlotte laugh. 'Oh, how I wish I'd seen them at it! Pa wouldn't stand an earthly with that old basilisk. What did he want anyway?'

'He wants you to come home, and that's where we're going now. He's not at all happy with your situation.'

Charlotte stiffened and experienced the

same tingle of apprehension that had disturbed her at the Grahams'.

'Papa knows how he can change my situation,' she said.

Ellen chose to take this in a way Charlotte did not intend.

'He wants to improve it and I hope with all my heart you'll reach an understanding with him. It would make me so happy, especially now we're having an addition to the family.'

'Yes, of course,' Charlotte agreed. 'I expect Papa is very pleased about that.'

'Yes, indeed he is.'

They fell silent, each with less than comfortable thoughts. Ellen wanted the birth to be over. She was sure she would love the infant once it was in her arms but the prospect of actually going into labour filled her with dread. People seemed to take a delight in telling her the most gruesome tales of difficult deliveries. She always tried to close her ears and remember her mother's easy-going advice. 'Take no notice, dear. Just refer them to what Shakespeare said.'

'What was that?'

'"Come what come may, Time and the hour runs through the roughest day."'

'Was he referring to childbirth?'

'I couldn't say, but why not? It's from *Macbeth*, I believe. But it's applicable in any painful circumstance, don't you think? I once quoted it to my dentist and he was most impressed and said he'd get it printed on a placard and hung in his surgery.'

Charlotte was thinking about her father. She was curious about his emotions. Not having been to school, she had never known girls from similar families to her own, so could not compare notes about the behaviour of fathers. Hers had always been aloof. A peck on the top of her head was all she ever got from him. Never an embrace, and yet she didn't think he was cold-hearted. It pleased her to see him with Ellen when he thought they were unobserved. He would take one of her hands in both of his and lean forward to kiss her. Then he would kiss her again and again and eventually hold her close with a prolonged kiss, and they would break away and laugh and come together again.

Mrs Vickery and the maids all remarked on the improvement in the household when Ellen came. 'He wanted a bit of you-know-what,' Mrs Vickery would say with a chuckle. 'It's all warm now where it used to be chilly.' But that was before Charlotte attained her eighteenth birthday and was marked off as the bride of Albert Morton. That, as Ellie had told her, was no longer a consideration.

Now, weighing up all this, Charlotte told

herself that Pa, in the light of his own experience, was perhaps ready to approve her engagement to Richard. How could it be otherwise? She snuggled up to Ellie and took her arm. 'Won't it be heavenly if everything comes right?' she said.

Ellie hoped with all her heart that it would.

Annie opened the door, Ellen went in and Charlotte grabbed Annie's hand, so pleased to see her again. Then she spied Mrs Vickery peeping out from the top of the kitchen stairs and rushed over to give her a great hug and say how spiffing it was to see her after all this long time.

'We're always talking about you, my lamb,' said Mrs Vickery. 'Don't ever think we forget you. If good wishes count for anything you can be sure of ours.'

'I'm so glad of them. Richard will be home in September and you'll be at our wedding, won't you?'

'Oh, Miss Charlotte, bless you both. The girls will dance a jig when I tell them.'

There was no time for more. Ellen had taken off her hat and was patting her hair in front of the hall looking-glass. She went into the drawing room, came out at once and said: 'Your papa is waiting, Charlotte.'

Charlotte took a deep breath. Her father

was standing by the mantelpiece. There was a huge copper jug full of flowers in the hearth. All kinds of flowers. It looked like a still life she had noticed at Mrs Graham's. She had wondered at the time how the artist contrived to paint a drop of dew on a petal. It must be difficult to paint water. But you could make the sound of it in music. Richard could. The Trout.

She found her voice. 'Good evening, Papa,' she said.

'Good evening, Charlotte. Pray sit down.' He glanced at the clock. 'Have you dined yet?' he asked.

'I've only just left work. I shall have supper when I get home.'

'I think we'll ask Mrs Vickery to send something up for you.' His hand was on the bell rope.

'Oh no, please don't trouble, Papa. Please don't. I'm used to my own ways now.' But his offer was surely a good sign, so she added quickly: 'Thank you very much, Papa.'

'My dear girl—oh, never mind.' He sat down, cleared his throat and said: 'You've been away a long time now, Charlotte.'

'Since February,' she replied.

'That's long enough to have learned your lesson, eh?'

'I've learned more than one,' she said.

'I'm glad to hear it. Now, listen. After

a great deal of thought I have decided to overlook your past bad conduct—' He paused as though expecting a grateful response, but she sat up very straight, compressed her lips and folded her hands in her lap.

'Charlotte! Are you listening?'

She was listening intently. He was going to lecture her and there were one or two things she wanted to say to him if he tried treating her as anything less than what she was.

'As I just said, I'm ready to overlook the shameful way you behaved and invite you to take your proper place as my daughter and companion to your stepmother again.'

'Thank you very much, Papa.'

'That's settled, then.'

'Not quite. There's a little bit more about the lesson I've learned.'

'And what is that?'

'I've learned that it's very hard to make a living, and for me it was sheer hard work. I know what it is to be cold, wet and hungry, and to count every farthing.'

'Then it's done you good. You'll appreciate your home all the more.'

'Ah, but I know what it is to have friends now, and it's wonderful. People with none of the advantages I've had accept me. They are kind and generous and helpful.'

He drummed his fingers on the arms of

his chair and said that would be something for her to look back on.

'I don't mean to lose them,' she said. 'They helped me through that horrible time when you confiscated Richard's letters. I was in despair. They helped me to keep my hopes high, and I made up my mind to endure all the hardships that came my way, for his sake. You see, Papa, I truly love him, and knowing how you love Ellie I'm quite sure you understand how I feel.'

'That is enough, Charlotte.'

'But I've seen how you look at her, how you kiss her. I'm not a little girl any more. I've grown up.'

This sent the colour to his face. His indignation made him splutter. That this girl, this impertinent chit should dare to address him as an equal was past bearing. Of course it was Amanda talking.

'It is most unseemly for you to speak to me in this manner, Charlotte, and I will not tolerate it. You forget your place.'

'My place is that of a workroom girl, Papa.'

'You are a saucy young woman. But you are my daughter. You must discard your working-class ways and learn respect. Let us leave it at that. You will, of course, need to pack your clothes and give notice at your place of work. You can do that tomorrow. Your stepmother is looking forward to having you here, particularly now.'

Had she won? Was he going to accept Richard? She had to be sure.

'Papa, in inviting me home again, and I do so want to be here, may I take it you agree to my marrying Richard Allen?'

'Certainly not!' he roared. 'You will give up all idea of it.'

'I will not,' she said, rising and drawing on her shabby cotton gloves. 'Unless you consent to my marriage, I can't live here, and after this conversation I don't want to.'

It was not Annie with her ear to the door, but Ellen who confronted Charlotte as she left the drawing room. Ellen looked so woebegone that Charlotte longed to be able to tell her that everything was all right and Pa was the most understanding of men. All she could say was: 'I'm truly sorry, Ellie,' before running out of the house to the Bayswater Road, where she stopped to ask a newspaper-seller the best way to get to Clapham.

Ellen found William fuming when she had collected herself enough to rejoin him. 'What on earth went wrong?' she asked.

'You should have heard the way that girl spoke to me! It will take me weeks to get over it.'

'Oh my dear, you really are distressed.'

'I'm shattered. She practically read me a lecture. Jawed about her friends. Called herself a workroom girl.'

'Well, dear, she is.'

'She's certainly caught their common ways. She referred to my feelings for you—'

'Whatever did she say?'

'I can't repeat it. She could have been one man talking to another. What are you laughing at?'

'I'm not,' said Ellen. 'But you know she's always been thrown with servants, so perhaps that's why she took to the people she meets now. She really loves Mrs Vickery. She's often told me so.'

'That's not my fault.'

'Of course not, dear. No one suggests it is. But she does say she learnt nothing from the governesses and everything from Mrs Vickery. She's very well read, you know.'

'Don't tell me the cook reads.'

'Indeed she does. And she always lent Charlotte her books. All the classics. Sixpenny editions.'

'I'll dock her wages.'

'Oh William! William darling, it's simply splendid. She's been a boon to poor little Charlotte.'

'Poor little Charlotte! I like that. What about me? Here I am, ready to take her back, and all I get is abuse from her and no sympathy from you.'

'Here's your whisky, darling. And I do feel for you. Really I do.'

'I'm glad someone does,' he said.

Charlotte saw no chance of a reconciliation, and regretted it. Now that she was a self-supporting woman and had a place in the world, no matter how lowly, she thought that her father should acknowledge it and allow her to express her feelings openly, not hide them because she happened to be his daughter.

Nothing would have made her happier than to resume the old comfortable companionship with Mrs Vickery and the maids, to say nothing of Ellie, but her father's intolerance prohibited it. Unless and until he consented to her marriage it was not in her power to mend matters.

Nanny agreed with her but pitied Ellen. Victoria said it was only what you'd expect of an old blighter like Mr Grant, and Algie echoed her sentiments. 'I'd say he's spiteful, and a spiteful man's worse than a spiteful woman,' Algie said. He was sharing a pint of porter with Victoria as he spoke. They took alternate swigs from an earthenware mug, not being able to afford tumblers as yet.

Most evenings Edward Graham met Charlotte after work and drove her to

Clapham. 'Why don't you bring him in?' Victoria asked.

'I don't think it would be a good idea.'

'A girl can't have too many strings to her bow.'

'You're more than contented with your one and only.'

'He's my husband. I've got Eustace as well, haven't I? And Mr Goode drops in now and then. It's nice to have a circle. When we're prop'ly settled I shall have Sunday tea parties.'

Charlotte called her a honeypot and loved to see her revelling in her new life. Although she was so soon to be married herself, the waiting made her intolerably restless and she was glad of any diversion.

One Saturday afternoon Edward drove her to Richmond before taking her to Nanny's. They got out at the top of the hill and found a seat. He had a new motor, much more comfortable than the primitive Sunbeam. It was Arthur Heston's cast-off, Arthur having bought the latest model for himself.

'He demands the best of everything and deserves it,' Edward said. 'He works hard managing the farm, you know. He's been in charge ever since my father died. It's amazing when you think how far afield our sheep are. New Zealand has flocks of them. Canterbury lamb.'

'That's what Mrs Vickery orders. I always thought it was Canterbury, Kent.'

'No. It all started at our farm in Dorset. Incidentally, my mother and I will be going down there soon.'

'For long?'

'A month or so. I shall miss seeing you, Charlotte.'

'I shall miss you too.'

'Not in the same way.'

There was a long, awkward pause, which she didn't like. He seized her hand and held it. 'You know how I feel about you, don't you?' he asked.

'Edward, you really are a chump. Let go,' she said, slightly alarmed and trying to laugh it off.

'You're teasing me.' He was angry, hurt. He thrust her hand away. 'You must have twigged I'm pretty fond of you by now,' he said.

'I thought we were friends.'

'A bit more than that, I hope.'

She didn't know what to say to that and he went on: 'Can't you see what a rotten time you'll have with Richard Allen? Don't you realise he's selfish to the core? He doesn't love you. He'd never have gone away if he did.'

'That's not true.'

'It is and you know it.'

'I won't listen to you saying such horrid things. Richard had good reasons for going and I understand them. I wish you could. But perhaps that's too much to ask. He lives in a different world from yours.'

'And from yours. Ask yourself if you can enter it.'

His words struck home and upset her. She could see the difference between Richard's life and Edward's clearly. If there was any argument about whose was the more comfortable, Edward would win every time. But that was not the point. It was her complete devotion to Richard that mattered.

'Would he give up his occupation for you, Charlotte?'

'That's an unreasonable question.'

'You daren't ask it because you know the answer.' He waited a minute. 'Don't you?' he asked.

She thought deeply of Richard, and of Mary, and of Hans. There was an accord between them, it was as though they belonged to a special order and it was impossible to imagine them in any other.

'Richard couldn't give up music,' she said. 'He wouldn't be Richard if he did.'

'And you think you can step into his world! You'd be much happier in mine.'

He took her hand again and she didn't draw it away.

She was remembering the three days Richard was home and her overwhelming disappointment at the little time he had to spare for her, the importance of rehearsing, the obligation to Hans and not to her. That recital in the half-empty hall. They had played the Kreutzer Sonata, the work he had enthused over in one of his letters, and although she had heard it, her mind wasn't on the music but on his coming departure.

Kreutzer. Why was it called Kreutzer? She didn't know.

At that moment, in the warm sunshine at the top of Richmond Hill, with the river sparkling below, she was in darkness. She heard the footsteps of people walking on the Terrace, voices, children skipping along, someone calling a dog. She thought of Ellie and of home, she thought of Mrs Graham and the strange chance that had thrown them together. And she was tired. Tired of the struggle, the daily grind. What joy it would be to give in, to live with this ordinary man she liked so much and who clearly loved her.

'Why don't you come down to Dorset with us?' he asked. 'You'd love the house. It's enormous and rambling and so ancient you get lost. It's beautiful. So are the grounds. There's a stream running through and if you can't sleep at night you can look out of the window and count real sheep.'

'Don't tempt me,' she said.

'Why not? You need a holiday.'

'Eddie, please don't. Let's go to Nanny's now. She'll wonder where I've got to.'

He didn't argue. He was sure she was thinking things over and would see the sense of what he had said, but it wouldn't do to press her too hard. Give her time to come round.

They stopped outside Nanny's. He left the engine running, got out and held her door open. As she alighted their faces were level and he brushed her cheek lightly with his lips. 'Don't marry Richard. Marry me,' he said.

He left her standing in the road, staring after him as he drove away.

'That's an impressive motor,' Nanny said when she went in. 'Did you have a nice drive?'

'We went to Richmond, and you know how lovely it can be at the top of the hill, but Edward's upset me dreadfully. He did his best to put me off Richard and ended up by popping the question.'

'Well, my dear, he has paid you a lot of attention. It's not a complete surprise.'

'It is to me.'

Nanny shook her head. She knew that Edward frequently met Charlotte after work, and motored her to Hammersmith almost every Saturday. It was obvious that he was taken with her, and had it not been for her prior engagement he would have been an excellent match. Good family, nice-looking, considerate—she thought of Lily—and well off. More important still, Charlotte liked him.

She had no doubt that Mr Grant would welcome a man like Edward as a son-in-law. He would favour an alliance with a family of the Grahams' standing. The Grahams, to put it bluntly, were just a cut above the Grants. Sheep farmers in a very big way, she understood, but moving in the highest circles.

The Grants were merchants, not to be spoken of in the same breath as trade, of course. From all accounts William was doing exceedingly well, much better than when he was so thick with the Mortons, Mrs Vickery informed her. There was talk of moving to a larger house in a more fashionable part of town by the end of the year.

'Why did Mr Graham speak of Richard in a derogatory manner?' she enquired. 'It was hardly likely to please you, was it?'

'He made out he was selfish and only thought of his music. He said I'd never be at home in Richard's world but I'd be happy in his.'

'And do you think you would?'

The question, put in a sharp tone, made Charlotte see Edward's world with surprising clarity. It was like the Mortons' and her father's, and all the other well-off families, with their good houses, their possessions, their servants. The boring existence they called life was brightened by little intrigues, scandals, tea parties, dinner parties, the relentless social round, and it was not for her.

How could she have wavered as she had done at the top of Richmond Hill? It frightened her to know she had even contemplated changing course, giving up, giving in, for it would mean losing Richard forever and that was unthinkable.

'What a fool I've been!' she cried. 'I couldn't live without Richard. I've been letting disappointment get the better of me. Because I was disappointed he didn't stay longer, Nanny.'

'But you didn't expect him back until September did you?' said Nanny drily.

'No, I didn't, it was a three month tour,' said Charlotte slowly, as it dawned on her that Richard's short visit was a gift to be cherished.

'Oh Nanny, what a darling you are! I'm seeing straight again. Shall I make us a pot of tea?'

'I rather think you'd better,' Nanny said.

'The kettle's been singing ever since you came in.'

Edward's proposal cleared Charlotte's head as effectively as a strong wind sweeps the sky. All this talk of Richard's world indeed! She would be as much at sea if he were an engineer or an architect or a doctor. As it was, she could listen and what was more learn, so she refused to let her ignorance haunt her, and much as she longed for Richard to come back she didn't wish the time away.

That Sunday she went on a househunting jaunt with Nanny. They took a picnic to Barnes Common, with Will going ahead on his bicycle. He had discovered a house to let in a beautifully secluded spot and had the keys from the agent.

It was not a large house but the rooms were well proportioned and the main one looked as though it had been made to accommodate a grand piano. Charlotte fell in love with it on sight.

'It was made for us,' she said, and walked from room to room, upstairs and down, feeling the atmosphere and knowing it was right. 'We simply must have it,' she declared.

Nanny agreed. She thought it the very thing, so long as the lease and rent suited them, and provided it was structurally sound. Charlotte said she would write to Richard immediately and ask him to contact the agent fast, before anyone else saw it.

The garden was overgrown but some roses were in flower. There was an old acacia tree and under it a bench, so they sat down to their picnic and enjoyed it all the more because a thrush was giving a concert nearby.

'It feels like home,' Charlotte said.

How exhilarated she was! She felt able to face anything, even the prospect of telling Edward she considered him a dear and valued friend and hoped he would always remain so, but that anything closer was out of the question.

It was strange to think that the uneasiness that had bothered her for so long originated with the Grahams. She had been wrong to mistake Edward's obvious affection for friendship, but, never having had a friend, she had enjoyed his companionship. It was fun being with him because he let her talk her head off, and she did. She told him how wonderful Richard was and what it had been like at the opera, but when he said he was not at all surprised at Mr Grant throwing him out of the house, she didn't think he was serious.

'I'd have done the same if I'd caught him with my daughter the way he caught you, Charlotte,' he said.

'You wouldn't!'

'I would.'

'You can't be as stuffy as Pa,' she protested.

'In such circumstances I certainly can. It puts you both beyond the pale, you know.'

'Is that how you think of me? A woman outside the pale!'

'You must know how I think of you by now.'

'Best friend?'

No answer.

'Second best?'

'Nothing of the kind. Now dry up.'

'Dry up yourself.'

Why hadn't she realised she was on dangerous ground? It was simply because it had never occurred to her, and even when Victoria threw out hints she turned a deaf ear. Now that Ellie was on visiting terms with Mrs Graham, she sensed danger. Her father would see advantages in the acquaintance and foster it, especially if he met Edward. It was a blessing Ellie had promised not to mention that very eligible young man to her father. But still. I was a pawn when Pa tried to saddle me with Albert Morton, and I'm not going to be a pawn now, she told herself.

As the evenings were lighter, she was

able to call on Clarice and Aunt Cassie occasionally, and was sorry to hear that Mr Heston was still taking far too much interest in Clarice.

'It isn't right,' Clarice said. 'Mrs Graham's sure to notice and she won't like it. I've told him so.'

'What does he say to that?' asked Charlotte.

'He just laughs and tells me not to worry. "I'll see you're never the loser," he says.'

Charlotte thought this promise had rather a sinister ring. So did Clarice. She was thrilled with her job: it had advantages she had never expected: a much better wage, shorter hours, good meals and the happiness of being able to provide for Aunt Cassie.

She walked to Curzon Street every morning and home again in the evening, and enjoyed it, until Mr Heston, on horseback, hailed her with a 'Good morning, Miss West.'

'Mr Heston!' she exclaimed. 'I thought you were in Dorset.'

'So I was until last night.' He dismounted, threw the reins to his groom and walked beside her.

'How remarkably well you look,' he said. 'And you walk beautifully. Did you know that? I suppose you practise with a pile of books on your head?'

'I do nothing of the kind.'

'You walk as a Greek goddess would.'

'I never saw a Greek goddess sitting, standing or walking, and I doubt if you did either.'

'Next time you pass a long mirror, look in, and you'll see the reflection of one.'

They had reached the house. 'Good day, Mr Heston,' she said, and went swiftly to the servants' entrance. He stood watching her until she disappeared inside.

Later on he came and leant against the doorpost of the workroom and said he wanted a portrait of her and had an artist friend who would paint one.

'Just as you are now, looking up from your work with the stuff trailing off your lap to the floor. Don't you think it would be ideal?'

'I'm employed to work here, not to sit for my portrait. Only actresses and ladies in high society have their portraits painted.'

'Then it's time there was an exception.'

Mrs Graham came along the corridor and saw Mr Heston lounging against the doorpost, and Clarice rather too pink in the face.

'Good morning, Arthur,' she said, taking in the scene and its implications at a glance. 'I have some matters to discuss with Miss West,' and so saying she went in and shut him out.

'I hope Mr Heston hasn't been disturbing you,' she said. 'You look a little *distrait.*'

Clarice was too embarrassed to reply.

'If Mr Heston, or indeed anyone else in the house, says or does anything upsetting, you must tell me at once,' Mrs Graham went on.

'I've nothing to complain about at all,' said Clarice. 'Everybody here is so kind—all the staff. I never expected to meet with such kindness and I enjoy working for you.'

'And Mr Heston? He can be a tease, you know.'

'He only passes the time of day, and so does young Mr Graham.'

'So long as it's kept to that and no more, Miss West.'

Mrs Graham knew her sewing woman was in no danger from Edward, but she was not at all sure of Arthur Heston. She hoped her implied warning was enough. Miss West was a sensible young woman who wouldn't do anything to jeopardise her position.

The Grahams always spent the summer on their Dorset estate, leaving town as soon as the season ended. A skeleton staff stayed in Curzon Street; the rest accompanied the family. The King's illness had affected the usual arrangements but his remarkable recovery meant that the Coronation was to be held early in August, so the exodus would not take place until it was over.

Mrs Graham gave Clarice the choice of going to Dorset or staying in town. She was to have a week's holiday and could then resume her work in whichever location she chose.

Most of the servants had been to Wool and told Clarice how lovely it was. They said it would do her all the good in the world to get away from London and enjoy the sights and sounds of the country, but she didn't like to leave Aunt Cassie and chose to stay.

The Coronation brought an enormous revival in trade, and Madame Last was swamped with orders. 'I reckon we'd better have the firm's outing the first Sunday after the crowning,' she announced at breakfast one morning. 'The annual holiday can follow on the Monday. So you'd better get on with the arrangements, Algie. It's to be the best of everything, mind.'

'Right, Ma.' said Algie. 'Champagne?'

'Of course champagne. And lobster. I leave it to you.'

'*Carte blanche?*'

'If that means the best of everything,

yes. This is a year to remember.'

It was indeed. Out came the flags, the triumphal arches, the bunting and all the paraphernalia befitting a Coronation. Back came the crowds to line the street and cheer themselves hoarse as the King was driven to the Abbey. Hotels and boarding houses filled up again, there was genuine rejoicing, and although the Eastern potentates and princes from faraway countries failed to return, many said the event was all the better for being homespun.

Clarice took her holiday at the same time as the workroom girls and looked forward to seeing them and perhaps taking a trip to the sea. Victoria spoke of Margate—Charlotte wasn't sure. She wanted to spend her time at Barnes and do some measuring, make enquiries about furniture, about hiring a piano, even acquiring a bicycle so she could get backwards and forwards quicker. Will had promised to teach her to ride.

But first there was the outing. The weather had been cold and overcast, not what was expected of August, but by one of those rare dispensations Sunday was an exception.

It was the perfect day for the river. Algie had hired a steam launch, and Madame Last was justly proud of her girls when she welcomed them on board at Maidenhead. Algie, like every other man on the river, sported a straw hat, white shirt and trousers and a bright-blue blazer, and never were so many punts to be seen or so many pretty girls reclining on cushions and trailing their hands in the water.

Algie had decided against having luncheon at Skindle's in favour of The Compleat Angler at Marlow. This was so they could enjoy cruising through Cliveden Reach, which Eustace had informed him was a must, as it was the most glorious of all. 'In my opinion,' he added.

Eustace was one of the party, at home in any kind of craft, especially a punt, and the companion of Algie's many fictitious weekends on the river.

None of the girls had ever been upstream, although some had been down as far as Ramsgate on the *Golden Eagle,* which was a very different thing. But Cliveden! Who among them could describe the wooded hills of Cliveden sloping down to the water or name the multitude of trees and the different shades of green?

'You may travel far and wide and never find a place to compare with this,' said Miss Prescot, in the manner of one giving a geography lesson.

The party disembarked at Marlow for the superb luncheon Algie had ordered.

Madame Last glowed with pride, to say nothing of the heat, when she took her place at the head of the long table reserved for them. Henry was on her right, Algie on her left. Eustace Bright and Wilfred were placed opposite each other halfway down the table.

The girls, many of whom had enjoyed the firm's outings in previous years, had never known one like this. To eat lobster and sip champagne in this delightful setting was the event of a lifetime.

'It's just heavenly,' said Miss Prescot, closing her eyes in ecstasy.

'Heavenly,' they all echoed, casting their eyes upward.

'We'll drink to His Majesty,' announced Madame Last at the end of the protracted meal, upon which they all stood, raised their glasses and wished King Edward a long and prosperous reign, although Victoria remarked that it might be prosperous, but wasn't likely to be long, as he was already over sixty.

The afternoon was to be spent as they wished, strolling by the river, exploring Marlow or just dozing in deck chairs until it was time for tea.

Madame Last had told Algie he was free to go punting once the luncheon was over. She knew he wouldn't want to be with a bunch of girls all the afternoon but didn't know how he longed to be with just one of them.

Eustace had hired a punt and suggested going further upstream and making their own way home by train, which Henry Last said was a good idea as then they wouldn't be tied down.

'I've done you proud, haven't I, Ma?' said Algie.

'You have indeed. And don't call me Ma. This is the second time today. I don't want to tell you again.'

He only laughed and took himself off, leaving his mother to remark that at last they'd set eyes on his famous straw hat which, considering the time he'd had it, looked remarkably new.

He only managed a word with Victoria, who was arm-in-arm with Charlotte. 'To-night's the night I spill the beans,' he said.

'Let's hope Madame doesn't blow up when you tell her she's my mother-in-law.'

'And almost a granny.'

'Shows now, don't it?' Victoria said with a little laugh that ended in a shiver, and with unexpected urgency she added: 'I wish you wouldn't go punting, Algie.'

'Must. It's expected of me.'

'Can't me and Charlotte come with you?'

'It wouldn't do in your state. There'll be another time. You've got to take care of yourself'

Charlotte wondered if he was slightly tipsy, but he was always lively and today of all days was very special for him and for Victoria.

'See you at home,' he said.

'Can't wait to get there.'

Charlotte wished the two of them could have a moment alone, if only to touch hands, but the rest of the party was so close and Eustace was waiting to bear Algie off, so it was impossible.

Twilight, dusk. Downstream to Maidenhead. Chinese lanterns, flower-bedecked houseboats with people lounging on the verandas, the glow of a cigar, the twang of a mandoline, a burst of song. Richness. What a day it had been! And no work tomorrow. A whole week's holiday.

Charlotte would be staying with Nanny and doing as much as she could to get the house ready to live in. There was so much to think about. Richard would be home in less than six weeks, so she must arrange for the wedding at the parish church and put up the banns. Sometimes she felt her head was spinning. There was linen to buy, sheets, blankets, towels. Help!

By the time she got to Hammersmith

late on that wonderful Sunday, she was dropping.

'You must have a lazy day tomorrow,' Nanny said.

'What bliss!'

She got up late, and in spite of all the tasks before her it was so good to dawdle, to sit chatting with Nanny, recalling the joys of yesterday and talking of those to come.

Halfway through the morning, Nanny answered a knock at the door and found a distressed Victoria on the step.

'Algie didn't come home.'

Charlotte heard, and was with her in a moment. Victoria was trembling. She clutched Charlotte's hand. 'I can't think what's happened. I knew he'd be late, seeing as he was going to tell his ma about us. I sat at the window all night and now I don't know what to do. Do you think he could have been took ill?'

'More than likely, after all that rich food and the excitement,' Nanny said.

'But he'd have let me know, wouldn't he? He'd know I'd be worrying. "See you at home", that's the last thing he said.'

'Yes, but it might not be so easy,' Charlotte said. 'He could be at your flat by now.'

'I left a note to say I'd come here. I just couldn't stay there wondering. You don't mind me coming, do you, Nanny?'

'No, my dear. I'm glad you did. Now sit down and rest yourself. Ten to one there's no need to worry.'

'I do hope you're right.'

'It's not so much a worry as a puzzle. Algie and Eustace were to come home by train. There could have been a delay,' said Charlotte. 'Suppose I go to Last's and pretend I've left something in the workroom. Wilfred's bound to tell me what's happened.'

'Would you?' Victoria jumped at the idea, and Nanny said there was nothing to lose, so Charlotte set off.

She didn't feel at ease as she approached the staff entrance. On any other Monday there would be comings and goings, but with the holiday break it was bound to be deserted. She rang the bell and waited. Nobody came. Give it ten minutes, then ring again. The minutes crawled. She rang again. Waited. At last the door opened and an old, grey-faced man peered out and stared at her without recognition.

Mr Last.

'I'm very sorry to trouble you,' said Charlotte. 'I work here and I left some of my belongings upstairs. I thought Wilfred would be here.'

'He's on holiday. You can go up and get your things.'

He stood aside for her to pass, and she couldn't resist saying: 'What a lovely day we had yesterday. I shall never forget it.'

'Neither shall I,' he said, and he leant his head against the wall and gave way to such awful sounds as she had never heard before.

She didn't know what to do. She had never seen a man cry. She had always been told men didn't cry, but this old fellow was convulsed. Should she pass him, make a pretence of collecting nonexistent possessions, or just wait?

She waited. He seemed to take a grip on himself and faced her.

'It's our boy,' he said. 'Drowned. Fell in the river.'

'Oh, no!'

'It was an accident.'

The obligatory words came out of nowhere. 'I'm so very, very sorry.'

She was more than sorry. She was staggered, knocked off her balance, stunned.

'You'd better get your things.'

'It doesn't matter. They're not important,' she said, and ran blindly away.

She had no idea how she reached Piccadilly but next thing she was sitting on a bench in Green Park, trying to take in what Mr Last had told her.

Algie. How could anyone so full of life as Algie be dead? Victoria won't believe it. But she'd have to, and Charlotte was the one to tell her. She was frightened, appalled at the effect this would have. Victoria had expected to give up work once Madame knew she was Algie's wife. But now. What now? It wasn't just the agony of loss that affected poor people. It was where the next meal was to come from, and who would pay the rent.

I'm just not equal to telling her, but who can I go to for help? Clarice. She was on holiday too. Clarice was the one. Hurry, run to Aunt Cassie's—take a cab, never mind the expense. I'll manage. I'll borrow if I run out.

It was a white, shaky Charlotte who knocked at Aunt Cassie's door and blurted out the news, which was met with a disbelief that matched her own. They sat, all three, trying to take it in, to think what to do. A little later, Clarice was saying she knew how she had felt over Mr Blades.

'But at least he wasn't dead—only put away for a bit, and that's bad enough. Poor old Victoria. And her so thrilled with her home and all her bits and pieces. Still, she'll have to be told. We'd better go, Charlotte.'

It was the most wretched journey and seemed to last for hours, yet they were there all too soon and the sight of Victoria's anxious face at the window had Charlotte fishing for her handkerchief.

They hardly had to speak. She knew by their faces, their tears.

'Nothing would have kept Algie away last night,' she said. '"See you at home," that's what he said. You heard him, Charlotte. I've been kidding meself. I knew all along.'

Nanny was there, her arms round Victoria, her heart full of sorrow and her head of fears, doubts, misgivings. The Lasts knew nothing of Algie's marriage. It would come as an unwelcome shock to find that their son had married one of their workers, a doorstep orphan, uneducated, just a cockney sparrow with the dust of the streets on her. They were not likely to appreciate her true qualities, her grit, her cheerfulness, her thought for others. Must they be told? Unless they were, she had no place as Algie's widow, mother of his unborn child.

The decision about whether or not to tell must be Victoria's, but not until she was in a fit state to make it and the Lasts to hear it. For now the chief consideration was her health, and helping her to bear the grief and trials that would beset her.

All Charlotte's ideas for the house at Barnes went out of the window. How could she go bothering about it while Victoria went back to Clapham by herself?

She couldn't. And Victoria was determined to go back and refused Nanny's invitation to stay, if only for the night.

'I'm all right, Nanny. Straight I am,' she said. 'I haven't taken it in. It's like me heart's gone paralysed. I ain't got no feeling in it.'

'It would do you good to cry, my dear.'

'I shall when I see his shaving brush. I gave it to him for a wedding present. Badger's hair. The best. I want to go now, please.'

'Very well, my dear.'

Nanny watched the three girls go down the road, Victoria walking between Clarice and Charlotte, her arms through theirs.

The house was empty. So much grief. The Lasts without their son. Perhaps she could comfort Bessy a little. She had known her so long and watched her create the distinguished fashion house of Madame Last. But she knew that deep down Algie had meant more to his mother than anything else in the world.

It was as well she went to Mayfair that afternoon. She was the one person Bessy wanted.

Victoria's tragedy threw Charlotte's life into disarray. Difficulties seemed to spring out of the walls and attack her in swarms.

She talked them over with Clarice, and they agreed that returning to work at Last's would be unbearable for Victoria. It would mean smothering her grief, for after the first day back at Clapham she was crying, breaking her heart. But what of her wages?

'We'll manage,' Charlotte said. 'Mine will be enough until the baby's born.'

Eustace Bright came in deep distress and poured his grief over Charlotte as they sat on the stairs leading up to the flat.

'Clarice is with her. She's just dropped off to sleep,' Charlotte told him. 'What happened exactly?'

'It was all my fault. Algie and I have been friends for years and I let him fall in and drown. How am I to live with myself?' He stumbled on, trying to recall everything.

It seemed they had both felt drowsy after lunch, so Eustace moored the punt to a tree on the bank. It was comfortable reclining on the cushions, and they were soon asleep. He didn't know for how long, but he was woken by a movement and opened his eyes to find they were in midstream. Algie had cast off. Eustace shouted at him to sit but he had the pole. He was gripping it dangerously hard with both hands, and although Eustace ordered him to put it down he only laughed and said, 'Watch me. It's easy.'

Laughing, he thrust it down far too close to the side and into deep mud. The punt slid away from him and he was left clinging to the pole. Then, with a shout, he was in the water. A moment more and he was under it.

Eustace dropped his head in his hands, and tears squeezed between his fingers as he told her.

'It wasn't your fault,' she said, her arm round his shoulders, comforting him.

'It was. I should have told him—warned him that it takes weeks to learn how to punt. He often bet me he'd do it first time, but I never thought...' He was living the scene over again. There was no spare pole, not even a paddle, and all he could see was Algie's straw hat floating as the punt drifted further upstream. He didn't know what a poor swimmer he was until he was in the water trying to reach the spot, hanging on to a skiff that was making for the place.

Several rowing boats drew near; men stripped off and dived. Eustace, frantic, weighed down by his clothes, was getting into difficulties and had to be rescued and taken ashore.

The search went on with the river police in charge. After a long time, when Algie's body was brought up, it was evident that he had bashed his head on a submerged tree stump as he went down and lost consciousness. One foot was entangled in some thick wire mesh at the bottom which had held him down.

It was a small comfort to know he wouldn't even have struggled, but that wouldn't ease the pain of loss for his wife, his parents and his friend.

Charlotte tried to persuade Eustace not to be so hard on himself and take the blame. Algie's charade of spending his weekends on the river with Eustace might have to be explained to his parents one day, but not now. Victoria, of course, knew all about that.

Each day brought another problem, as the facts of Victoria's situation grew clear to Charlotte and Clarice. Algie had saved some money to tide them over his wife's lying-in. There were three sovereigns in an ornamental jug in the sitting room. The one suit he kept at the flat could be sold, together with a pair of shoes, his bowler hat and his walking stick, Clarice said. That would bring in a little.

'No!' shrieked Victoria when Clarice offered to sell them. 'I'm not parting with his bowler. Not ever. You just leave it where it is, Clarice.'

'He won't be wanting it,' Clarice protested.

'*I* want it. I'm keeping it. And the stick.'

It was a nightmare of a week. Nanny came with Lizzie Wilson, who had readily agreed to take care of Victoria when the time came. Will Goode called with a bunch of flowers from the garden. Aunt Cassie came. Eustace was there every evening.

'How's Madame?' asked Victoria.

'She's knocked flat.'

'I bet she is.'

'Don't you think you should tell her?' Eustace suggested.

'No, I don't. Don't any of you ever tell her. I forbid it.'

It was useless to argue. It was her secret and Algie's, and she wasn't going to risk incurring his mother's wrath. Madame would be sure to reject her as his wife, even though she had the lines to prove it. All right. She couldn't go to the funeral. So what? She'd put some flowers on his grave as soon as she knew where it was.

Monday came. Victoria had declared her intention of going back to work, but not for a few days. There would be too much chat about the tragedy and she'd never keep her end up. She'd expect him to breeze in like he so often did. But go she must once she'd got a proper grip on herself. In the meantime she'd get on with making the baby's clothes. The poor little blighter would have to be clad, no matter what happened, and Aunt Cassie was coming to keep her company as Clarice had finished her holiday and would be at Curzon Street again.

Madame Last's girls knew nothing of the tragedy until they arrived at the staff entrance and read the notice pinned to the door. It stated that due to the death of Mr Algernon Last in a boating accident, the establishment would remain closed for a further week.

The news caused dismay, surprise and sorrow, for they all liked Mr Algie. He was so bright and lively and not a bit above himself. They couldn't believe it. And after such a wonderful day as they'd had, too.

Charlotte was already so upset by Algie's death that it was a relief to shed a few quiet tears with the others.

Miss Prescot was upstairs with Mr Last. Madame was too distressed to see anyone and he was extremely worried about her. 'I've had the doctor to her but what can he do?' he asked helplessly. 'Algie was the apple of her eye, Miss Prescot.'

'We must all do what we can, Mr Last. You may rely upon me,' said Miss Prescot and she went down to tell the others what he had told her, adding some details of her own to spice the story up.

'Mr Algie came up three times before he finally sank, and his last words, carried on the breeze, were, 'Sorry, Ma.''

'That isn't true, Miss Prescot,' Charlotte said quietly.

'Oh? And what do you know about it, pray?'

'Only what Mr Bright told me, and it wasn't like that at all.'

'So you've seen Mr Bright, have you?' Miss Prescot turned to the others and said: 'We must all remember that Miss Grant moves in higher circles than the rest of us, girls.'

'Oh, please!' cried Charlotte. 'I'm sorry, but I just happened to see Mr Bright. It's a terrible tragedy and we mustn't have words about it, must we?'

'Not if you keep quiet,' said Miss Prescot.

Miss Sharp was impatient. 'This is all very well,' she said. 'It's very sad for Mr Algie's mum and dad, but what about us? What about our wages if we don't work this week?'

The same idea had occurred to most of the others, and after much debate Miss Prescot agreed to go and enquire. 'Though one hardly likes to mention money at such a time,' she said in a simpering tone.

'One's driven to,' snapped Miss Sharp. 'One's only got a couple of bob to see one through to Sat'day, and that one's me.'

'Me too,' chorused the others.

'It'll be bread and point for me,' piped up the oldest worker.

'Lucky to have bread,' retorted Miss Sharp.

Miss Prescot departed and someone asked where Victoria was. Charlotte said she wasn't very well and would be glad of the week's respite. Inwardly she wondered what she would do if there were nothing at the end of it. Her funds were running low.

Miss Prescot returned, looking smug. Madame Last did not wish her girls to suffer on account of Mr Algie's untimely death. They were to return at noon next Saturday and would be paid in full, just as though they had worked.

It was an extraordinarily generous offer and Miss Prescot was dispatched once more to express everybody's thanks and appreciation.

'I don't think many employers would be so considerate,' Charlotte remarked as she left the premises with Miss Sharp.

'The Lasts can afford it. Must be rolling,' said Miss Sharp.

'Yes, but still...'

'There will be changes. You'll see. It wouldn't surprise me if they pack up.'

Charlotte didn't respond. She disliked

Miss Sharp and was glad to get away from her. Knowing Victoria wasn't alone, she went to see Nanny and found Mrs Vickery with her.

'Why, Miss Charlotte, what a treat it is to see you. It's been such a long time now.'

'Yes, hasn't it? Much too long,' Charlotte said, returning Mrs Vickery's hug and kiss. 'How are things at home?'

'Looking up, my dear. Your pa and stepma are spending a few days in Dorset with Mrs Graham. What do you say to that?'

'I really don't know what to say.'

'Mrs Graham's taken a fancy to your stepma, my dear. She's been to dinner with us twice, and her son, young Mr Edward, too. Your pa's quite flattered by their attention, and nothing's good enough for them. I've told Annie she'll get donkey's ears the way she has to stretch them to listen.'

'I suppose you'll tell us what she's heard,' said Nanny, pausing as she laid the table for lunch.

'I don't vouch for the accuracy. Twice-told tales always gather extras on the way. Still, it's a fact you've been mentioned, Miss Charlotte.'

'Have I? I don't suppose that pleased Pa.'

'I don't know so much. Mrs Graham cracked you up to the skies. Says she's never met such a brave girl the way you went to see her about your poor friend. She thinks you're full of character. He wouldn't contradict a guest at his own table, would he now?'

'I suppose not.' Charlotte felt a strange little shiver. 'I wish they wouldn't talk about me,' she said.

It was odd to feel apprehensive about the Grahams, but she did and was glad the conversation turned to other things, for Mrs Vickery wanted all the latest on Richard: where was he, what was he doing and when would he be home?

'September,' Charlotte said. 'He writes every day and Will's going to make me a box to keep all his letters in. Not just an ordinary box.'

'Nothing Will makes is ordinary. This one is to be of sandalwood,' Nanny said in the tone she used for announcements of great importance.

In the afternoon Charlotte took Mrs Vickery to Barnes to see the house, and she declared it just perfect for a very special young couple. 'The atmosphere's right. You can sense it the minute you come in,' she said.

'It almost seems to be waiting for us, doesn't it?' said Charlotte. 'I can't wait for

Richard to see it. Oh, Mrs Vickery dear, I do love him so. But I shan't feel safe until we're together for keeps.'

'But you've nothing to be afraid of, have you?'

'It's just a funny feeling,' said Charlotte, and although Mrs Vickery's reassuring words were a comfort, they didn't dispel it entirely.

The pattern changed for the three girls. Clarice spent as much time as she could at Clapham, especially at weekends, but there was one in particular when she couldn't be there, although afterwards she regretted it.

With the Grahams away in Dorset she could work without fear of Mr Heston bothering her. His remarkable resemblance to Herbert Blades disturbed her, and she didn't know how to counter the hints he kept throwing out. Now she was safe until September.

But one morning there he was, lounging against the doorpost. She was startled out of her skin and looked it.

'It's all right. I'm not a ghost,' he said.

'I thought you were in Dorset, Mr Heston.'

'So I was, Miss West. I see I've alarmed you.'

'You have rather.' She had to swallow

hard, because for one mad moment she almost thought it was Herbert standing there, and when she knew it couldn't be she wanted to cry.

Mr Heston drew up a chair and sat, something he had never done before.

'Will you do me a favour?' he asked.

'That depends what it is.'

'I've taken a house at Sheen. It's quite delightful there and you could think yourself a thousand miles from London. It's furnished but needs curtains, hangings, cushions. All the things that make rooms attractive. Would you advise me?'

'One of the special shops could help much better. Why don't you try Hampton's?'

'Everything they do is cut and dried. That's why I'm asking you.'

'But I'm busy here, Mr Heston.'

'Not at weekends. Couldn't you spare a Saturday or Sunday?'

'Well...' She was thinking about Victoria, but of course Aunt Cassie could go there, and Charlotte would always stay, as she was doing more and more since poor Algie... 'I suppose I could manage a Saturday. You want me to choose curtain material? I'm not an expert and I don't know when I'd have time to make them up.'

'I wouldn't dream of asking you. The

making is for an upholsterer. I just want advice on design, colour. You've done such wonders for Mrs Graham with the colours you choose, the way you put them together. You have a talent for it.'

'Thank you,' she said.

'You'll be recompensed, naturally.'

It was difficult to refuse. He wanted her to see the house, for the task would be impossible unless she did. He would send a carriage to take her there on Saturday afternoon and convey her home when she had made her recommendations...

'Will there be someone to let me in?' she asked.

'Yes. The housekeeper.'

She was pleased about this, and surprised when Mr Heston opened the door to her himself when she rang the bell.

'I expected the housekeeper,' she said.

'She had to go to the shops.'

They had passed a few shops miles away.

'It's a long way to go,' she said.

'She has a dogcart. Come along in. I expect you'd like some tea?'

After the long drive Clarice was gasping, so she didn't say no. There was a tea table set with fine china and silver tea things. A kettle was singing on a spirit stove. She was bewildered. The drive, once clear of the main roads, made her think of the sylvan glades she had read about but never seen, and the house, standing back in its own grounds, looked enchanting. Noble trees. Yes, noble. That was the word they used in books.

Now they were in a tastefully furnished drawing room, and Mr Heston was leading her to a sofa, then making the tea himself and asking her if she preferred milk to lemon.

'Milk,' she said weakly, and after a few sips, 'you make lovely tea.'

'I have a few accomplishments.'

She agreed that he had if he'd made the cucumber sandwiches himself, and he admitted he had. She had never tasted such delicious ones, the bread cut so thin it was almost transparent. They were irresistible. Still, why hadn't the housekeeper made them?

'She didn't have time,' he said.

She leaned back, relaxing. This must be how the rich lived, she supposed. It was bad manners to stare at objects and ornaments and fine pieces of furniture, but she knew without looking that they were there. She sensed the grace of the room.

He sat on the other end of the sofa and began talking about his quest for a house and the number he had inspected before finding the one that was exactly right. He asked if she liked it, and seemed pleased when she said it was lovely, but what about the curtains?

'What about them?' he said. 'There's plenty of time yet. Let's take it easy. You won't mind if I call you Clarice, will you?'

She hesitated. Only close friends called one another by their Christian names, and she was certain Mrs Graham would disapprove.

'Come along! We're not in Curzon Street now,' he said.

'Very well. But I shall continue to call you Mr Heston, of course.'

'I daresay you'll invent something a bit less formal when you know me better.'

'About the curtains, Mr Heston.'

'You said that before.'

'That's why I came this afternoon. I've been looking at the carpet—trying to choose one of the colours.'

'Let's take a turn about the garden. I want you to see the house from the outside. It will give you a better idea about curtains.'

'I don't think it will. They'll be lined.'

But he insisted, and it was still a beautiful afternoon, although time was going on.

The garden was extensive, with slopes

and hills, gravel paths, steps to different levels. He took her arm and began talking gently, drawing her out, asking her if she had parents, brothers, sisters, and how it was she came to be a dressmaker. She told him everything, far more than she intended or even realised she had said.

From having thought he was rather sinister, she now found him kind, sympathetic and likeable. They sat on a garden bench and she felt peaceful. The garden was tranquil, so far from the world she forgot why she had come. The shade from a nearby tree deepened, and he said they had better go in before the dew began to fall.

'You'd like to see the other rooms, wouldn't you?' he asked when they were in the hall. 'I shall leave you to explore. You'll find me in the drawing room.'

She tiptoed upstairs. There were four bedrooms: the largest had an enormous bed with shell-pink silk curtains, full-length looking glasses, a large walnut dressing table with silver accoutrements. She thought the bed far too beautiful to sleep in.

The other rooms were plainly furnished by comparison, but still far better than any she had seen. There was a large bathroom which left her gasping. Next door she discovered what most people she knew called a dub. She would have liked to use it but feared he would hear the flush, and that was embarrassing. A lady would never let a gentleman see her going to or coming from the dub. Madame Last, who had no such inhibitions, often spoke of a client who had spent her entire married life dodging her husband while on such expeditions. Clarice decided to wait until she got home.

Downstairs she peeped into the dining room, where the table was laid for a meal. She had an impression of silver, crystal, flowers. Mr Heston must be having friends to dine and it was high time she left.

She went back to the drawing room. He rose, took her hands and drew her to the sofa. An ice bucket with a bottle of champagne had replaced the tea tray.

'Do you like the house?' he asked.

'It's absolutely beautiful.'

He could uncork a champagne bottle as expertly as the best of butlers. He did so now and she watched, fascinated.

'I should be going,' she said.

'Should you?' He handed her a glass.

'But I haven't done anything about the curtains!'

'Never mind. Let's drink to the house.'

He raised his glass, she did the same.

'And to my visit here,' he said.

She sipped delicately, thought, was

411

puzzled. 'What do you mean by *your* visit?' she asked. 'I'm the visitor, or rather the person you asked for some advice.'

'My dear, dear Clarice, you're not going to play cross-purposes, are you?'

Something in the tone of his voice and the way he was looking at her changed everything.

'This house is yours, Clarice. I'm the visitor. A frequent one, I hope.'

She put down her glass. She hoped she had misunderstood what she had so clearly heard.

'I don't know what you mean,' she said.

'I think you do. You must have realised how much I want you. I've wanted you since the first moment I saw you. That's why I took this house for you. When I visit you I want you in the right setting.'

She was frightened and started to shake. She didn't know how to respond, except in the obvious way.

'How could you? How dare you? You were having me on about the curtains. You don't care tuppence for me. You've got your feelings, I daresay, and they have a very ugly name.' She seemed to have lost her dignity and be speaking in the way of any common girl when faced with an affront to her virtue.

'You can call my feelings what you

like. Be sensible. Think for a moment. I'm not seducing you. I'm offering you my protection, and that's not worthless or dishonourable.'

'You're asking me to be your fancy lady.'

'Don't use that abominable expression. It doesn't become you.'

She knew her colour had gone. She had looked handsome all day. Now she was ugly. She sat down because her legs were giving way. 'I wish I hadn't come,' she gulped, tears threatening. 'I wish I was home.'

She shouldn't have let him put his arm round her and say soothing things, praising her, telling her how he admired and wanted to help her. He said she could have Aunt Cassie to live with her if that would make her happy. 'You'll have a wonderful life,' he said.

Oh, if only he didn't look so like Mr Blades!

'You'll get married one of these days,' she sniffed.

'It won't make any difference to us if I do. I shall always want you. And you'll be well provided for whether I'm single, married, alive or dead. You need have no fears on that account. Think about it.'

'No,' she said, drawing away, standing. 'There isn't anything to think about.'

She had regained her composure but he was angry.

'You don't want to spend the rest of your life plying a needle, do you?'

'Only until Mr Blades comes out of prison,' she replied.

'That's years away.'

'But it's bound to happen. Will you please order the carriage, or must I walk?'

'Stay where you are,' he said, and went away. Presently she heard wheels crunching over the gravel. The carriage was at the door. She went out and asked the coachman to take her to Clapham.

Mr Heston was nowhere to be seen.

Charlotte was horrified when she heard about Clarice's adventures at Sheen. It was Mr Heston's deception and low cunning that disgusted her so much. No wonder Clarice looked ill when she arrived at Victoria's flat, where Aunt Cassie was waiting for her, that Saturday night.

They could all see there was something wrong before she said a word. It was not like Clarice to flop into a chair and ask for a drop of water. After all, she had come home in a carriage, it was not as though she'd had to take a bus.

After some time she managed to tell them what had happened, describe the house and come to Mr Heston's proposal.

'Doesn't he want to marry you?' asked Charlotte, and was surprised when the others laughed.

'We all knew you was born yesterday, Charlotte, but not the day before,' said Victoria.

'Gentlemen don't marry girls like me,' Clarice said. 'Not unless they want to get kicked out of their clubs and cut dead everywhere.'

'Oh,' said Charlotte, who didn't see how anybody could object to Clarice as a wife.

'Did he say as I'm to live there too in all that luxury?' asked Aunt Cassie after they had chewed over the results of misalliances that turned out badly.

'Yes, if it would make me happy,' Clarice said.

'I'd be a fish out of water. All grass and trees and no shops. You can count me out.'

Victoria, considering the situation, told Clarice she should do what he said and think about it.

'It's the best offer I ever heard, and you'd be daft to turn it down. He looks like Mr Blades, he's a proper toff and he don't stink. So why aren't you jumping at it?'

'Because it's wrong,' said Clarice, who was furious with herself for being almost

415

as green as Charlotte. 'You all seem to forget I'm engaged to marry Mr Blades.'

Victoria sniffed, Aunt Cassie tutted and Charlotte spoke. 'Did he say he loved you?' she asked.

'No,' said Clarice slowly, thinking back to all he had said and how close she had come to falling in love with him when they were in the garden. She sat up straight. 'No. Not once. He didn't even kiss me,' she said.

'Then you can't go and live there. Of course you can't.'

'Oh, bless your dear heart, Charlotte! You really understand, don't you?'

'I should hope so,' said Charlotte, for she remembered how Edward had tried to make her change her mind and marry him instead of Richard. She had been tempted for an iota of a second, but that was enough to make her appreciate the danger Clarice was in.

It was a very real danger, as Clarice began to realise before very long. Mr Heston must have spent a fortune on the house, and if he didn't get the return he expected he would exact his revenge. She hardly dared think what it might be but of one thing she was certain. She would have to give up working for Mrs Graham and never go near Curzon Street again.

The gloom at Madame Last's was thicker than a pea-soup fog when the establishment reopened. Wilfred was subdued, Miss Prescot unusually quiet and Miss Sharp didn't put in an appearance. Everyone seemed to be thinking.

Perhaps it was because the house had been closed for an extra week that so few orders came in, or perhaps it was because Madame Last was unable to see clients herself. Those who came were not pleased to be met by Miss Prescot and asked for Madame Last or no one.

There were the standing orders to deal with, and those taken before the annual holiday, just enough to go on with.

'You'd better do the best you can, Miss Prescot, only don't come bothering me,' Madame said, with none of her old vigour. She was uncorseted, wore a shapeless dressing gown, and her hair, always so splendidly coiffed, was twisted up in an untidy chignon.

'She's a broken woman and her figure's gone to pot,' said Miss Prescot, when the staff gathered for their midday meal. 'Does anyone know why Miss Sharp hasn't shown up?'

Somebody suspected she had found another job.

'Oh, has she! And what about Victoria?'

'She'll be here tomorrow,' said Charlotte.

Victoria had no choice but to work for the sake of the money.

'Algie would expect it of me,' she said, but it was hard going now that she was so large, and waddled along, clinging to Charlotte's arm. Passing the front door and going up to their workroom took all her courage.

'I'm a burden to you, Charlotte,' she said.

'No you're not. Don't ever think that,' said Charlotte warmly, although getting Victoria on and off buses was not easy. But she considered herself indebted for much more than she could ever repay, and often told Richard so when she wrote. She would never forget how Victoria had taken charge of her when she ran away from home, showing her the ropes and even insisting on taking her to live at Clapham when she left Mrs Blunt.

But what would happen when she lived at Barnes with Richard? Victoria never asked, but it occurred to Charlotte over and over again, especially when Victoria conceded that she really couldn't go to work any more. The journey, the hurtful remarks of people like Miss Prescot, and the mental pain of Madame Last's establishment with all its associations were more than she could bear. She had never had to seek help from the authorities; now she meant to find out where to go for outdoor relief.

There were letters from Richard by every post, and now that it was less than a month before he came home he told Charlotte he was counting the days. The banns had been read for the first time at the parish church, and Charlotte and Nanny went to hear them.

'Can I be married from your house, Nanny darling?' she asked.

'Where else?' said Nanny, who was enjoying the part of bride's proxy mother and spent days at Barnes waiting for deliveries and weeding the garden.

The reception was to be at Barnes, just a small gathering, rather like Victoria's, but as long as all the people dear to her were present she would rejoice. Nanny, Mrs Vickery, Annie and Tilda, Clarice, Will Goode, Victoria if her nerves were strong enough to bear it, with Eustace Bright to escort her. It went without saying that Mary would be there, and Hans Braun, Richard's best man. Ellie? What about Ellie? The answer came when Charlotte left work one evening and found Ellie beckoning to her from her carriage window.

'I've got such wonderful news for you,' she began, almost before Charlotte was inside. 'Did you know your papa and I went to stay at Wool with Mrs Graham?'

'Mrs Vickery told me. What was it like?'

'Unbelievable. The house, the grounds —oh, how I wish you'd been there. And Mrs Graham made our stay one of those things you can't stop talking about. I shall simply say glorious. But now...!'

'Now?' queried Charlotte.

'Now for the best thing of all. Mrs Graham was so extraordinarily good with your papa. Where you and I and even Aunt Mildred failed to make him see that poor Richard's unfortunate birth shouldn't debar him from matrimony, Mrs Graham succeeded. What do you say to that?'

Charlotte was not nearly so pleased with this piece of information as Ellie seemed to expect. It was not exactly flattering to be told that a stranger had succeeded when those so close to her father had failed. And what of it, anyway?

Apparently Mr Grant was now persuaded that he must accept the inevitable. Richard Allen's parentage, although illicit, was nothing to be ashamed of. Mary Allen had never disclosed his father's name to anybody, but there were those who knew, and Mrs Graham was one of them. Wolves wouldn't drag the secret from her, save to say that he was a man of the highest standing, forced into a marriage which united two great families and this debarred him from marrying Mary.

Charlotte had never known Ellie to rattle on so. It was just as though she was bewitched, and so, apparently, was Pa.

'Ellie, this all sounds quite dottily romantic and needs to be taken with a peck of salt. Where does it lead to?'

'Why, my darling, don't you see? You're to have a splendid wedding and your papa intends to give you away!'

Indignation and anger swamped Charlotte's brain and she gave way to it. 'Does he indeed? I never heard such a thing in all my life. Pa is a snob and you can tell him so from me. And as to giving me away—why, whatever next? He'd be the last one, I can tell you that.'

'Charlotte! What on earth are you saying!'

'What I mean, Ellie. I'm to be married from Nanny's and I'm only having the people I love at my wedding. That includes you, of course, for I do love you, and I shall love my little brother or sister when it's born.'

'Oh dear! You're making me miserable. How can you talk like this?'

'Because I have reason to. And where are you taking me?'

'Home, of course.'

'My home's in Clapham, and if you'll put me down I can take a bus.'

But Ellie was crying. There she was, almost in the same stage of pregnancy as Victoria, only so becomingly dressed that her condition was not nearly so obvious.

Charlotte was sorry to see her upset, especially as she had tried so hard to change her husband's attitude towards his daughter.

Neither wife nor child could see deep into the heart of William Grant, the victim of his own narrow mind, his prejudices, his conviction that everything he did was right.

Who could tell how much he had suffered at the hands of Amanda, so wretchedly in love with her as he was and so distraught when she died. Was it because he failed to make her conform and become a conventional, obedient wife that he tried to turn Charlotte into a spineless daughter?

He didn't know the answers to these questions himself. He honestly believed he could choose a better husband for her than she could for herself, and saw shades of Amanda in every wilful step she took. How he would have welcomed a suitor like Edward Graham! How gracious was the old house at Wool, and its beautiful mistress.

It was almost impossible for William to cling to his rigid ideas in Mrs Graham's enlightened company. She took a broad view of the world and considered art supreme. Music, books, painting—he had trouble trying to hide his own inadequacy in these fields and found it better to give in and confess that no, he had never read Keats, or Shelley, and certainly not Byron.

'But you must!' she cried. 'Byron especially. Naughty young man that he was, but so very, very young. We have to forgive youth, don't we, Mr Grant?'

Shelley, it seemed, was even worse, but he too had to be forgiven for conduct Mr Grant considered so unspeakable it was as much as he could do not to splutter.

Still, he found it soothing when Mrs Graham read Keats aloud, although he would have preferred nightingales to be left out. He always blamed that beastly songster for Amanda's death, and they hadn't even heard it sing. Now he hoped he never would.

But the surprise of this Friday-to-Monday with Mrs Graham was her admiration for Charlotte. 'Your beautiful young daughter,' she called her.

She seemed to know a great deal more about his beautiful daughter than he did himself. His beautiful daughter's courage in helping a distressed friend, running through the worst parts of town at dead of night to fetch a doctor for her, keeping her in food and drink and attending to her needs while working a twelve-hour day were only a few of the examples Mrs Graham described.

And although Mr Grant disapproved of Richard Allen, what fortitude Charlotte had shown in her constancy to him! Think of the strength of character that demanded, especially when she had another, more eligible suitor.

'My poor Edward couldn't shake her faith in Mr Allen, although he tried hard enough, Mr Grant. He said he wouldn't give up hope until the knot was tied, but I think he realises he has lost.'

'Indeed?' This was the first William had heard of it.

'Yes indeed. When Charlotte came to tea I tried to point out the disadvantages of marrying a man of Mr Allen's profession. But could I shake her? I could not.'

William was learning all the time, and suffering intense mortification. To think the stupid girl had rejected such a splendid chance! Could it mean that Richard Allen had even more to offer? He began to wonder.

All this and much more Charlotte learned from Ellie while they drove to Clapham, for Ellie insisted on taking her there.

'Please don't be hasty, Charlotte dear,' pleaded Ellie.

'I won't,' said Charlotte.

'Promise you'll think it over.'

'Very well.' Charlotte felt obliged to say that.

'Why not leave work and come home? You must have so much to do, and I'd like to help.'

'You're a dear darling, Ellie, but it's impossible.'

'Why?'

'Victoria can't earn just now, you see, so my wages have to keep the two of us,' said Charlotte as she got out and ran in, leaving Ellie to go back to Lancaster Gate alone and make up some story for William, as she hadn't the heart to tell him the truth.

Nanny often went to see Bessy Last after her first visit. She thought she knew her well, but the bereaved mother's abject state of despair was so desperate she didn't know how to treat it. It might lift as time went on. She knew the enervating sense of loss, the terrible longing and hopelessness only too well. These would never go away, but usually a second strength came and enabled people to go on.

Bessy didn't want to go on and told Nanny she couldn't.

'Everything was for him,' she said. 'We worked this business up to what it is but it was all for Algie. Now he's gone, what's the use?'

'A lot of use,' said Nanny. 'You employ people, and that's good whichever way you look at it.'

'They can find work elsewhere.'

'There aren't many employers as considerate as you, Bessy.'

'I've always said a good light, airy workrooms and a midday dinner get the best results.'

'But it takes a woman like you to run the place and get the orders in.'

'Well, I'm giving up, closing down, putting the shutters up. Don't try to talk me out of it.'

But Nanny couldn't help trying. Victoria and the child she was carrying were always in her mind, and she longed to tell Algie's mother so. It was on the tip of her tongue many times but she always remembered Victoria's injunction and thought it only right she should decide if and when the Lasts were to be told.

One day Nanny accompanied Bessy to the cemetery. There were always flowers on Algie's grave, but on this particular day Bessy noticed a small bunch of white daisies. They were tied with a narrow blue ribbon and had a card attached. She picked it up. The words, written in large, round letters, were: NEVER MIND, ALGIE.

'What's the meaning of this? Who did this?' Bessy was purple in the face with indignation.

'I don't know,' said Nanny, although she knew very well.

'Neither do I and I don't like it. Impudence, I call it. Where's the reverence?'

'Don't say that, Bessy. They're probably from some poor person Algie helped.'

'Never mind, indeed! What a thing to put on a card. And the daisies look second hand.'

'It's the thought that counts, remember.'

'Seems I'm not aware of everyone Algie knew.'

'I expect he had friends everywhere. Put them back.'

'I've a good mind to throw them on the rubbish heap.'

'Don't.' Nanny took the flowers from Bessy's hands and laid them down. 'Whoever put them there must have thought a lot of Algie,' she said.

'I'd like to know who it was.'

'Perhaps you will one of these days.'

Later on, Nanny thought of Victoria buying the stale flowers and tying them with a bit of baby ribbon before making her way to her husband's grave, and she couldn't help crying. Someone would have to help that poor girl, and nobody had much to spare.

Charlotte was practically keeping Victoria now, but that would have to stop when she married, although, knowing the girl, it wouldn't surprise Nanny if she tried to keep on working. And now, of all things, came the news that Mr Grant had been persuaded to give her away.

Nanny was keeping Victoria company when Charlotte came in and told them. 'Pa's a pig and I'm not having him,' she said.

'Then you're a bigger mug than I took you for,' said Victoria after the astonished pause that followed the announcement.

'I second that,' said Nanny.

'What? After the way he's treated me? And how about the horrible name he called Richard?'

'There's nothing worse than a family feud. Be a sensible girl and make it up.'

'We shall see what Richard has to say.'

And then Richard was home. Charlotte came in from work one Saturday afternoon and there he was, with a skein of wool stretched between his hands and Victoria winding it.

'Oh!' she cried, dropping all the parcels

and packets she had collected on the way. 'You're here!'

'It rather looks like it,' he said, skilfully transferring the wool on to the back of a chair and taking her in the embrace she'd been dreaming of. It was a very discreet hug, for they both knew how Victoria must feel and tempered their ardour accordingly. But it was the reality that mattered after the long wait, during which many sad and disquieting things had happened.

What pleased Charlotte so much was Richard's way with Victoria. He had only met her once outside Madame Last's, and that was when she had everything to live for. Now he treated her as an old friend, making her laugh over some of the more comical events on his travels, telling her he would expect her to stay with them when she wanted a change, and promising to deafen her with his piano. He made her feel included, wanted.

'You haven't seen your house yet, have you?' Victoria asked.

'No, and I don't know what to do first. My mother can't wait to see Charlotte. I want to see Nanny, and I must see the house.'

'Mothers come first,' said Victoria.

Charlotte had been basking in the sheer joy of Richard's presence. She loved him, loved him, loved him.

So off they went to Green Street, where Mary had managed to secure a lease on the same house. They took a hansom so they could have all the kisses they'd been missing, and took it in turns to talk as each had so much to tell the other.

'How well did you do? Were there any fiascos like the Wigmore?'

'That wasn't a fiasco. *You* were there. That made it a celebration.'

'But I wasn't listening. I was too miserable to hear a note with you going away again. I didn't think I'd ever go to sleep that night.'

'And did you?'

'Must have done. I woke up and felt sort of empty.'

'So did I.'

'Did you? Did you really?'

'Honestly, truly, with my hand on my heart. But we're going to make up for it.'

'Are we?'

There came one of those strange silences, and without knowing why, Charlotte suddenly burst into tears.

'What is it? What's wrong?'

'Nothing. Nothing.'

He stopped the cab. They were in Park Lane, and there was Hyde Park, trees, grass, strollers, perambulators. He took her arm, walked her to a grassy slope and sat. Her head was on her knees. She was sobbing.

'What's wrong?' he asked again.

'Everything's right. Oh!' she cried. 'You can't think what it's like for me to have someone of my own.'

He thought he knew, or could at least guess, but only Charlotte really knew what it was to be an unloved child. She loved Mrs Vickery, Nanny, Ellie and her workroom friends, but they didn't entirely fill the empty place in her life. It was not until that very afternoon in the hansom cab that she knew exactly how much Richard meant to her, and it was overwhelming. Hearing his voice, feeling the touch of his hand, knowing they were to step into a new life, struck her with something approaching awe.

She tried to tell him, tried to put it all into words, but they didn't fit. Listening, looking at her lovely tear-streaked face, he understood exactly what she meant.

A little while longer and they were walking arm-in-arm, keeping in step.

Very soon they were with Mary, drinking tea from delicate porcelain cups and talking. How they talked!

'Tell me everything,' said Mary.

So Charlotte began, and soon had Mary laughing with an account of her stay at Mrs Blunt's, her despair because she hadn't

431

heard from Richard, and what Victoria did to help. 'She's my friend for life, and Clarice is another,' Charlotte said.

'I should think so too. What dear, good girls.'

'They were so kind to me. And poor Mr Blades. I wish you could have seen him. And to think he's doing time, and Clarice means to wait for him. Years and years.'

'I think you helped Clarice, didn't you, dear?'

'With some of the sovereigns from that lovely purse you gave me. It was such a boon.'

Mary wanted to hear all about it, and Charlotte was eager to know more of Richard's tour. She knew it had been a success, but there were so many details to fill in, and what about the future?

'I'll tell you,' he said. There was a full programme with Mary for the autumn—all in cathedral cities in the south and west. In the winter a series of recitals with Hans Braun was planned. They would be playing violin and piano sonatas and in addition Richard was to give some solos. Schumann, he said.

'He's hard, isn't he?'

'Listen.'

He went over to the piano and began to play. Those magical opening bars! She was entranced and found her hand was in Mary's, and they were both so still. He only played a little, stopped and swung round. 'The rest when we're in our own home with our own piano, Charlotte,' he said.

'What's it called?'

'Papillons.'

'That's French for butterflies, isn't it?'

'Yes, but not this time. These are two ethereal beings searching for each other at a masked ball, nearly touching then swept apart and carried away like leaves in the wind.'

'Like us?'

'Like we might have been.'

She couldn't bear to think what her life would have been if they had never got together again, but here they were, with the whole evening to enjoy. They chose to have dinner at the mysterious little restaurant Hans had taken them to, but this time no dread of parting hung over them, so it was a Saturday to remember.

Sunday was even better, for Richard was ecstatic when he saw the house, especially the room that was made for a grand piano.

'How clever of you to find it,' he said.

The acoustics were right, he could see exactly where the members of the trio, quartet, quintet, however many, would sit.

There was to be music, music, music!

'Will cycled all over the place to discover this. It's all thanks to him,' she said.

'He must have been led to it. It's magic. Don't you feel it the moment you walk in?'

'That's what everyone says. Come and see the garden.'

They found two old deckchairs in the conservatory, which was full of aged flowerpots containing withered leaves. When they went in, a toad hopped out.

Richard brushed the cobwebs off the chairs and they sat in the garden and argued over which flowers to have.

'You can't do any digging. You'll spoil your hands,' she said.

'I shall scatter seeds. Packets and packets of them. Where's the lemonade Nanny gave us?'

She produced it and they drank a toast to the house, then ate the pasties that Nanny had packed for them.

It was peaceful, dreamy, with nothing but the occasional creak of a tree against the fence, a burst of song from the resident thrush and the sound of wings as birds flew across the garden.

Nanny and Will came in the late afternoon, and later still Mary arrived to see the house and give it her approval, which she did with genuine enthusiasm.

In the early evening they all went back to Nanny's in Mary's carriage. It seated four comfortably, five with a squash, so Charlotte perched on Richard's knee and they both laughed at their secret thoughts and wouldn't tell the others why. They were remembering the last time she'd sat on his lap, and the disastrous consequences.

Nanny could always conjure up a meal without notice, and that evening she excelled herself. She stuffed wafer-thin pancakes with a savoury filling. Peas from the garden glistened with butter.

'Let me make the salad. It's my speciality,' said Mary when she saw the lettuces Will brought in. They were all heart. 'Like me,' he said.

'Where's Richard?'

No one knew. They had all been too busy mincing cold chicken, slicing onion and chopping parsley.

He had nipped out for a bottle of wine from the off-licence and was back just as everything was ready.

It was a never-to-be forgotten meal at the kitchen table, and the accord between them all made Charlotte think she was living in Arcadia.

Will gave her a bunch of roses for Victoria, and she took them back with her to Clapham.

'He ain't half thoughtful,' Victoria said

as she put them in water.

As Mary was preparing for her autumn recitals, Richard expected to spend the best part of Monday with her. Charlotte was worried about Victoria's financial position and had already decided to go to Last's that day and for the ensuing week.

She had been able to add to the little store of money Algie had left, and every penny counted. If they could only scrape enough together to last a month or two! Will Goode surreptitiously slipped a florin into the jug when he called, and Eustace Bright found the occasional threepenny bit, but his means were very restricted while he was training. His father, an eminent surgeon, dangled the carrot of a handsome allowance once he was qualified.

'But that's not now,' Eustace groused. 'My nose will be ground off by the time I'm a registered quack.'

'You won't miss a bit off the end,' said Victoria.

Charlotte arrived at Last's to be greeted by Wilfred. 'The old man wants to see you up in his office,' he said.

The miserable tone of his voice prepared her for an unpleasant interview, and she wondered if she had ruined an expensive blouse and was to have her pay docked.

Mr Last, sitting at his desk, told her that

Miss Prescot was leaving and hands were being laid off, and as she was one of the last to come, she must be first to go.

'Madame's in no condition to speak to staff herself but she's done you a reference, and here's a week's pay in lieu of notice.'

'Thank you,' she said.

So that, without any action on her part, was that. She was out of work.

She met Miss Prescot on the stairs and told her what had happened.

'What! You got a week's pay?' exclaimed Miss Prescot nastily. 'If that doesn't beat cockfighting! Here's me having to work the week, and all because I gave notice Saturday.'

'Oh dear,' murmured Charlotte.

'Here's you picking up the cash without so much as dropping a pin. Favouritism. That's what it is.'

'I don't get the same wages as you, Miss Prescot. Mine's much less.'

'Maybe it is. Anyhow, Madame will be in the bankruptcy court if she doesn't pull her socks up.'

'Goodbye,' said Charlotte, hoping she would never see Miss Prescot again.

She went home to tell Victoria about the sad state of affairs at Last's.

'Madame ought to pull herself together same as what I'm having to,' said Victoria crossly. 'Old cat. She's got a husband and pots of money, and if she hadn't been such a tartar Algie could have told her about me.'

'I never thought to hear you talk in such a hard-hearted way,' Charlotte said.

'It's true, what I said.'

'But she hasn't got the one thing that matters now, and you have.'

'I suppose you mean the baby.'

'Of course I do.'

Victoria's lip trembled. 'Poor little blighter. Look at the sock I just knitted for him!' She held up the tiny little sock made of the finest wool. 'Oh, Charlotte, I do miss Algie so. I long for him. If I could just hear his voice! Every time Eustace comes I expect Algie to be with him.' She was choking on her words, sobbing them out in disconnected jerks. 'It will be a boy, won't it? It's got to be a boy.'

Charlotte wished there was a better way to comfort her than with the usual threadbare platitudes. There must be something, some consolation somewhere. The one possibility and the only one was Madame Last. Victoria had forbidden anyone to tell her the truth and she was adamant. It wouldn't do any good to mention it again and might upset her even more, but everyone thought she was wrong and told her so. Nanny, Clarice, Aunt

438

Cassie, Eustace—they had all reasoned with her and been smacked back.

But weren't there times when you had to act for another person's good, even if it was against their will? Suppose Madame Last greeted the facts with anger and rejected Algie's wife and child? If that happened, the situation would be unchanged. Victoria would be in exactly the same position.

But if Madame welcomed the news and it gave her a real reason for living, what a difference that would make. It was worth a try, wasn't it?

Charlotte made up her mind there and then to tell Madame Last the whole story.

As Lizzie Wilson, the midwife, came to see Victoria in the afternoon, Charlotte went to Green Street, where Mary and Richard had just finished work for the day.

They were glad to hear that she had left Last's, and Mary said they really must start making arrangements for the wedding without further delay, and besides that, there was the whole house to furnish.

'Why don't you go shopping now?' she asked.

'But shouldn't we take some measurements first?' asked Charlotte. 'We don't want furniture all the wrong sizes.'

'We know the size of the bed, and that's our first buy. Come on,' said Richard.

The bed department in the store they visited looked bigger than the Albert Hall, with row upon row of every conceivable type of bed, from the enormous four-poster complete with hangings to the narrowest imaginable couch.

An assistant, a rosy little man with a black curl carefully plastered to the middle of his forehead, showed them round. He was an enthusiast and stretched himself out to his full five foot two inches whenever they showed a gleam of interest. He looked like Cupid dressed up in a morning suit, and twinkled at them wickedly from a recumbent position.

'Try it for yourselves. Otherwise you may not be satisfied after purchase.'

They declined, but in the end Richard lay down on the bed they kept coming back to and declared there was no doubt about it. 'Test the springs,' cried the little man, so Richard bounced and Charlotte was convulsed. She refused to try it herself and told the assistant that she trusted her fiancé's judgement implicitly, whereupon the little man shook Richard's hand, bowed to Charlotte and said: 'If he chooses as well and wisely in everything else, he will be a model husband.'

'I don't want a model husband, I want a real one,' Charlotte told Richard while the account was being made out.

She was beginning to discover that furnishing a house was a very tall order indeed, and few girls did it unaided, especially in such a short time.

And then there was the problem of Pa. She didn't want him to have any part in their wedding after the abominable way he had treated Mary and Richard, but she would have to tell them about his offer sometime.

The thought kept returning to her, but when they got back to Green Street, tired but hilarious, she simply couldn't bear to spoil the day by talking about Pa. Besides, she meant to tackle Madame Last in the morning. She must get that over first.

Madame Last couldn't keep away from the cemetery. She went there almost every day. Sometimes Henry went too, but more often Nanny accompanied her.

There were always flowers on Algie's grave, she saw to that, but she was still angry over the miserable bunch of daisies someone had put there, with that unsuitable message. If anything like it happened again she meant to take steps to find out who it was. She'd post Wilfred there to watch. She'd find some way.

She stood there, a lonely, unhappy, angry woman, and that was where Charlotte found her, having been told by Wilfred of Madame's daily pilgrimage.

She approached slowly and with increasing trepidation, for she was not enjoying the role of informer, although she had chosen to take it regardless of its consequences.

'Madame Last?' she said quietly.

Madame turned and looked puzzled for a moment, Then she said: 'Yes? You're Miss Grant, aren't you? It's no good asking for your job back, for I can't give it to you.'

'That isn't why I'm here,' Charlotte said.

'Oh? Then you've no business with me and I'd thank you to leave me with my sorrow.' She turned away and stood looking at the flowers, all prim and beautiful, straight from the florist, except for a bunch of garden roses tied with a piece of blue baby ribbon. She picked it up and wheeled round on Charlotte. 'Perhaps you know something about this,' she said, her puffy white face turning red and ugly.

Charlotte knew they were the roses Will had given Victoria. She must have brought them here, and it was her big round writing on the card, 'ONLY CUPLA WEEKS NOW, ALGIE,' it read.

She couldn't help her eyes filling with tears. 'Yes, I know who put those flowers on Algie's grave. You know her too,' she said.

'One of the workroom girls, I suppose. I like her impudence, whoever she is.'

'She was a workroom girl but she's not with you any more.'

'You seem to know a lot about it. Referring to my son by his first name like you did. He was young Mr Last, I'd have you know. Not Algie.'

'He was to me. I'm sorry it upsets you but I knew Algie outside working hours. The roses are from Victoria, the girl who worked with Clarice West and me.'

Madame Last looked at her hard. 'You're trying to tell me something, aren't you? Well, don't beat about the bush. Out with it. Did she lead him on?'

Charlotte hesitated, but Madame had asked a question, so she should have the answer.

'Algie was married to Victoria,' she said. 'She'll be having his baby very soon.'

Madame's eyes bulged so dangerously she looked like a bullfrog ready to explode. 'You're lying,' she shouted. 'You're saying it was my son gave her a big belly, and expecting me to fork out. Well, there's nothing doing. Tell her that.'

Madame Last had reverted to the language and manner of tough young Bessy Weller, and Charlotte was shocked and frightened. She hadn't done any good. They said the path to Hell was paved with good intentions, but whatever kind of Hell was she descending into?

She shouldn't have come without telling Nanny. She had unleashed goodness knows what fury in this already overstrung woman and damaged poor Victoria. There was a bench nearby. She'd better sit down until her legs stopped shaking and she could go and ask Nanny what to do next.

Oh, why had she been such a fool? What on earth had possessed her to come here without telling Richard what she intended? What a horrible mess she'd made of everything. But for her Mr Blades wouldn't have been caught, Clarice wouldn't have worked for Mrs Graham and been pestered by that horrible Mr Heston, and she wouldn't have met Edward Graham and led him up the garden path. Above all, Mrs Graham wouldn't have gone poking her elegant nose in and persuaded Pa to give her an outsize wedding when all she wanted was a nice quiet little affair.

It's me, she thought, sobbing. I'm at the bottom of it all, interfering, upsetting people, making trouble wherever I go, and she cried into her miserable little handkerchief.

'Now, now, now. What's all this about?' The voice, trained to reach the back row of the gallery but now soft and gentle, was Nanny's, and there she was with such a look of compassion on her face as Charlotte seldom saw. It was clear she knew what had happened.

'I wish someone would shoot me,' Charlotte snivelled. 'I've spoilt everything for every single person I ever met.'

'Come now, that's stretching it,' Nanny said. 'I really can't agree with you, though you may be a bit hasty now and then.'

Madame Last was still at the foot of the grave, pulling the petals off the roses and grinding them under her heel.

'She's in a terrible temper,' Charlotte whispered.

'I know, dear. I come here with her most days, and it's a shame she left without me today. Never mind. She'll calm down.'

So saying, Nanny approached Madame Last and spoke with great firmness. 'Behave yourself, Bessy,' she said. 'You are desecrating the flowers that were put on your son's grave by a dear, good girl who loved him with all her heart.'

'They were put here by a common little slut who taught him to say ain't. Oh, I thought it very odd the bad ways he was getting into. Calling me Ma, never home till after midnight, out on the river every weekend no matter what the weather.'

'He was never on the river, Bessy. That

last time was his first. It was the excuse he made so he could be with his wife.'

'Then why wasn't I told? Why did he keep it from me?'

Nanny took a deep breath and then said slowly and deliberately: 'He kept it from you because you are such a tartar, Bessy.'

Madame Last's face began to crumple up. She looked like a very ugly baby bracing itself to howl.

'Me? Me a tartar?' Big tears ran down her face. 'I never was a tartar. Not to him. Never.'

Nanny led her to the bench and sat her down. 'I know this is a shock and a hard one to take, but you had to know some time and it's best to get it over.' She went on talking in a quiet, soothing voice until Madame Last stopped hurling cruel words at the woman who had led her son astray and began to listen.

It seemed the right time for Charlotte to slip away and go to Green Street, leaving Nanny to continue her peacemaking. She felt wretchedly low. When she saw Richard she told him how wrong she had been to go against Victoria's wishes, and he had to use all the arguments he could think of to console her.

'It must be right for Madame Last to

know she's to have a grandchild,' he argued. 'Victoria's bound to see that once she gets used to the idea.'

Mary had joined them and agreed with Richard, so between them, Charlotte began to feel better. But she still had that other field to cross, and there were bulls there waiting to toss her.

'There's something else,' she said.

It wasn't easy to tell them of her father's extraordinary change of heart and her own reaction to it. When she finished the silence seemed to go on for ever, and then Richard simply said, 'Oh.'

The atmosphere was charged with emotion. Richard and Mary had not expected to meet Mr Grant again, and neither had Charlotte, but there were so many considerations.

'Let us think about it individually,' Mary said. 'My feelings are my own. I'm not going to influence either of you.'

Was the quiet little wedding from Nanny's house to be displaced in favour of a fashionable one? Once again Charlotte felt the power of Curzon Street impinging on her life.

She had seen Edward once more before he went to Dorset and had made her refusal perfectly plain. It was the Saturday after his odd little proposal when he'd left her at Nanny's saying, 'Don't marry

Richard. Marry me.'

He had been waiting for her outside Last's. 'I'm going straight to Clapham,' she said.

'Hop in. I'll take you there.'

They scarcely talked on the way, but when they stopped outside the house he only had to say: 'Well?' and she knew what he meant.

'Eddie, I like you very much but it isn't the same,' she said. 'I'm going to marry Richard. I can't live without him so it's no use trying to make me change my mind.'

'I see,' he said.

'We'll be friends, won't we?'

'Of course.' But he didn't mean it. How could he be just friends when he was burning to kiss this girl who had come to mean so much to him? He couldn't even look at her, and the hell of it was he'd stopped the engine thinking they would have a long talk. Now he'd have to crank it up again.

She left him turning the handle, and was so sorry he was disappointed she made herself run in quickly or she would have started saying mollifying things instead of just goodbye.

And now, after her dreadful meeting with Madame Last, there was another decision to make. She did not want her father at the wedding, and was sure Richard would refuse to meet him, but they agreed not to discuss it as they went to Barnes that afternoon.

It was an important day for Richard. The piano was being delivered and he had to be there when it came. It arrived at the appointed time and was taken in through the French windows. The piano tuner came with it, and once Richard was satisfied with the position of the instrument the tuning began.

Charlotte realised that her role was to supply them both with tea, for which she boiled water on a Primus stove. She rather enjoyed doing it, for she had become an expert at Mrs Blunt's.

The recollection of those days always amused her. When she took the tea in, the two men were so busy sounding notes they were scarcely aware of her, so she put the cups on the floor and took hers into the garden.

How long did it take to tune a piano? Hours, apparently. Now and then she would hear the tantalising sound of a few chords, but then it was back to single notes struck over and over again. Once Richard came to close the doors and she asked why.

'It's that damn thrush shouting. It interferes,' he said abruptly.

So birds had to keep quiet when a piano was being tuned. Another surprise for her. But at last came the sound of something lovely, and she knew that Richard was at the keyboard. When she hurried in, she saw that it was the piano tuner.

'How wonderfully you play,' she said.

'I don't play at all. Only that bit to test it,' he said.

Richard refused to touch the piano after he'd left, and said it was time for them to go.

There were all kinds of delights in Barnes. Plenty of friendly little shops, a pub called The Sun, an old church, the common itself, and above all the pond. Charlotte had been enchanted by it from the first, the water, the willow trees and the ducks. That late afternoon she walked Richard there to see it.

They sat on the grass. He threw stones into the water, trying to make them skim along the top, and she leaned back on her hands and listened to the sound of the leaves stirred by the wind.

Then, out of the blue, Richard said: 'You must make up the quarrel with your father, Charlotte.'

She had expected him to be hard against a reconciliation, so this surprised her. 'Is that what you honestly think?' she asked.

'I don't have to think. You'll never have

another father so you might as well make the most of this one.'

'Have him to our wedding?'

'I suppose so.'

'He'll spoil it.'

'We mustn't let him. Just think how unpleasant it will be as the years go by if you are still at odds with him. You could never go to see Ellie, and what about your half brother or sister? Had you thought of them?'

'I can only think how beastly he was to you and Mary, and that's not counting the misery he caused me.'

'It's all in the past. Don't let it ruin our future. Come on. Be magnanimous.'

She knew he was right. What was it that made him different from other men? Was it his looks, which never struck you until you got used to them and saw the distinction—his voice, his hands, an ineffable something? Perhaps it was his generous spirit.

'Very well. I give in,' she said.

'Just this once.'

She wanted to hug and kiss him there and then, but there were too many people about—thirsty workmen going into The Sun for a pint, clerks in city suits hurrying home, shop girls exchanging backchat with the men.

The bus was coming. Richard ran and

stopped it, and off they went, ending up in Green Street where Charlotte found that Mary used exactly the same arguments as her son. All she had to do now was to come to an agreeable arrangement with her father.

It was late when she returned to Clapham, and as she didn't know what kind of reception to expect from Victoria, Richard went with her.

'I'm not sure I'm speaking to you, Charlotte,' were the words with which Victoria greeted her when they went in.

'Aren't you? Why not?'

'You know very well why not. Nanny was here this morning. She told me you spilt the beans. Madame took it very hard.'

Richard sat beside her and took her hand. 'Only to start with,' he said. 'She'll get over it and be glad. You'll see.'

'I don't want her being too glad and trying to pinch my baby, thank you very much. It's my baby. Mine and Algie's and I'm keeping it.'

'Of course you are.'

But Victoria was in distress, moving restlessly in her chair. 'Ooh, I've got such a pain in me back,' she gasped. 'It's awful. I've had it on and off ever since Nanny went. Must be lumbago.' Her colour had gone and she looked frightened. 'Don't let

452

go me hand, Richard. Hold me hand. It's coming back.'

'It isn't lumbago—it's the baby coming,' Richard whispered to Charlotte.

'How do you know?'

'I've seen it happen before.'

Victoria was writhing.

Charlotte had a fleeting acquaintance with Mrs Rogers, the woman who lived with her husband in the ground-floor flat. Not knowing what else to do, she ran down to ask for help. Mrs Rogers hurried upstairs, took one look at Victoria and sent Richard off to Hammersmith to fetch Lizzie Wilson and Nanny.

Mrs Rogers informed Charlotte that she'd had six of her own, and there wasn't much you could tell her about giving birth.

'There, my dear, soon be over,' she said soothingly to Victoria, but aside she mouthed: 'Won't be over for another twelve hours. Ten with luck.'

'What can I do to help?'

'Fetch some towels, make us all a good cup of tea, then stay within call until wanted.'

Charlotte did as she was told.

It was at least two hours before Richard came back with Lizzie Wilson and Nanny. He had sent Mary a message telling her he didn't expect to be home that night, and she responded by sending a cab with a consignment of sheets and towels, guessing that Victoria would only have a limited supply.

There was nothing for Charlotte to do. Richard made her curl up on the black horsehair sofa in the sitting room, while he catnapped in an easy chair.

She swore the next day that she never slept a wink, but as she hadn't heard the comings and goings, or the groans and gasps that kept Richard on the alert, he told her she must have dreamt she was awake. It was a subject they argued about for years afterwards.

Algernon Charles Last, a very small baby, was born at seven o'clock in the morning. He was three weeks early but none the worse for that, according to Lizzie Wilson, who said Victoria had probably got her dates wrong anyway.

'I'd never have left you yesterday if I'd known,' said Nanny.

'How was you to know if I didn't know?' asked Victoria. She was sitting up in bed enjoying the best cup of tea of her life. 'Saucy, ain't he?' she said, referring to her son, who looked so like his father she laughed and cried and said: 'Oh, if only Algie was here. He'd be tickled pink.'

Lizzie Wilson, having allowed everyone in to see the baby, now ordered them out so her patient could rest. Charlotte, the last to leave, said quietly: 'Have you forgiven me, Victoria?'

'Course I have. The Charles is after you. Nearest I could get to Charlotte.'

What a strange mixture of emotions filled Charlotte's heart as she left the house and went off to tell Clarice all about it. Richard, after seeing her into a cab, went home for a bath and a shave, and Nanny went to see the Lasts, with what she optimistically hoped would be good news for them.

Charlotte dreaded meeting her father again and approached her old home wondering what kind of reception he would give her.

She went down to the side door for a reassuring chat with Mrs Vickery first, and was welcomed as a lamb restored to the fold.

It was strange and yet so right to be back in the kitchen with the three women who had befriended her in her childhood and stood by her ever since. They talked of those times.

She noticed familiar things: the well-scrubbed table, the stove Tilda polished with black lead till it gleamed, and the shelf with Mrs Vickery's precious books. What a solace they had been, and still were!

It was as though she had never been away, and yet so much had happened in the months between.

'I'm to patch things up with Pa, Mrs Vickery,' she said.

'And a good thing too, Miss Charlotte. Your stepma's been so put out with you being away from home. She's been worried stiff for you off and on. Still, you've done wonders and we're right proud of you down here.'

'Is Pa home yet?'

'No, but he's expected soon.'

'Then I'll go and ring the front door bell.'

Mr Grant was just getting out of a cab, so he didn't see her emerging from the basement, which was just as well. They came face to face at the gate and Charlotte felt a little thrill because her father raised his hat.

'Good afternoon, Charlotte. I'm pleased to see you here,' he said.

'Thank you, Papa.'

She preceded him up the steps and he noticed that the soles of her shoes had large holes in them.

'You will find Ellen in the drawing room,' he said when they were inside. 'I will join you in a moment.'

'Thank you, Papa,' she said again. He had said Ellen, not 'your stepmama' as in former days. That must mean something.

Ellen was reclining on the sofa and more delighted to see Charlotte than she could say. It was such a relief having her home, and in much happier circumstances than last time, she said, making just enough room for Charlotte to sit on the sofa and holding her hand as though she didn't mean to let her go again.

She wanted to know everything fast, and Charlotte did her best to tell her. But what came first—the wedding only three Saturdays away, the house, the rush to get everything done, Victoria's baby, Richard?

Richard, of course. Charlotte was ecstatic about him and could have gone on forever, but Mr Grant came in so she desisted and returned to practicalities.

Ellie expected to give birth in November, so she would be all right for the wedding. Exactly what was planned?

'A quiet wedding without many guests,' Charlotte said, although the numbers were growing, for Richard wanted the other members of the quintet to come. So it would be those four, Mary, Nanny, Will, Clarice, Aunt Cassie, Eustace, Victoria, Mrs Vickery, Annie, Tilda, and now with Pa and Ellie—it was getting on for twenty. And she hadn't counted herself and Richard.

'Why are you frowning?' asked her father.

'I was just thinking of how many to cater for. We're having the breakfast at Barnes, and Clarice and the others have promised to help me get it ready. Will is making the cake, just like he did for Victoria, and we thought if we cut lots of sandwiches and things—' She was thinking aloud, forgetting where she was for the moment. Fish paste, meat paste, sardines. Clarice had suggested cider.

'Shall we begin again?' said Mr Grant. 'Have the reception at Barnes by all means but allow me to arrange for the catering.'

'You'll have enough to think of without that,' said Ellie.

'You're not taking it out of my hands, are you, Papa? I do so want it simple. They all love salmon and shrimp paste.'

'I think you can rely on the caterer to provide whatever you want,' said Mr Grant, and Ellie murmured something about Gunter's and went on to say that it would be a good thing for Charlotte to move back home, 'so you can be married from here.'

'But I'm getting married from Nanny's. I asked her ages ago.'

Her father was speaking, saying that she seemed to have taken a great deal upon herself, far too much in the circumstances,

458

and he hoped she would allow her parents to play their traditional part in the marriage of a daughter. He would give her away and if she wanted to go from Nanny's, very well, that was where they would go from.

'Aunt Mildred is coming to stay. She arrives tomorrow and she's going to make your wedding dress,' said Ellie. 'Just think of that.'

Aunt Mildred! Everybody knew what an expert dressmaker she was. Charlotte certainly did, for she owed her own skill to her great-aunt. She realised Ellie was still talking and saying she must come for fittings.

'I think we had better have some tea and then perhaps we can go to Barnes to see the house,' said Mr Grant.

This was a new papa, an amiable, considerate man, but surely it wasn't all due to Mrs Graham's influence?

After tea, when Ellie went up to put on her hat, Charlotte went with her and had just enough time to ask.

'Mrs Graham can't speak too highly of you, dear, and that probably helped. But you know that day when you came and had such an argument with him?'

'I'll never forget it. It was awful.'

'Well, I believe he thought about it. About you and about himself as your father. He realised that you were a young

459

woman to be reckoned with.'

'That puts a much better complexion on things.'

'Yes, doesn't it? I honestly believe that when he realised you were never going to give in, he accepted defeat.'

'It must have been a struggle for him.'

'I think it was. Now, you won't go and antagonise him, will you?'

'Not so long as there are no recriminations.'

'There won't be.'

The carriage was at the door and they were soon on their way, with Charlotte pointing out landmarks. 'There's our church, and there's Hammersmith Bridge.'

Ellie had never seen the suspension bridge and thought it fantastic. They drove round by the pond so that Ellie could admire it, and then on to the special part of the common where their house nestled among the trees.

'Quite picturesque,' remarked Mr Grant.

Charlotte had the key in the door, but she heard the piano even before she opened it. Richard was there practising and she had not expected him to be. She couldn't speak because her heart was choking her.

'Aren't you going to take us in?' her father asked.

She led the way.

Richard stopped playing, looked up, stood. As always, when distressed, the little colour he had fled, leaving him ashen.

Charlotte held her breath. If there was a scene she'd die.

Her father stepped forward, hand outstretched. 'Mr Allen, I deeply regret what I said at our last meeting. Can you overlook it?' he asked.

There was one of those loaded pauses. Then Richard said: 'For Charlotte's sake I'll try.' He did not offer his hand.

And so, with those few words, a rather uneasy peace was born.

Ellie, having lagged behind to admire the black and white tiled hall, didn't notice the tension. She expressed her pleasure at seeing Richard again and told him how much she was looking forward to the wedding.

Charlotte was amazed by Richard's attitude after all he had said. She sought to cover it up by offering to show her parents the rest of the house. Ellie enthused over the features that enhanced it, the panelled ceiling in the small but well-proportioned drawing room, the stained glass in the front door that threw such lovely colours on the floor when the sun came round.

'It's absolutely beautiful, Charlotte. A nice little cloakroom by the front door, too. Excellent bedrooms and a kitchen looking on the garden. Don't you agree, William?'

'I do. They were lucky to find it,' he said, and asked how they proposed furnishing the house.

'Bit by bit, I suppose, but that will be fun.'

Mr Grant produced a card from one of the more exclusive London shops. 'Go there and choose whatever you want, Charlotte. I'll tell them to expect you. They can furnish the whole house, so don't stint anything.'

'Papa! That's more than generous. It's simply ripping. I don't, know what to say.' She was quite overcome.

Ellie glowed with pleasure. It was a truly remarkable day for her, because William was proving himself to be the great-hearted man she knew he really was.

From the music room came the sound of scales and arpeggios played at breathtaking speed. The Grants heard and decided not to interrupt, although it was time they left.

Charlotte waved them goodbye and watched the carriage until it turned the corner. Then she went in to see Richard.

'Are you alone?' he asked.

'They've just gone.' It was clear that their visit had been an ordeal for him that

462

she had not foreseen. He was still pale and tense. 'I thought I should be able to meet your father without feeling such a surge of anger,' he said.

'But you wanted us to make it up. You gave all kinds of reasons.'

'I know.'

'Well then?'

'I suppose you think I'm contrary.'

'You are. You quite shocked me.'

'Let me get on with my practising,' he said.

Her mood darkened. She took a deck chair to the kitchen and sat there, brooding. It disturbed her to see Richard as she had never seen him before. Sort of prickly, so she couldn't get close, was how she thought of it.

Her father had been obnoxious in the past. It could be said that he wanted to protect her when she reached marriageable age, but there was no excuse for the way he had treated Richard.

Well, one could dwell on that until it became a spring of poison killing everything it touched. Now it seemed he was trying to compensate by showing great generosity. He had extended his hand to Richard but Richard had not taken it.

She understood why Richard cringed from the touch of a man who had called him a bastard and his mother a whore.

The playing stopped. She heard him close the piano lid and come in.

'Are you ready to go?' he asked, but it wasn't Richard who spoke. It was this hurt, angry man. She put the deck chair away.

'Hammersmith or Clapham?' he asked.

'One after the other.' She longed for Nanny's wisdom, Victoria's common sense. Most of all she longed to put her arms round him and tell him: 'Never mind.'

It was almost dark when they passed the pond and saw a cab outside The Sun waiting for a fare. Next thing they were in it and on their way to Hammersmith. This was her chance to do what she wanted. She put her arms round his shoulders and said those soothing, comfortable words: 'Never mind,' and she felt him relax, felt the tension lift until he was himself again, and presently he began to talk.

He told her as much as he knew of the man who was his father. It was the same story as Mrs Graham had told Mr Grant. 'I don't know my father. Never met him and never shall. It was worse for him than for Mary. His family made a settlement on her so she could go on training. He had to marry a girl he hardly knew. Just think of that.'

'Why didn't you tell me all this before?'

'Because it hurts. I've never told anyone.'

'But me? Aren't I part of your life?'

'You are my life.'

'Me and the music?'

'Charlotte! That goes without saying.' He was beginning to laugh, telling her they need never talk about it again and he was thankful to have it off his chest.

Nanny was amazed to hear that Mr Grant had actually apologised to Richard, and told him she would never have believed it possible. 'It's a very good thing,' she said. 'You've had your sulks and I don't blame you. Now go and shake hands with him.'

'Just like that?'

'It will please everyone, especially Ellie. She's the one in the middle and that's not a comfortable position.'

Nanny had a lot to say about the value of peace in a family and the folly of spurning conciliatory offers.

Charlotte didn't take part in their conversation. Will had just given her the promised sandalwood box and she was admiring it. Watching her, Richard thought of the way she had comforted him and felt an even deeper love. He knew then that he must steel himself to meet Mr Grant and make up their quarrel. Nanny was right. He would go in a day or two.

A few days later Annie opened the door to Richard Allen, and a broad smile spread across her face when she saw who it was.

'Hallo, Annie. You look better than ever,' he said.

'Mr Allen! Oh, I'm that glad to see you.' She looked so pleased. 'Miss Charlotte's been here today trying on her wedding dress. We're all thrilled to bits, I can tell you. Am I to announce you?'

'Perhaps you had just better say I'm here.' He had such a peculiar feeling inside that he had to fix his eyes on an ornamental dish that graced the hall table to keep him steady while he waited.

Voices. Annie's, Mr Grant's, Ellie's, and another as yet unknown to him. Then Mr Grant came out, and this time it was Richard who extended his hand. Mr Grant clasped it. Neither spoke. It was a prolonged handshake, with Richard's hand enclosed in both of William's. The ice cracked and melted as the thaw set in. Richard couldn't have spoken. His throat felt so constricted he had to keep swallowing, but William said: 'Mr Allen! I'm very glad you've come. My wife will be delighted to see you. There are all kinds of things she wants to talk about. Come along in.'

He led Richard into the drawing room where he had so frequently taken tea with Ellie and Charlotte at the beginning of their acquaintance. This was where he

466

had met the unattractive Albert Morton, with his mouth full of tea and scone, and discovered he was to be Charlotte's husband.

Ellie was on the sofa, looking very comfortable and contented, and a stately, much older-looking lady sat at a small table with a large work basket beside her and some kind of soft white material in her hands. She looked at him over the top of her spectacles. He guessed she was Aunt Mildred.

There was a warm welcome for him from Ellie and a more restrained one from Aunt Mildred, who was introduced as Mr Grant's aunt. She put down her needlework and said she hoped the preparations for the wedding were almost completed, and might she be permitted to enquire where the honeymoon was to be spent.

'We haven't even talked about it,' said Richard. 'At Barnes, I should think.'

'Ah.' There were depths in that monosyllable.

Mr Grant was pouring Madeira, to which Ellie and Aunt Mildred were partial. They drank the usual toast of good health all round, and sipped.

Ellie did most of the talking, telling Richard that the wedding dress was a sheer delight, it fitted to perfection and was almost too beautiful to wear. There was a sense of well-being in the room.

'As you are spending your honeymoon in your new home, Mr Allen, may we assume you have engaged staff to take care of your comfort?' Aunt Mildred asked.

'Staff?' He echoed the word and it hung in the air.

'Staff. Who is to get breakfast in the morning, for instance?'

'I really don't know,' he said. 'Perhaps I could. Or Charlotte might.'

'And clear the grates and light the fires?'

He was lost and looked it. Never in his life had he been faced by such problems.

'Good gracious, Aunt, what a lot of queries,' said Ellie.

'Very necessary ones,' responded Aunt Mildred, but Ellie managed to steer the conversation into smoother waters which were far easier for the men.

It was natural and right for Mr Grant to get to know the man who was soon to be his son-in-law. Having overcome his strong aversion to Bohemians, as he automatically called artists, musicians and poets, he was beginning to realise that they had as much right to recognition as bankers, merchants and industrialists. He was surprised to discover how diligently Richard worked, with long hours of study and the continual striving for perfection.

He began to see him as a man dedicated to his profession and sincerely in love with Charlotte.

There was still the matter of his unfortunate birth, but again, if people like Mrs Graham and Aunt Mildred could ignore it, so must he.

Nothing like that was mentioned or even touched upon that evening. The domestic matters that troubled Aunt Mildred were forgotten in the far more absorbing subjects that emerged, and by the time they had lingered over another glass of Madeira they were all in harmony.

Richard refused an invitation to stay to dinner. He couldn't wait to see Charlotte.

She didn't have to ask how he had fared at Lancaster Gate, because he came bounding up the stairs two at a time and looked as pleased as he felt. 'Your father and I shook hands,' he said. 'We are in accord. Are you pleased?'

Charlotte was thankful. Her resentment towards her father had given way to kinder feelings, and Victoria voiced her own satisfaction by saying: 'Great. Seems quite a few people have come to their senses at last.'

Richard didn't mention the domestic questions Aunt Mildred had asked. These problems were not for Charlotte. She had enough to think about without them.

Algernon Charles Last was two weeks old and a constant surprise to his mother. Everything about him was unique. No other baby had such perfect fingers and toes, such beautiful eyebrows, such a variety of expressions to put on his face. She was amazed by how he frowned, smiled, puckered his features and knew exactly what was going on in every corner of the room. And the way he gripped your finger! The strength of it.

A good deal of this might have been due to Victoria's imagination but it made her happy and helped her to bear the pain of Algie's loss.

She had scarcely dared to look further ahead than the next day before Charlie, as he was to be known, made his appearance, but the support of her friends was beyond telling. People she never expected to help rallied round. Mrs Rogers was always coming up with a 'little something'. Will Goode called frequently with flowers for her and a gift for Charlie. And Richard Allen and his mother—those beautiful towels and sheets were for keeps. Richard had told her so.

'We're so lucky. We don't want for nothing,' she kept saying.

But the thing that surprised her most

of all was the visit from Henry Last. Mrs Rogers, being near the street door, had taken it upon herself to admit Victoria's callers. She knew them all by now, but when Mr Last arrived carrying seven teddy bears she ran ahead with a warning.

'I think he's all right. Name of Last,' she said.

In came Mr Last, the practically unknown partner of Madame Last, who went quietly about in his unobtrusive way and managed the business side of the establishment without thanks or recognition.

Mr Last, even more than Madame, was devastated by the loss of their only child, but he knew better than to show it. Now there was a grandson. Algie's boy was the hope of the world.

Victoria held Charlie tight and said, 'Oh my!'

Mr Last stood in the doorway clutching the teddy bears and said: 'I thought the little fellow would like these.'

'He's a bit small for 'em,' said Victoria.

'I'll put them on the shelf.' He arranged them in order of size, then sat down on an upright chair and said: 'This isn't such a surprise to me as you may think. I used to see you walking arm-in-arm with our Algie.'

'You never said.'

'Why set the cat among the sparrows? You both looked so happy—'

'We were, Mr Last. Me and Algie. Oh dear.'

'I'm sure,' he said, and he sniffed and blinked and wept inwardly for Algie.

If there was any trace of wariness on Victoria's part to begin with, it soon vanished and she found herself talking pleasurably with Mr Last, telling him all kinds of things about her life with Algie and finding him so easy to get along with as she never would have believed.

'What about Madame?' she asked eventually.

'She'll come round,' he said. 'Doesn't like Mayfair any more, though. Says she can't abide our house and we'll have to find somewhere out of town.'

'The business isn't doing too well then?' said Victoria.

'It's gone to pot, my dear. She's got no heart for it, you see.'

'That's a pity,' said Victoria.

She was going to have a lot to tell Charlotte next time she came, and as she came almost every day there wouldn't be long to wait.

Madame Last intimated her intention of calling on Victoria with the object of seeing her grandson. It had taken all

Nanny's and Henry's combined powers of persuasion to bring this about, and Victoria was consequently in a state of twitters.

'I wish you'd be here to back me up, Charlotte,' she said.

'I will,' said Charlotte, but she was rushed off her feet with the wedding now less than a week away. She had been to Mr Grant's favoured shop with Richard and chosen several pieces of furniture. They were attended by the manager when they arrived and treated as persons of consequence.

Acting on his advice, they did not attempt to fit out the whole house. 'Choose the essentials now and give yourselves time to cogitate over the rest when you've settled in,' he advised. 'May I suggest carpets and rugs to begin with? And then perhaps a dining room suite? A sofa or two? An occasional table? We mustn't overlook the kitchen.'

Dazzled by the choice, they paid more than one visit together. Then Charlotte went with Ellen. Eventually they selected enough to begin with, and when the pieces were put in place at Barnes they looked as though they had been expressly designed for the house.

But Charlotte couldn't neglect Victoria and went, as requested, to give moral support. 'Although Madame Last doesn't like me much,' she warned.

'She doesn't like me either,' said Victoria. ''Ere, don't you start crying, Charlie, for Gawd's sake.'

Charlie obligingly blew bubbles.

Footsteps were heard on the stairs, and voices. Madame Last's and Nanny's. Charlotte opened the door and stood back for them to enter. Nanny treated her to a conspiratorial wink.

Madame advanced into the sitting room, took one look at Charlie and was conquered.

'Why, if he isn't my little Algie!' she exclaimed.

Victoria's nervousness vanished. She asserted her rights without delay. 'He ain't your little Algie. He's my little Charlie,' she said.

'Oh? Well, he's the dead spit image of my Algie at that age. I'll hold him for a minute, if I may.'

Victoria couldn't refuse to hand him over, and Charlie didn't object. He was a very placid baby but Nanny could have sworn he looked surprised at the sight of Madame Last, and after one long stare into her face closed his eyes and went to sleep, as though this was enough for one day.

'I think he's taken to you, Bessy,' remarked Nanny.

'He'd better. I'm his grandmother, let nobody forget.'

Charlotte, in the kitchen, listened hard. Nanny was guiding the talk into peaceful channels and before long a three-sided conversation was in progress. Madame kept a dignified distance from Victoria and spoke to her in a condescending way, but at least she spoke. It would be some time before she could accept her as a member of the Last family, although Charlie was already well in.

'Rest assured, Charlie shall want for nothing,' she said. 'For the matter of that, as his mother neither will you. Mr Last will be making arrangements.'

'Thank him from me,' said Victoria stiffly.

'Do you intend to go on living here?' asked Madame.

'Course we do. It's our home, ain't it, Charlie? Mine and Algie's. We gathered all these bits and pieces between us. I wouldn't leave it. Not for a palace.'

This had an unexpected effect on Charlie's grandmother. She began to cry. 'I do wish I'd known,' she said. 'I wish Algie had told me. I wouldn't have objected.'

'Oh yes you would,' said Victoria. 'Only natural. Only son marrying a brat from an orphanage. If I'd a' been you I'd have

475

objected. Leastways to start with.'

'Now, now, now,' boomed Nanny. 'Enough. Peace. In other words, shut up, both of you.' And in an even louder voice: 'How about some tea, Charlotte?'

'Coming,' said Charlotte, who had already made it and now brought it in. It had a wonderfully calming effect. The sleeping Charlie was put in his cradle so Madame could sip her tea unimpeded, and the talk turned to the state of affairs at Last's.

'It's finished,' Madame said. 'We're closing down.'

'You're being short-sighted,' said Nanny.

'I can't face it. I've told you so before,' said Madame.

'*You* can't face it? How about little Charlie? What's he to come into if you shut up shop?'

Madame only shook her head, but Nanny had her in a corner.

'You hadn't thought of him, had you? It's very easy to retire, and very selfish. If you don't do better I shall be ashamed of you, Bessy.'

'What can I do? Tell me that!'

'You could get someone.'

'Who, I'd like to know?'

'Advertise,' said Nanny. 'Henry knows the business like the back of his hand. You only need a figurehead. Somebody who understands fashion, can advise clients and looks the part. There must be such a person.'

'Huh,' said Madame Last dismissively.

Charlotte was holding her breath. She had put her foot in it with Madame at the cemetery. Dared she risk it again? She was outside the circle and had not entered into the conversation. Now she must. Come what may, she must. She gripped the arms of her chair, dug her feet into the floor, sat forward and said in a loud, clear voice: 'Why not Clarice West?'

They all looked round. She was fixed by three pairs of eyes. Then they spoke as one: 'Clarice? Clarice West?' and immediately: 'Yes!' from Victoria and 'Yes,' from Nanny.

Madame looked from one to the other, mystified, but before she could say a word Nanny told her that Clarice was made for the job.

'She has the presence and the skill, Bessy. She'll salvage Last's. She'll put it on the map again.'

'Well, I don't know. I'm sure I don't,' said Madame.

'Yes you do, Bessy. It's worth trying. For Charlie's sake.'

'I'll think about it,' said Madame.

'Don't think. Act. She happens to be

free now. Snap her up before someone else does.'

'I remember her,' said Madame slowly. 'Diddled by a con man. Yes, I can see her now. Distinguished. Ladylike. Very well, Nanny. I'll write to her tonight.'

Somehow the vision of Last's rising like the phoenix from the ashes put new heart into Madame. After more discussion, all favourable to Clarice, she took an almost gracious leave of Victoria, tucked a guinea into Charlie's cradle, and with a nod to Charlotte, departed.

Nanny, following, was able to convey her satisfaction with another expressive look.

If Charlotte considered herself rushed, Richard was even more so. They both had clothes and personal belongings to take to Barnes and spent so much time travelling there from points as far apart as Green Street, Hammersmith and Clapham that they were continually missing each other. We'll be lucky if we manage a wave in passing, she said.

The day before the wedding, with everything in hand and nothing else to do, she sat on the side of her bed at Nanny's and looked at her wedding dress. It hung outside the wardrobe, a perfect specimen of Aunt Mildred's art.

Aunt Mildred had been kind, and so

indeed was Papa. He had organised carriages for everyone, ordered her bouquet and the buttonholes. It was to be simple, as she wanted it, but nothing was neglected or forgotten.

She hadn't seen Richard since yesterday and he seemed strangely remote and faraway. It was late afternoon and she was restless, with nothing to do and longing for company.

Nanny had gone up West to buy a new hat and didn't intend to hurry. Victoria would be out for her afternoon walk with Charlie. Clapham seemed a long way off, Barnes much nearer, and she felt drawn there.

It was not too far to go and a fine day for a walk. Autumn, with the leaves changing colour. There was a magnificent copper beech across the road from their house and she had never seen a tree in such beauty. She wondered if it could be as lovely as this in its spring colours.

It was almost eerily quiet in the house. There were trestle tables waiting in the hall to be erected, and stacks of little gilt chairs. She tiptoed into the music room and saw piles of music on the piano stool, the piano, the floor. There was a violin stand, several stands in fact. Hadn't Richard said the room was ideal for rehearsing?

The fireplaces were ready laid with paper,

sticks, tiny pieces of coal. There were large pieces in the copper scuttles and logs in the hearths.

Upstairs in their room the bed was already made up. Nanny must have done that. A scarf lay on the bed, and the Russian-style tunic Richard wore when he was practising. These were his things. His handkerchiefs in a drawer, his shaving kit in the bathroom. So he had been and gone and she had missed him. The house was full of his presence and he wasn't there. It made her feel lost.

She went sadly downstairs, dragging her hand on the rail, and heard a wonderful, heartening sound that meant more to her than any music. His latchkey in the door.

And there he was, dropping parcels on the floor so he could take her in his arms. 'I'm so glad you're here,' she kept saying, between laughter and tears. He told her he had only been down to the village for a few things. 'The fact is, I can't keep away. I love it here. But I really must tidy up my muddle,' he said.

The first thing was to stow the music in its cabinet, and he set about it straight away, working methodically. He didn't want any help so she went back upstairs to put her own things away. Her best dress next to his evening suit. It was so ordinary and yet so extraordinary. All kinds of odd thoughts struck her. The wonder of having a home of their own, followed by the realisation that she hadn't even got an ounce of tea, a loaf of bread, some butter, anything at all, and it was much too late to go shopping now. No milk. Well, it wasn't any use weeping over that. Much better to laugh.

If she had but known, Richard had taken care of everything. Prompted by Aunt Mildred's questions, he went shopping for commodities he had never expected to buy and found the experience most exhilarating. He meant to begin married life by cooking the breakfast, but that was his secret.

Charlotte had put all her things neatly away when he went up to find her.

'Did you try the bed?' he asked.

'No.' They both thought of the funny little salesman with his kiss curl testing the springs and trying to persuade her to do the same.

'Which side would you like?'

'I don't know,' she said. 'You choose.'

'I will.' He took off his jacket and shoes, removed his things from the bed and turned down the quilt.

'Come on. Try it,' he said.

She only hesitated for a second, then they were side by side, and how could they help turning to each other, so much in love

481

as they were? How could they resist the most wonderfully exciting embrace they had yet had, and how long it would have gone on and where it would have ended they never knew, for they were disturbed by a man's heavy tread in the hall. Somebody had come in.

Richard shot up, combed his hair, straightened his cravat, hustled into his coat and thrust his feet into his shoes. Then he walked nonchalantly down the stairs and surprised Will Goode, who had brought the cake, packed in three separate boxes, and was wondering where to put it.

All this gave Charlotte time to smooth her hair and restore her appearance to that of the elegant young lady everyone knew. Presently she joined the men in the kitchen. They had decided to label the boxes for the caterers.

'Nanny wondered where you'd got to, Charlotte,' said Will.

'Oh dear, I should have left a note. Did she get a nice hat?'

'Magnificent. Wait till you see it.'

'It won't be long now,' she said.

Will had his bike and went off. They had just missed a bus at The Sun and decided to walk, as it was one of those mild, balmy evenings that have to be treasured.

It was tempting to stop on Hammersmith Bridge and look down at the dark river underneath, watch a little boat tooting along and see the lamps on the shore.

Richard put his hand over Charlotte's on the rail. 'Mr Grant called on my mother this afternoon,' he said. 'There won't be any tension at the wedding.'

'That's the one thing that worried me,' she said.

For a young girl to throw her arms round a man in the street and give him a long, long kiss was not a proper thing to do. Two women passing by chorused, 'Disgusting!' in loud voices.

'No it isn't,' said Charlotte. And to prove it wasn't, she did it again.

It was Saturday and Clarice looked superb, for she was going to Charlotte's wedding in the dress she had made specially for the occasion and a positively daring hat. So stylish, so fashionable, she could have passed for a duchess anywhere. Mr Grant was sending a carriage for her and Aunt Cassie, so there would be no scrambling for buses today.

But first she had to get Mrs Graham's dresses back to Curzon Street. After Mr Heston had disgusted her with his proposal she went back there only once, for she felt compelled to finish work already in hand and didn't know how it was to be managed.

'Do it at home,' Victoria told her.

'How am I to get it there?'

That was a poser but Victoria solved it by telling Eustace Bright, who borrowed his father's motor car and took Clarice to fetch it. Now it was finished, and only just in time, for Madame Last's letter had come and changed her life. She had been for an interview, was thrilled with the offer, and on Monday she would start her new career. She didn't have any qualms about going back in the exalted position Madame offered. By the time Herbert's free I could be a leading light in the fashion world, she told herself, and that strengthened her determination to shine.

Victoria had told her that she had Charlotte to thank for this. Charlotte had dared to suggest Clarice as the ideal person to take Madame's place and had actually said it to Madame's face. The courage of it! Oh, Charlotte, Charlotte, bless your darling heart!

'You had better take those things in a cab,' Aunt Cassie told her. 'You need only hand them in.'

Clarice thought a lot about Mrs Graham on her way. She had so much to thank her for and would always be grateful for her help. She would never forget the way Mrs Graham had come to her aid when she was in despair, and treated her with generosity and consideration. If Mr Heston hadn't spoilt everything she would most likely have gone on working for her. She wouldn't tell Mrs Graham she was leaving on his account. She would write a letter of appreciation and thanks for all this, and say that she was resigning to manage Madame Last's establishment and would be honoured if Mrs Graham consented to become a privileged client of the firm.

By the time she had composed and recomposed the letter in her head she was there. She told the cabbie to wait, carried the dresses in their protective satin covers to the door and gave them to the maid.

The girl was disposed to talk, but Clarice was in too much of a hurry to get away. She almost ran back to the waiting cab and was getting in when she heard a voice and almost stopped breathing.

Mr Heston.

'Oh no!' But there he was.

'I'm only just back from Wool and was coming to see you,' he said. 'My dear Clarice, how entrancing you look. I've been thinking of you so much.'

'I can't stop. I'm in a hurry. Drive me back home, cabbie,' she said, trying to close the door. He held it open and got in too.

'Get out at once. This is my cab,' she said, but it was moving.

485

'I want to talk to you,' he said. She turned her head away.

'Listen. You must listen,' he said.

'You can't say anything I'd like to hear. Please don't spoil my day.'

Oh, how terribly like Herbert Blades he looked. Herbert in his most pleasing mood, Herbert when he was about to snap open a velvet case with a precious jewel for her.

'Clarice, just let me tell you something. You know my family has sheep farms in New Zealand, don't you?'

She nodded and he went on: 'I'm going out there.'

'To New Zealand?' She brightened. He couldn't be any trouble to her from there. 'I do hope you'll like it,' she said.

'I shall if you'll come with me. Will you, Clarice?' He was serious. Begging her to go with him, telling her there were no class barriers there, no distinctions. They would be free, happy, living together in a state of blissful harmony. He went on and on.

'I set off next week. It's short notice, I know, but can you be ready?' he asked.

She heard all he said and thought he was crazy. 'Of course I can't go with you, Mr Heston. You're just as bad as ever you were. I don't hear you make an offer of marriage.'

'In my position—'

'Oh, don't go on. I know all about

486

your position. And I wouldn't accept if you did ask me. You know very well that I'm engaged to marry Mr Blades.'

'I can do much more for you than he ever could. And I want you so desperately.'

'Wanting isn't loving, Mr Heston.'

'It's all the same to me.'

'Then you'll have to learn different, won't you?'

'Clarice!' This in his pleading tone, which didn't fool her.

'I'm getting out here,' she said. 'There's the carriage waiting for me.'

'Won't you even think it over?'

'How many more times do I have to say no? I wish you well, Mr Heston, but now it's goodbye.'

He was angry because he had been thwarted, so she didn't feel any pity for him. She only wished he hadn't made such a nuisance of himself.

Still, she wasn't going to let that upset her. She was off to Charlotte's wedding, and there was Aunt Cassie all in her best beckoning to her from the carriage Mr Grant had sent.

'Who was that man who got out of your cab?' Aunt Cassie asked as they drove away.

'Just someone who wanted a lift,' said Clarice.

Charlotte was almost ready. Her bouquet of lilies of the valley had just arrived, and although she had often said they were her favourite flowers, she didn't expect to see them in the autumn.

'Your pa must have ordered them specially,' said Nanny, who was helping her dress.

'That was kind of him,' said Charlotte, wondering why this made her feel like crying when she was so happy. She laid the bouquet on the bed and told Nanny not to sit on it.

'And don't you sit on my hat,' said Nanny, fussing round and trying not to get flustered.

Charlotte kept talking about Richard and their plans. They would only have a week at home before going to Bath for the first of Mary's recitals. Nanny feared she might have to spend a lot of time alone, but Richard had told her she would have a wonderful chance to explore the city. 'Keep a journal. Then we'll be able to read it when we're old and remember all the things we'll have forgotten,' he said.

That was one of the things she meant to do, but she wanted to learn as well. He had promised to tell her how the Kreutzer Sonata had got its name, and all kinds of other things. Once he said they were a bit like Schumann and his Clara, who were separated by her hostile father.

'Richard's so wonderful, Nanny. Do you suppose he's thinking about me now, this minute?'

'Note the time and ask him when you next meet.'

'At the altar?' They laughed at the idea.

There had been a lot of excitement and nerve-calming that morning, but now she was alone. Nanny and Will had left for the church, she could hear the clip-clop of hooves trotting away. It was time for her to go too.

Papa was in the hall, immaculate in his morning suit, tall, handsome and remarkably cool, although he had been at Barnes earlier to make sure the caterer had carried out his instructions.

He found everything in order there: masses of flowers were banked in the hall; the long trestle tables, disguised with a linen cloth, were overlaid with lace and set with Gunter's silverware and sparkling glasses. Will's cake, the centrepiece, was a work of art and looked magnificent. He doubted if the repast would equal it, but it was to prove a triumph for the caterer. The everyday fare the workroom girls liked had been prepared in a way that made it a gourmet's delight. This, with other, more sophisticated dishes, would satisfy everyone. All this was planned as a surprise for Charlotte and he hoped it would please her.

Now he was at the foot of the stairs and she was coming down. For one frozen moment he could have sworn it was Amanda. His heart all but missed a beat. He gulped, squared his shoulders, straightened his back and looked again. This time he saw a Charlotte he had never seen before. This Charlotte was her own self, and she was beginning to smile as though she was pleased to see him. It was an enchanting smile.

He felt a rush of pride. This exquisite, almost fragile-looking girl had a will of iron and nerves of steel, and was, as she had once said, as tough as a soldier's boot. He put his hands on her shoulders and took a long, admiring look.

'Will I do?' she asked.

'You'll do,' he said, and kissed her.

'I never thought it would be like this, all friendly and cosy. Isn't it lovely?' she said.

'It is indeed.' He offered his arm, and out they went to the carriage drawn by two white horses. Inquisitive neighbours came into the street to stare.

Charlotte's emotions were so strong that day. Love, gratitude, joy. All her friends were in the church, turning to see her as she walked up the aisle on her father's arm. Their faces were gentle, full of kindness and affection.

She felt she owed a debt to each one of them for all they had given her of themselves, and that kind of debt was precious. Victoria held Charlie so that he was looking over her shoulder, small, perky, chuckling. Mrs Vickery, with her dear shiny face, and Nanny, short but regal, in her new hat: where would she have been without them?

She saw Ellie on one side of the church and Mary, looking radiant, on the other. For a moment it was all too much. The solemnity of the occasion almost overwhelmed her. She was in this sacred place to marry the man she truly loved, and he was at the altar rails waiting for her.

The moment they had lived for was now.

Now it was all beginning.

This Large Print Book for the Partially sighted, who cannot read normal print, is published under the auspices of

**THE ULVERSCROFT FOUNDATION**

---

**THE ULVERSCROFT FOUNDATION**

. . . we hope that you have enjoyed this Large Print Book. Please think for a moment about those people who have worse eyesight problems than you . . . and are unable to even read or enjoy Large Print, without great difficulty.

You can help them by sending a donation, large or small to:

**The Ulverscroft Foundation,
1, The Green, Bradgate Road,
Anstey, Leicestershire, LE7 7FU,
England.**
or request a copy of our brochure for more details.

The Foundation will use all your help to assist those people who are handicapped by various sight problems and need special attention.

Thank you very much for your help.